ALL THAT REMAINS

a novel by

ROBERT L. LeBRUN

INKWATER PRESS

Portland • Oregon
INKWATERPRESS.COM

Scan this QR Code to learn more about this title

Edited by Holly Tri
Cover and interior design by Masha Shubin

Photos & illustrations: Titanic © Andrea Crisante (dreamstime.com); Rough Texture Background © David Broberg (bigstockphoto.com); Fancy scrollwork © Ozerina Anna (bigstockphoto.com)

Publisher: Inkwater Press | www.inkwaterpress.com

LeBrun, Robert L. (Robert Lee)
All that remains / Robert L. LeBrun.
pages cm
LCCN 2013945052
ISBN 978-1-59299-983-5 (pbk.)
ISBN 978-1-59299-984-2 (hc)
ISBN 978-1-59299-985-9 (eBook)

1. Titanic (Steamship)--Fiction. 2. Detective and mystery stories. 3. Adventure stories. 4. Bildungsromans. I. Title.

PS3612.E332A45 2013 813'.6
QBI13-600119

Paperback ISBN-13 978-1-59299-983-5 | ISBN-10 1-59299-983-2
Hardback ISBN-13 978-1-59299-984-2 | ISBN-10 1-59299-984-0
Kindle ISBN-13 978-1-59299-985-9 | ISBN-10 1-59299-985-9

Printed in the U.S.A.
All paper is acid free and meets all ANSI standards for archival quality paper.

1 3 5 7 9 10 8 6 4 2

Dedicated to my savior, Jesus Christ,
to whom I give all glory.

Have you ever had a dream? A dream that never goes away. It follows you. It haunts you during the day and keeps you up at night. This is my dream.

CHAPTER ONE

On 31 March 1909, in Belfast, Ireland, Harland and Wolff Shipyard began working on the largest and, certainly, the most luxurious passenger liner ever built in its time.

RMS *Titanic* was owned by the White Star Line and was completed 31 March 1912. She was 882 feet and 9 inches long and weighed in at 46,328 tons. The first sea trials took place on 2 April 1912. An *Agreement and Account of Voyages and Crew* was signed by Mr. Francis Carruthers, who deemed the *Titanic* to be seaworthy.

Titanic began her maiden voyage across the Atlantic Ocean on 10 April 1912 with Captain Edward J. Smith in command. She left Southampton, England bound for the United States. She never made it.

Everyone would hear the story of a rogue iceberg striking the starboard side and sending *Titanic* to her grave. But, in fact, there were several iceberg warnings preceding the night of the sinking, and they had caused Captain Smith to alter his original course.

An iceberg may have contributed to the sinking of RMS *Titanic,* but it was arrogance, ignorance, and incompetence that led up to the disaster.

As *Titanic* left her berth on 10 April 1912, one family in particular watched her wake as her enormous displacement caused the SS *New York*, which was docked nearby, to break away from her moorings. Mr. Victor Carnelius Kotter, his wife Elizabeth, and their four-year-old son, Jack, were watching with excitement as crewmen scrambled on deck to try to keep the two massive ships from colliding.

After a four-hour delay, *Titanic* continued on, making several stops, including Cherbourg, France and Queenstown, Ireland, in order to pick up more passengers.

Victor Kotter happened to be in England on a business trip and had brought along his wife and son with a plan to be part of the maiden voyage on their way back to the United States. Victor had some shares tied into the shipping industry and into imports and exports. He traveled to England in order to strengthen his position with other shareholders, and at the same time, took his family on vacation.

After a week of agonizing over the rising cost of shipping freight, the Kotter family boarded *Titanic* en route to New York. Although Victor wasn't considered wealthy, he was a well-to-do businessman, which earned him the privilege of conversing with passengers such as Macy's co-owner Isidor Straus, industrialist Benjamin Guggenheim, millionaire John Astor, and other wealthy businessmen on board for the maiden voyage. Also on board was Denver millionaire Margaret Brown, who often enjoyed the company of Elizabeth and Jack.

Day hours were considered family time and spent with Elizabeth and Jack, but the evening hours, after dinner, Victor had the honor of lounging with the business class and talking shop. Usual subjects included banking, stocks, and whatever happened to be in the business section of The Wall Street Journal. Elizabeth and Jack would usually wander the ship in amazement at all the new technologies then make their way back to sit with the ladies.

On 14 April 1912, as the Kotter family lay sleeping, RMS *Titanic* struck an iceberg. As ice fell on the starboard deck, the massive ship shook and rumbled as First Officer Murdoch ordered "hard to starboard" and "full reverse." The incident awoke the Kotters and many other passengers, so they made their way out of their rooms and up on deck. Many of the businessmen took advantage of the opportunity and went to the lounge area for drinks.

After being awakened by the impact, Captain Smith arrived on the bridge and gave the order "full stop." As Elizabeth and Jack sat with friends, Victor leaned over and kissed Elizabeth on the cheek. He then gave Jack a smile and quietly slipped away to find out what happened.

As rumors spread throughout the ship, some passengers began to panic. Shortly after midnight, Thomas Andrews, a naval architect who helped design the ship, and ship officers conducted an inspection of the damage. *Titanic* was designed to stay afloat with up to four watertight compartments flooded, but because water was rushing into at least five compartments and was also rising from the ship's bottom, which no one could account for, it was soon realized RMS *Titanic* would eventually sink.

On 15 April 1912, shortly before 1:00 a.m., the first lifeboats were ordered into the water. As passengers began to filter out to the decks and into lifeboats, Elizabeth and Jack sat quietly in the lounge waiting for Victor to return. As time passed, more and more passengers became hysterical and some even violent. Elizabeth knew she couldn't risk waiting any longer. She picked Jack up and reluctantly made her way to the deck area, bouncing off people as she tried to keep Jack covered.

With all the mass hysteria, she could still hear the officers yelling "women and children." Through the pushing and shoving, Elizabeth and Jack were helped into a lifeboat just before it was launched. She asked the officer about the men. The officer, with a distraught look, shook his head no and kept shouting for women and children.

While sinking, a ship that size could very easily suck down anything around it, so as the lifeboats were lowered, oarsmen tried to put as much distance as possible between them and *Titanic.* But as the stern rose from the water, all the lifeboats stopped and the passengers watched in horror as the massive ship broke apart. Not knowing where Victor was, Elizabeth held Jack close and wouldn't let him look.

At 2:20 a.m. on 15 April 1912, RMS *Titanic* sank beneath the water and was gone. Although the oarsmen had brought the lifeboats to a safe distance from the ship, Elizabeth could still hear the screams of passengers in the frigid water. She begged the oarsmen to go back, but their lifeboat was one of the few filled to full capacity. He didn't want to risk the chance of being overturned by more people attempting to climb in. Through the entire experience, Jack never flinched. He never complained or cried. As the water calmed and the night became quiet, Jack finally pulled away from his mom and asked, "Where's Daddy?"

At 4:10 a.m. RMS *Carpathia* arrived on the scene. By 8:30 a.m. *Carpathia* had picked up the last of the lifeboat survivors. It then continued on to New York. During the trip back, Margaret often sat with Elizabeth and encouraged her to find comfort in the fact that she still had Jack to take care of. *Carpathia* arrived at New York Harbor on 18 April 1912 and docked at Pier 54 on Little West 12th Street. Elizabeth looked out at the thousands of people waiting for their arrival. Although she wasn't sure of Victor's survival, she couldn't help but feel grief for the families waiting to know if their loved ones were on board *Carpathia*.

According to newspaper articles, the White Star Line chartered the CS *Mackay-Bennet* to try to retrieve the deceased. Several other ships, including the *Montmagny*, the *Algerine*, and the *Minia* also joined in the search. Even with the extra help, Elizabeth was still not optimistic Victor's body would be found, either alive or dead.

In the weeks that followed, many charities were formed to help the survivors, as so many families lost the husbands and fathers who supported them. Elizabeth was offered help on several occasions, but she respectfully declined. She was an educated woman and, through the years, had often paid attention to Victor's business exploits. She knew how to handle the investments he had, and she also relied on a life insurance policy and several bank accounts Victor had set up.

Elizabeth and Jack eventually moved from their busy New York apartment and bought a small house outside of New York City, in the peaceful suburbs. They lived quietly out of the public eye as Elizabeth devoted most of her time and energy to raising Jack. She did stay in touch with Margaret Brown and would often get together with her to discuss business ventures. Jack also enjoyed those times, because he was able to travel and see places most kids his age could only talk about.

Through the years, Elizabeth impressed upon Jack the importance of education in succeeding in life. Jack missed his dad very much but learned a lot from his mom. Despite all the schooling, Jack chose not to pursue college. In 1927, at the age of 19, he secured a small business loan from the Bank of New York, using his inheritance as collateral, and bought two old stake body trucks. He convinced his best friend, Sergis, to be his partner, and together they came up with the name Up and Down Hauling, in memory of Jack's dad. The name represented the times when Victor would have a bad week and would tell Jack that life was full of ups and downs. They began contracting themselves out hauling steel to and from the steel mills. They quickly gained capital and reinvested it back into the business.

Some of the qualities Elizabeth instilled in Jack were "never be greedy" and "bigger isn't necessarily better." So when Sergis wanted to expand the business, Jack called on his mom for advice. Afterwards, he followed his heart and decided to keep the company small and simple.

This turned out to be a sound decision, because shortly afterwards, in 1929, the stock market crashed, and the United States economy sunk into its darkest financial days. Because Jack decided not to expand, his business was small enough and lucrative enough to not be affected like the bigger corporations.

Stress took its toll on many people, including Elizabeth. Although she was smart enough to have money set aside, she did lose a lot with the various investments she had. Nevertheless, her strong will took over and she still remained diligent in the charities she shared with Margaret. More often than ever, Elizabeth visited Margaret, and both ladies worked on ideas to try to make it through the depression and still be active in what they considered to be important, things such as education and workers' rights. During the Depression, Margaret became sick, and in 1932, at the age of 65, she died of a brain tumor while lodging at the Barbizon Hotel for Women in New York City.

After what had seemed like a lifelong friendship, Elizabeth was devastated. Both she and Jack mourned Margaret's death. Elizabeth lost a close friend with whom she'd shared a horrific experience. Because Margaret had personal differences with both of her children, she grew close to Jack and often told Elizabeth he was like a son. Margaret was buried at the Cemetery of the Holy Rood in Westbury, New York. Elizabeth often visited her grave to lay down flowers and to reminisce about times past. Because friends of Margaret would sometimes refer to her by the nickname Molly, after her death, she was dubbed "The Unsinkable Molly Brown" because of her experience on *Titanic.*

Elizabeth was never the same after Margaret died. Her health began to decline and the energy she once had was gone. At the age of 68, she was still active with various charities, but sold most of her stocks and investments. She wanted to make sure Jack was well taken care of. In 1935, at the age of 69, she passed away peacefully in her sleep. Because he'd lost his dad at a young age, Jack had to be strong and make it through losing the mom who'd saved his life and guided him to adulthood. She was laid to rest at the Cemetery of the Holy Rood so she could visit Margaret Brown whenever she wanted.

In 1941 the United States was swept into World War II, and the Great Depression came to an end. Many government contracts depended on the steel industry to supply their manufacturing needs, such as weapons, planes, and military vehicles. Jack and Sergis decided it would be the right time to finally expand. They purchased an abandoned steel mill that had gone out of business during the Depression and had no shortage of willing laborers. Sergis quickly went to work securing contracts from the Maritime Commission, which was building small cargo ships to haul troops. They also bought a fleet of trucks to expand the hauling side of their business. Sergis decided to hire his much younger brother Benjamin, who had dropped out of high school. Ben was a street-smart kid who was in and out of trouble. Sergis knew he would be a risk, but just when the court system had had enough of seeing the name Benjamin Marcus, Sergis made a deal with the judge. It helped that Sergis was well-connected at the time.

Ben started off learning how to work the machinery then gradually worked his way up to being a truck driver. By the end of the war, Up and Down Hauling had expanded coast-to-coast, and the small steel mill expanded into Kotter Industries, which consisted of Up and Down Hauling, four steel mills, and six other small parts factories that supplied replacement parts for vehicles. Ben was a hard worker and a quick study. He eventually moved up to management and was making decisions along with Jack and Sergis.

In 1950, at the start of the Korean War, Kotter Industries once again expanded. This time, overseas. Benefiting from post-war protection from the United States, Japan's economy experienced an economic boom. Sergis often traveled to Japan in order to manage the company's contract negotiations. By 1954 Kotter Industries was well on its way to international success. That same year, while flying back from Japan, the flight Sergis was on crashed at Idlewild Airport, killing

26 out of 32 passengers. At the age of 45, Sergis was dead. For the first time in his life, Jack was alone. With his dad and mom gone and the passing of his best friend and business partner, he had to make the painful decision of giving up private ownership of the company.

Combining his street toughness with the business sense that Sergis had taught him, Ben flourished into an intelligent and resourceful businessman. At the age of 24, he inherited the 49 percent of Kotter Industries Sergis controlled, which made him Jack's new business partner. Both men agreed the company would benefit more if a board of directors was established. By 1955, after selling off a limited amount of the company stock, an executive board was voted in and, once again, Kotter Industries was moving forward.

It took a few years for Ben to finally feel comfortable stepping into his brother's shoes, but by 1957 he was on top of his game and going head-to-head with the best. Whether it was hostile takeovers or handling million-dollar contracts, Ben was a tyrant among the best.

With the executive board in place and Ben running most of the day-to-day operations, the time came for Jack to finally slow down and concentrate on some of the more personal projects he frequently entertained. Along with his strong business sense, Jack also inherited his dad's strong family values. He never forgot the smile his dad gave him 45 years earlier during the tragic night he stood up and walked away. Every now and then, as a pet project, Jack would invest time in reading legal documents from the three inquiries into the sinking of *Titanic*. He would often obsess over the fact that the radio operators, Jack Phillips and Harold Bride, ignored the warnings from other ships in reference to large icebergs in the path of *Titanic*. He was also distraught that a ship close enough to be seen off the port side of *Titanic* ignored the CQD, which was the international distress signal sent out. The ship's officers also attempted to contact the mysterious ship using a Morse lamp and flares, but were ignored. A lot of controversy existed in Jack's heart. A lot of unanswered questions. Why didn't his dad return after the lifeboats were ordered into the water, and where did he go? During the May 2 and July 3 inquiries from England, it was thought that the SS *California* was the mysterious ship off *Titanic*'s port side. It was also charged that Captain Stanley Lord failed to give proper assistance to *Titanic*.

Jack knew some of the bodies that were recovered couldn't be identified and most were buried at sea, but they were the bodies of second and third class passengers. As far as Jack was concerned, his dad was still on *Titanic.*

After the sinking, there was widespread of misinformation concerning where *Titanic* went down. With that in mind, Jack often thought how great it would be if someone could locate her and bring his dad home.

CHAPTER TWO

In 1958, at the age of 50, Jack was in attendance at a charity ball. There were a number of charities he was involved in, just another trait given to him by his mom: *When you have many blessings, try to help the people who don't.* At the ball, he locked eyes with a woman, Ms. Bianca Eleanor Chase. She was a dark-haired beauty who'd been born on Crete, which was part of the Greek Islands. With her dark olive skin, dark eyes, and long, thin frame, the attraction was instant and started a yearlong courtship. Bianca was from a well-to-do family that had ties to the shipping industry. Her family was originally from Baltimore. Her father, who was a master shipbuilder, received an offer from the New York Shipbuilding Corporation. He moved his family to Camden, New Jersey in 1922 and started work. The family bought stock in the company and, during World War II, became very wealthy.

In 1959 Jack asked Bianca to accompany him to San Francisco on business. Bianca was all too pleased to go. Between all the board meetings and business trips, she didn't get much alone time with Jack. She'd always wanted to see the west coast, and this way, she had the chance to see it with Jack. After a brief rest at the Fairmont Hotel, Jack told Bianca he had to meet with some important men and their wives. Not thinking it was strange to bring wives to a business meeting, Bianca agreed to go with him.

After contacting some friends and pulling some strings, Jack finally located the sportiest car he could find, a black 1959 Ferrari 250 GT Spyder convertible still in port waiting for the rental company to pick it up. He made arrangements to have the car for the week and didn't waste any time having it delivered to the Fairmont.

When Bianca came down to the lobby, she saw the valet pull up and park the Ferrari. She waited in the lounge area for Jack to come down and periodically looked out to admire the car. When Jack finally arrived, he had one hand behind his back and was wearing casual clothing that was more for leisure than business. When she questioned him about it, he pulled his hand from behind his back and handed her freshly picked flowers. He smiled and told her how beautiful she was. Bianca wondered if she should change out of her formal attire into something more comfortable. She inquired about the meeting, but Jack just played it off and told her it would be an informal day.

After a brief delay Bianca came back down to the lobby dressed in a more comfortable look. Once again, Jack greeted her with a smile and, that time, a kiss on the cheek. It seemed that it didn't matter the situation, with her free spirit and soft looks, Bianca was always easy on the eyes, and Jack melted every time their eyes met.

They walked hand in hand like a couple of kids out to the area where the valets were. As they stood waiting, Bianca once again admired the Ferrari and told Jack how exciting it would be to drive it. As Jack turned and gave the signal, the valet who originally parked the car pulled up in front of them. He quickly stepped out and made his way around to the passenger side and opened the door.

Bianca stood in awe as Jack stood next to her gleaming with pride. He informed the valet that he was no longer needed by thanking him with a nice tip. As the valet excused himself, Jack held the door for Bianca. Without a word, she hesitated and then stepped into the car and quickly made herself comfortable. As Jack made his way around to the driver seat, he glanced over at Bianca, because she was the one gleaming with pride now.

At last, Jack was just where he wanted to be. With the beautiful woman he loved, in the coolest car he could find, and on the Pacific Coast Highway. Jack's thoughts raced for a minute as he shifted the car into gear. How nice it was to finally be able to enjoy all he'd worked for. With all the hard work and the drama of life, he hadn't felt that good since he was a young boy growing up.

Jack really didn't have a set plan. Sergis often came to the west coast on business trips and would always try to sell Jack on the idea of moving their company to California. He would always pester Jack about how clean the ocean air was and how free a person felt just being in a non-stressful environment.

Jack missed Sergis very much and always thought he would see the west coast with his best friend. The situation he was in with Bianca never even entered his thought process before. Nevertheless, he was enjoying the trip and feeling completely relaxed as he shifted the gears up and down as he drove around every twist and turn of the highway.

After a brief period of silence, Bianca finally confronted Jack. She tried to be subtle, but she wasn't exactly that kind of woman. Her aggressive but kind soul would often propel her into questioning Jack about his business, whether it was personal or professional. Jack didn't mind, though. He enjoyed that Bianca expressed herself with grace. Knowing he could rely on her to provide a difference of opinion gave him comfort.

Once again, Bianca asked about the trip and why he'd asked her to come along. She also confronted Jack on the little road trip he'd put together. She always chose her words carefully, placing Jack on the defense in a playful kind of way. Knowing the drive would be a long one, Jack had no choice but to tell Bianca there was no business trip. But being the shrewd businessman he was, he just simply made up another story to throw her off. A simple need to get away so he could see how Ben would handle business on his own. Bianca accepted the excuse and let Jack wiggle off the hook. Besides, she was enjoying the ride too much to pursue an argument.

As they weaved their way down the coast, they took in all its beauty and sights. Jack often pulled to the side just to smell the clean air Sergis had bragged about. Bianca took those opportunities to stretch her legs and needle Jack about seeing more of the country as a tourist rather than a businessman.

After making a few rest stops at some roadside inns, Jack finally arrived at his first destination. Although he really hadn't planned every detail, he did have an idea of the area where he wanted to end up.

Carmel, California. It was a coastal township established in the early 1900s. Because of its gorgeous land and seascapes, it had always attracted local and international artists. After touring the town and admiring the local art, Jack and Bianca visited the set of *A Summer Place*, which happened to be filming at the time. Although Jack wasn't connected in the film industry, he was a well-known businessman. When he introduced himself to the director, Mr. Delmer Daves, Mr. Daves was pleased to let them watch while filming was in progress. They even had the chance to meet two of the actors, Richard Egan and Sandra Dee.

After leaving Carmel, they visited the famous 17-Mile Drive created in the late 1880s by the Pacific Improvement Company. It was originally used by horse-drawn carriages and later made famous by car excursions for tourists from the Hotel Del Monte. Real estate along the 17-Mile Drive had always been desirable, whether private or business related. As for Jack and his tentative plan, he finally made it to his last destination, where he planned to let Bianca in on all the secrecy.

The sun was starting to set as he pulled off to the side of the road at one of the many lookout points along the route. Jack didn't really plan for the sun to be setting, but he was excited it was just the same. He down shifted and brought the Ferrari to a stop. Realizing no one else was around, he considered how perfect it was that no one happened to be at that particular point of interest at that time. Jack and Bianca both sat quietly and enjoyed the breeze and the spectacular sunset over the ocean. After a brief calm, Jack stepped out to stretch and Bianca followed. They walked as far as the landscape would allow.

Although Bianca had been enjoying the past few days, she knew Jack and knew he had something on his mind. She figured he would tell her eventually. That was why she didn't push too hard when she cornered him during their conversation about the trip. Just as the sun set and the daylight bowed down to the dusk, Jack casually struck up a conversation about the trip. Being genuine in his words, he asked Bianca's opinion of the last few days. He already knew the answer, but he wanted to hear her sweet words. She gave Jack a smile and gently took hold of his hands.

Thinking this might be Jack's way of trying to tell her something undesirable, she paused for a moment then gave him a hug. She then explained how wonderful life had been since they met and that the trip was what dreams were made of. She continued, telling Jack no matter what he was going through, she would stay by his side and they could work it out together. Trying to keep himself from laughing, Jack didn't want to string her along anymore. He quickly changed the conversation to the less emotional subject of real estate.

The quick change threw Bianca off and she became quite annoyed. He asked her what she thought about all the nice property they saw along the 17-Mile Drive. Bianca couldn't hold her temper anymore. She lashed out at Jack for being so deceitful. She couldn't believe he brought her across country to look at property that Kotter Industries was interested in.

Jack stood and watched in awe as Bianca tensed her body and was gearing up for a second attack. He knew if he didn't quickly defuse the situation, she would probably storm off in a fit of rage. Then he would lose his one and only opportunity to bring his plan to a close. Before she could get another harsh word in, Jack, in his subtle voice, asked how she would feel about having a summer home somewhere nearby. Before she could swoop down for her second go around, Bianca stopped for a moment to let Jack's words sink in. Her temper calmed for a minute, but then, in a disappointing voice, she explained that her family would never permit her to be single and live with a man. For the first time, Jack could hear in her voice how upset she was at him. Bianca turned away in disgust as tears started to fall.

Jack reached down into his pocket and pulled out a small ring box. He opened it up and the moonlight shined down on a one carat diamond ring. As Bianca turned back around, Jack didn't waste any more time. He motioned the ring towards Bianca and simply said, "Then marry me."

Bianca had no words. She still had tears falling, thinking their relationship was going to end. When she saw Jack with the ring, it took her breath away. Her tears of sorrow turned to tears of joy as she jumped into Jack's arms and held him tight. A few minutes went by and she still had no words. Normally a woman who had no problem expressing her opinion, Bianca just couldn't gather herself enough to let go. She finally pulled herself away and managed to breathe out just one soft word. "Yes."

It wasn't exactly how Jack imagined it and it definitely wasn't the plan to make Bianca cry. When everything was said and done, though, Jack was too busy enjoying the moment to care anymore. He knelt down on one knee and formally proposed. Bianca sat on Jack's knee and put one arm around him. She smiled then started to laugh, because they both already knew the answer. Jack picked her up and twirled her around as Bianca laughed with joy.

After a brief celebration, Jack once again asked about a summer home somewhere close. Bianca was very intuitive when it came to conversations. She would hang on every word of whoever happened to be talking to her. She noticed that twice Jack referenced the word "close." With her devious smile and some persuasive body language, she started inquiring about the location of the house, but Jack just laughed. He wasn't about to try to play any more games. He simply took her by the shoulders and gently spun her around. He pointed out a beautiful ten-acre lot across the road that backed up to miles of woodland. It was situated on a hill overlooking the lookout point where he proposed marriage.

Once again, she had no words. Bianca just couldn't believe Jack kept all that secret during their trip. She tried to play it off for a little revenge, but Jack wasn't having it. To avoid any more unforeseen heartache, Jack suggested they both start designing the house when they arrived back in New York. Bianca was all too happy to agree, so they stayed the night at another little, quaint inn along the route.

In the morning, they made their way to Pebble Beach. Jack had business dealings with the owner, Samuel F. B. Morse. They were good friends and Jack had called ahead to make plans to meet with him and his daughter, Mary Rose. Jack also made arrangements to have the Ferrari delivered back to San Francisco. After spending some time with Samuel and his daughter, Jack and Bianca took a private jet back to New York.

Jack had his driver waiting at the airport, but little did Bianca know Jack was scheming again. Knowing Bianca would be tired from the trip, he knew he wouldn't have any problem talking her into making a quick stop before going home. Fortunately for Jack, they hadn't eaten dinner yet, so he suggested stopping at the new Four Seasons Restaurant. He told Bianca he was curious to see what the excitement was. The owner, Mr. Samuel Bronfman, had spent 4.5 million dollars to build the Seagram Building, where the restaurant was located.

Bianca was tired but not tired enough to let Jack try to prank her any more. She had been reading about the building and knew the restaurant wasn't open yet. When she questioned Jack about it, he made the excuse that a private celebration was taking place and he happened to be on the guest list. Once again, Bianca let him wiggle off the hook, but only because she knew Jack had a lot of wealthy friends and he just might be telling her the truth.

When they finally arrived at 52nd and Park, Bianca could see people entering the restaurant, but really didn't take notice of who they were. As the driver pulled up to the curb, a porter stepped to the door to help them out. Bianca realized there was something going on, but she gave Jack the benefit of the doubt. As they stepped through the door, Ben approached and greeted them. Bianca didn't think it was out of the ordinary for Ben to also be there, so all three of them made their way into the dining area.

That's when Bianca saw her entire family waiting for her and realized Jack had tricked her again. It was an engagement party. She quickly turned to Jack and brought up the fact that his California trip didn't really go as planned.

"So what if the proposal didn't work out?" she asked.

Jack really didn't have an answer for her, but suggested she take comfort in knowing that it did and enjoy the party. They did just that.

After three months of planning, Jack and Bianca were married in a small ceremony. Since Jack's only family was Ben, the wedding was held in Baltimore where most of Bianca's family still lived. They honeymooned in Greece, where her parents met.

The turn of a new decade brought more fortune for Kotter Industries. The United States had been lagging in its efforts for a space program in 1957, when the Soviet Union launched *Sputnik 1*. It wasn't too long afterward, in 1958, that President Eisenhower signed The National Aeronautics and Space Act, establishing NASA.

On 5 May 1961, NASA launched its first manned rocket into space. It wasn't too hard for Jack and Ben to convince the board of directors to invest in this new area of industry. After buying out the smaller companies that were supplying materials to NASA, Kotter Industries went to work outbidding their competition for various government contracts.

As the 1960s came into full-swing and the younger generation was protesting, rioting, and enjoying their sexuality, Kotter Industries was business as usual. Jack and Ben divided the responsibilities of business travel, contract disputes, and confronting the board of directors with new ideas.

Because Jack engrossed himself in his business, it left very little time for Bianca. She was okay with this, because she knew Jack was mostly about business, and she had also been aware of what life would be like when she was married to him.

The one thing she did desire, and thought would be good for Jack, was a baby. So many times, she and Jack would have conversations about starting a family. Jack wasn't opposed, but it seemed like every time vacations or weekend getaways were planned, business interrupted and diverted Jack away. Bianca knew Jack wasn't getting any younger, so after a decade of wishful thinking, she decided to give up her quest for a family.

With the assassination of President John F. Kennedy in 1963 and his brother Robert Kennedy in 1968, the turbulent '60s finally ended on a positive note. In 1969, Apollo 11 landed and broadcasted man's first steps on the moon.

The year 1970 ushered in a new era for the United States. The first Earth Day was created. Politicians started to focus on protecting the environment and created various recycle and clean-up programs. Since a family was no longer an option, Bianca decided to meet Jack on his own playing field. At the very least, she could share Jack's enthusiasm for business.

Knowing Jack had an important business meeting concerning future projects, Bianca stormed into the boardroom and demanded to be heard. Jack found her interruption to be quite refreshing, knowing how those meetings usually wound up. Ben was not in a laughing mood and suggested Jack take her home. The rest of the board members had mixed emotions, but were like deer caught in headlights. They just stared.

Bianca had a briefcase and some poster board. Before anyone could get a word in, she quickly set up and started a presentation. She handed out some paperwork so everyone could follow along with what she was talking about. She concentrated most of her efforts on investing in recycling facilities. She'd even had a real estate agent investigate some existing companies. At the end of the presentation, the room was quiet. Everyone was absorbed in the logistics presented to them.

Ben was the first to get up. He stretched his legs then walked over to Bianca. With his usual not-so-happy look, he handed her the schematics and told her, her interruption was the boldest thing he had ever witnessed. He congratulated her on one of the best presentations he'd ever had the pleasure of being forced to listen to.

Bianca was asked to step out of the room while the board expressed their opinions. Jack was the first to speak. Aside from the fact Bianca was his wife, he thought it was definitely a good direction to look into for Kotter Industries. Ben was in total agreement. After a brief discussion, the board was almost unanimous in its vote. Kotter Industries had always forged ahead with the changing of times and the '70s was going to be no different.

The meeting rapped up much faster than expected, so that left Jack the rest of the day to spend with Bianca. Knowing that was a rarity, Jack didn't waste any of it. Dinner, the Broadway musical *Company,* and a late night walk through Time Square. Then, after everything was said and done, they went home for a romantic evening.

Kotter Industries eventually bought controlling interest in several recycling companies that had started to falter. Not very long after that, Ben worked his magic and secured several government contracts and a number of private contracts. Jack and Ben were the golden boys of industry. It seemed like everything they touched turned to money.

Bianca seemed to be enjoying her new-found projects. Ben actually gave her control overseeing all operations concerning recycling. Just like previous decades, the '70s had a great start. One evening in 1972, Jack came home from a late-night meeting. As he strolled up the sidewalk, Bianca greeted him at the door. He noticed she had a different look about her. He gave his usual kiss on the cheek, and she quickly grabbed his hand and pulled him into the house. She sat him down in his favorite chair, which he often fell asleep in. As tired as he was, Jack knew she had something to say. He just didn't know if it was good or bad.

As Bianca stood in front of Jack smiling, she asked him how he thought she would look wearing maternity clothes. Jack kind of giggled and thought she was just getting back at him for the many pranks he'd played on her. She then turned to the side, showing Jack her hands rubbing the profile of her stomach. After a brief pause, Jack realized the different look was the glow of a pregnant woman. He jumped to his feet with eyes as big as silver dollars. At the age of 64, he was suddenly going to be a father. Although late in life at the age of 51, Bianca finally received her wish. To start a family.

Nine months later, Jack Carnelius Kotter II was born. In memory of his father, Victor, Jack gave his son his father's middle name. Because Jack's father died when he was a boy, Jack always tried to spend as much time as possible with Jack Jr. Over the years, Jack had poured all his time and efforts into building Kotter Industries into the success it was, but after Jack Jr. came, he gave all his attention to Bianca and his son.

Ben was very happy for Jack and his new family. He was even asked to be Jack Jr.'s godfather. Of course he accepted. He tried to do as much as possible so that Jack could concentrate more on his family rather than the business. Between all the family time, vacations, and holidays, Jack still made a point to stay tuned in to what was going on with the inner workings of his company. No matter what, he still owned controlling interest in Kotter Industries.

Like all the previous decades, the '70s weren't without drama. Kotter Industries had to contend with several issues. The resignation of a United States President, the end of the Vietnam War, and the Iranian hostage crisis were just some of the ongoing problems, but Jack also had a new son and his life was forever changed.

Over the years, Jack often took his son to work with him. Once there, Ben was all too happy to steal him away for hours at a time. Jack Jr. was the apple of everyone's eye. Secretaries couldn't get enough of him. And Ben would always get a wink or two as he proudly pranced him around the office complex. Ben would spoil him rotten, buying an occasional ice cream cone and making the weekly trip to 5th Avenue where FAO Schwarz was located. Ben made sure Jack Jr. had every toy any kid could ever dream of.

Jack Jr. attended one of the oldest private schools in New York, Trinity School. Its motto reminded Jack of his father and himself: *Labore et virtute,* hard work and moral excellence. By the age 12, Jack Jr. was distinguished, respectful, and very intelligent, but every now and then would find himself in a bit of trouble, along with his friends. Whether it was just plain silly stuff kids do in school, such as fighting, or the more troublesome things they do out of school, like breaking nuisance laws, he would always count on Ben to pull strings and get him off the hook. Jack had high expectations for his son, so Jack Jr. never wanted his dad to know about his troubled times and be disappointed.

Connie Saunders was Jack Jr.'s best friend and was always around to help him get into trouble. They were two peas in a pod. Warner Jenks was the school clown and usually the beginning of all the trouble. Everyone knew this trio was inseparable, and if one was around, then the other two weren't too far behind.

Connie's family was very wealthy. His father was a stock market analyst on Wall Street. He invested in a company called Atari, which eventually paid off in the early '80s. Warner's family was also professional. Her parents were college graduates. Her father was a surgeon at New York University School of Medicine and her mom a lawyer with her own private practice. She specialized in business law and had represented Kotter Industries on several occasions.

On 1 September 1985, Jack was at his desk researching new projects, when his secretary connected a phone call to his private line. Jack's private line was reserved mainly for his family or Ben, or sometimes the questionable people he used to acquire various types of information. He picked up the phone expecting it to be Bianca, but soon realized it wasn't. The voice on the other end didn't identify himself, but Jack knew exactly who it was. The caller proceeded to tell Jack that a joint American-French expedition had finally located RMS *Titanic.* Jack sat back and slumped down in his chair. He couldn't believe after all the years of researching any and all material he could find, he would finally be able to lay his father to rest.

When it came to business and his personal life, Jack was a rock. He worked on many business-related and personal projects without anyone taking notice. *Titanic* and his father was definitely one of those projects. Jack told his source on the phone to keep at it and to find out as much information as possible. He definitely wanted to know how the expedition was going to proceed.

Later that same afternoon, the phone rang again. Jack was anxious and quickly picked it up. The news was bad. Jack's source informed him the decision was made to not move the ship. He also told Jack the terrible news that the ship had broken apart as it sank and it was now in two pieces.

Jack was devastated. Once again, he sat back in his chair. As tears started to form, he wiped them away, but more kept coming. At 77 years of age, he couldn't remember the last time he cried, if ever. He took a minute to remember the night of 14 April 1912 and he remembered his dad's smile.

On 3 September 1985, the media broke the story to the world. Jack, like the rock he was, kept his emotions in check. It was easy for him because he never told the story about his family being on *Titanic*. Not to his friends, not even to his wife or child. He knew it was time to move on.

As it turned out, Bianca's good business sense, combined with many government programs and media coverage, recycling gained momentum through the 1970s and into the 1980s. In December 1986 Bianca attended a meeting in Washington, D.C. to pressure the Reagan Administration for better environmental laws. She had also made plans to visit family in Baltimore during the Christmas holiday.

As the holidays came and went, Bianca felt good about the trip. She visited with family, including her father, who was long retired, and she felt the Washington trip made positive steps towards a better future for the environment. She was looking forward to the train ride back to her husband and son.

On 4 January 1987, Amtrak train 94 left Washington's Union Station headed for Boston. At 1:04 p.m., while passing through Chase, Maryland, it collided with a set of Conrail locomotives, killing 13 people. Bianca was injured severely enough to be airlifted to the Shock Trauma Center at the University of Maryland Medical Center.

Just as paramedics were preparing her for the ride, Bianca started to hemorrhage uncontrollably. She passed out and never regained consciousness. At the age of 66, Bianca was the fourteenth death of the tragic accident.

The incident made local and international news. Employees of Kotter Industries followed the story all afternoon, not knowing Bianca was on the train. Later in the day, Jack realized he hadn't talked to his wife all day. After meeting with Ben and some of the board, he called his secretary and asked if Bianca had called. The secretary had no messages and assured Jack she hadn't received any calls from Mrs. Kotter.

After conducting business all day, Jack finally had a chance to take a break. He saw some other secretaries hovering around a television and walked over to see why. Being the graceful person he was, it wasn't too long before he was talking and laughing with everyone.

When the news came back on, Jack stood watching as some of the ladies filled him in on what was going on. He knew Bianca's trip involved travel by train, so he quietly slipped away and started making phone calls. He would normally know her travel arrangements, but because of the personal plans she had, he wasn't quite sure what trains she had planned to be traveling on.

The media flashed a phone number across the screen in order for relatives of the victims to call and receive information. When Jack called, he was placed on hold for a few minutes. Afterwards, he spoke to a representative of Amtrak. Jack identified himself and inquired about the passenger list. He was informed that Bianca Kotter was one of the passengers, but Amtrak personnel couldn't give any further details.

Jack called Ben and had him come to his office. Ben could hear the trembling in Jack's voice and hurried down the hallway. He entered Jack's office and found him pacing in panic. Before Ben could say anything, Jack started to mumble about the accident. Ben couldn't understand him at first, but when Jack told him about the train wreck, Ben started piecing everything together.

After making Jack a stiff drink, Ben kicked into overdrive. He had contacts in just about every industry, including the medical field. He made a phone call to a doctor Kildero at the University of Maryland Medical Center. He was a surgeon at the Shock Trauma Center and a good friend of Ben's. Dr. Kildero was well aware of the day's events involving Amtrak and had no problem getting the information Ben needed. It was going to take some time, but Dr. Kildero assured Ben he would have some answers soon.

Jack and Ben sat in Jack's office with their eyes glued to the television. By that time, rumors started to spread throughout the office complex. The five o'clock hour was quickly approaching, but no one had plans of going home. Kotter Industries was family and everyone had the highest regard for Jack and Bianca.

When the phone call finally came, Jack could barely hold the phone. He sat listening as Dr. Kildero relayed the details of the accident. He even had the names and phone numbers of the paramedics who worked on Bianca in her final moments. As the tears rolled down his face, Jack thanked the doctor and hung up the phone. Ben had a tremendous amount of respect and love for Bianca. All he could do was hug Jack as all his sorrow and frustration came out.

After an exhausting afternoon, Ben arranged for one of the company limos to take Jack home. With his arm around him, Ben escorted Jack to the elevator. All the employees were still there in support. Jack stopped for a moment but just couldn't bring himself to say anything. Through all the pain, he placed both hands over his heart letting everyone know his warmest appreciations.

Ben also made sure Jack Jr. was excused from school and picked him up. When they arrived at the house, Jack was already inside resting. After such a traumatic day, Ben knew Jack didn't have the strength to tell Jack Jr. his mom was dead, so Ben thought it best if both sat Jack Jr. down to tell him. Ben wound up spending the night as the Kotter family coped with their loss.

After a few weeks, the media was still covering the story as lawsuits were eventually formed. Jack didn't feel the need to pursue any compensation, because it wouldn't bring Bianca back. He also knew Jack Jr. would never have a shortage of finances. With the death of Bianca, the constant hounding of the media, and the burden of moving forward, Jack and his son remained strong in their bond together.

Although he kept controlling interest, Jack eventually withdrew himself from Kotter Industries, leaving Ben with power of attorney to make all decisions concerning the company. Ben did exactly that.

Thinking they might try to force him out, he kept the executive board on a short leash. Knowing Jack's health was in question, Ben needed to be certain that when Jack Jr. became of age, he could step in and take control without any threats of a corporate takeover.

As the '80s came to an end and 1990 ushered in a new decade, Jack Jr.'s time at Trinity School soon came to an end. In 1991 Jack sat in the audience and watched his son graduate on stage. Jack Jr., Connie, and Warner walked arm and arm as they made their way down the aisle. Ben looked on as proud as he could be. Through the years, he was all too familiar with their many shenanigans, but nevertheless, he was proud of all of them.

Knowing he was being groomed to take over Kotter Industries, Jack Jr. didn't take any time off. He enrolled in Harvard Business School and started working his way towards a master's degree in business. In his spare time, he familiarized himself with industrial and labor laws and business economics.

In 1995, only one year before Jack Jr. was to graduate from college, Jack Kotter Sr., at the age of 87, died of natural causes. Like his mother, Elizabeth, it happened peacefully in his sleep. Jack's death came as no surprise, but that didn't make it any easier on Ben or Jack Jr. During the funeral, it became apparent just how much Jack Kotter Sr. was loved, respected, and well-known. The media covered the service as friends, employees, and Bianca's relatives stood in line to pay their respects. Kotter Industries completely shut down and made arrangements for everyone who wanted to attend.

Through the years, Jack Sr. had formed many friendships and helped many people. Friends living both in the States and overseas came. Even local politicians made sure the local and state police escorted the hearse to the cemetery. Jack Sr. was laid to rest next to his wife, Bianca. Just like his first company, the head stone simply read "Jack Kotter Sr. 1908-1995, Hauling life's ups and downs." Dedicated to his father even in the end.

CHAPTER THREE

At the age of 22, Jack Jr. inherited controlling interest of Kotter Industries. His father also left him the real property and all the investments, stocks, and bank accounts. Although power of attorney was previously given to Ben, it was Jack Sr.'s wish, according to his will, that the power of attorney be given to his son. Being of age and of sound mind, Jack Jr. became the president and CEO of Kotter Industries.

Jack was young, but was very intelligent. He decided not to finish his degree, and instead, took on the responsibility his dad had left him. Almost on a daily basis, he spent time with Ben to make sure he was up-to-date with everything going on within the company. Jack would often meet with Ben behind closed doors so Ben could counsel him on how to deal with the executive board members on difficult subjects.

For the most part, Kotter Industries had no real problems. The company's stocks always remained strong through turbulent times, mainly because Jack Sr. made sure the company would never over-extend itself. There were many perks for company executives, but even they were always monitored.

Soon after the death of Jack Sr., a meeting was held. For the first time in years, Ben and the board members were in full agreement with a decision to place new projects on hold. The stock market was booming and the company was doing just fine. Kotter Industries started as a hauling company then moved to the steel industry. After connecting with Bianca's family, Kotter Industries became strong in shipping, and then jumped on board with the government and NASA. They rounded everything out with their investment in recycling. Even during the late '80s and early '90s, when the United States steel industry was in a decline, Kotter Industries remained successful in its operations.

The company's success was particularly good for Jack, because his young age could be used against him if Kotter Industries ever became weak. During board meetings, Jack would just listen and learn. He never interrupted and always let Ben speak on his behalf. He took in as much information as possible. Like his mother, Jack was very intuitive. He hung on everybody's words as they spoke, and he always kept an eye on reactions of various board members during any disagreements.

With the creators of Microsoft, Bill Gates and Paul Allen, ushering in the computer era, the '90s became a full-blown battlefield. Companies such as IBM, Hewlett Packard, and Dell were racing to be the biggest and the best. It wasn't long before Kotter Industries saw an opportunity to, once again, expand, and Ben could no longer use the death of Senior as an excuse not to capitalize on an already profitable industry.

Since the board's creation in 1955, executive board members had come and gone. Some pursuing new avenues, some handing over the reins to a younger generation, and others just passing away. The only constant was Ben. When the board was created, it was treated as a democracy. Neither Jack Sr. nor Ben felt the need to have a chairman. When the company started to invest in various ventures, the board became divided, and in 1965, Ben was voted in as the chairman and had remained strong in the position ever since.

In 2001, the new millennium had come and gone, without global disaster, and Ben was still at the top of his game. Still sharp as a tack, and when push came to shove, could be ruthless among the best.

He knew the board was scheming and wanted to expand the company into the computer industry, but he held them off as long as possible. Ben had allies on the board and so did Jack, but Ben knew they couldn't wait too long and called for a meeting. The day of the meeting was definitely going to be a long day, and most likely, nothing was going to get resolved. Over a six-year period Ben had instilled as much information into Jack as possible, in terms of corporate rules, laws, and what the executive board could and could not do. The more information at Jack's disposal meant the more ammunition he had to defend himself and Kotter Industries.

All the board members were stockholders. In fact, over the years members of the board had managed to somehow buy back most of the stock sold off back in 1955. Two days before the meeting, Ben met with Jack to review whom he would have to confront and what the issues were going to be. One of the most important strategies Ben taught Jack was to know his opponent. Know their strengths, and more importantly, know their weaknesses.

Through the years, Ben fought many boardroom battles, winning most and losing few, always leaving the battlefield in one piece, but the older he grew, the younger the board members became. Back in the day, the board members were old and stuffy. They were always friends and had nothing but respect for each other. In current times, as he sat at the head of the table, he saw more youth. Young go-getters who were hungry for power and money. Not necessarily in that order. He wanted Jack to know what he was up against.

Nicholas Cummings. His father, Carroll Cummings, was one of the original board members. Carroll's health had become an issue, so he'd passed his wealth and knowledge on to his only child. Soon after, he'd passed away. Nicholas was a good friend of Jack's.

Ethan St. John. Also Jack's age and a good friend, he was a college graduate with business degrees. He'd started at the bottom and worked his way up. He was very bright and was voted into his position and remained a good ally to Jack.

William Holden. Not to be mistaken for the actor back in the '50s. At 53 years of age, he'd bought stock in the company and then decided to weasel his way into a management position. He eventually made his way into the boardroom. He was a backstabber, but also a conservative.

Linda Roth. Linda was drop-dead gorgeous, but a conniving bitch. If a man wasn't careful, she would steal his heart and laugh in his face when she ripped it out. She would do anything to get to the top. Anything.

Jonathan Rourke. He also inherited his fortune through his father's good investments. His father, Charles Rourke, had died under mysterious circumstances shortly after adding his son to his will. Just a coincidence? Who knows? Jonathan was always looking to make a power move.

Stanley Albrek. Stanley was a conservative, but could also be bought for the right price. Known as the "deal maker," he made deals all the way to the boardroom, laying waste to anyone who stood in his way.

Robert Alders. He was Ben's age and conservative. He was very impressive when it came to business sense, as he was well versed in business law and was an economic genius. He remained good friends with Ben even though they didn't always see eye to eye.

Kathy Webb. She was very snooty, but also conservative. She'd obtained her money the old-fashioned way: She'd won it. Her father was once a board member, many years before, but chose to sell off all his shares and go over to the competition. He'd bought stock in Bethlehem Steel, which turned out to be a bad move.

Anthony Steiner. Anthony had time invested in Kotter Industries. He was 60 years old and had been with the company for 30 years. He was a bright and funny man who'd become old and grumpy, doing nothing in recent years but grumbling about how he should be the chairman of the board.

Lewis Rawlings. He was a regular Alex P. Keaton. He'd been politicizing all his life. He usually went with the majority, but every now and then, he'd make a stand, as long as it benefited him.

Richard Bender. Richard had a lot of friends in low places. He was always trying to maneuver his way into power plays. They very seldom work out, but he was a smooth operator. He could sweet-talk most of the board when he needed something.

Fitzgerald Voulke. Fitzgerald was from Germany. He was a very laid-back man. He was part of an upper management team for LERO International Forwarding, based out of Germany. When it came time to share the profits, he was left out, and that's when he walked out. But not before he microfilmed all the company secrets. Legal and illegal. Not that Kotter Industries promoted industrial espionage.

Jack already had some idea about their personalities because he spoke to all of them on a regular basis, just not about business. Ben made sure he kept Jack away until the time was right. Ben's last words for Jack before the meeting were: "It's good to know a person, but it's better to know what they're about."

Ben and Jack emerged from Ben's office and made their way down the hall to the boardroom. Both men were heavily armed with briefcases and notebooks. Ben stopped at the glass doors and turned to Jack.

"You ready, kid?"

Jack looked at Ben and gave a soft smile. "Come on, Ben, you and my dad groomed me for this. I'm not going to let you down."

Ben gave him a gentle pat on the back. "Okay, kid. Ding, ding the bell has been rung."

Jack and Ben were the last to enter the boardroom. Everyone else was there and seated and, of course, already trying to line up their last-minute alliances. Jack walked in with a very confident look.

"Hello, everyone." He was dressed to impress and everyone stopped bickering to notice.

Ben said his usual nothing and walked straight to his seat. He slammed his briefcase down to get everyone's attention. With his raspy voice, he barked out the order, "Okay, shut your traps and let's get this party started."

They all knew Ben wasn't pleased with the direction the board members wanted to take, but they also knew he had to at least entertain them. Besides, the majority only took eight votes.

Ben pulled out some paperwork from his briefcase and held it in his hand. He looked at the top page briefly and laid the stack on the desk.

"Let me just begin by saying this. Most of you have been with this company a long time. Some of you a little less time. Robert and Anthony, both of you have been here the longest. I'm not going to take the time to name names, but I did not appreciate certain board members trying to pressure this company into making decisions that could eventually cripple us. And for what? Quick money? That's not why or how this corporation got its start and that's not how we operate today. So, with that said, Jack, you have the floor."

Jack stood up and adjusted his suit. He also had his briefcase, which was filled with paper, open on the table. "Why don't we start by finding out where everyone stands. Obviously, buying into a different field of interest isn't going to happen overnight. Robert, we'll start with you. What say you?"

Robert could always support a good argument and had the good sense and intelligence to back up his words. "Listen, the idea of computers has been around since 1939. Usage was strictly industrial. In the late '80s they started creeping into households, and now the industry is just a full-blown war. I can tell you this, with each decade comes technological breakthroughs that used to be considered science fiction. It stands to reason this field has unlimited potential. I say we move forward to capitalize on its success." As Robert sat down, he could feel Ben burning a hole through him with his eyes.

Jack didn't seem fazed and moved on to the next person. "Fitze, tell us your opinion."

Fitzgerald didn't bother to get up. He leaned back in his chair then spoke something in German. He smiled and looked down the table at Jack. "You Americans have a saying: If it's not broke, then don't fix it. Why do Americans feel the need to dominate everything? I say we stick with what we have."

"You're right. Good point, Fitze." Jack smiled and moved on. "Kathy, you're next."

Kathy really didn't care about board meetings, business, or what the other board members thought. Her interest involved getting the best results for her money. "My father was a fool and wasted the family fortune on a dead company. I won't be following in his footsteps. I agree with Fitze."

Jack sat down and spread out his paperwork. He paused for a minute then was ready to get back on track. "Anthony, what say you?"

Of course Anthony stood up. He was always trying to be the professional and to outdo Ben. "I'm thinking about Jack Sr. He was innovative and a doer. He wasn't afraid of taking chances and he wasn't afraid of failure. I think he would have jumped at the opportunity to invest in today's technology. I say we don't hold back, and take Kotter Industries into the future. Thank you."

Jack listened but didn't take offence. He knew Anthony didn't mean any harm by guessing what his dad might have done. "Lewis, what say you?"

Lewis took a deep breath. "I've been listening to all the arguments today and over the past few years. There's no doubt the computer industry is well on its way to bigger and better things. It's already a proven and successful technology. I say it would be a win for Kotter Industries to invest its resources and buy into it."

Once again, Jack looked at his notes while he pivoted his chair around in half-circles. He straightened his chair out so he could pick the next person. "Stanley, how are you today, sir? Tell us your opinion."

Stanley sat up straight and leaned over the table. "I agree with Lewis. I think the potential is great and the risk minimal. There's a large financial gain to be made here."

Jack sunk his eyes into Linda and couldn't help but blush. Thoughts of eye candy raced through his mind. "Linda, the floor is yours."

With her leather skirt looking like she had to use mink oil to get it on, and the two top buttons on her see-through blouse looking like they were about to pop, she peered into Jack's eyes and gave a come-hither smile. "Jack, you know I don't like to be difficult, but I don't sit on this board to lose money. Besides, if you would have taken me up on my invitation to Italy, we may have been able to work something out. I'm going to have to agree with Robert."

After that eye contact, Jack had to take a minute and recover. He loosened his tie and took a breath. "Richard, let's hear from you."

Being the smooth operator that he thought he was, Richard gave his best ten-dollar smile as he stood up. "I've done a little research on my own. In today's world, technology is where it's at, and if we don't get in now, ten years from now, Kotter Industries will be no more."

Ben grumbled a little then covered it up with a cough. He couldn't stand Richard. He was too stupid to actually know anything, but then he tried to make it sound like he knew what he was talking about. If he had spent half the time investing in himself as he had trying to get into Linda's pants, Ben may have had more respect for the guy.

After Jack finished scratching his head in confusion, he wrote a couple of notes on some paper and decided to move on. "Jonathan, you're next."

Although Jonathan could come off as sleazy, he actually understood business and, at times, could be very useful. "Well, Jack, I think Kotter Industries has enough to chew on right now. There's no doubt the technology available today is valuable, but if you take a step back and look at the big picture, you can see it's moving way too fast for anyone to keep up with. Kid games, cell phones, computers. As soon as a new product comes out, a year later, there's an up-to-date version to replace it. I don't think we should try to jump on something that's moving way too fast."

Jack was truly surprised. He was sure Jonathan would try to backdoor him. He was actually impressed. Ben's jaw had dropped in the middle of Jonathan's impressive speech and was still hanging after he finished.

Jack stood up to get a glass of water. "Would anyone like a drink?"

As usual, Linda liked to play. "Sure, Jack, but I would like for you to serve it at my house."

Jack was just as vulnerable as the next guy when it came to beautiful, horny females. Whenever Linda set her sights on him, he would just think about his longtime girlfriend Bria.

Bria was stunning. She was tall and had a body any woman would kill for. She had long black hair, dark skin, dark eyes, and could very easily take down any female in her path. Bria knew about Linda, and Jack did everything in his power to keep them apart.

Watching Linda as she tried her best to undress him with her eyes, Jack sat back down and took a long sip of water. "Alright. Let's get back to business. William, you have the floor."

William was already upset that it took so long to bring the meeting to order. He was a weasel, but he did have a mind for business. "I think it's despicable we didn't get in on the ground floor years ago when computers for the average everyday Joe were being developed. Jack, your father was a good man and I'm not going to speak ill will towards him, but he could be stubborn. Now, I've given Kotter Industries time to mourn and I would like to say my peace. Even though we missed our golden opportunity, I still think we can salvage a bad situation before it becomes terminal. I say we take our chances and buy."

Ben was very sensitive when it came to Jack Sr. He normally wouldn't stand for any comments made about him, but he felt since Jack was in the room, it wasn't his place to say anything. But he thought, *There is always another day.*

Jack didn't let the comments bother him. In fact, he kind of went with it. "Yeah, you're right, William. As the years went by, my dad may have become a little stubborn, but my dad, along with Ben and his brother

Sergis, built this company from the ground up. Leading this company into profits for 68 years, I think he could afford to be stubborn."

Ben sat back in relief and enjoyed the show. He felt an overwhelming sense of pride watching Jack handle himself through the situation. Jack was managing the meeting with such confidence, Ben actually started to become bored. He stretched out his arms and yawned. "Oh, excuse me. Sorry, not used to just sitting here. Please continue."

Jack just laughed. He knew Ben was just toying with the members. "Nick, you have the floor."

"Well, I was really impressed with Jonathan's opinion. I was on the fence with this, but I think Jonathan put it in perspective for me. I say no."

Jack thought he knew Nick's answer already, but became a little worried about the fence comment. Still, he was glad to hear the word no.

"Okay, Ethan. You're up."

Ethan was a little glad to be last, because he was able to hear everyone's comments and ideas, and knew he could express his opinion and not be worried about standing alone. "I think that both arguments hold merit. I also know this company voted a few years ago not to take on any new projects or tap into any new industries, mainly because of the passing of Mr. Kotter, so I'm going to have to go with no."

After hearing everyone's opinions and ideas, Jack looked at his watch and realized a few hours had passed. He stood up and looked around shaking off the stiffness in his legs. "Okay everyone, let's take an hour break and we'll reconvene back here and talk about an official vote."

Not everyone caught the wording Jack used in his last sentence. While all the board members were making their exit, Robert stopped to talk with Jack. He had a wondering look as he sat on the corner of the table.

"What does that mean?"

Jack put on his best puzzled look. He knew Robert was sharp, but didn't want to get trapped with his own words. "Robert, you're always reading too much into things. What does what mean?"

Robert paused for a second to try to break down Jack's poker face. "'Talk about a vote.' What does that mean?"

Jack laughed as he was placing his notes into his briefcase. "My mom was like that. She hung on every word when someone was speaking to her. She could catch even the tiniest piece of information and use it against you. Drove my dad nuts. I just meant that when we come back, we'll sit and talk about what's best for Kotter Industries and how we're going to proceed."

Robert became a little flustered as he stood up and straightened his tie. "Don't mess around, Jack. There's too much at stake here. I don't know why Ben wasn't running this meeting. I don't think you have a clue about what you're doing." He stormed out leaving Jack and Ben bewildered.

Jack closed his briefcase and looked down the table at Ben who hadn't moved since the first break. "Well, what do you think, Ben?"

Ben usually had no shortage of words for Jack, but chose to stay quiet and let him get his feet wet. "I hope you have this situation contained. These members might look like a bunch of clowns, but don't take them too lightly. They'd roll you and take your wallet if they thought they could get away with it."

Jack smiled as he walked down to the end of the table. "Between my dad and you, don't you think with all that experience I can handle a bunch of gold diggers?"

As he stood up, Ben just played off the ass kissing. "Listen, kid, your dad and I taught you everything you needed to know and then some in order to run this company, but unless you use all the resources available to you, you will eventually be overrun, and then what? Kick back and let someone else just come in and take what took a lifetime for your father to build?"

Jack could think of nothing to say. He knew Ben was right, and he also knew Ben didn't give people a chance to voice their opinions, as during the meeting. Jack walked around Ben and headed for the door. "I'll see you in an hour, Ben. Don't be late."

As Jack walked out, Ben grabbed his notes and hastily shoved them in his briefcase. As he gathered himself to walk out, he realized what Jack had said. Don't be late? Who the hell did he think he was talking to?

As Ben walked out of the boardroom, he was approached by Nick and Ethan. They didn't have to say a word. Ben knew exactly what they were thinking. With frustration written all over his face, Ben raised his hand in the air. "Hold on, boys. Let's go in here and we'll talk." They stepped into one of the empty meeting rooms and locked the door.

Nick was upset because it seemed like Jack wasn't taking the meeting very seriously. "Damn it, Ben, did you meet with Jack at all before today? Don't you understand this company could take a serious nosedive if these greedy bastards have their way?"

Ben tensed like a concrete statue ready to crack as he slammed his briefcase down on the table.

Before he could say anything, Nick continued his assault. "Why is Jack even talking? You're the chairman. You should be running the show. You're just sitting there like a bump on a log."

After hearing Nick, Ethan made the grave mistake of getting into the conversation. "Nick is right, Ben. Can you get in on this meeting so we can divert this approaching disaster? At the very least, you should be voicing your opinion."

Ben could feel his temper about to explode, but decided to take a breath to cool down. It didn't help much. He chose Nick to be his first target. "Little man, your dad and I were very close friends. He was intelligent and knew how to play the game. It's out of respect for him that I'm not ripping your head off right now." Like a drill sergeant, he turned his anger towards Ethan. "As for you, butt boy. Who the hell do you think you are? His sidekick? I don't see a cape. And I sure don't see someone who knows what the hell he's talking about."

Ben's voice grew louder as he continued his counter attack against the two men. The secretaries down the hall stopped working so they could enjoy the spectacle. It was always entertaining when Ben chewed someone's head off. Scary, but entertaining.

Ben finally realized he was out of control and walked over to the window to take another breather. He knew Nick and Ethan were Jack's friends and that they were just worried about the future of Kotter Industries. As his blood pressure came back down, Ben was able to put things in perspective. "Sit down, boys. Go ahead, have a seat. You're right. I am the chairman, but I wanted to give Jack an opportunity to address the board so he could see just how greedy these pigs are. Listen, Jack needs all the help he can get, and to answer Nick's question, yes, of course we went over strategies and talked about various outcomes before today. I'm not as old and senile as I look."

A feeling of relief came over Nick and Ethan as they both sat listening to Ben's attempt at humor. Ethan stood up and walked over to the window. He stood with his hands in his pockets as he watched the cars in the distance moving up and down the highway. "Maybe we shouldn't have waited this long to have this meeting. I know the death of Jack's dad was a huge blow to the company, but as a company, we should have moved on. Because of our personal feelings, we placed ourselves in a bad position."

Ben sat on the edge of the table and crossed his arms. He thought about the words he was going to say before he blurted them out, which didn't happen very often. "You're absolutely right, Ethan. Jack Sr. would've understood. I remember when Sergis died. Jack was almost systematic in his grieving process. After everything was said and done, he went right back to work like it was nothing. I guess I just don't expect Jack to be like his dad."

Nick still wasn't feeling any better about the day's events. Ben could see he was still troubled. "If it makes you feel any better, Nick, I do have back-up plans just in case things get out of control in there."

Nick shot Ben a sarcastic look and took a deep breath. "I think we're past that point, Ben. The majority could swing us if just one person changes their mind."

Ben snickered and shook his head. "I think you're wrong. Although I don't agree with giving that much leeway to people, I do think Jack had it under control. I didn't interrupt because it just seemed to me he had an ace up his sleeve."

With a look of interest, Ethan sat back down. "What do you mean? Did he tell you something before the meeting?"

Ben stood up and walked back over to the window. "No, he didn't say anything. But there was something. It's hard to explain. Back in the sixties, his dad and I were involved with the hostile takeover of Magna Corp. It was a small corporation that supplied the government with materials to build launch pads."

Nick's gloomy look quickly left his face as he sat up to pay attention to Ben's story. But he committed the ultimate no-no. He interrupted Ben. "So, what happen?"

Ben shot him one of those looks that could kill. "If you shut your face long enough for me to finish, I'll tell you. Anyway, I remember Senior wouldn't tell me anything. He just told me everything was going to be fine. I remember being so angry. I knew if we didn't get that company, our chances of competing in the race for space were out the door. But what I didn't know was that he had some friends in D.C. who made some calls and some threats, which eventually put the deal over the top for us."

Nick waited until he knew for sure Ben was finished. "So, what is your thinking on this? You think Jack has something going on like that?"

Ben paused for a few seconds then let out a small laugh. "No, Jack isn't old enough to have friends like that, and if he did, I would know them. But what I do see in Jack is the same look I saw in his father. He's got something. I just haven't figured out what it is yet."

Ethan stood up and fixed his tie and jacket. "I hope you're right Ben. I also hope you figure out what it is before we get back to the boardroom."

Ben just hung his head and realized how hungry he was. "Come on, boys. Let's grab some lunch. My treat." The three men walked out and closed the door. The secretaries quickly grabbed papers and some even placed their phones to their ears. As Ben walked down the hall, he gave everyone the okay. "Alright, ladies, the show is over. I should dock every one of you an extra half-hour, but you're all lucky I'm a nice guy." Ben could be a charmer sometimes. "So," he said to Ethan and Nick, "anything you boys want, as long as it's under 10 dollars."

With an hour break, Robert Alders knew he had a small window of opportunity. He asked Stanley and Kathy to join him for lunch and a private meeting. Robert gave Stanley a courtesy call to let him know the invite wasn't a heartfelt gesture.

As the ringtone started, Stanley answered with a confident voice. "Hello, Robert. Don't worry, I'm coming."

Robert really wasn't in the mood to hear the cheesy remarks Stanley always conveyed, but he needed him to help convince Kathy to change her vote. "Listen, you moron, this isn't *Fun with Dick and Jane*. I need you to help me woo Kathy to vote our way."

Stanley wasn't expecting cheap jokes, especially coming from Robert. It took a second for him to realize Robert had an agenda.

"Damn, Robert, you really know how to burst a guy's bubble. I was actually looking forward to having lunch with you."

Uptight and stressed, Robert tried to keep his patience intact. "Listen, Stanley, opinions are about even and I'm already looking into legal means to take action. We can't afford to take the chance of someone changing their mind against us, and we certainly can't delay the vote any longer. You and I are going to eat light while Kathy listens to our reasoning."

Stanley was the equivalent of a greasy salesman, but he also had an intelligence about him. He knew Robert was making sense and he also knew Robert chose him over everyone else. Using a combination of charm, salesmanship, and good old-fashioned bribery, it was, once again, time to broker a deal.

Knowing most board members would elect to eat at the several restaurants within the office complex, Robert chose to meet at the diner out on Route 110. When he pulled onto the lot, he noticed Kathy was just walking in. Stanley was nowhere to be found, so he waited. A few minutes later, Stanley pulled onto the lot and parked his car. Robert stepped out and walked over to greet him. "You must drive like you're 'Driving Miss Daisy.' What took you?"

Stanley couldn't help but laugh. "You're really on today with those jokes. I've never seen this side of you before."

Robert was getting more tense by the minute. "Just follow my lead and do your thing."

As they walked into the diner, they saw that Kathy was already seated. The greeter promptly seated them as they exchanged pleasantries.

Robert took his menu and started the conversation. "Thank you for meeting me here, Kathy. What a day it's been."

Kathy might have been snooty, but she was by no means stupid. She knew Robert was up to something. Besides, none of the board members actually liked each other, so why would Robert suddenly, out of the kindness of his heart, invite her to lunch?

One thing Stanley didn't believe in was dillydallying around, so he decided to be blunt. "Listen, Kathy, I'm not going to patronize you, so I'll get straight to the point."

Kathy smiled and politely interrupted. "Before we get down to business, boys, can we order first? I'm starving."

Robert just shook his head in disgust, thinking his plan just went up in flames. He wasn't expecting Stanley to be so honest. "Sure, we can order, but we need to really talk about what went on in that meeting."

Kathy agreed as she placed her order with the waitress. "I'll have the ham and cheese on rye and the soup of the day, and may I have a refill on my water please? So, for what do I owe the honor of having lunch with you two fine gentlemen today?"

Stanley knew sarcasm when he heard it, but didn't pay it any mind. "You voted against moving into the computer industry earlier today. I don't really buy that lame excuse you gave about your dad. So tell me, do you always turn down money or is this a woman thing you're going through?"

Robert couldn't believe his ears. This guy was supposed to be turning on the charm and all he had done so far was insult the woman.

As the waitress placed the food on the table, he couldn't help but wonder why he recruited the idiot sitting across from him. Since Stanley obviously was incapable of doing the job, he decided to play the part of the good guy. "Woe, Stanley. Cool your jets. Jack asked our opinions and Kathy gave hers based on personal experience."

Kathy was impressed. She knew the tactics of good cop, bad cop, but she figured Stanley would come off smooth and Robert would be the ass. "Listen, fellas. Let's not jerk each other around. We're running out of time, and we still have to finish eating and then get back to the boardroom. So let me follow Stanley's lead and be blunt. Robert, you want me to change my feelings on how I'm going to vote. You somehow talked numb-nuts here into sweet-talking me and he did the exact opposite. I need to get you boys in the poker room so I can bankrupt the both of you. You guys suck at this."

Robert just sat with his mouth open. He didn't know if he should applaud or just get up and leave. "I'm sorry, Kathy. I feel very strongly about this decision and I didn't want to take the chance of a hung jury. Your vote would put us over the top and I don't think you would have any regrets."

As Kathy was finishing the last bite of her sandwich, Stanley decided to throw a little motivation into the mix. "Listen, Kathy, we don't doubt your sincerity, but do you think it's economically sound?"

Kathy gave a smile and laughed. "Stanley, you need to stop using big words you don't understand. Let me tell you what's economically sound. Kotter Industries is doing just fine and is making us millions. Why should I risk what I already have and wind up getting burned like my broke-ass father? Did you guys have plans to offer me any incentives, or did you think I would just hand over my vote out of the goodness of my heart?"

Stanley took a drink of his water and gave Robert a small nod.

"Of course we have an idea to run by you. I think Robert would agree there are millions to be made if we make the move, so we are prepared to offer you controlling interest in the companies we decide to buy."

Kathy sat back for a moment and gathered her thoughts as she contemplated what was being said. "That's it? That was your plan? Are you stupid, or do you just think I am? There are fourteen members of the board, including Ben. There's no guarantee control over the ladies' room, let alone any companies we may or may not buy." Kathy took one last drink of water and stood up. "I don't know how the hell you boys managed to get to the positions you're in. By the way, one or both of you can pick up the check."

After Kathy stormed out of the diner, Stanley stood up and wiped his face with his napkin. "I'll be back. I have to use the restroom before we go."

Robert was still in awe. He wasn't sure just how his great idea slipped away from him so quickly. He gathered himself together and walked over to the cashier. "Hi, sweetie, in a minute there's going to be a jackass coming out of the men's room. Just give the check to him. Oh, by the way, he said something about giving a fifty-dollar tip. Make sure he doesn't forget."

Back at Kotter Industries, Ben was in his office making some notes and talking on the phone, when Jack walked in. He waited a few minutes as Ben finished his conversation and hung up.

"I know you're the big cheese, kid but have you ever heard of knocking? Have a seat."

Jack smiled as he unbuttoned his jacket and sat down. "Don't worry, Ben, I already know all your little secrets. Besides, most of the secretaries don't want to be alone in here with you."

As Jack laughed, Ben could feel his blood pressure rise. "Will you get serious? All your life you're always jerking people around. Anyway, that was a friend of mine on the phone. Seems that some of your executive board had a small meeting down the road. I think Robert may have been trying to swing more votes over to his way of thinking. It's already in a deadlock. Doesn't surprise me a bit that he's trying to make a move." Ben sat down at his desk with a very distraught look. "Most of the time he's a straight up kind of guy."

Jack stood up and buttoned his jacket. "Look, Ben, you said it yourself. This company isn't what it used to be. It's not family orientated anymore. Nowadays, it's 'all about the Benjamins,' no pun intended. Before we reconvene, why don't you talk to him? I know you consider him a friend. Be blunt. If he's your friend, he'll be honest with you."

Jack was about to walk out when he stopped and turned around. "I understand why you and my dad went public with Kotter Industries, but since then, you could say we're back to being somewhat private. You and I hold the majority of stock. The executive board scarfed up most of what's left."

Ben suddenly felt a sick feeling in his stomach. He jumped up from his desk with a frightened look. Jack actually became scared. He thought Ben was about to keel over. "What's wrong, Ben? You suddenly look worse than you usually do."

The light bulb in Ben's head lit up like Christmas. "I can't believe I didn't see this coming." With one hand on his head and the other on his hip, Ben started pacing.

Jack's joking mood went into panic mode. Very rarely had he ever seen Ben uptight. "Ben, you look white as a ghost. Tell me what you're thinking."

Ben went to his desk and pressed a hidden button. A secret compartment slowly began to emerge and he pulled out a key chain with too many keys to count. "I knew there was something funny about how the board members managed to buy up most of the remaining stock that was available. I started to build some case files on each board member so I could track their movements by monitoring financial transactions and even checking out who they were associating themselves with. I got distracted when your father passed away. The past few years haven't yielded too much information, so I locked the files away and forgot about it."

Jack was more confused than when Ben first went into his panic mode. "Ben, slow down. What are you talking about?"

Ben walked over to a huge file cabinet. It was very old with a type of lock that might be on a pirate chest. "Listen, kid, I know you're young, but you really need to start thinking in corporate terms if you're going to keep your father's company. Your dad and I agreed when Sergis died to let the company go public. That way we could vote in an executive board in order to take away some of the day-to-day pressures. When we went public, we sold off a small percentage of our stocks. Don't you find it strange that thirty-nine years later, the current board members somehow managed to get their hands on most of the available stock?"

Jack sat down for a minute to think about what Ben was telling him. "I don't think it's that strange since most of the members either bought into Kotter Industries or inherited their stock from relatives."

Ben finally pried the old lock off and pulled out one of the drawers. He selected several folders and handed them to Jack. "Skim through the folders and I'll show you what I'm talking about."

Jack looked at his watch. "Ben, we're late. We have to get back to the meeting."

The last thing on Ben's mind was finishing a meeting he didn't care too much about in the first place. "Listen, kid, we can't go back in there now. I need to check out a few things first."

Jack stood up and placed the folders on Ben's desk. "What do you want me to do? I have to go back in there. They're expecting a vote to be made today."

Ben became flustered and started to ramble. "I don't give a rat's ass about what they expect. Our main priority is to protect this company. Just go back in there and tell them I ate something bad for lunch and got sick. I ate downstairs at that awful café anyway. They'll believe you."

Jack was looking forward to finishing the business of the day, but could see how upset Ben was. He agreed with Ben and walked out. He walked down the hall to the boardroom and saw that the blinds were open. Jack peered through the window and saw everyone waiting. He could see Fitzgerald speaking to Robert and Stanley arguing with

Kathy. Everyone else was just lost in space, waiting on the meeting to resume. As he walked through the door, all heads turned.

Never short of angry words, Anthony decided to speak his peace. "Your younger generation just doesn't understand the meaning of being on time. You think the world revolves around you. Well, it doesn't. And I don't appreciate being forced to wait."

Jack wasn't normally an uptight person, but after all that just happened, he could feel the pressure. "I apologize, Mr. Steiner. Ben got a little sick after lunch so he won't be back. As for you waiting, you will do as I say and like it. I know you don't agree, but I still run this company. Now, does anyone else want to form an opinion about my habits?" Everyone could see Jack was upset about something so no one else said anything.

Jack walked over and stood at the head of the table. "Okay, I know we don't like each other, but I'm sure everyone here has a mutual respect when it comes to illnesses. We will reconvene next week and conclude our business." Jack walked out of the room before anyone could say anything.

Anthony stood up with his usual grumblings. "To hell with him. To hell with Ben, too. The day will come when I run the show, and when it does, that boy will no longer be part of this company."

Nick and Ethan walked out behind Jack as the others gathered up their belongings.

Although Robert headed the charge to reinvest the company, he was still Ben's friend. "Shut up, Anthony. You're an old fool that got passed by. Get over yourself and move on. And if I ever hear you speak ill will towards Ben again, I'll make sure you're no longer with this company." With that said, Robert walked out with everyone else, leaving Anthony to sit and ponder Robert's words.

After speaking with his secretary, Jack made his way back to Ben's office. Just before he opened the door, he remembered being scolded by Ben about knocking first, so he stopped himself from walking in and knocked. Just then, Anthony was leaving to go home and saw Jack in the hallway. He hid in a small corridor and listened as Ben yelled for Jack to come in. He waited a few more minutes to see if Jack would come back out, but he didn't so Anthony scurried down the hall to the elevator.

When Jack walked in, Ben was still rummaging through his file cabinet and pulling out folders. "Sit down, kid, and start going through these folders."

Jack took his jacket and tie off because he knew when Ben sunk his teeth into something, it would be a long night. He rolled up his sleeves and grabbed the top folder. "Is there something in particular we're looking for?"

Ben pulled out more folders and laid them on his desk. He saw that Jack had made himself comfortable and realized it might be a good idea. "Yeah, I'm looking for the history of the stock. Who first acquired it and how the stock made its way to its current owner."

Jack already had a folder open and was looking through the notes Ben had written. He also noticed the name. Richard Bender. Ben peered over Jack's shoulder as his eyes scanned the folder. "Yeah, kid. A really greasy character. He bought into the company back in 1990 when one of the original shareholders, Mr. Franklyn Summit, passed away. His death was ruled suicide, but he wasn't the type. He had no relatives and no will, so by law, his stock went public. Richard just happened to be on the floor of the New York Stock Exchange when it did. Luck or coincidence? Unknown. He had Robert's endorsement for the executive board." Ben couldn't wait to dig into the pile of folders and grabbed one as Jack finished reading his.

"So, Ben, why don't you think Mr. Summitt committed suicide?"

Ben put his folder down and gave Jack the "I'm positive" look. "Come on, kid. He was older than me. He loved life and would constantly invite your dad and me over to fish off his pier. Very smart man. The police said he passed out from exhaust fumes while he was in his garage."

Jack placed the folder on the floor by his chair and laughed. "Okay, he was an old man. Maybe he just took too long one day getting out of his garage."

With a frustrating sigh, Ben just shook his head. "He helped your mom establish her recycling companies because he was a damn tree hugger. He drove one of those ugly Yugos, for Christ's sake, and his garage door was always up because it was broken. Now shut the hell up and pay attention."

"I have William here. This clown is a real character. He bought his stock back in eighty-five when it went down due to the poor performance in steel manufacturing. Now get this, he didn't buy it straight up. He was dating a woman who already had it in her portfolio. She was just an investor and not a board member. But the funny thing was, he paid her less than what it was worth. Shortly afterwards, she left town. I used to think he was just a weasel, but now I'm thinking there's more to it."

Jack took the folder from Ben and placed it on the floor with the other one. "Ben, you know I love you dearly and I would never question your judgment, but it's seems too farfetched that all these board members, with various backgrounds, somehow know each other. Another reason I have doubts is that you're talking about a long-term plan. With you and my dad at the helm, I don't see where it would have been possible."

Ben knew Jack wasn't doubting his judgment and was momentarily proud that the young man was thinking on his own, but nevertheless, Ben was Ben. "That's enough of your opinion, kid. Let's get down to business. Grab another folder."

Jack just shook his head as he reached over to the pile and grabbed a folder off the top.

Ben glanced at the name on the folder and laughed. "Linda Roth. Drop-dead gorgeous, but also dangerous. She was the mistress of a board member that happened to be a dirty old man. That little quality cost him. She somehow managed to get a hold of his bank account numbers and ran through them like Mean Joe Greene through an offensive line. He's actually still alive, though penniless and in a nursing home. Once most of the money was gone, she used the rest of it to hire a top-notch law firm to go after the stocks. Somehow, she wound up with a corrupt judge. One of my contacts within the court system told me he still keeps a pair of her panties in his chambers."

Once again, Jack placed the folder on the floor as Ben grabbed another. "Come on, Ben, I'm tired and it's getting late. Bria is going to kill me. We're supposed to have dinner tonight."

Ben understood. He could be a ruthless tyrant when he needed to be, but he also had a big heart. "Alright, let's read one more and we'll call it a night."

Ben looked through the pile as the wheels started to turn in his head. Why would Robert try to backdoor me? He pulled out Robert's folder and opened it.

"This guy is really bright. I also consider him a good friend. I couldn't really find anything bad on him. He comes from a wealthy family. His dad was once a heavy hitter with the government."

Jack was itching to leave, but he suddenly became interested. "What do you mean 'heavy hitter'?"

Ben yawned and realized it really was getting late. "He was a ghost for the CIA. He must have been good because he's still alive. That would make him a very dangerous man if his own government was afraid of him. Thanks to his dad, Robert has a full-time staff taking care of his every need."

Jack's mind turned completely from his date and back to work. "So Kotter Industries gets a lot of government contracts. You think there's a link?"

Ben shook his head no. "I don't think so. Whatever he was into or is into, my connections in the federal government would have definitely told me something."

Jack shook his head and laughed. "You're kidding me. You have people that high up?"

Ben snickered and paused for a second. "Kid, I have people on top of people. That's just how this world works. It's not who you are; it's who has the most leverage. So anyway, I have some notes that say he went to China on a vacation."

Jack leaned back in his seat and shifted back into confused mode. "China? Why would anyone go to China on a vacation?"

Ben just flipped through the pages as he looked for more notes. "He had mentioned to me one time how he wanted to take a trip through China to tour their industry."

Jack thought about the little meeting Robert held with Kathy and the light bulb came on. "You think his dad, being ex-CIA, would have contacts in China?"

Ben placed the folder on his desk and sunk into his chair. "I see where you're going with this, kid. Hell, yeah, with China being a communist country, I would say he had many contacts."

Jack stood up and paced the floor as he tried to put together a big picture in his mind. "You know as well as I do, since China adopted continuous casting, they've been a force to be reckoned with. They're pretty competitive in the worldwide market."

Ben stood up and scratched his head as he sat on the edge of his desk. "The U.S. and China have been at each other forever and a day. We should never have aided those communist bastards during WWII. What the hell do they have to gain with our steel companies?"

Jack stopped pacing as he finally put the pieces together. "No, Ben. Not our steel companies. You were on the right track all along. Think about it. Relations between the two governments were going okay while the Soviet Union was intact. The Russians clashed with both China and the U.S. You know the saying, 'My enemy's enemy is my friend'? It was when the Soviet Union finally collapsed that the United States became the undisputed superpower. China's been trying to catch up ever since."

By that point, Ben was furious with himself for not following through with all his background investigations. "Kotter Industries has its hands in just about everything, including government space projects, not to mention all our contracts in other countries and our thousands of contacts. And if this vote goes through with the computer industry, there's no limit on what a foreign country could do with those kinds of resources."

Ben grabbed some of the folders from his desk and asked Jack to help him clean up. Jack grabbed the rest of the folders and helped Ben place them back into the file cabinet. As Ben clamped the old lock back on the doors, Jack collected his jacket and tie. "Well, Ben, this is your specialty, right? This is what you live for. Industrial espionage. Except the stakes are a bit higher than usual."

Ben was back to being calm and cool. He was no longer fighting an invisible opponent. He knew the players and what their plan was. "You know, kid, I feel good. I haven't had this much excitement since 1993 when I helped Nations Bank Corporation take over Maryland National Bank."

As Ben placed the keys back into his secret drawer, Jack just looked bewildered. "You were part that merger?"

Ben put his jacket on with a smile and walked towards the door. "Well, kid, I was asked by a person I'm not going to mention to kind of assess the situation and orchestrate a plan of action. But legally, I was just a consultant."

Jack opened the door as the two men walked out. Everyone was gone for the day. With the eerie quiet of the halls, Jack and Ben made their way to the elevator. As Ben pushed the button he turned to Jack. "Listen, kid, go pick up your girl and have a nice time. Don't mention any of this to anyone. That also means Bria."

Jack smiled and agreed. He just wanted to forget the day and was looking forward to spending the night with Bria.

CHAPTER FOUR

JACK HAD ABOUT 45 MINUTES TO GET HOME, SHOWER, CHANGE, AND pick up Bria. No problem. He had always been a speed freak, and when he turned 16, his dad had bought him the dream-car he'd always wanted: a 1973 Pontiac Firebird Trans Am complete with a Super Duty-455 Pontiac big block engine. It was considered to be one of the last true muscle cars. When Jack was younger, he stayed up one night watching the movie *McQ* with John Wayne. He fell in love with the car Wayne was driving and begged his dad for years to buy it for him. The car was so cool, even Chuck Norris got in on the action. He drove one in his 1981 film *An Eye for an Eye*. Of course Jack needed to have that car, but he found out later the car was demolished in the movie. He wound up having Ben make some calls, and it just so happened that one of the cars used as a double was available, though it wasn't in very good condition due to the owner having a few fender benders and then storing it away for years.

Jack spent three years bringing it back to life, and yes, he even had it painted Brewster Green. He also added personal touches. He named the car *Lunatic Fringe* and had the words painted on both sides in place of the words "Trans Am." He also had "Super Duty-455" on the hood scoop. He modified a few other details of the engine to his satisfaction. With an impressive 503 horsepower, he had very few worries about being late.

With Ben already gone, Jack was the last to leave the parking lot. As he turned his key, the roar of his horses came to life. He sat for a minute just to listen to his car hum with a low rumble. So smooth that every time he started the car, it became a part of him. As he shifted the SuperMatic transmission into first gear, the massive torque motioned the car forward and off he went.

As he made his way out to Route 110, Jack noticed there weren't too many cars on the road. His windows were down and a good tune graced his stereo system. He kicked back and just cruised along. All the business dealings were done for the day and the only thoughts that entered his mind were of his dream car, the cool breeze, and the great tune. Better than a cigarette after sex.

As the song came to an end, Jack suddenly had a strange feeling, as if someone was watching him. He stopped at a red light and looked around. Nothing. When the light turned green, he shifted gears and pressed the gas. He loved the sound of his engine as he shifted up into overdrive. Just when he was about to turn his stereo back on, a set of headlights appeared in his rearview mirror. The car wasn't that close behind, but it was following close enough to get on Jack's nerves. Feeling somewhat annoyed, Jack started talking to himself. "Who are you and why are you following me?" He downshifted once to see what would happen and the strange car also slowed down. Every time Jack shifted gears up or down, the strange car matched his speed.

Jack knew he had little time, if any, to play, so he switched lanes to try to get a better look at the car. "Now I see you."

A 1969 Plymouth Road Runner. Pretty car. Hemi, no doubt. "Now, what is it that you want with me?" Suddenly, it dawned on Jack who that Road Runner belonged to. He'd heard ghost stories, and now he had the pleasure of seeing it for himself. A mysterious 1969 Plymouth Road Runner, black with red pin stripes down the sides. She liked to challenge all who dared to race her. She was supposedly driven by a woman, but no one really knew because the windows were tinted pitch black. She was an unknown with the nickname Lilith. Jack didn't know who gave her that name, but somehow, it was linked to an ancient text that described a female creature that predated Eve.

Jack's heart started to pound because he'd always heard she was an urban legend. The sudden appearance of the car seemed to prove the gossip wrong. As he pulled up to the next red light, Lilith pulled up beside him. Jack didn't know what to think. He was almost afraid just to look over, but finally mustered enough nerve to do it. Lilith had pulled so close that her passenger side window was within Jack's reach. As his eyes squinted to try to pierce the tint, the window suddenly came down. It was only a couple of inches. Just enough to see a pair of eyes staring back. "Hello, Jack Kotter. I've been longing to meet you."

Jack almost popped his clutch, but held it together just enough. "How do you know who I am?"

Lilith pressed her gas pedal and her engine roared. "Your license plate. There's only one car I know of with the name *Lunatic Fringe* and the plate that says 'Jack 2.'"

By then, the light had changed several times, but no other cars were in sight. Jack was feeling a bit more relaxed, but was still concerned about why she was following him. "So what's the deal, Lilith? I'm sorry, I shouldn't call you by that name. That seems to be what everyone calls you, though."

The mysterious woman paused for a minute and then winked at Jack. "That's okay. I know what these young boys call me out here. I don't mind."

Jack smiled, but was still curious. He also knew his curiosity could sometimes get the best of him. "Why are you following me?"

With the moonlight shining down into the car, Lilith's eyes had a slight glow to them. "Do you know who Lilith is, Jack Kotter."

Once again, the light turned green, but this time a few cars were waiting behind them. Jack looked over and smiled. "No, but I'm sure you'll tell me at the next light."

They let the other vehicles pass while they drove side by side to the next intersection. Jack was actually looking forward to the answer. That way, he'd have a good story to tell his friends.

As he pulled his car to a stop, Lilith pulled up beside him. Her window was still only down enough to see the moonlight hit her eyes.

"So, Jack, according to some ancient scrolls, Lilith was Adam's first wife, but because she wanted to be the dominant one of the two,

God became angry and cast her out into the world. It's said she roams the world in search of male souls to mate with."

Jack was so intrigued with the story, he forgot all about the time. He could hear her licking her lips as she chuckled. "Well, that's all fine, but that doesn't explain why you're following me."

The '69 Road Runner rumbled as Lilith hit the gas. The custom duel exhaust system kept the noise to a minimum. "You haven't figured it out yet, Jack Kotter? You're next."

Jack played it off, mainly because he was feeling pretty confident. "I didn't hear the bet."

Lilith looked at Jack for a moment with a slight squint. "The bet is you and me. Let's see whose car moans first, and afterwards, you and I can slap skin in a dark room, and we'll see which one of us moans first."

Jack looked up at the green light as a bad feeling rushed over him like a dark cloud. "I don't know. I've heard a lot of things about you."

Lilith was intrigued. "Oh yeah? I hope they were all bad."

Jack just smiled a little and laid his head back. "Yeah. I think it was the good kind of bad though."

Lilith was beginning to become impatient and told Jack she expected his answer at the next light. As the two cars approached the light, they both came to a stop at the stop line. The nose of each car was exactly in line with the other. Lilith looked over with a gleam in her eye. "Well, Jack Kotter, you wanna sink the pink?"

Jack kept the clutch in as he placed the car in first gear. "So where's the finish?"

Lilith paused and thought about it. "Past the rural cemetery to Holdsworth Drive."

Jack glanced over at Lilith and gave her one last smile before he rolled up his windows. "Ghost or no ghost, you won't catch me or my soul."

Both cars sounded fierce as they waited for the green. As they anticipated the light, a police car pulled up behind them. It was an officer from the Huntington Police Department. He could tell what the two cars were going to do and he wasn't about to let a race happen while he was on duty. He gave a short blast of his siren and turned on his overhead lights. As the light turned green, both cars waited. The officer didn't get out of his car, but instead, also waited.

Jack rolled down his window to talk to Lilith who already had her window cracked. "Well, Lilith, maybe some other time. I don't think Officer Friendly is going to let us go."

Lilith let out a small giggle. "Okay, Jack Kotter. If you can't outrun a police car, then maybe I'm wasting my time with you."

That pushed Jack's last button, and he certainly wasn't going to stand for it. "You bitch. What'ya say I take you and this cop for a ride?"

Lilith rolled her window back up and revved her engine. Jack took that as a yes and waited for the next green.

Little did they know the officer was calling for back up and attempting to set up a roadblock. As the red light went out, both cars roared through the intersection before the green could come on. The officer tried to keep up, but his bottom-of-the-line vehicle just couldn't handle the speed. Jack thought for sure he would have no problem, but as he shifted through his gears, Lilith stayed by his side. Both cars had no problem getting up over one hundred miles per hour, but as the street signs started to blur, it became increasingly difficult to navigate between the traffic.

Jack saw the cemetery coming up and saw police cars filling in space to create a blockade. He was already hell-bent on beating Lilith and he sure wasn't going to get caught doing it. He downshifted just enough to make a squealing left turn onto a side street. As Lilith blew by, he thought for sure she would get caught. Just as he straightened out the car, he had to make a right turn. As Jack cruised along, suddenly Lilith came squealing out of a right turn from the intersection, just missing Jack's car. Jack immediately shifted down to pick up power then shifted up to create speed. He couldn't help but think out loud. "Crazy bitch, where the hell did you come from?"

As both cars rambled through the small neighborhoods, they barely rounded the corner onto to another small street, just missing some parked cars and each other. Jack knew if he couldn't get in front of her when they turned back onto Route 110, he was going to lose. When they approached the intersection, Jack tried to take the inside but lost control when Lilith purposely clipped his right front wheel-well, spinning him onto the shoulder of Route 110. Lilith didn't miss a beat, and her brake lights never came on once. She raced out of sight, disappearing in all the smoke.

Jack sat for a second while all the police cars converged on him. He couldn't go anywhere because his tire had gone flat as his car spun to a stop.

Besides the damage to his car, his ego took a big hit. He thought about the old wise tail and realized how lucky he was that his curiosity didn't kill the cat. At least not this time. A quick thought came to mind. If only he was still a boy, he could call on Ben to make everything okay. He had an outburst of laughter until an officer approached.

Jack stepped out of his car to greet the officer. It was his friend Dale. "So, Dale, how is your night going?"

Jack and Dale had been friends ever since they played sports together as kids. It didn't matter which sport, they always competed with each other. Dale shook his head and laughed. "Obviously, better than yours. Looks like *Fringe* is going to need some work."

Angry and embarrassed, what could Jack say? "I'm really pissed off."

Dale paused and gave Jack a smile. "Well, you know what they say. Better to be pissed off then pissed on."

Jack was already furious, and he knew Dale was loving every moment. Most of the police were gone by then, with the exception of Sergeant Lactgan. He'd never liked Jack because Jack always called him "Sergeant Lactose" as a joke. Lactgan threatened to put Jack in jail once, but as it turned out, Jack was a major contributor to the police and firefighter unions. Obviously that wouldn't have gone over too well with his superiors.

As Lactgan came walking up, he was waiting for Jack to say something stupid, but Jack's anger was still in the red. With his hands on his hips, Lactgan walked around the car and stopped in front of Jack.

"What's wrong, rich boy? Did you get smoked by a woman?" Lactgan's laugh was loud and obnoxious.

It took all of Jack's manners not to punch him in the throat. Instead, he took a deep breath and started to relax. "Yeah, Lactose, a woman did this. Did you come here to gloat or did you have something productive to say?"

Lactgan stepped to Jack and stood face to face with him. "You think money can protect you from the law, but you're wrong, rich boy."

Jack cringed as he took a step back. "I know I have some mints that can protect me from your breath. Here, take the whole pack."

Lactgan didn't want to get into it with Jack. Besides, he'd had his little fun. "Alright, Kotter, but one day, it's going to be just you and me and no car cam."

As Lactgan walked back to his car, he tripped over some roadside debris. That brightened Jack's mood enough for him to temporarily forget about Lilith. That's when he remembered where he had been going.

"Oh my God, Bria is going to kill me."

Dale ordered a tow truck and was just getting off the radio with his dispatcher. "Don't tell me you shrugged off Bria to race that maniac woman?"

Jack suddenly felt really disappointed with himself. "That wasn't the plan. It just turned out that way. She approached me and made me an offer. By the way, what was all this about? You guys don't usually do blockades for a couple of racers."

Dale turned to walk back to his car. "Come on, I wanna show you something." As they made their way over to the squad car, Dale started asking questions. "Do you know that woman at all?"

Jack didn't answer right away. He just thought for a second. "No, but I've heard stories about her before. People I know in certain circles that socialize in the local racing clubs told me about her. They say nobody can beat her. But the way they tell stories, it always sounded more like a ghost story. I thought she was an urban legend, until tonight."

Dale reached into his car and pulled out some photos and some reports. "Look at these."

Jack took the photos from Dale and skimmed through them. "Those are some really nasty looking accidents."

Dale took the photos back and started reading from some of the reports. "Black Plymouth Road Runner with tint all around. A '69 Road Runner with dark windows. Old dark colored car with tint. These are just some of the police reports from the stupid kids who accept her challenge. Here, these photos are from a fatal we had two weeks ago."

Jack looked at the photos and recognized the area. "This is two miles south, down 110. I remember that accident. It was all over the news."

Dale took the photos and put them and the reports back in his car. "Yeah, it's a really bad section where Woodhull, Academy, and Olive converge into 110. And then just when you come around that corner, you have Church Street that comes out. Three people died that night, including a child."

Jack suddenly became very interested in the mysterious woman and wanted to know more. "So what happened?"

Dale leaned back on his car and folded his arms across his chest. "There was a family traveling home to Ohio. They were lost and trying to find a place to stop for the night. Witnesses say two cars came racing down Route 110 when they sideswiped each other and the kid driving the Corvette lost control. He hit the Ohio family's station wagon as it was coming off Church Street. The father said he never even saw them coming. The Corvette exploded on impact. The kid never had a chance. The station wagon rolled a couple of times before it came to a stop 100 feet down the highway. The force of the impact was so strong, it tore the old, rotted seatbelts, and the mom and baby chair were ejected from the car. They died instantly. The father is still in the hospital. He's so distraught, he's already tried to kill himself twice."

Jack couldn't believe what he was hearing. "So, why am I still standing here? That was Lactose's big chance to do me in."

Dale shook his head and smiled. "It wasn't you we wanted. Witnesses from that fatal say they saw a black Plymouth speeding away from the scene. Damn, Jack, we haven't had any problems with these kids since the early '70s. Nowadays, these kids meet up on some vacant lot and show off the toys their parents bought them. They didn't start racing until this woman showed up one night and started these challenges. You know how these kids think. They're not gonna back down from a woman. At least not in front of their friends."

Jack's thoughts raced as he tried to put the scenario together in his head. "So you think this woman is purposely causing these accidents? That doesn't make any sense."

Dale stood up from his car and stood beside Jack. "Talking to these witnesses and victims, I think she does it to win the race. How did she approach you? Did she say anything to you?"

Jack thought for a second. "She was following me and I wanted to find out why. She kept playing cat and mouse games until she finally pulled up beside me. She rolled her window down and called me out by my name."

Dale looked surprised and stepped right up close to Jack. "She knew who you were? You saw her? Who is she?"

Jack put his hand up and backed away. "Whoa, no. I don't know her. Never saw her before. I asked her how she knew me, but she said she knew my car."

Dale was still operating in full-court press mode. "But you got a good look at her? What does she look like?"

Once again, Jack put his hand up. "No, no, no. She's a smart one. She only rolled her window down just enough for me to see her eyes. I couldn't make out anything else." Jack suddenly felt his emotions running wild. "I can't believe that bitch ran me off the road."

The tow truck arrived. It was a flat bed, so *Fringe* wouldn't be damaged anymore then it was. As the driver was hooking up the car, Dale asked Jack to keep his ears and eyes open and to let him know if his friends or car clubs had any new information. Jack agreed and Dale went back to work.

After Dale left, Jack had to think of a story to tell Bria. He dialed her number and listened to the ring. As she answered the phone, Jack could hear the excitement in her voice. Before she could talk, Jack spoke up. "Hey, Bria, it's me."

There was a short pause and Jack could hear Bria start to breathe a little heavier. "Damn it, Jack. I should have known. What is it this time? You hanging out with your racing buddies? Or are you working on some secret project with Ben? What is it?"

Jack expected Bria to act this way. There had been a number of times when they'd made plans only to have them canceled by Jack.

"Bria, I'm sorry. I was in a rush trying to get home and I caught a flat. You know *Fringe* doesn't have a spare."

Bria cooled down just enough to speak in a rational voice. "First off, Jack, I know how you are with *Fringe*. Second, you're a lying ass. A news helicopter caught your little race on camera. I just wanted to give you the chance to be truthful with me." Jack could hear the shaking in her voice, and just before she hung up, he could hear the crying.

As usual, Jack called Ben to bail him out. As the phone rang, he thought about what he could say, but then he thought, what was the use?

Ben finally picked up. "Hello?" Jack didn't speak right away. He still had his mind on Bria. Ben spoke up in his usual scratchy voice. "Don't worry, kid, I know just where you are. I'll be there in a few minutes."

Jack walked across the street to an all-night diner. As he walked in, there was a surprisingly fair amount of people there. Most of the heads turned as the waitress sat him in a window booth. "So, sweetie, what'll it be?"

Although he had been saving his appetite for dinner with Bria, he really wasn't hungry. "I'll just have a coffee, please."

As she placed her pen and pad in her pocket, she attempted to make Jack feel better. "Don't worry sweetie, that car is a menace. It races up and down this strip all the time. You're not the only one that's been driven off the road."

Jack heard what she was saying, but didn't even look up to acknowledge her.

As the waitress walked away to get the coffee, the bell on the door jingled and Ben walked in. He walked over and stood at the booth shaking his head. As he sat down, he motioned to the waitress. "Hey, Dee, if you're getting coffee, make it two."

Jack looked over at Ben and let out half a laugh. "Is there anyone you don't know?"

Ben grabbed the placemat and looked at the advertisements. "Come on, kid. I've been around a long time. Probably know most everybody." Ben lightly pounded his fist as he leaned across the table. "Besides, we had a one-nighter. She can really make those hips dance."

Dee placed the coffee down just as Ben was about to get nasty. She placed her hand on Ben's shoulder as she cracked her chewing gum. "You better not be talking about me, Ben."

As she walked back to the kitchen, Ben couldn't help but watch her butt cheeks shake side to side. "Hm, hm! I know some hula dancers in Hawaii that can't shake like that."

Jack was already halfway through his coffee when he decided to lighten up. "How old is that chic? She can't be more than 25."

Ben poured some cream into his coffee and added some sugar. "She's 27, if you must know." As he took a sip, he gazed out the window at the sight of the accident. "So, kid, want to tell me what happened or should I give you my educated guess?"

Jack drank the last of his coffee and placed the cup down on the edge of the table. He glanced over at Dee and gave her a head nod for more. "Sometimes, I think I'm too sure of myself. I had it all worked out today. I planned on giving the board members their say during the meeting. After lunch, I was going to slam them with my research and make them understand that the computer industry wouldn't be cost efficient. That didn't work out. Then my plans with Bria got derailed when this woman challenged me on the way home."

Ben stared at Jack like a father stares at a son who needs help. "Listen, kid, don't worry about those jackasses on the board. That will all work itself out. Now, this woman you got involved with tonight. She's driving a black '69 Plymouth Road Runner?"

Jack just shook his head in disbelief. "Damn, Ben. Don't tell me you slept with her too."

Dee walked over and Ben grew silent. She refilled both coffees and quickly retreated back behind the counter, where she was watching a documentary about *Titanic* on the history channel. With an angry look on his face, Ben started tearing open more packets of sugar and cream. "I was driving home late one night and I see these headlights in my mirror. I wasn't in any hurry. I had my new Zagato and those damn cops were just itching to grab me."

Jack took another drink as he started to perk up. "Your Lamborghini? That's what happened to your Lamborghini?"

Ben didn't have to say anything. His facial expression said it all. "Anyway, I got over so she could pass, but the bitch stayed behind me. So I decided to pick up speed and get away from her, but she stayed right on my ass. As we pulled up to the red light, I glanced over, and she had her window cracked."

By then, Jack was leaning across the table and hanging on every word Ben said. "Don't tell me. You could only see her eyes."

Ben tilted his head to one side and raised his eyebrows. "Yeah, I thought maybe she saw the car and wanted to try to coral me. But instead, she starts talking about racing through traffic. I called her a crazy whore and took off."

Jack was so intrigued with the story, he forgot all about Bria. "Let me guess, she followed you to the next light and offered sex after the race."

Ben looked down at his coffee almost in a humorous shame. "You know me, kid. I'm a damn sex fiend. She definitely pushed the right buttons. The light turned green and we took off like maniacs. I don't know what I was thinking. We got about a quarter mile down the road and she clipped my left rear quarter panel. I must have spun around at least six times before I flipped over. When the cops came, I told them I got cut off by a tractor trailer. They took the report and towed what was left of the car: $250,000 gone. I didn't even have it for a week. That night, I wound up in here. That's when I hooked up with Dee."

Jack finished the last of his coffee and motioned for Dee to come to the table. "Hey, Dee, I think I'll order now. I suddenly got my appetite back."

Ben grabbed a menu and opened it up. "Are you in here, Dee, or do I have to place a special order for you?"

Although it was late, Dee still had some humor left. "If I was on there, I'd be the special of the day. Both of you could enjoy me."

Jack wouldn't even look up. He kept his nose buried in his menu, which happened to be upside down.

Dee snapped her gum and laughed as she reached down and grabbed the menu from Jack and turned it upright for him. "Just let me know when you're ready to order."

As she walked away, Jack glanced over at Ben with his red face. "How do you keep finding these girls?"

By then, just about everyone had left the diner except Jack and Ben. After getting through a few more of Ben's sexual harassment jokes, Dee finally took both their food orders. As the night went on, the two men sat quietly and ate. Neither one really wanted to talk business. Halfway through dinner, Ben decided to break the silence.

"So, what happen with Bria?"

Luckily, Jack had food in his mouth, because it gave him a minute to think about what he was going to say. "Well, I thought I would bend the truth just a smidge, but it didn't work. She said one of the local news stations caught the race on camera. They must have been broadcasting it live. I've never known her to watch the news. Now I know better."

As Ben wolfed down the last bite of his steak, he called Dee for a refill of water and the check. Jack was already finished and was reaching for his wallet, when Ben slapped down a Ben Franklin. "I got this one, kid."

Jack knew Ben had never offered to pay for dinner, so he didn't say a word and graciously accepted. Dee refilled the waters and took the money over to the register for change. When she returned, Ben told her to keep it. "So, are you busy tonight?"

Still cracking her gum, Dee placed the change on the table. "Benjamin, I know you're not trying to buy my company tonight."

Ben gently slid the money towards her. "No, sweetie. I'm just asking you if you wouldn't mind stopping by tonight."

Dee picked the money up with a smile. "Sure, I'll be there around midnight."

Because Ben was trying to get home as soon as possible, he didn't waste any time dropping Jack off at his house. Before Jack climbed out of the car, Ben told him to take a few days off while he contacted some friends still with the CIA. That was all Jack needed to hear. He knew in the past Ben and his dad had some shady dealings, and he knew it might come back to haunt him one day. Jack said his goodbyes and went in the house.

As he picked the phone up hoping to hear messages from Bria, he could hear Ben ripping and roaring down the road. He smiled, but then realized there were no phone calls made to the house. Jack looked at his watch and went upstairs for the night. After a long, warm shower, he climbed into bed and closed his eyes. As he lay in bed going over the day's events, he fell into a deep sleep.

Jack started to breathe hard as his heartbeat grew faster. Suddenly, out of nowhere, he was at the top of a large beautiful staircase. As he looked around, people were in a panic and seemed to be running in all directions. He was knocked to the ground, and as he lay still looking up, he noticed a huge glass dome. A young man with blood on his face helped him to his feet, but as he stood up, the young man disappeared. Jack woke up in a sweat and jumped up out of bed. He looked around his room for a moment then walked over to the window. Jack had had dreams in the past, but nothing so real as that night.

CHAPTER FIVE

The next day, Ben was at work early, making calls to people he hadn't talked to in years. He contacted Roy Dobbins, an ex-CIA operative who was in Beijing, China a few years before Robert's vacation. "Hey, Roy. It's Benjamin Marcus."

There was a long silence, then a voice finally spoke. "Ben? How did you get this number?"

With a mixture of pride and arrogance, Ben sat back in his chair and smiled. "Come on, Roy. Just because you're retired doesn't mean I can't find you. Let's not go into all the sentimental how do you do's. I need some info."

Roy was involved with a network of counter intelligence. One of his jobs was to monitor and even eliminate people who the government thought might be a threat to national security. He had access to any and all names of people who visited or had relations with communist countries. "Ben, you shouldn't have done this by phone. You know there are ears everywhere."

Still wallowing in his pride, Ben stood up with determination and gave Roy the bottom line. "My phone is secure and I'm sure your phone is too, so cut the bull. I'm in a bind and I need a favor. I have someone within Kotter Industries who was in China back in the early '90s. His name is Robert Alders. He said he was on vacation, but I think he might have been meeting with someone within the China Steel Corporation."

Ben could hear Roy sifting through papers and punching computer keys. "Okay, Ben. I owe you anyway. Give me some time and I'll get back with you. We're going to have to set up a meeting somewhere."

Ben was already ahead of the game. "Now you're talking. I already have a place in mind. I'll expect to hear back from you in a couple of days."

As he hung up the phone, Ben paged through an old black notebook that he also kept hidden in his file cabinet. He turned page after page until he came to some notations. He paused as he read to himself. *China, plan for expansion*. There were names written at the bottom of the page. Two brothers, Chang and Changpu, and a woman, Liling. These weren't real names but code names in reference to contacts within China Steel Corporation.

Ben closed the book and walked down the hall to Jack Sr.'s office. Except for the cleaning crew, no one had been in the room since his death. As he entered, he stopped and looked around, thinking about his old friend. He spoke out loud as he walked across the room trying to shake off the sadness. "I can't believe we didn't catch this, Jack. We must really be getting old."

Ben pulled the desk chair out but didn't sit down. He just stood there looking at it. He reached down and pressed a button from beneath the desk and a secret drawer popped out. Within that drawer, he reached all the way to the back and pressed another button, and one of the wall panels slid open.

Behind the wall panel was a safe, and of course, Ben knew the combination. After he opened the safe, he paused and stood staring at an old lockbox. He reached in and pulled out the metal box and some files. He placed the files on a nearby table and then reached back into the safe and pulled out an old satellite phone. Taped to the inner roof of the safe were two keys to the lockbox. As some employees walked past the door, he quickly shoved the files back into the safe and closed the door. He made sure the panel closed and the desk was back in its original condition.

Ben made his way back to his office quickly without talking to anyone. As he closed the door behind him, he locked it, and then closed the blinds on his window. He sat at his desk as he stared at the box. He remembered having a conversation years before with Jack Sr. about a project he had been working on since 1927. He never went into details with Sergis or Ben, but just before he died, he gave specific instructions for Ben to give the lockbox to Jack.

Ben didn't open the box, but just laid it on his desk. Not much frightened Ben, but he didn't want anything to do with what was in the box. It gave him an eerie feeling. But, at the same time, his curiosity was peaked.

As the satellite phone was being charged, Ben called his most reliable asset, Hellen. She had been his secretary for more years than he cared to admit to. Sometimes, she knew what Ben needed before he would have a chance to ask. "Hellen, I need you to book a flight for me."

As Ben listened for an answer, a sassy voice came back over the phone. "Do you know how many messages I've been holding for you?"

Ben already knew she would be angry. He hadn't returned anyone's phone calls in two days. He held the phone away from his ear knowing she was going to tear into him. As the voice became louder, the further away the phone went. Finally, silence. He placed the phone back to his ear, and in a surprisingly calm voice, asked Hellen to come into his office.

Almost immediately, the door opened and there she was: 115 pounds of fury about to explode. "Benjamin Marcus! Do you understand you have a company to run, or has that idea completely left your mind?"

Ben stood up with a smile on his face. Hellen was the only person who could ever get away with that kind of attitude towards him.

"Please, have a seat. I need to book a flight to China. Just don't tell anyone where I'm going. Not even Jack. I'll be gone for at least a few days, maybe more."

Hellen had her pen and pad in her lap while she took notes. "Please review your messages and act accordingly, or at the very least, for my sake, act like you're somewhat interested. How soon do you want to leave?"

Ben didn't think for a moment. "As soon as possible. Preferably tomorrow morning. Have a limo meet me at the house. Tell them to send an older driver. Someone I can relate to. These young kids they send can't hold a damn conversation." Hellen stood up and started walking towards the door.

Ben stood up with his hands on his hips. "Hey, I might not be finished with you."

Hellen turned around and pushed her glasses up from her nose. "One of these days, Ben, you're going to appreciate that I know you better than you know yourself."

Ben walked out from behind his desk and sat on the corner. "One of these days, you're going to appreciate that I let you keep your job. You're not exactly Miss Moneypenny. You can be replaced."

Hellen laughed and walked out. Just before she closed the door, she turned back around. "You're not exactly James Bond." With that, she shut the door and went back to her desk.

As Ben sat back down at his desk, he thought back to when Jack Sr. was still alive and thought about all the deals they'd made through the years. The steel industry had always been the backbone of Kotter Industries. Back in the early seventies, China Steel Corporation developed 100 percent continuous casting and was on its way to being a dominant force in the steel industry. Jack Sr. and Ben tried to convince the executive board to expand into China so they could compete. That way, China Steel Corporation might possibly offer a deal to work together. Both companies could have benefited more from working together rather than against each other. The only board member that would listen was Carroll Cummings.

In 1977 China Steel Corporation became state-owned and that put a stop to all negotiations. With China being a communist country, the United States government threatened to cut off all federal contracts with Kotter Industries. And, of course, each individual state would have followed suit. There wasn't even an argument. All ties with China were cut and any plans that were made were considered taboo. Both Jack Sr. and Ben knew it was a missed opportunity, but they were alright with it. Carroll was more bitter. Normally Ben or Jack Sr. would negotiate the expansion of the company, especially into another country, but they both wanted Carroll to head the project. He'd spent time in China while in the military and was familiar with their culture.

In 1995 China Steel Corporation was reprivatized. The state

owned less than a quarter percent. But by that time, Carroll Cummings had passed away and Kotter Industries made its own advancements in the field, so there was no interest in China.

Ben glanced over at the satellite phone and saw it was charged. He reached over and dialed a code that unlocked the phone. This gave him the ability to dial anywhere around the world. He sat back in his chair as he dialed some numbers. As he listened to the ringtone, he wasn't sure if anyone would even pick up after so many years. Suddenly, a Chinese voice came on. Ben was a little rusty, but it didn't matter. He remembered the Chinese code words and proceeded to use them.

After Ben finished, there was a brief silence. He was about to hang up when the voice came back in English. "It's been a long time, Benjamin. How have you been doing?"

Ben's nerves came to a calm and a sense of relief rushed over him. "Well, I could be better. But then we wouldn't be having this conversation. So, tell me, is this Chang or Changpu? I could never tell you guys apart."

After a brief sigh the voice came back. "Ah, Benjamin, even with old age you're still filled with sarcasm and laughter."

With that, Ben knew it was his old friend Chang. With the overwhelming happiness, he almost forgot why he called. "You old dog. How the hell are you?"

Chang was also glad to hear from an old friend like Ben, but he knew he had to get down to business. "Benjamin, my brother and I are so sorry for your loss of Mr. Kotter. Obviously, it wouldn't have been wise to attend the funeral. But we did try to contact you several years ago concerning one of your potential problems."

Ben understood why Chang couldn't attend Jack Sr.'s funeral and he was okay with it. Back in the '70s, Chang and his brother Changpu were high ranking employees of China Steel Corporation, and they were acting as insiders, shuffling company information to Kotter Industries. There was also a female named Liling. She was the daughter of one of the executives. Her father was careless and often left important documents at home and, on occasion, combinations to various company safes. The Trojan Horse. This was how Kotter Industries had been going to ensure success in China. Come in as friends then gain control using inside information.

Ben's covert way of thinking, from his throwback days, kicked in as he mentally prepared himself for what he hoped would be an informative conversation. "Well, old friend, I'm hoping we're on the same page. You said something about trying to contact me?"

Chang had information about someone possibly selling company information to China Steel Corporation. "What's the saying you Americans have? Oh yeah, you have a fox in your hen house."

Although alarmed, Ben was relieved to hear Chang was still looking out for the well-being of Kotter Industries. "So you do know about our problem. How long do you think it's been going on?"

There was a silence. Then Ben could hear Chang lighting up a cigarette and blowing out the smoke. "Like I said, Benjamin, we tried to contact you several years ago. We kept trying, but these satellite phones can be useless when only one end is working."

Ben stood up and started pacing his office floor as he thought about the days when he and Jack Sr. wouldn't be without the satellite phone. "I'm sorry, Chang. After being shut down by the Carter Administration, I didn't really see the need to keep up with our arrangement. It might sound funny, but it was like we had our own private Cold War going on."

Chang laughed as he continued puffing on his cigarette. "Yeah, those were some fun days we had. Just like you, Benjamin, my brother and I have eyes and ears everywhere. After the company was reprivatized, it came to our attention that someone from your organization was trying to make some backdoor deals. I didn't really take it seriously because our two countries would never allow any cooperation between our companies. Too much at risk."

There was a brief silence as Chang finished his cigarette. "I'm gonna take a wild guess that I'm wrong since we're now having this conversation."

Ben grabbed his files and sat back down at his desk. He pulled out Robert's file again and skimmed through the folder. "I got a guy on our board who supposedly took a vacation in China several years ago. I'm not sure exactly where he went, but I have a friend working on that as we speak. I'm not all together convinced that he's the same man you're talking about. Although we sometimes clash on various subjects, I do consider him a friend."

Chang let out a small laugh as he lit up another cigarette. "Come now, Benjamin. You know the first rule in business. Keep your friends close and your enemies even closer. Your friends can be some of your worst enemies."

Ben knew the rules all too well. Jack Sr. and Sergis had taught him everything they knew, legal and illegal. Through the years, he'd been recognized on several occasions for his business savvy. Ben had also been featured on the covers of magazines such as *Forbes* and *Business Today*. He had the *Forbes* framed because he was named the year's most successful businessman, edging out Donald Trump by a small margin.

Still looking through the folder, Ben just couldn't believe Robert would try to backdoor Kotter Industries. "Chang, I know I'm getting old, but I still think I can read people pretty well. The guy I'm looking at just doesn't fit the bill. Tell me you have a name for me."

By then, Chang was on his laptop punching in information. "I don't have a name yet, but my brother is working on that. Do you really want to talk like this, Ben? How secure are we?"

Ben closed Robert's folder and breathed out a sigh. "We have these satellite phones just for security purposes. The technology was originally created for the military. It's one of the most secure ways to communicate by phone."

Ben checked his watch and saw it was early afternoon. "Listen, Chang. I have a flight out early tomorrow. I'll be flying into Beijing. Can you send a car to pick me up?"

Chang lit his third cigarette. He was glad to hear his old friend was coming to visit, even though it was under bad circumstances. "Of course, Benjamin. I'll arrange everything, and I'm hoping by that time, I'll have more information."

Ben hung up with Chang and gathered his thoughts. He had Hellen clear his calendar so he could leave work early. He had a lot of information to gather and he needed to pack. He also had to stop to see Jack on the way home.

Ben grabbed the old lockbox and stopped at Hellen's desk on the way out. "I know I'm wasting my time, but did you make my arrangements with the airlines?"

Hellen didn't even say a word. She pushed her glasses up from her nose and handed Ben copies of his itinerary. She then continued on with her work.

Ben took a moment and looked over the paperwork. "Alright, then. I'll see you next week. Aren't you going to wish me a safe trip?"

Hellen stopped for a moment then continued back with her work.

Ben turned to walk away, knowing she was just waiting for the right time.

"Have a safe trip, 007. See you next week."

Ben smiled as he walked down the hall. He received a few stares from some of the other employees. They didn't see him smile very often.

As he made his way down Route 110, he made a few phone calls before he arrived at Jack's house. First up, the company law firm. He had a direct line to Mr. Lawrence Winder, one of the senior partners at Schonfeld and Weinstein, LLP. Kotter Industries wanted the best and that's who they had. Corporate law was one of the law firm's many specialties, and they'd helped make Kotter Industries earn the title of one of the leading companies in America. Mr. Winder didn't pick up, so that meant he was in court. Ben left a message. "Hey, Larry, Benjamin Marcus here. I'm on my way out of town, and when I get back, I need to meet with you. Call Hellen and give her the appointment, and I'll see you when I get back."

Ben was hanging up the phone when he noticed two cars speeding towards him on the other side of the median. They blew by at a high rate of speed, but not so fast he didn't notice who it was. The black '69 Road Runner. Talking to himself, he let out a low grumble as he watched them race away in his rearview mirror. "They still haven't caught that bitch? Damn cops. Couldn't catch a cold in winter, but I bet they could finish off a dozen donuts in record time."

Ben finished his phone calls and made his way to Jack's house. As he pulled to the front of the house, Jack was waiting with two beers in his hand. Licking his lips, Ben grabbed the lockbox and stepped out of his car. "Not bad, kid. You're getting good at thinking ahead of the game." No "hello, how are you" or "are you enjoying your days off." Ben just grabbed the beer out of Jack's hand and took a healthy swig. "So grab a seat, kid. I need to go over a few things with you."

Jack turned around and asked Ben if he wanted to step inside. "Oh, by the way, good to see you too."

Ben took one more drink and the beer was gone. "Why don't we sit outside? It's a nice day and I'm tired of being in a stuffy office."

Ben placed the box on the table and grabbed the other beer from Jack He sat down and made himself comfortable as he took a small drink. "I didn't know you were a Sam Adams guy."

While Ben stared at the box, Jack smiled and took a seat next to Ben. "That's okay. I wasn't thirsty anyway. I've been buying Sam Adams for a while now. They make good beers. So, what's with the old box?"

Ben stared at the box for a few seconds as he continued sucking down the second beer. "Damn good beer, kid. What other good tastes do you have that I'm unaware of?"

Suddenly, Jack felt a lump in his throat. "What are you not telling me, Ben? You're a pretty direct guy and I can see you're avoiding something."

Ben knew he had to get serious for a moment and he could always be honest when it came to Jack. As he looked Jack in the eyes, he took a few seconds to gather his thoughts. "Look, kid, nobody's perfect. Sometimes life can throw a change-up at you and you just have to deal with it the best you can. You can say it's God's building blocks for strengthening your character."

Jack didn't say a word. He remembered all the life talks his dad and Ben gave him as he grew. He also knew never to interrupt. Ben paused for a moment to wet his whistle. He finished off the second beer and just held the bottle in his lap. Being the considerate host he was, Jack took a chance while Ben was thinking about what he was going to say next. "Would you like another beer or six?"

That made Ben chuckle for a minute, but that was okay. He knew Jack was used to getting his little jokes in every now and then.

Ben set the empty bottle down and picked up the old box. He kept it in his hand but gave Jack one of the keys. With a little confusion, Jack looked at the key and wondered where Ben was going with the wisdom speech. "Ben, you're not making any sense. Does this have anything to do with China or Kotter Industries?"

Ben was disappointed in himself, but knew Jack would give him a chance to explain. "I'm sorry, kid. I guess not having children of my own makes it somewhat hard for me to try to step in where your dad should be."

The lump in Jack's throat was gone as a good feeling overwhelmed him. "You've always been there for me when my dad couldn't be. That was one of the great qualities about my dad. He knew he could always count on his best friend when he wasn't around. It was almost like I had two dads growing up."

Ben felt a sudden rush of pride and handed the box to Jack. He stood up and walked to the end of the porch. As he turned to face Jack, he leaned against the column. "I know your dad was 87, but he was healthier than any man half his age. It was a devastating surprise to everyone when he passed away. He was working on something big. I never knew what it was."

Jack stood up and laid the box on the chair. "My dad actually had a project you didn't know about? What about Sergis?"

All Ben could do was look at the ground and shake his head. "I don't know, kid. If Sergis knew about it, he took it to his grave. Anyway, I knew he was working on something, but I never pressed the issue. I knew your dad to be an honest man and that was always good enough for me. Whatever it was, it took a good portion of his time."

Jack walked over and picked the box up. "So, is that what this little visit is about? My dad left me something and now you're giving it to me?"

Ben walked over and took the box from Jack and laid it on the table. "No, kid, not exactly. I have no idea what the contents are. Your father had that in his wall safe. I was supposed to give it to you upon his death as long as you were of age, but I didn't exactly plan on your dad dying. Hell, I didn't even remember it until I opened the safe and saw it. My guess is, whatever is in the box has something to do with what he was working on."

Jack pulled the key out of his pocket and saw how old it looked. "You're not the least bit curious about what it is?"

Ben looked at the key then looked over at the box. "After all this time, you would think I would have opened it, but truth is, it gives me the heebie-jeebies."

Jack laughed. He enjoyed watching Ben become squeamish. "The great Benjamin Marcus afraid of a box? I never thought I would see the day you were afraid of anything."

Ben wasn't laughing. And he certainly wasn't feeling very good about whatever was in the box. "Listen, kid, I loved your dad like I loved my own brother. I had a tremendous amount of respect for his business sense and judgment, but whatever he was working on should remain with him. I just don't like surprises."

With all the talk about secret projects, Jack's curiosity started to build. "Well, together we own the majority of the company, so don't you think it's both our responsibilities to find out what my dad had in store for us?" He walked over to the box and picked it up.

Ben wasn't a spring chicken, but he was fast enough to snatch the key out of Jack's hand. "Wait a minute, kid. Before you go opening Pandora's box, I'm on my way out of town. I'll be gone for several days."

Jack set the box down and waited for Ben to go on, but that was it. "So, are you going to tell me where you're going?"

Ben placed the key in his pocket and walked back to the edge of the porch. "No, I think it's best you don't know. That way, no one can point a finger at you if something goes wrong."

Jack suddenly felt the lump come back and he started to worry. "What do you mean, Ben? What the hell are you going to get into?"

Ben smiled as feelings from the old days came rushing back. "Been a long time, kid, since I felt the way I do. Now listen, this is what we're going to do. You keep the box and I'll hold on to the key. Take time to think about what I've said, and when I get back, if you still want to open the box, we'll do it together. Deal?"

Disappointment settled into Jack, but he was okay with it. "Do I really have a choice?"

Ben turned to walk to his car. "No, you don't. See you when I see you."

As Ben left to go home and pack, Jack grabbed the box and took it inside the house. His curiosity was still peaked, but he had enough patience to be able to wait. He placed the box on the fireplace mantel and softly

spoke out loud some of his thoughts. "What did you do dad and why all the secrecy? What's in the box that Ben is so afraid of?" Jack had other problems to take care, so he turned and walked away.

He walked into the kitchen and fetched the beer he didn't get to drink earlier. "Wow! A few days without Ben on my ass. What to do? What to do?"

Jack thought about it for a minute, then, suddenly, it dawned on him. With all that had been going on with Kotter Industries and Bria, he hadn't had a night out with the guys in a while. So he grabbed the phone and made some calls. Of course Connie came to mind, but he was living abroad. He called Nicholas and Ethan. Nick politely declined, but Ethan was definitely in. He'd been looking for a girlfriend lately and he wasn't going to pass up a good opportunity. And, last but not least, Dale. Police always liked to party. Women and drinking are their two favorite things to do.

As Jack was getting ready to go, he thought about his last fight with Bria. She hadn't called or returned any of his messages. But as time went by, he became more involved with thinking about where the boys were going. Manhattan's Upper West Side China Club. It had a VIP section and it was also a cool place where celebrities hung out. Jack groomed himself in the mirror and adjusted his clothes accordingly. He smiled thinking about how much fun he was going to have.

Later that night, the stretch limo pulled to the front of his house. Jack walked through the living room and past the fireplace, glancing at the mysterious box. As he walked out the door, the limo driver, Casey, already had the door open and waiting. Jack climbed in as he was met by Dale and Ethan, both already with beers in their hands.

"I see you guys aren't wasting any time, so hand me one so I can catch up."

Dale reached into the fully stocked icebox and handed Jack his drink. "So, what kind of trouble are we going to get into tonight?"

Ethan laughed as he finished off his beer. "Yeah, Jack, the last time we went out, Dale wound up getting slapped by some chic who happen to have a very large bouncer as a boyfriend."

Jack downed half his beer while he laughed about their last outing. "Well, I thought tonight we could hit the China Club."

That peaked Dale's interest. "Wow! Hope you brought enough money for me. That's Upper Manhattan's West Side."

Ethan smiled as he grabbed another beer. "Yeah! Heard some pretty awesome women go there. Tonight, I'm feeling lucky, boys."

As the three men toasted themselves, the limo finally arrived at its destination. Knowing the club had a reputation for celebrity visitors, Jack reserved a space in the VIP section. "Are you ready, boys?"

Jack placed his beer in the cup holder and swung open the door.

Although there was a swarm of people attempting to get in, Jack led the way through the crowd and into the nightclub.

Ethan was trying to keep pace, but he lagged behind. "Give me a break. Wait up, guys. I can't believe we walked right in."

Dale headed straight for the bar as Jack made his way through the crowded dance floor and up the steps to the very top level. "What do you think, Ethan? They don't call this place Eden for nothing."

Ethan's heart started to pound, keeping pace with the pounding music. As he stopped to look around, he had a hard time taking it all in. "I still can't believe we walked right in. I'm guessing they know you here."

Jack had already had a few beers and was feeling pretty good. "I've been known to drop some money here every now and then."

Just then, a vivacious blonde with legs up to her neck crept up behind Jack and wrapped her hands around his eyes. Jack was startled at first, but quickly felt at ease when he felt the hands of a female.

"Okay, I'll play the guess who game. Give me a minute." He placed his arms by his sides and slowly reached around to the female's legs. As he worked his fingers up her thighs, he blurted out a name. "Monica?"

He turned around into the arms of the tallest Southern belle he'd ever laid eyes on. "Damn, girl. Haven't seen you in a long time."

Monica leaned forward and gave Jack a little tap-kiss on the lips. "You haven't been around for a long time, Jack."

Jack took a step back and tried to keep his composure. "Well, I've been somewhat busy. Hey, let me introduce you. This is Ethan, a friend and colleague of mine."

Ethan was still trying to absorb his surroundings and presented himself as nervous, at best. "Hello, I'm, uh, uh, I'm really glad to meet you."

Monica gave a half-smile and turned her attention back to Jack. "Where's Bria tonight?"

Jack felt his heart sink and couldn't think of anything quick to say. "Well, we decided to give each other a break, so I came out with my friends tonight."

Monica turned to walk away then looked back at Jack with a devious smile. "Come find me before you leave. Maybe we can get together later tonight."

Dale finally made it upstairs, and he found Jack and Ethan still trying to shake off the effects of Monica.

"Hey, guys, where the hell did you go? I thought you guys were right behind me."

Dale handed them each a beer and they walked over to a lounge area. No sooner had they sat down than a bachelorette party arrived at the top level. As the music was pumping, the women grew louder. A few of the girls made their way over to Jack's table and pulled Dale into their little dance group. Dale was all too pleased to accommodate them.

Ethan and Jack tried to sit and talk quietly, but it wasn't working. Every time a gorgeous woman passed by, Ethan lost his concentration. Dale never made it back to the table, so Jack left Ethan to his fantasies and stood up to walk around. He walked over to the bar and tried to get the bartenders attention. Just when he was about to give up, another bartender came from the opposite end of the bar and handed him a beer and a note. The note read, "Finish your beer and meet me at the front door." Jack thought maybe it was Dale joking around, but so what. After a couple of minutes, he finished off his beer and worked his way through the crowds to get downstairs.

Jack finally made it to the front door and walked out. He stood off to the side, away from the hordes of people still trying to get in. Just then, Bria came from behind and wrapped her hands around his eyes. Once again, Jack was startled, but quickly breathed a sigh of relief when he felt a woman's hands. Thinking that it was Monica, Jack turned and found himself in Bria's arms.

"What are you doing here? I've been trying to call you to apologize, but—"

Before Jack could finish, Bria leaned forward and kissed him, and kept kissing him.

"Hello, Jack Kotter. I got all your messages, but I wanted to make you squirm a little for lying to me." She pulled Jack around the corner and pushed him up against the wall. She then started to undo his pants, but Jack quickly stopped her.

"What are you doing? Are you nuts?"

She took a step back and unbuttoned her top three buttons. "What's wrong, Jack Kotter? Lost your nerve?"

Jack buttoned his pants and walked over to the curb. A taxi pulled over and Jack opened the door. Before Bria climbed in, Jack gave her one last passionate kiss. During the ride home, they held hands and didn't say a word.

CHAPTER SIX

WHEN THE TAXI PULLED TO THE FRONT OF THE HOUSE, JACK STEPPED out and paid the driver. When he finished, he turned around and saw that Bria was already sitting on the porch. He walked over and sat down beside her as he reached over and took her hand.

"I'm really sorry, Bria. It wasn't my intention to race that night. That bitch just knew how to push my buttons."

Bria leaned forward in order to look Jack in the eyes. "I thought I was the one who knew how to push your buttons."

Jack blushed and gave her a smile. "You know what I mean."

As the two sat quietly enjoying the nighttime breeze, the sky started to change colors. A pending storm was brewing and the winds were bouncing the fading moonlight from cloud to cloud. As the clouds became darker, the last of the moonlight disappeared. Jack gazed at Bria as he gently rolled her fingers into his.

"I think it's time to go in now. It's not looking too good." Jack looked out into the yard and saw it was starting to drizzle. Then, with the crack of the thunder, the sky opened up and the downpour started. As Jack and Bria stood up, they kissed once more before they went in the house.

Bria walked to the kitchen and filled a pot with water. "Jack, would you like some tea?"

Jack was busy hanging up the jackets and thought tea would be nice. "Sure. Make more than usual. I might want a second cup."

When he finished hanging the jackets, he walked into the kitchen and found Bria waiting for him. She had no pants and just wore her top and panties, with a tea bag hanging from her belly button ring.

"So, Jack Kotter, would you like some sugar with this tea?"

Jack stopped dead in his tracks with his eyes open wide. "Whoa, girl! Of course I want some sugar. You could probably get a eunuch to want sugar."

He made his way across the kitchen floor and kissed Bria as he slid one hand down her thigh and the other up her blouse.

"Damn, girl, you should warn a guy first."

Before Jack could finish what he was saying, Bria slipped her tongue into his mouth and wrapped her legs around him.

The minutes went by and all of Bria's clothes came off. As she unbuttoned Jack's shirt, she stared at him with her dark eyes. "Jack Kotter, what big hands you have."

Jack's shirt slipped off his shoulders as he placed his hands above her hips. "Yes, I know. All the better to lift you onto the kitchen counter with."

With her arms and legs around Jack, Bria leaned back and Jack softly laid her on the countertop.

"Jack Kotter, what big eyes you have."

Jack leaned over and kissed her neck, working his way down to her breast. "Yes, I know. All the better to see all of you with."

As the thunder became louder and lightning dominated the sky, Bria's passion became overwhelming. "Oh! Jack, what a big ego you have."

By then, Jack was nonstop. "Yes, I know. All the better to please you with, over and over."

Another crack of the thunder and lightning followed, and the lights went out as Jack and Bria's exploits came to a climactic end. They had one last passionate kiss as they looked out at the rain pounding on the kitchen window.

As Jack sat on the counter, Bria jumped down and squeezed in between his legs. She wrapped her arms around his neck and got right up in his face. "So, Jack Kotter, would you like another cup of tea up in the bedroom?"

Jack was just catching a second wind as he slid down off the counter. "Hm, if I didn't know any better, I might think you have a touch of nymphobia. I better take you upstairs to check you out further and make sure you're taken care of."

Jack and Bria felt their way through the dark and made it to the steps. Jack turned and picked Bria up and carried her up and into the bedroom. He laid her on the bed as they engaged in a passionate kiss. With her aggressiveness, Bria rolled Jack over and climbed on top.

"So, Jack Kotter, now it's time to step up your game. Think you can handle it?"

Jack had his hands on her waist and maneuvered her into place. "Get ready for round two. We'll see who screams first."

As the rain fell, thunder and lightning went on through the night. Eventually, Jack and Bria wore each other out. They fell asleep listening to the rain beat against the roof.

The storm didn't let up at all. It was one of those storms that came alive in the nightmares of little children. Suddenly, as it happens with some dreams, Jack's thoughts became ominous. His adrenaline started to rise and his heart started to beat faster. He found himself on the deck of *Titanic*. After what felt like a long while, the dream turned to *Titanic* at the bottom of the ocean and Jack was standing at the top of the famous fore Grand Staircase in the first-class section. After a few minutes of looking around, he was thrust upwards until he hit the ceiling and was dragged across to the other side of the ship.

After the dream, Jack woke up shaking. He jumped up out of bed as the sweat poured down his face. Bria woke and sat up in bed. "Are you okay? What's wrong?"

Jack stood at bedside shaking. "I'm not sure. Guess I had a nightmare."

Bria crawled over to Jack to try to comfort him. "Baby, you're soaked. Go wash up and come back to bed."

Jack just stood at the side of the bed. He was only half-listening to Bria. "That's the second dream I've had like that. It was so real." He sat down on the edge of the bed and tried to wipe the moisture from his brow.

Bria reached over and gave him a hug from behind. "So, what happen? What was the dream about?"

The thunder and lightning had stopped, but the rain was still coming down. Jack walked over to the window and looked towards the sky. "Looks like the storm will end soon." It was four o'clock in the morning and it was going to be awhile before the sun came up. "It's too early for coffee or tea. What'ya say we sleep in this morning."

Bria climbed out of bed and walked over to the window with Jack "What about work?"

Jack took hold of Bria's hand and led her back to the bed. "I'm the boss. I pick my own hours." As the rain continued to fall, they slipped back under the covers and fell asleep.

Later that morning, Bria woke up and Jack was gone. She could smell something cooking so she threw on some sweat pants and t-shirt and quickly ran down stairs. Sometime during the morning, the electricity came back on and Jack was cooking Bria's favorite breakfast, banana nut pancakes and sausage.

As Bria entered the kitchen, she stopped to watch Jack hover over the stove. "Hey, Jack Kotter, nice ass."

Jack turned around and smiled. "You're not supposed to be up yet. But that's okay. You're just in time to save me a trip up those steps. Have a seat."

It doesn't happen often, but when Jack cooks, Bria always eats. As she watched him load up her plate, she grabbed her fork and prepared to dig in. "Are you going to tell me what your dream was about last night?"

Jack laid the plate down in front of Bria and walked back to the stove. As he made his plate, he paused and turned around. "I don't know where to start. Out of nowhere, I was standing on the deck of the *Titanic,* just staring."

With a mouth full of food, Bria stopped chewing just long enough to get out a few words. "What were you staring at?"

Jack finished making his plate and sat down. "Nothing. I was just staring. I remember I was standing at the bow and staring back at the ship. Then, all of a sudden, the ship was at the bottom of the ocean and I was at the top of a staircase."

Bria took a drink to wash down the first round of food. "So how do you know it was the *Titanic*?"

Jack was cutting up his food and stopped. "I guess I recognized it from pictures. When I was younger, I read about it in school. The teacher told us one day we had to do a book report, so she took us to the library to pick out a book. I came across the story of the *Titanic*, and it must have struck a chord inside me because I read the first few pages and it fascinated me."

Bria sat back in her chair and laughed. "You actually read a book in school?"

Jack played off the comment and kept talking. "Do you want me to finish the story or do you wanna harass me after I made you this nice breakfast?"

Bria went back to wolfing down her food. "Okay, Jack Kotter, please continue."

Jack smiled as he continued eating his food. "You're lucky you're so sexy and that I love you. So anyway, I remember when they found it, but I wasn't really into the story, probably because I was too busy getting into trouble with Connie. I really liked the book so I decided to do my report on *Titanic.*

"I got home that day and told my mom about it, and she was glad I was actually excited about doing a book report. I remember reading for about half an hour when my dad walked in. He had on his usual happy face when he kissed my mom. He walked over to the table to see what I was working on and nearly fell over."

Once again, Bria couldn't help herself. "Why, because you were doing schoolwork?"

Jack laughed it off as he finished eating. "Ha, ha. No, smart ass. I don't know why. He just froze like a deer in headlights. He asked me why I had that book and then took it from me."

"I told him it was for a book report and then he closed the book and laid it on the table. He told me to pick out a book worth writing about. I remember the angry look he gave me. I didn't think he was mad at me; I just thought maybe he was upset that I picked out a book that wasn't complicated. My mom got right up in his face. I thought she would be all over him, but she wasn't."

Jack stopped talking for a minute. He stood up from the table and started gathering the dishes. Bria sat waiting for the rest of the story. "Come on, Jack Kotter, what happened?"

Jack took a breath and gathered his thoughts. "Something happened that day. My mom just backed away. I'd never seen her back off from my dad before. She saw something in his eyes that scared her. It's hard to explain. My dad took the book and walked away with it. My mom asked me if there was any way I could pick out another book. It scared me a little. I don't know why. At the time, it wasn't a big deal to me.

"The next day, I found the book next to my dad's favorite chair. It was open to the page where everyone went into panic mode and was trying to get off the ship."

Bria stood up to help with the dishes. "So, didn't you think that was kind of strange? Your dad takes your book and bans you from reading it and then reads it when you're not around?"

Jack just shook his head with uncertainty. "I know. Sounds strange, and my dad wasn't a strange guy. He came downstairs as I was about to leave for school. He saw me with the book in my hand. I tried talking to him about the report, thinking he might change his mind, but he got really angry. He told me to get the book out the house and not to ever bring the subject up again."

Jack sat back down and leaned his elbows on the kitchen table while supporting his head. "I never saw him so mad. In fact, up until that point, I'd never known my dad to get angry at anything. Well, except when he lost out of that Nabisco buyout back in '88. I ran out of the house. I was so upset. I thought he would've been happy I was showing so much enthusiasm for a project."

Bria finished filling the dishwasher and sat back down. She reached across the table and took Jack's hand. "I'm sure your dad had his reasons. He couldn't have been mad at you. It was just a book." As much as Bria tormented Jack, she always listened with an open heart when he needed to talk. Knowing Bria was a comfort to him, Jack stretched across the table and placed a soft kiss on her cheek. Bria still had Jack's hands, and she gave them a little squeeze then shot him a quick smile. "I love when you do that. So, what happened with the book report?"

Jack leaned back in his chair and shrugged his shoulders. "I wound up getting *To Kill a Mockingbird.* It was okay. I got a B+. I went back to the library after school one day and checked out everything I could find on the *Titanic.* They even had some documentary videos. I took it all. I didn't let anyone know what I was doing. I wanted to try to figure out why my dad got so upset."

Jack paused for a moment and laughed. "Connie and Warner saw me coming out of the library during summer vacation with a bunch of videos and some books. They busted me about it for a week. But I made them promise not to say anything in front of my parents. They spent more time at my house then they did their own."

In a playful kind of way, Bria stood up and brushed up against Jack as she walked over to get some coffee. "Did you find out anything good when you read the books?"

Jack just shook his head no. "They all said pretty much the same thing. The video footage was cool. It's really spooky the way it just sits there in the dark. As the submersible comes up on it, it literally appears out of nowhere. I gave up on it after that summer. The thought never crossed my mind again until last night when I had that dream."

Bria sat back down with her coffee. "Yeah, what about the dream? You never told me the end of it."

Jack looked across the table and threw out some sarcasm. "Don't worry, I didn't want any coffee. So anyway, I was standing at the top of the Grand Staircase when all of a sudden some unknown force picked me up and slammed me upwards against the ceiling. Then it dragged me across the ceiling to the other side of the ship. Just before I was about to fall, I woke up."

Bria looked on with intensity, like a little kid around a camp fire. "When you woke up, you jumped up out of bed shaking. You really worried me. I've never seen you shake like that."

While Bria was talking, Jack went over the dream in his head. "Yeah, it was so real. I've never experienced anything like that before. I would almost swear I was there."

While Bria finished her coffee, Jack finished his storytelling with some more sarcasm. "Well, I know you wouldn't understand, but I have to get ready and go to work. I know I said I was the boss, but I still have to make grown-up decisions."

With that, Bria grabbed a dish towel and flicked Jack on his butt cheeks. Afterwards, he chased her upstairs and finished off the morning by picking Bria up and getting her dizzy with a helicopter twirl. Jack knew she hated that.

CHAPTER SEVEN

LATER THAT EVENING, BEN'S PLANE ARRIVED AT BEIJING CAPITAL International Airport. He made his way through the crowd and picked his suitcases up at the baggage claim. Ben glanced around, but saw nobody holding up a sign with his name, so he quickly hailed a taxi. As the driver loaded the luggage, Ben glanced over at two American men who were watching him. As the taxi exited the airport, Ben stared out the window at the two men. "Take me to the Fengniao Apartment please." As the taxi picked up speed, Ben laid his head back and closed his eyes.

Thirty minutes later, the taxi cab shook as it pulled onto a dirt road. Ben woke up to see the taxi pulling up to an old, abandoned warehouse. "Where the hell are we?"

Two men quickly opened the old sliding doors and the taxi pulled inside. As the driver slowed to a stop, the two men closed the doors just as quickly as they'd opened them. Ben attempted to get out, but the door wouldn't open. The driver turned around and looked at Ben. "Someone will be with you in a moment, Mr. Marcus."

The driver smiled then climbed out and shut the door. Ben looked around, but didn't see anyone. Suddenly, out of nowhere, his door opened. His old friend Chang held the door while Ben stepped out. "Benjamin, it's been too long, my friend."

Ben breathed a sigh of relief when he saw Chang, but he was

equally upset. "Chang, what the hell is going on? I thought we agreed to meet tomorrow."

Chang handed Ben a locked briefcase and escorted him into the next room where a stretch limo was waiting. "Benjamin, please forgive me. I wanted to try to make it as much like the old days as possible. I hope you don't mind; I canceled your reservations at that dirty apartment and set you up at the Aman at the Summer Palace. I've stayed there a number of times. It's one of the finest hotels in Beijing."

Ben's blood pressure started to come down, but he still had questions without answers. "What are we doing, Chang? We'll both hang if we get caught together."

Chang laughed as the limo made it out to the road. "Here, Ben, have a drink. If I remember correctly your favorite was Jack Daniels with a hint of Coca-Cola, and hold the lemon. I have some news for you, old friend, but it's going to have to wait until tomorrow. I've made arrangements for a limo to pick you up tomorrow at twelve o'clock. That should give you enough time to rest and get rid of any jet lag you might have. But, for now, please enjoy your accommodations, and I promise all of your questions will be answered tomorrow."

The limo pulled up to the front of the hotel and one of the doormen opened the limo door to let Ben out. A bellhop rushed over and took care of the luggage as Ben checked in at the front desk. "My name is Benjamin Marcus."

Usually, the desk personnel would look a guest up in their computer, but not this time. The woman simply shot Ben a smile and waved over one of the bellhops. "Welcome to the Aman, Mr. Marcus. We've been expecting your arrival. Please follow this gentleman and he'll show you to your room."

Ben turned and followed the bellhop as he stepped onto something resembling a golf cart. The driver took Ben through several areas of the resort and then to his private suite. Just outside was a pool with several women swimming. When Ben finally took his eyes off the women, he turned to find the bellhop waiting with the door open.

As he walked through the door, Ben noticed his luggage was already waiting for him. He tipped the bellhop and the driver fifty dollars each, and told them to give another fifty to the bellhop that delivered the luggage. He closed the door and made his way into one of the bedrooms. As he sat down, he could hear sounds coming from the other bedroom. He went to investigate and found two gorgeous women waiting for him on the bed. One of the women stood up. She was wearing nothing more than a black, silky, lace pair of panties. "Hello, Benjamin. We've been waiting for you. Chang told us you might need some TLC when you arrived, so we're here to take care of your every need."

Ben was tired, but not that tired. With a sigh of relief, he laughed to himself. That Chang really knew how to treat his friends. Ben turned the lights off and closed the door.

While Ben was finding pleasure in China, Jack went to work. When he arrived, he found a meeting involving Robert, Nicholas, and Linda in progress. He watched through the glass as Robert was obviously upset at something. Linda was slumped down in her seat as Nick argued with Robert. Linda finally noticed Jack through the window and sat up straight with a smile. Robert stopped yelling just enough to glance over and see Jack watching. He motioned for Jack to come in.

When Jack walked in, Nick became really quiet. As usual, Linda couldn't keep her eyes to herself. Without even saying a polite hello, she looked Jack up and down. Robert stood up and greeted Jack with a handshake.

"Hello, Jack. I wasn't expecting you in today."

Jack smiled as he shook Robert's hand. "I see. So, what's going on? You want to let me in on what you and Nick were arguing about?"

Robert sat back down and closed his briefcase. "Nothing important. Just a difference in opinions on how we should proceed with our current situation. By the way, Ben is nowhere to be found and Hellen won't say where he is. I find that to be unprofessional and inconsiderate, considering this company is at a crossroad."

Jack sat down next to Robert and politely asked Nick and Linda to leave the room. Nick was all too glad to get up and leave, but Linda was a little offended. Nevertheless, she stood up and followed Nick out the door. Jack stood up and quietly shut the door behind them. As he sat back down next to Robert, he made sure he collected his thoughts before speaking.

"You've been with Kotter Industries a long time. My dad and Ben were like two peas in a pod. If you were friends with one, you were friends with both. I know you and Ben have a mutual respect for each other. So, did that respect extend to my dad?"

Robert stood up and briefly thought about walking out. But just like his father, Jack was a pretty straight forward guy. Robert admired that in a person. "Your dad and I were very good friends. Just like Benjamin and myself, we had a great respect for each other. Your dad valued my input and one can't place a price tag on that kind of friendship. I can see some of your dad's qualities in you, so I want to try to give you as much room as possible with whatever questions you're going to ask."

Jack knew he wasn't obligated to feel sorry about the questions he was about to ask, so he didn't. He set out to be direct and he knew Robert would lose any respect he had for him if he wasn't. "Listen, I truly don't know where Ben jetted off to, but I kinda have an idea. There's a lot going on right now and I'm hoping I can make the right decisions for Kotter Industries. So, with that said, would you mind if I ask you about your vacation to China?"

Robert pushed his chair back from the table and let out a laugh. He stood up and pulled out his pocket watch as though he was checking the time. "Your father gave this to me. It's English, from the mid-1800s. He told me he was in China and bought it off some old Chinese merchant. If you're interested, I'll tell you the story."

Jack was somewhat thrown because he'd never known Robert to be a storyteller. "Sure, I love to hear about things my dad did."

Robert handed the watch to Jack and paused to gather his thoughts. "Your father was visiting a marketplace, when he saw the old man trying to sell some beaded necklaces. He watched the old man for a while until the old man grew tired and started to pack up for the day. Your dad was about to walk away, when out of nowhere, these three little kids came running over to the old man. As your dad stood watching, another merchant leaned over the counter and told him the old man came to the market every day to sell the necklaces that his grandkids made, but that not too many people bought them. Your dad asked the merchant about the parents, but they were both killed during a robbery. The old man lost his wife when she was beaten to death by one of the local gangs. So now he had to care for the grandkids on his own.

"Now, I'm not sure how or where the old man got the pocket watch, but he had it in his vest when your dad decided to walk over and talk to him. The old man didn't speak much English, but one of the grandchildren did. Your dad asked how much for the whole collection. As the child was translating the question, the old man noticed your dad was wearing a plain leather wrist watch. The old man's asking price for all the necklaces was $50.00, and he wanted to trade for your dad's watch. When the old man pulled out the pocket watch, your dad tried to decline his offer. He told the child to let the grandfather know his pocket watch was worth a lot more than the wrist watch. I think the old man knew that, but was thankful your dad was attempting to help him in his time of need.

"So your dad, being the type of person he was, traded watches with the old man, but instead of giving him $50.00 for the necklaces, he handed the man $300.00, which was all the money your dad had on him at the time. He walked away so the old man couldn't refuse. If you notice, the watch has medieval battle scenes engraved on both sides. With all the past violence the old man had to endure, it's my guess he didn't mind getting rid of the watch.

"The week before your dad left for China, we got into a heated argument over how management was becoming too relaxed. He said some pretty harsh words to me. When he came back, he invited me into his office to apologize to me. He shook my hand and told me how much he valued our friendship. He handed me a small case, and when I opened it, the watch was inside. He'd had it engraved on the inside. 'Friendships are priceless.' Your dad was a very proud man, but not too proud to say he was wrong."

Robert took the watch back from Jack. He looked down at the floor for a moment as he thought about his next words. "I miss your father. He was a wonderful man. No matter who he came in contact with, he always had happiness to give. I valued our friendship very much. So before you ask anything else, I can tell you my vacation to China was exactly that. A vacation. Besides wanting to see certain sights, I wanted to tour some of their industry. On a more personal note, I attempted to track down the old man your father got the watch from. I wanted to meet him, but he had passed away several years earlier. I couldn't locate the grandchildren. I'm most certain they were probably split up and placed into some kind of foster care system. So, may I ask about this inquiry?"

Jack wasn't really prepared to answer the question, but he felt obligated after Robert broke down and told him such a personal story. "Well, I know you're trying to gain support for this vote we're going to have. I just can't figure you out, though. You just told me something very personal about you and my dad, but yet you seem to want to take this company down a path of destruction."

With a stern face, Robert sat back down and looked Jack in the eye. "You're still young. Although I know you're in good hands with Ben, I just don't think you have what it takes to run this company. At least, not yet. When Ben comes back from wherever, you and I are going to have a sit down with him to discuss the future of the company and why he thinks I'm trying to do him wrong." With that, Robert stood up and walked out. Jack still wasn't able to determine if Robert was genuine or deceitful.

Jack wasn't sure what kind of progress, if any, Ben was making, so he had his secretary, Bonnie, send out a memo to all the board members. He planned to finish the meeting without Ben, knowing Ben would blow his top if something went wrong. Afterwards, he called the repair shop to see if *Fringe* was ready, but he didn't have any luck. The damage was extensive and they were still waiting for parts to arrive. Upset and embarrassed that he still had to drive a rental car, Jack left work to go visit his car club friends at the Wiley Roadster.

The Wiley Roadster was an old-time drive up where car enthusiasts would park and congregate. As he pulled onto the lot, he noticed a purple '74 Cuda and an orange '74 Challenger. The owners were two Mopar enthusiasts, who happened to be brothers and also friends of Jack's. Walley and Jimmy watched as women wearing daisy-duke shorts skated around delivering food to the customers. Jimmy turned his attention away long enough to see Jack walking towards them. "Hey, Jack, what'ya got there? That's a real sharp looking family car you have."

While Jimmy and Walley found humor in Jack's car situation, Jack wasn't laughing. "One of these days, you clowns are gonna stop fooling around with this Mopar junk and get some real hotrods. So, what's up? Where is everyone?"

Jack waited for an answer, but neither brother wanted to speak up. Walley finally forced the lump out of his throat in order to tell Jack the bad news. "I'm guessing you didn't see the news last night." Jimmy stepped out of his car and walked around to Jack. Walley climbed out of his car so he could look at Jack face-to-face. "Bobby died last night."

It took a second for Jack to realize Walley wasn't kidding. "What? What the hell happened?"

Walley leaned back on his car and took a few breaths. "We don't know the full story, but we know enough. We were all just hanging out last night, having a good time during that storm. Bobby was wired as usual, itching to get into something. As the night started to wind down, Bobby looked across the lot and saw that black Road Runner just sitting there. No one even saw it pull onto the lot. It just appeared out of nowhere. You know Bobby. Always fooling around. He said he finally wanted to get a good look at the driver so he walked over."

Jack felt a headache coming on, but he knew it was from the anger he had for Lilith. "Why did you guys even let him go near that bitch? He was your friend. You should have stopped him." Walley felt bad as it was and Jack could see it. "I'm sorry, Walley. Go on. What happened?"

Walley gathered his thoughts and continued with the story. "We sat here for a few minutes watching Bobby, but we couldn't really see if he was actually talking to her because of the rain. We could see him standing next to the driver side window, but that was it. Suddenly, the car started to shake and rumble as she revved her engine. Bobby came running over shouting something about finally taking her down. Jimmy and I tried to grab him, but he shook us off and jumped into his car."

As Walley took a few moments, Jimmy continued to piece the events together. "We figured he would come back and tell us some story about being the first person to beat Lilith, but he never came back. After waiting for a while, we all jumped in our cars and went looking for him. I thought maybe he didn't come back because he got embarrassed. As we headed down 110, we started seeing fire trucks and police all over the place. It was still raining pretty hard and the traffic was backed up, but we were still able to make it all the way down to about the cemetery. They had the west-bound lanes blocked off, so we got out and stood off to the side to see if we could see anything, but all we saw were lights. After a few minutes of waiting, we saw a medevac take off. The only reason we found out what happened was because your friend Dale happened to be listening to his police radio on his way home from the China Club. He saw us on the side of the road and stopped to talk. He said Bobby had lost control of his car and hit the guardrail. They don't think he was wearing the custom harness he had in his car, and he was ejected."

By then, Jack was feeling sick. "So, how do you know it was Lilith?"

Walley was finally able to jump back in with his thoughts, although at that point, it was all speculation. "Dale told us some witnesses saw Bobby hit the rail, but didn't really see anything else. But one little girl said she saw a black car hit the back of Bobby's car just before he lost control. We kinda figured Bobby was winning the race, so she ran him into the guard rail. We asked Dale where the medevac was taking him, but Dale said it was empty. Bobby died just before it landed. When he got ejected, his body must have somehow wrapped itself around the guardrail. Both his legs were severed right above the knees."

Jack leaned over and gave both Walley and Jimmy hugs. "Are there any funeral arrangements yet?"

Jimmy shook his head no as he stooped down to pick up a penny. "Look at this. Remember when Bobby swore that every time he pulled onto this lot, he would be able to find a penny?" Jimmy gave the penny to Jack and shook his hand. "Here's to Bobby and his last penny."

Jimmy and Walley said their goodbyes as Jack climbed back into his car and went back to work.

CHAPTER EIGHT

As Jack was winding up his day, Ben was just waking up from a long night of pleasure. As he sat up in bed and focused his eyes, he noticed one of his female companions was still sleeping and the other had just emerged from the other room with nothing more than a G-string. She climbed onto Ben's lap and gave him a short kiss on the lips. "Good morning, Benjamin. Chang is sending a limo to pick you up, but not for another hour. How about we play for a while?"

Ben placed his hands on her hips as he leaned his face forward between her breasts. "Why couldn't I have known both of you 25 years ago? I would love to spend some more time with you girls, but I have to get ready. By the way, I didn't get either of your names."

The Asian beauty stood up with a smile and walked over to the closet. By that time, the other companion had woken up and was getting dressed. "We don't usually use our names. We go by the name of Double Trouble."

After a small laugh, Ben stood up and walked over to the dresser. He took $1,000.00 out of a gold money clip and placed it on the night stand. As the girls were getting dressed, Ben retreated to the bathroom to shave and shower. When he finished, he peaked his head out and saw that the money and the girls were gone.

Ben dressed and grabbed the mysterious briefcase Chang had

given him. He made his way over to the lobby, and when he arrived, he saw the limo was already waiting for him. That Chang was really efficient. As Ben walked out, the driver had the door open and waiting. For the long ride, there was a fruit basket and coffee, teas, and orange juice. Ben went straight for the minibar. After helping himself to a drink, he looked around and found the intercom system. "Hey, driver, how long of a ride is it?"

The driver paused for a minute as he thought about it. "I would say about forty minutes, Mr. Marcus." After downing his drink, Ben placed a pair of sunglasses on his face and laid his head back. He hadn't really had much sleep the night before.

The limo finally arrived at its destination, a 25-story office building in downtown Beijing. Ben waited for the driver to open his door. When he stepped out of the limo, he was met by Chang and Changpu. Ben shook hands with Chang and gave Changpu a hug. "It's been a long time, my friend."

Changpu smiled with joy and shook Ben's hand. "Yes it has, my friend." As the three men turned to walk into the building, Ben couldn't help but feel something was out of place. "I don't ever remember conducting business this way. I seem to remember all the hole-in-the-wall bars and empty warehouses we would meet in."

Chang laughed as he opened the door for Ben. "I told you, Benjamin; times have changed."

As the three men entered the elevator, Changpu leaned over and quietly whispered to Ben. "I heard about the joke Chang played on you. If it was me, I probably would have added some fake gunfire just to spice it up some."

As Changpu laughed, Ben looked at Chang and shook his head. "You had me going, Chang. Especially when the taxi driver jumped out and left me there with the doors locked."

As more people were getting on and off the elevator, it took a few minutes for it to reach the 25th floor. Since it was an outside elevator with glass, Ben was enjoying looking out over Beijing. When the elevator finally reached the top, the door opened and the first thing Ben saw was a name in big bold letters: China Steel Corporation.

Chang and Changpu stepped off the elevator and held the door for Ben. Ben didn't move. He just stood in confusion, looking at the brothers. "What is this all about? I thought we had some business to take care of."

Chang smiled and asked Ben to step out so they could talk. "Benjamin, remember when you first arrived, I told you all your questions would be answered today? So here we are. Finally able to meet without persecution. We can also, how do you Americans say … oh yeah, kill two birds with one stone. You Americans have so many funny sayings."

Ben gathered his composure and stepped off the elevator. They walked down the hall and through two large glass doors. They were met by a receptionist who escorted them to one of the conference rooms. Along the way, Ben noticed photos of various projects hanging on the walls. He briefly thought about the days he worked in the steel mill as a young man. As the men entered the huge room, Ben realized he was still holding the briefcase Chang gave him the day before. "What's the deal with this briefcase, Chang? Why would you give it to me knowing I couldn't open it?"

Changpu slid one of the chairs out for Ben to sit. "Benjamin, we are waiting for some very important people to arrive, so we can get this meeting started. Let me relieve you of the burden of carrying this briefcase." Changpu gently took the case from Ben and placed it on the table.

Chang walked over to a beverage cart and poured three cups of coffee. "If I remember correctly, Benjamin, you like two creams and two sugars."

Ben turned his head and watched Chang as he was about to drop the sugar cubes into a cup. "Not anymore, Chang. My doctor advised me to switch to Sweet'n Low."

Chang placed the cubes back in the bowl with a smile. He knew Ben didn't completely trust him. "Sounds like a wise man." He walked over to Ben and handed him his coffee with two creams and two Sweet'n Lows. "Whether or not your doctor really told you to switch is irrelevant. Please believe me when I tell you we are not here to harm you, but to help you, Benjamin."

Ben looked at the coffee then examined the prepackaged cream and sugar supplement. "We have a lot of history together, Chang. Right now, it looks like the rules have changed, and I feel like I'm sitting in the lion's den."

Just then, the door opened and in came a women dressed in business attire. Ben worked his eyes from her feet up to her face. After so many years, he still recognized her. Ben knew her as Liling. She had grown into a beautiful woman and obviously had worked her way up the corporate ladder. As Ben stood up, Liling walked over and gave him a hug. "Hello, Benjamin. It's been a long time. I hope your stay at the Aman was acceptable."

Ben didn't say anything. He was still trying to process how much Liling had changed. "Your English? I remember when you didn't speak it very well. Now look at you. All grown up and working these corporate bastards like dogs."

Ben turned to Chang as though he was expecting something to happen. "Well, we're all here, just like old times. Now what?"

Once again, the conference room door opened and in walked an entourage of men. The first three were obviously some type of bodyguards. Very large with muscle on top of muscle. The next three men were older and very distinguished looking. Obviously, some sort of management team. While the larger men took up positions around the room, the older gentlemen sat down at the table.

Ben watched as Chang and Changpu stood up out of respect when the men entered the room. He decided not to extend the courtesy, due to the fact he wasn't sure what to expect at that point.

Liling bowed her head then approached the man at the head of the table. She leaned over while he whispered something in her ear. Ben noticed he was the eldest out of the three and had Coke-bottle eyeglasses. His hands were somewhat shaky, but nevertheless, he seemed to be the one in charge. The man to his right motioned to Changpu to bring the briefcase over to him. As Changpu picked the case up, he ran his finger along the side and pressed a hidden button, which opened the two locks near the handle.

Ben watched as Changpu walked the case to the other side of the table. Although he still had an uneasy feeling, he couldn't help but throw some sarcasm in Chang's direction. "Ah yes, the old hidden button in the briefcase trick. An oldie but a goodie." Chang smiled as he tried to hold back his laughter.

Changpu placed the case down in front of the three men and stood off to the side. Liling was then motioned to the front of the room to introduce the three men. "Benjamin, I want to introduce one of the senior management teams of China Steel Corporation. To the left is Jianguo, which means 'building the country.' To the right is Guoliang, which means 'may the country be good.' And at the head of the table is Huizhong, which means 'wise loyalty.' None of these gentlemen speak English, so I will translate all dialogue."

Ben stood up and bowed his head as a traditional hello. Then, with his raspy voice, he started the meeting. "Can you ask them what the hell is going on?"

With an embarrassed look, Liling turned to Huizhong and spoke to him in their native language. Huizhong became quite offended and stood up. He then spoke back to Liling in a stern voice. When he finished, Liling bowed her head as though she was being reprimanded. She then turned to Ben. "Huizhong wishes you to refrain from using inappropriate language at this meeting. He has extended to you the courtesy for this meeting out of respect for Mr. Jack Kotter. He was good friends with Mr. Kotter and was very sad to hear of his passing."

Still frustrated about being in the dark, Ben sat back down in his chair. He knew if he was going to get any usable information, he was going to have to be patient. "I apologize to Mr. Huizhong and his colleagues. Please continue." Liling informed the three men of Ben's apologies and asked that they continue.

Huizhong reached into the briefcase and pulled out a photo and some paperwork. He then spoke to Liling in reference to the papers. After a lengthy conversation, Guoliang motioned to Changpu to collect the photo and paperwork. As Liling turned to translate the information, Changpu walked the material over and placed it on the table in front of Ben. Ben skimmed through the paperwork as Liling translated what Huizhong said.

"After the passing of Mr. Kotter, the man in the photo took it upon himself to come to China in order to sell certain information. He contacted some of our lower management in order to set up a line of communication. We are certain that he was working alone."

Ben just stared at the picture in disbelief. It was a surveillance photo of Nicholas Cummings. "Is this a joke? I know this kid. He's on our executive board. Very bright. What the hell kind of information would he be trying to sell?"

Liling once again translated Ben's words with hesitation. Huizhong leaned over and whispered something to Jianguo. He then stood up, along with Guoliang. Huizhong motioned to two of the bodyguards and all four men walked out, leaving Jianguo behind.

With a confused look, Ben stood up as he watched the men leave. "What the hell is going on? That's it?"

Liling walked over to Ben to let him know that Huizhong was once again offended by his words. She informed him that it showed a lack of respect. She also told him Jianguo would continue the meeting and answer any questions he might have.

Since Huizhong was gone, Chang and Changpu were able to sit at the table next to Ben. Jianguo stood up as he closed the briefcase. He then took a seat closer to Ben in order to make Ben feel more comfortable. Then, in a soft quiet voice, he spoke some words to Liling. Afterwards, he opened the briefcase and took out some more paperwork. Liling asked if Ben wanted some time to go through the information or if he wanted to move on with questions. Once again, Ben skimmed through the information and saw most of it consisted of customer information, accounts, and some very old documentation, such as names of people within the China Steel Corporation who were involved in industrial spying back in the '70s and early '80s.

With a degree of sadness, Ben breathed a heavy sigh. "I knew this kid's father. He was a very good friend of mine. This has to be some kind of mistake."

Jianguo spoke to Liling at length and then he spoke to Chang and Changpu. He then stood up and motioned to the last bodyguard that he was leaving. As the bulky man opened the door, Jianguo bowed to Ben and walked out.

Liling sat down at the table in order to explain what Jianguo said. "Jianguo wanted to apologize for all the secrecy. He understands your frustration. He said he was a young employee back when China Steel and Kotter Industries were talking about a possible partnership. He also remembers Mr. Carroll Cummings touring the facilities quite often. As laborers, he says they were all excited about the talks of joining together with the Americans, because it would have meant more jobs and much more money. It was a real disappointment to all of us when China Steel became state owned. He also says it was only by chance we found out about young Mr. Cummings. The surveillance cameras were being updated the week that photo was taken. They were conducting a test on one of the new cameras and it snapped the photo of young Mr. Cummings meeting with one of our lower management, Chen Guang."

Ben slumped down in his chair for a moment while he tried to take it all in. On one hand, he was relieved because it wasn't his friend Robert trying to sabotage the company, but this meant he had to deal with even a bigger problem. Nick was good friends with Jack, and he was trying to sell information to one of Kotter Industries biggest competitors.

Ben sat back up and turned his attention to Chang. "Why didn't you try to contact me back when this all started?"

Chang just looked at Ben in disbelief. "When you contacted us, I informed you we tried to contact you using the satellite phone with no results. So we decided just to wait for you to contact us. Since Mr. Kotter had passed away, my superiors thought it best not to try to get involved."

Ben's face turned red as his blood pressure started to rise. "Get involved? How the hell do you not get involved?" As his voice became louder, his hands became very active, striking the table several times. "Damn it, Chang. You were my friend. You too, Changpu, and you, Liling. All that we did for you."

Just then, Changpu had heard enough. He stood up with fury in his eyes. "Benjamin! They knew what we were doing. China Steel knew about us all along. All the documents we risked our lives to get to you. All the meetings we had. Even the secret phone calls that they weren't supposed to be able to track. They knew it all." As he sat back down to catch his breath and calm down, Chang stood up to continue on.

"He's right, Benjamin. They knew all along. When the state took over in 1977, they pulled everyone's files. Word somehow leaked back that we were stealing valuable company documents and handing them over to Kotter Industries. But instead of us being shot for treason and our families punished, they saw an opportunity to manipulate us. They wanted us to act as double agents. Before we could set it up, you cut off all communication. We found out later Kotter Industries was being threatened by your own government."

"When China Steel was reprivatized in 1995, Changpu, Liling, and myself had already secured our positions. Both Kotter Industries and China Steel had advanced their technologies and there was no longer a need for industrial spying. This is why we didn't take this matter with seriousness."

Ben sat calmly listening to what Chang was saying. He realized he'd not only made the mistake of not seeing Nick for who he was, but he was an old fool for thinking he could relive the old days. "I'm sorry, Chang. I really am."

Ben stood up and placed all the information back into the briefcase. He had a look of shame on his face as he turned to Changpu. "Please give Huizhong, Guoliang, and Jianguo my most sincere apologies. Liling, you've grown into such a beautiful woman. It was so very nice to see all of you again. Chang, don't worry about making arrangements. I have some other business to attend to before I fly back to the states."

As Ben turned to walk towards the door, he stopped and turned with a smile. "Oh, by the way, may I keep this very nice, expensive, hidden button, double locked, top secret briefcase?"

Chang and Changpu broke out in a laugh as Liling walked over and gave Ben a hug. Chang reached out and shook Ben's hand. "Benjamin, so nice to see you again. Please, let us accompany you downstairs."

All four friends stepped onto the elevator joking and laughing like a bunch of children. As they walked to the front of the building, it was time to say their goodbyes. Chang leaned into Ben one more time. "Benjamin, you can call me by regular phone now." Ben laughed as he gave Chang a hug. Everyone knew it would be a long time before they would see each other again, if ever, but at least that time they wouldn't have to part ways in secrecy. After the hugs and handshakes, Ben climbed back into the limousine. It was still early, so he had some time to waste. Because of the legality of the subject, strip clubs, brothels, and sex shows didn't exist in Beijing, but Ben, being a perverted man of the world, knew exactly where to go. Though closely monitored, massage parlors were legal, and Ben had the resources to get more than just a happy ending.

CHAPTER NINE

As Ben prepared to get lucky, Jack was just waking up. After a late breakfast, he was back in his office contemplating what Ben was working on and wondering when he was coming back. He decided to make a few phone calls to Bobby's family. After talking with his mother and father, he called Dale to find out if there was any progress on Lilith and to ask about Bobby's case. The phone rang twice before Dale picked up.

"Hello?"

Jack could hear sirens in the background. "Dale, it's Jack. What's going on?"

Dale could barely hear over the sound of traffic and sirens. "Jack, listen. I'm on an accident scene. Give me about fifteen minutes and I'll call you back. Keep your phone handy."

After Dale hung up, Jack had a bad feeling. He stepped out into the hallway and asked Bonnie to clear his schedule for the day. That didn't exactly make Bonnie happy since she'd worked very hard to schedule various meetings for Jack. "Jack Kotter! Are you running this company or should I just reroute all your business over to Benjamin's office?"

Jack smiled because he knew she was frustrated, but just kidding at the same time. "You're priceless, Bonnie. When Secretary's Day comes around, I might let you go home early." Jack laughed and walked back into his office.

As Jack sat quietly waiting for Dale to call, Bonnie buzzed in telling him he had an incoming call on line one. Jack looked at his desk phone and saw line one blinking. He knew Dale wouldn't call on a business line, and Bonnie would have told him if it was Ben. He picked the phone up more out of curiosity than anything. "Hello, this is Jack Kotter."

A female voice came back that Jack didn't recognize. "Hi, Jack. This is Dee. Ben's friend from the diner."

It took Jack a moment to think, but he definitely remembered Dee. "Hello, Dee. How are you?"

Dee started in with some small talk to get the conversation going then asked if Ben was back in town. Jack just listened to her talk, and then it dawned on him. "Hey, Dee, Ben's not back in town yet, so I'm guessing you know where he went."

There was a brief silence, but Dee finally told Jack she didn't exactly know where he went, but before she left Ben's house the other night, he told her he would bring her some Oriental beads.

That was all Jack needed to hear. "Listen, Dee. I would love to sit and talk, but I'm waiting for an important phone call."

Dee cracked her gum as usual and gave Jack a small giggle. "Okay, Jack. Hey, maybe we can get together sometime."

Jack didn't say it, but he definitely thought it. *First Ben, then me.* What a sick girl. "Sure, Dee. Maybe I'll see you in one of the clubs downtown."

After saying goodbye several times, Jack was finally able to hang the phone up without sounding rude. He stood up and paced the floor in a fury. "Son of a bitch, Ben. You went to China without me."

He peeked his head out the door and barked out an order to Bonnie. "Let me know the minute Ben calls or gets back in town." Just then, his cell phone rang. He picked it up thinking it might be Ben, but it wound up being Dale.

"Hey, Jack. Sorry I couldn't talk before, but I was on the scene of a serious accident."

That bad feeling Jack had before had never left, and with Dale's words, it became worse. "What happened, Dale?" Jack could hear Dale shuffling through some paperwork and was preparing himself for bad news.

Dale didn't answer right away, but then he found what he was looking for. "Sorry, Jack. Some of your friends got involved with that '69 Plymouth."

Jack's heart sank as he plopped down in his chair. "Oh God. Dale, please don't tell me that woman killed someone else."

This time, Dale had no hesitation. "No, Jack. But a couple of your friends, Walley and his brother, Jimmy, chased that Road Runner and caused a major accident. Both of their cars were destroyed and some other people wound up with some minor injuries. They were transported down to Suffolk County Correctional Facility. I'm sorry, Jack. I just thought I would give you a heads up."

Jack breathed a sigh of relief as he stood back up. "I just saw those two knuckleheads yesterday. Do you know if bail's been set?"

Dale laughed because he knew it didn't matter. Those boys were going to spend as little time as possible in jail. "No, I don't know. It'll probably be a while before that's even determined. But I'm sure you're going to make sure it's paid if they do."

Jack smiled because Dale was absolutely right. "Thanks, Dale. I appreciate you calling me."

After a brief pause, Dale came back with condolences for Bobby. "Jack, I'm sorry about your friend Bobby. I was going to call you, but I figured Walley and Jimmy probably got to you first."

Jack was okay with that. He knew Dale had a lot going on with all the accidents lately. "So, I got some of the story from Walley, but tell me what really happened."

Dale didn't hold anything back. He thought Jack deserved the truth. "Well, after gathering all the witness information, it seems that Bobby was winning most of the race. But I have a statement from one witness towards the end that says the Plymouth blew by Bobby like he was standing still. Then, out of nowhere, she let up and got back behind him. Afterwards, she rammed him hard and pushed him into the guardrail. I don't know, Jack. It doesn't make any sense."

Jack didn't have any words. He felt sick to his stomach. "Thanks for the info, Dale. I'll catch up to you later." As the phone call came to an end, Jack just stood in the middle of his office floor with his hands on his hips shaking his head. "Christ, can anything else happen today?"

Jack left his office and walked down the hall to the men's room. As he pushed open the door, Anthony was at the wash area drying his hands.

"Hello, Jack. I know this isn't the proper place, but I've been wanting to talk to you. You're a hard guy to pin down lately."

Jack had little respect for Anthony, so he nodded his head as he walked towards the urinal. As he pulled his zipper down, he turned his head towards Anthony. "So, what's on your mind?"

Anthony was somewhat disgusted, but he knew he probably wouldn't get another chance to get Jack alone before the board met again. "Well, I saw you and Ben the night after the meeting. It seems to me you both might have something going on that the executive board needs to know about. Not that I'm trying to hold anything over your head."

Jack was tired and he just about had enough of too many bad things happening. As he finished his business and closed his zipper, he turned around to face Anthony. He could feel the anger building deep down inside. "You want to know what I think, Anthony? It doesn't matter. I'm gonna tell you anyway."

Jack walked over to the sink and started washing his hands. "I think that's exactly what you're trying to do. You think because I'm young, you can manipulate and control me by using your worthless threats. Go ahead and tell everyone Ben and I met secretly that night."

Jack walked over and opened the door to leave, then he stopped halfway out the door and turned. "The difference between you and me is that I'm not going to waste my life waiting for good things to happen to me." Jack turned and let the door close. As he did, Anthony could hear him talking out loud to himself. "Stupid old fool." Anthony had heard that phrase too many times.

As Jack made his way back to his office, Bonnie informed him Ben had called. "Your surrogate father is coming in on a late flight tomorrow night around midnight. He asked if you could pick him up. I told him you weren't having a pleasant day, but you know Ben. Would you like me to have a limo on standby?"

Jack was already tired. Worn out mentally more than physically. As he stood there contemplating, his cell phone rang. It was Bria. Jack walked off to the side so he could talk in private. He answered, but he didn't have that excitement he usually had when talking to her.

"Hey, Bria. How are you?"

Bria could hear the difference in his voice but didn't pay it any mind. "Hey, handsome, wanna get together tomorrow night? Me and the girls are looking to hook up with you and the boys."

As tempting as that sounded, Jack knew if he didn't pick Ben up, he would never hear the end of it. "I'm sorry, Bria. Ben's out of town and he's coming in tomorrow on a late flight. For some reason, he wants me to pick him up."

Bria was disappointed, but she understood. She knew Ben well enough to know when he wanted Jack to do something, Jack wouldn't say no. "Well, maybe after you pick Ben up from the airport, I can meet you at the house."

Remembering their last encounter, Jack was definitely not opposed. "Sounds good. I'll see you then."

After Jack let Bonnie know he would pick Ben up, he left work. As he walked out to the parking garage, he saw some familiar vehicles parked next to each other. Robert, Nicolas, Anthony, and Kathy's cars. As he opened his car door, he noticed some other familiar cars parked next to his. William, Linda, Stanley, Lewis, and Richard's. He laughed as he climbed in and started the rental car. Jack caught himself talking out loud. "You would think they wouldn't park together when meeting with one another." As Jack left for home, he couldn't help but think how ridiculous the board members were.

As it was, some of the board members decided to have their own meeting. In one of the conference rooms upstairs, Robert was about to begin. "Everyone get whatever refreshments you need and take a seat."

William walked over and closed the curtains as everyone filled their cups with coffee. When everyone sat down, all eyes turned to Robert. "As everyone knows, we're in a battle to try to get Kotter Industries to enter the computer industry before it's too late."

Kathy stood up and looked around the table. "I don't know why I was invited to your little party but I have better things to do."

Robert respected Kathy's position and understood why she would be upset. "Please, Kathy, if you would, stay just to hear me out. Maybe you might change your mind."

Kathy paused and thought about leaving, but decided to stay just in case there was any information she could pass along to Ben and Jack.

Robert opened up his briefcase and pulled out some folders. He also gave everyone a copy of some research that was conducted over the past year. Mainly profit margins on some of the main competitors in the computer industry. "As you can see, this research was conducted by an independent company at my own personal cost. These profit margins alone make a bold statement. Now, I know most of you in this room already agree with me on making this move."

Kathy looked through the paperwork and was unimpressed. "Listen, Robert, I understand that people like to make money and they like to be part of everything new that comes along. I'm not disputing the fact this industry is making millions, but I stand by the fact that making this move will cause our infrastructure to become vulnerable." That's when the light bulb came on. Kathy stood up with a sudden feeling of betrayal. "That's what you want, isn't it? It looks to me like you're trying to stretch this company too thin so it becomes weak. This would give you reason to force out Jack and Ben." With haste and disgust, Kathy walked out.

Robert ran out behind her, hoping to get her to come back in. "Wait up, Kathy. Please, just hear me out." Kathy was walking at full-pace and showed no signs of being interested in what Robert had to say. Robert finally gave up when the elevator door closed in his face.

Disappointed, Robert made his way back to conference room. When he walked back in, he started back where he left off. He handed out business cards of a law firm he'd hired. McBeavey, McBeavey, MacLan, and Associates, LLC. "I've taken steps to hire a New York law firm to protect our interests. I think we have a good chance of proving negligence on the part of Kotter Industries. Now, up until recently, we were at a stalemate. But Mr. Cummings has changed his vote and is now voting our way. This means we now have the majority vote. If need be, I might be able to get Jonathan on board. So, does anyone have anything to add?"

Of course Anthony stood up. He was always complaining about something. "Why would you hire a law firm without consulting us first? I thought we were all working for the same cause."

Robert couldn't stand Anthony, but tolerated him because he needed his vote. "First off, I don't have to consult anyone when I decide to bring a lawsuit I'm paying for against this company. Second, you're just along for the ride. And third, I'm running the show. Now, any more questions?"

As usual, Anthony stuck his tail between his legs and sat down. Robert was disappointed Kathy left, but it didn't really matter with Nicholas on board. "Listen, I'm going to meet some of the law firm partners later on this week. If nobody has anything else to add, I will call everyone by Friday and set up another meeting to let you know how strong our case is."

As the members adjourned for the day, Ben's limo was almost to the airport. Suddenly, the limo phone rang. Ben just stared for a minute wondering who it could be calling. He reluctantly picked the phone up. "Hello?"

The voice on the other end told him to stop at the Yoshinoya restaurant bar before getting on the plane then hung up. When the limo driver informed Ben they had arrived, he pulled the limo into the area of outgoing passengers and quickly made his way around to Ben's door and opened it. "Your bags will be taken care of, Mr. Marcus. Have a nice trip."

Ben stepped out and looked around for a moment. "Tell me, driver, do you know where Yoshinoya is?" The driver thought for a minute and gave Ben directions.

Ben checked his watch as he made his way into the crowded airport. He knew it wasn't Chang playing one last joke, so he constantly surveyed the area around him as he walked through the long corridors. When he finally arrived at the restaurant, he glanced over at the bar and noticed the same two men that were at the airport when he arrived. He casually walked over and sat down next to them. "You cheesy bastards don't exactly blend in with the scenery. Don't you have any other clothing besides black suits?"

As the bartender approached, Ben noticed he already had a drink in his hand. He set the drink down in front of Ben and walked away. Of course it was Ben's favorite. Jack and Coke, hold the lemon. "Hey, you guys are pretty good. Thanks for the drink. Now why the hell am I here?"

Suddenly, Roy Dobbins came from behind and sat down next to Ben. "Hello, Benjamin. Long time, no see."

Ben shook his head as he gulped down the drink he had. "Damn,

Roy. I should have known you didn't retire. I knew this set up looked too familiar."

Roy was dressed in a pair of Bermuda shorts, a multi-colored shirt, and a pair of sandals. "So, Ben, you really caught me off guard when you called me. My number has been changed so many times I don't even know what it is."

Ben chuckled as the bartender set another drink in front of him. "If your plan is to get me drunk, we're gonna be here all night."

Roy pulled out a fairly large envelope and placed it on the bar, then slid it over to Ben. "I remember the last time I tried to out-drink you back in '82. I'm still feeling the effects of that night. Anyway, I found some information, but not really anything of significance."

Ben picked the envelope up as he drank down his second drink with one swig. "As usual, Roy, you're a day late and many dollars short. I already have the information I was looking for, and by the way, I thought I was supposed to pick the meeting place."

Roy stood up from the bar and shook Ben's hand. "Well, Ben, it's been nice seeing you. We'll have to get together in another 15 years. By the way, I'm semi-retired. You might want to look inside that envelope. You might be surprised."

As Roy walked away and disappeared around the corner, Ben turned and noticed the two men in the suits were already gone. Then he glanced at the bartender who was staring at him. "I guess this means no more free drinks." Ben looked at his watch and saw it was almost time for his plane to board. He decided he would check out the contents of the envelope once he was in the air and settled.

Ben made it to his gate just in time to board his flight home. He was seated in first class by the stewardess and offered refreshments. Ben graciously declined as he made himself comfortable in his seat. He had the envelope in his hand, but decided to wait until the plane was in the air. As with every flight he was on, Ben bowed his head and recited a prayer for his brother Sergis. Afterwards, he reached into his pocket and pulled out the key to the mysterious box. He gazed at it for a moment then placed it back into his pocket.

CHAPTER TEN

As Ben's plane jetted across Europe en route to New York, Jack was home attempting to rest before making the trek to the airport. It had been another long, frustrating day, and the only thing on his mind was sleep. Jack would soon find out his subconscious had other plans. With all that was going on, he couldn't help but toss and turn. As he finally faded into a deep sleep, his mind started to wander. Once again, he was on *Titanic*. This time, the ship was already at the bottom of the ocean. He was standing at the top of the famous staircase watching bodies as they floated by with no life. Suddenly, he felt a hand on his shoulder. It jolted him awake, and he jumped out of bed in a cold sweat. "Damn, what the hell is going on with these dreams?"

He glanced at the alarm clock and noticed Ben's plane wasn't due to land for another four hours. Still shaken by the dream, he decided not to go back to sleep. Instead, he rinsed himself off in the shower and had his driver, Casey, pull the limousine around. Jack figured he would just get to the airport early and maybe have some dinner before confronting Ben.

As Jack made his way downstairs, he glanced over at the mysterious box sitting on the mantle. He had forgotten all about it until then. He thought about taking it with him, but decided not to. He remembered what his dad once said. If at all possible, try to take on one problem at a time. That way, a person usually ends up with better results. Jack left the box behind and walked out the door. He stepped into the limo and headed for John F. Kennedy International Airport. Along the way, he contemplated what he was going to say when he saw Ben. But then again, Ben wouldn't listen anyway. He would just yell back even louder. Jack usually talked with Casey on long rides, but he was still tired from the day, so he rested his head back and closed his eyes.

When the limo finally arrived, Casey had to wake Jack. "Mr. Kotter, we're here." He gently shook Jack's shoulder and Jack finally opened his eyes.

Jack was a little disoriented when he stepped out of the car. "Sorry, Casey. Haven't had much sleep lately." Jack gathered himself together and walked in to check Ben's flight status. He wasn't due for another two hours. That definitely gave him time to relax and get some dinner. Jack made a beeline for Sammy's Beach Bar and Grill. It was one of his favorites. Created by the Red Rocker himself, Sammy Hagar, and just a cool place to be. When the waiter approached, Jack was all too eager to order. No menu needed. "I'll start with an order of Cabo Wabo Classic Ceviche." As the waiter wrote the order, he asked Jack about his drink.

"I could use a nice I Can't Drive 55 and can I get a Corona please. For the entrée, I'll have the center-cut New York strip, medium-well, please."

When the waiter left to place the order, Jack sat back in his seat and let his mind wander off, analyzing the past few days. Out of nowhere, he felt a pair of hands wrap around his neck and cheeks. He jumped to his feet flipping over his chair. When he turned to see who it was, he was shocked to see Bria standing there.

"Bria? What are you doing? You scared the hell out of me."

Bria laughed as she gave Jack a hug. "I'm sorry. I thought you would be happy to see me."

Jack smiled as he bent over to pick the chair up. "I'm always glad to see you. I've just been on edge lately." Jack leaned forward and gave Bria a kiss. "I'm sorry. How did you get here?"

Bria sat down and leaned across the table to hold Jack's hands. "Well, I got bored with my friends. It's just not the same when we go out without you guys. So I had them drop me off here, and I thought

I would catch a ride back with you and Ben so I could save you from his corporate mumbo jumbo. Now, tell me what you're so stressed out about."

Jack leaned back in his chair and pushed his hair back. Bria could tell he was under a lot of strain. Jack paused for a second to try to gather his thoughts. "Well, this thing with Ben and corporate spying, along with certain people on the board of directors plotting against me, is really weighing heavy on my mind. We have Bobby's funeral to attend, and on top of everything, I keep having these damn dreams about *Titanic*. I can't seem to focus lately."

Bria knew Jack was upset, probably more over the death of Bobby than anything else. "Listen, I know Bobby was your friend. I didn't know him very well, but we had talked a few times. He made a choice. No one forced him to race that night."

Jack became quiet and just stared off into space. His mind was focused on remembering Bobby. "I know what you're saying, but she forced him into the guardrail. She was winning the race, but then she let up and got behind him. She purposely forced him into the guardrail. It just doesn't make sense."

Suddenly, the light bulb clicked on in Jack's head. Bria could see Jack's mind working. "Your eyes just lit up like Time Square. What are you thinking?"

Just then, the waiter arrived with Jack's food. With Bria being there, Jack had forgotten all about eating. "I'm sorry, Bria. Did you want to order something?"

Bria laughed with her usual answer. "No, I'll just eat some of yours." Bria grabbed Jack's fork and helped herself. After asking the waiter for a glass of water, she handed Jack the fork. "Tell me what you were thinking."

As Jack took a bite of food, his mind was still contemplating what he was going to say. "I'm not sure yet. I have to talk with Dale and get some more information."

As sexy as Bria was, she had no couth. She started picking through Jack's food with her fingers. "So, what about these dreams?"

Jack sat back and took a drink of his Corona while Bria gulped down his I Can't Drive 55. "What about them? They're just dreams. They don't mean anything." As Bria finished off Jack's drink, she stared at him with a devious look. "They mean something. You told me about your father and that book he wouldn't let you read. Maybe all this stress is bringing back old memories."

Jack took another drink of his beer and thought about it. "Yeah, maybe you're right. That night I crashed *Fringe*, I was in that little diner with Ben. We talked about some things, and in the background, I could hear the television. I think it might have been some kind of story about *Titanic*. I don't know. I wasn't really paying attention to it. Anyway, whatever it is will eventually go away. Once Ben gets back, I'll be able to focus a little more on what I have to do."

Bria finished off the last of the food then drank the last of Jack's beer. "So, if you don't have any plans for dessert, why don't you meet me in the men's room so I can pleasure you in one of the stalls? I can be your dirty little girl. What'ya say, Jack Kotter?"

As intriguing as that sounded, Jack had to decline. "Why don't we just wait for Ben to land then we can drop him off and have the rest of the morning to ourselves."

Bria wasn't one to take no for an answer. "Why can't we do both? You scared?" Bria always had a way to relieve Jack of stress, whether it was just talking with him or physically working it out of him. For the moment, Jack forgot all about his worries and followed Bria into the men's room.

Twenty minutes later, Jack and Bria emerged with smiles on their faces. They got a few looks on the way out, but that didn't bother them. They decided to window shop as they made their way through the airport to the gate Ben was due to land at.

Finally, a few minutes after midnight, Ben's plane landed. To Ben's surprise, Bria was with Jack, waiting at the end of the tunnel. Being the womanizer that he was, he gave Bria a hug with a little sarcasm for play. "So, Bria, when are you gonna dump this loser and hook up with me?"

As usual, Bria laughed it off and came right back. "You better start popping a hell of a lot more of those little blue pills if you wanna keep up with me, old man."

As they made their way out to the car, Jack noticed the envelope Ben was holding. "I'm guessing you found out some information during your trip. Oh, by the way, how come you could tell a one-night stand where you were going, but you couldn't tell me?"

Ben could hear the mixed emotions in Jack's voice and didn't really care to give him an answer, but he did anyway. "Yes, I did find out what I needed to know in Beijing, and if you're referring to Dee, I didn't really tell her any specifics about the trip. All I said was I would bring her back some Oriental beads. And why the hell are you talking to Dee?"

Bria had been half listening to the conversation, when it suddenly peaked her interest. "Yeah, who the hell is Dee, and why are you engaging in conversation with her?"

When they made it to the limo, Casey was ready with the door open. Bria climbed in, then Ben, and Jack last. "First off, Dee called me looking for you, Ben, and as for you, Bria, she is nothing to me. She happens to be one of Ben's booty calls. So both of you can climb down off my back."

Ben stared at Jack for a moment and realized he was somewhat on edge. "Whoa, kid. No one is accusing you of any wrongdoing. Just relax and have a drink." Ben reached over to the minibar and handed Jack a beer.

Bria just sat quietly. Jack had always been an easy going guy. That was one of the qualities she loved about him. She wasn't use to being around him when he was upset.

Jack took a nice hefty drink then apologized for his outburst. He gave Bria a kiss on the cheek then turned his attention towards Ben. "I'm really sorry, Ben. There's been a lot going on since you left. Robert has been having his little get-togethers at work with his cronies. And that damn Anthony. You believe he tried to muscle me? I walked into the men's room and he was in there. He tells me he saw me meeting with you the night of our vote. I can't believe he thought he could use the information to try to somehow manipulate me. What a jackass."

Ben listened, but he knew there was something more going on. "Don't worry about the opposing board members. Tomorrow afternoon, you and I are going to have a meeting with Robert. We have a lot to talk about. We were on the right track, but we weren't looking at the right person. I don't want to get into it right now, but it's going to be an interesting day. So, tell me, kid. What else is eating at you?"

Jack noticed Bria had fallen asleep, so he finished off his beer and gathered his thoughts. "Bobby was killed the other day. That bitch Lilith ran him into a guardrail. He was ejected and sliced in half. That could have very easily been you or me."

Ben knew there was nothing comforting he could say, so he just leaned over and handed Jack another beer. "Listen, kid, that bitch is bad news. Everyone knows to stay away, but those young boys let their pride get in the way. As you can see, sometimes that can be a fatal mistake. All your friends have a damn 'y' at the end of their name. Which one was Bobby?"

Although it was no laughing matter, Jack found amusement in Ben's analysis. "He had the blue Camero. Remember when you teased him about having that harness installed?"

Ben thought for a moment and smiled. "Oh, yeah. I remember that. How the hell did he get ejected wearing that thing?"

Jack just shrugged his shoulders. "I don't know. Walley told me Bobby talked to Lilith for a few minutes and then ran across the lot and jumped in his car. I guess he didn't think to hook himself in."

Ben didn't really know Bobby too well, but he knew Jack was hurting. "I'm sorry, kid. I'd like to know what the police are doing to catch that maniac. What about your friend Dale. Can you get any information from him?"

Jack finished off his second beer as he thought about Walley and Jimmy. "Well, Dale called me yesterday. The police don't really have anything to go on, and with everything else going on, the Mopar brothers apparently chased Lilith and totaled both of their cars. They're in jail right now."

Ben just shook his head and laughed. "Those two idiots need to stay in jail for a while. Maybe those two stooges will learn from the experience. But I have a feeling you're not gonna let that happen."

Jack smiled because Ben knew him so well. "Yeah, I don't really think there's any lesson to be learned. I'm sure they had Bobby in mind when they went after her."

As they took in the scenery, both Jack and Ben leaned back and took a break from talking. As Bria slept, Jack thought about the list of things he needed to address later on in the day with Ben and Robert. He also needed to post bail for Walley and Jimmy then contact Dale.

He had a long day ahead of him and he was really hoping Bria would sleep the morning away.

After what seemed like forever, the limo finally pulled in front of Jack's house. As Casey brought the car to a stop, Jack woke Bria and told her he would be a few minutes talking to Ben. Bria was still half-asleep but managed to drag herself inside the house. As Jack watched Bria walk in and shut the door, Ben stepped out to stretch his legs.

"Well, kid, welcome to corporate life. I haven't been gone that long and already you're complaining about company problems." Ben wasn't being insensitive to Jack's mourning over Bobby, but he knew they had a lot of work ahead of them and he needed Jack to be at his best. "So, kid, not that I'm trying to overwhelm you, but have you made any decisions about your father's secret box?"

Jack thought for a second trying to come up with a good answer, but he was just too tired. "To be honest with you, Ben, I forgot all about it until I glanced over at it tonight."

"Don't worry about it, kid. Just hang on to this key." Ben pulled the key from his pocket and handed it to Jack. "That box sat in your father's safe for this long, it won't matter if we wait a little while longer."

Jack was tired and without thinking, shoved the key deep into his pocket. He said his goodbyes and went in the house. He thought Bria would be waiting for him, but there was no sign of her on the first floor. The lights were out and the house was quiet. He walked over to the mysterious box and picked it up. There was definitely something rattling around inside, but Jack's curiosity was overtaken by his exhaustion. He made his way upstairs to find Bria already in bed and fast asleep. He smiled as he thought out loud, "Thank God." After taking care of his hygiene, he flopped down beside Bria and fell asleep.

Ben relaxed as Casey drove him home. He laid his head back and thought about what the day was going to bring. He also had to think about the daunting task of handling the China Steel situation and the information he now had.

CHAPTER ELEVEN

As the morning faded into history, the afternoon began with a bright array of sunshine. When Jack's alarm clock went off, neither Bria nor Jack moved. Jack finally mustered up enough energy to get out of bed. After he completed his daily routine, he saw that Bria was still out cold. He jotted down an "I love you" note and headed off to meet with Ben.

As he rushed out to the garage, he was surprised to see *Fringe* was back together and waiting for him. Once again, thinking out loud was able to get the best of him. "About damn time. Must have been delivered last night when I was at the airport." Jack didn't waste any time jumping in and starting her up. All he could think about was how nice she sounded, and then Lilith entered his thoughts. He thought about calling Dale, but he knew he had a hefty load of work to take care of, plus he knew Ben wouldn't be too happy if he was late for his meeting.

Before Ben left his house, he made sure Hellen contacted the members of the board to inform them all the current issues would be resolved by the end of the business week. He had Jack meet him at the 110 Diner to go over some of the issues that were going to be covered. When Ben pulled into the parking lot, the first thing he noticed was *Fringe*. As he stepped out of his car, he walked past *Fringe* shaking his head.

Ben walked into the diner and noticed Jack was in the same booth he'd been in the night of his accident. "I see you've claimed this booth for yourself. If it's any consolation, kid, I sat in this same booth the night that bitch flipped me over."

Jack was happy just to have *Fringe* back on the road so he didn't mind laughing about it. As Ben took a seat, Jack leaned across the table. "So, why all the secrecy about China?"

Ben had the same familiar envelope he'd had when he stepped off the plane. He placed it on the table in front of Jack. "Listen, kid, your father and I taught you just about everything we know about the business and then some. You know I've never had children of my own so I'm not going to sit here and pretend that I know what fathers are supposed to do. Your father was gracious enough to let me help guide you, at least through the business aspect of your life. I guess what I'm trying to say, kid, is there are some things in life you just can't prepare a child for. Instead, you just have to let them experience these things and hope for the best."

Ben reached into the envelope and pulled out some papers. He didn't show them to Jack. Instead, he flipped them face down so Jack couldn't read them. "Now, remember when I told you we were looking at the wrong person?"

Jack just glared at Ben with a lost look on his face. "I don't know what we were doing. You kinda just ran with this project and left me behind."

Ben took a deep breath in order to keep his composure. "Pay attention, kid. One of the few things in business that can't be taught is when a close friend you trust violates that trust and tries to hurt you personally and professionally."

Suddenly, Jack had the feeling Ben was about to drop a bomb. So he leaned back and took a breath. "Why are you trying so hard to ease into whatever you're going to tell me? What exactly did you find out in China?"

Just when Ben was about to explain, the waitress interrupted by pouring two cups of coffee. "Hey, Ben, long time, no see." She turned her attention to Jack and gave him a big smile. "Who's your nice-looking friend?"

Ben momentarily swallowed the lump in his throat in order to introduce Jack. "Bobby Jo, this is Jack Kotter. He owns Kotter Industries up the road. Jack, this is Bobby Jo. This is the friend I told you about who called and warned me about that little meeting Robert had with Kathy."

Jack held out his hand and gave Bobby Jo a smile. "Nice to meet you, Bobby Jo, and thanks for the heads-up."

Bobby Jo locked eyes with Jack while she cracked her gum. "Sugar, you just call on me anytime and I'll come running." She turned and walked away shaking her rear, hoping to catch Jack looking.

After momentarily watching the eye candy, Jack started preparing his coffee. "Does all the hired help here chew gum?"

Ben followed Jack's lead and started dumping the sugar and cream into his coffee. He thought he could use the time to ease into what he had to tell Jack. "Listen, kid, instead of me trying to save you some heartache, I'm just going to give you what I have." Ben flipped over a picture and handed it to Jack. It was the same photo that was given to him in China.

Jack looked at the picture, but nothing was clicking. "What is this?"

Ben's blood pressure shot up and he snatched the photo out of Jack's hands. "This is your boy Nicholas meeting with a couple of nobodies in China, you idiot. A security camera caught him with some lower management flunkies at China Steel."

Things still weren't clicking for Jack, but that was probably because Nicholas was his friend and Jack valued his friends over business. "I don't know, Ben. Where did this information come from? Nick doesn't have any information to do anything with."

Usually Ben would lay into Jack pretty hard, but they were in a public place, so he had to take a couple of deep breaths so he could talk in a rational voice. "Listen, kid, do you really think your dad and I survived for so long in the business world with naive attitudes? I used several sources to get this information, including the CIA and China Steel. They didn't have to meet with me. They didn't have to volunteer this information, and they certainly didn't have to entertain the fact that despite our two companies being competitors, they knew it would be better to squash this problem."

Still in a haze, Jack started reviewing the rest of the paperwork Ben had retrieved. Most of the documents were CIA records of

Nicholas and his trips to China. Others were documents supplied by China Steel concerning meetings between Nicholas and some of the lower management. Ben just sat quietly while Jack reviewed the paperwork. After a few minutes, Jack placed the papers down on the table with a dismal look.

Just then, Bobby Jo walked back over to refill their coffees. "Let me know when you boys are ready to order." As Ben and Jack sat in silence, Bobby Jo took the hint that she should just walk away.

Ben peered over at Jack waiting for a response, but Jack didn't have anything to say. He was in disarray, almost questioning himself and his ability to lead Kotter Industries into the future. Ben knew Jack was hurting, but he wasn't going to sit back and watch him self-destruct.

"Alright, kid, before you start feeling sorry for yourself, I want you to listen to me. No one ever said life would be easy. Especially in the business world. If you allow yourself to drop into a self-pity state of mind, you're never going to be successful, and all the work and knowledge your dad and I instilled in you will be for nothing. Now you have to ask yourself one question. Are you going to sit back and let some cheesy little punk wreak havoc on your father's lifetime accomplishments?"

Jack finished off his coffee and motioned for Bobby Jo to come over. "Hey, sweetie, can I get a refill and a menu?"

After placing their food orders, Jack felt he had a new mission in life. "Alright, Ben. Tell me everything you have on Nick."

Ben smiled with pride as he reached down and opened up his briefcase. "Alright, kid, now you're talking." He laid out some more paperwork and some folders and started going over some of the details. "As far as I know, your little friend didn't really get anywhere with China Steel. He was attempting to sell information on our interests around the world. He also somehow tapped into a list of our corporate contacts and some of our client information. We're going to have to review our security network to find out how he got in. Anyway, we were very fortunate that China Steel had a tremendous amount of respect for your dad. During my trip, I had the pleasure of meeting with some of their top executives. Very honorable men. Also very intelligent. They came to the conclusion our two companies have outgrown all the nonsense of dealing with industrial espionage.

Although those days were fun, I understand it's a whole new world now. The bottom line is, they were more interested in their honor than the petty information Nick had."

Jack listened and more questions flooded his mind. "I'm sorry, Ben. You're much better at this than I am. I recognize greed when I see it, but I'm not seeing it with Nick. What benefit would Nick have to try to destroy Kotter Industries?"

Ben took a drink of water to wash down his food. He sat back and gathered his thoughts in order to explain to Jack why the events unfolded the way they did. He needed Jack to understand his father had no choice in the matter. "Listen, kid, I've told you time and time again about making the right moves at the right time. Your father knew that timing was everything in this industry. Back in the early seventies, China Steel had made some significant developments in the steel industry that catapulted them way ahead of the game. Now listen. This is what I'm talking about with timing. Your dad and I convinced the board to try to expand into China. Not to be competitive, but to be a pain in the ass. We figured once China Steel found out, they would possibly counter with an offer of a partnership. Well, the plan worked all too well.

"Now, usually either your father or I would handle the expansion into another country, but we had Carroll Cummings on the board. He had spent some time over there during the war and was quite fluent with their language and culture. I don't have to tell you how valuable that was. Well, after a few years of working out all the logistics and contracts, we were finally in the closing stages in 1977 when, out of nowhere, China Steel became state-owned. To this day, nobody knows for sure if it had anything to do with us."

Jack knew his history from school books but had no idea about the history between the two companies. "How is that possible? You successfully orchestrated a partnership. How can a third party just come in and wipe everything out?"

Ben just shook his head in frustration. "I don't know, kid. I'm still trying to figure that one out. In my opinion, I don't think their government wanted us over there. Anyway, it was a done deal. All the work that went into it was for nothing. We actually thought about trying to salvage the situation, but Carter got elected into office and his administration put a stop to everything. They threatened to cut off all our government contracts. Nobody would have done business with us after that."

Ben paused for a minute to take a bite of food. "Now, here's where it gets bad. Although your father and I knew it was a missed opportunity, we could walk away and be alright. Carroll was another story. We didn't know Carroll had some backdoor deals going on. Your father and I found out later he had transferred most of his portfolio over to China Steel. Then, after the deal went south, it was too late. China Steel somehow took everything from him. Luckily for us, he kept his Kotter interest here in the States. Despite all the greed, your dad still considered Carroll a good friend and kept him on the board. He passed away in 87. Now do you see what I mean, kid? Timing is everything."

Jack finished his food, but still wanted to hear more. "So, China steel is a private company now."

Ben washed down the last of his food and lounged back like an old grizzly bear. "Yeah, they were reprivatized in 1995, right before your dad passed away."

Jack still had questions and was looking towards Ben to fill in the blanks. "Nick inherited the stock from his dad. Why ruin the only thing his dad had left?"

Ben knew Jack was having a hard time trying to understand, mainly because of Nick's friendship. "My guess, Nick blames Kotter Industries for his dad's downfalls. After that whole fiasco, Carroll's finances and health really took a nosedive. Funny thing is, two decades ago, China Steel would have welcomed Nick with open arms."

Ben stood up to stretch his legs. "Listen, kid, I have a plan to deal with Nick and to stop this battle going on with the board. I'm going to the restroom. You think about what you want to do. Go with my plan or come up with one of your own."

As Ben walked away, Jack lay back in his seat and thought about all the times he and Nick had hung out together. Just when Jack was about to shed a tear, Bobby Jo walked over and sat down. "Hey, Jack. I'm just getting off work. Maybe you wouldn't mind buying a girl a drink."

Jack sat up and pretended he was wiping his face with a napkin. He'd barely heard what Bobby Jo was saying. "Um, I'm sorry, Bobby

Jo. I think Ben and I are going to continue our meeting back at the office. But maybe some other time"

Bobby Jo reached over and squeezed Jack's hand. "That's alright, sugar. It was Ben's idea for me to come over here and try to cheer you up." As Ben was making his way back from the men's room, Bobby Jo leaned over the table and whispered to Jack. "Hey, listen. I work mostly the same hours here. If you ever need an ear, you know where to find me." As Ben approached, Bobby Jo stood up and gave Ben a hug goodbye.

Jack stood up and gathered himself together. "You know how to pick'em."

Ben smiled. "Yeah. That sweet little girl can really knock'em out with her strip show. If you get a chance, you should go see it."

Jack paused because he thought Ben was joking, but he soon realized he wasn't. "Damn, Ben, you really do know how to pick'em. Listen, I don't exactly have a plan, but at the same time, I know how you are with your plans. Before we do anything, can we give Nick a chance to explain?"

Ben and Jack shook hands and Ben promised he would give Nick every opportunity to explain himself. "Now listen, kid. I want to wrap this up as soon as possible. Why don't we plan to meet with the board tomorrow so we can put this mess behind us?"

Jack scratched his head and thought for a second. "No. Bobby's funeral is tomorrow. I don't think I'll be in any kind of shape to face the board."

Ben was all too glad to give Jack some time to mourn. "Alright, kid. How about this? You remember Lawrence Winder, don't you?"

Jack thought about it and remembered Lawrence was one of the partners with the company law firm. "Yeah, really nice guy. Intelligent."

Ben motioned for Jack to follow him outside. "Well, I contacted him right before I went to China. I haven't talked with him yet, but we might not need to if my plan works. He can be our back-up plan. Now, if by chance my plan fails, which I don't think it will, I know for a fact he's handled several cases involving board members with hostile intent. Just like what we're dealing with now. He's an ace and hasn't lost a case yet." As Ben opened the door to his car, he glanced back at Jack and smiled. "Don't worry, kid. Either way, we'll be alright."

After relaxing in *Fringe* and listening to some music, it was dark by the time Jack rolled off the diner lot. He planned on meeting with Bria for a late-night drink. Suddenly, out of nowhere, Lilith appeared alongside *Fringe.* Jack immediately pulled to the side and let her pass. As she did, she also pulled to the side a couple of car lengths in front of him. Jack sat quietly and waited while his engine purred. Just as fast as she appeared, Lilith revved her engine and was gone.

After his brief encounter, Jack picked Bria up and drove down to Manhattan where they met some friends at the Vig Bar. It was very low-key and elegant, and Jack and Bria liked to meet there just to get away from the hassles of life. After a night of relaxation and remembering Bobby, Jack and Bria drove back to Jack's house. They knew they had an early day with the funeral, so they drank a small glass of wine and chased it with a beer for Bobby. They crawled into bed and fell asleep holding each other.

CHAPTER TWELVE

Inevitably, the morning arrived faster than Jack and Bria wanted it to. It was a somber morning with an overcast sky, but it didn't matter to Jack. He had to bury one of his good friends. While Bria was taking forever, Jack decided to go downstairs and start some coffee. As he sat at the kitchen table in silence, he went over in his head the night he met Lilith. So many questions and no answers to go with them. Jack knew Dale would be at the funeral, so he decided to put aside his theories and get through the day.

Jack could still hear Bria fumbling around and knew she would be awhile. He made his way into the living room where the mysterious box was still up on the mantel. As he walked over and picked it up, he had the strange feeling he should've opened it by then. But with all that was going on, Jack knew he couldn't afford anymore drama at that time. He felt bad that it belonged to his father and whatever was in the box should've been taken care of by then. Unfortunately, the string of events leading up to the discovery of the box seemed to be more important. He shook the box and tried to listen to what was inside, but he just couldn't tell what it was. All he knew was something was rattling around and he wasn't going to find out until after he dealt with the board.

Finally, Bria emerged from the bedroom and made her way downstairs. She made a quick cup of coffee as Casey pulled the limo around. Jack placed the box back on the mantel and walked out to the car with Bria. The couple sat quietly sipping on their coffee as Casey drove to the church. While at the church, Jack had to navigate his way through Bobby's friends and family. After sitting awhile with Bobby's parents, he finally locked eyes with Dale, who had found a quiet spot in the rear. Jack excused himself and quietly maneuvered his way to the rear of the church.

"Hey, Dale, wasn't sure if you were going to make it." Although Dale was a police officer, he and Jack shared the same friends.

"I'm really sorry about Bobby. He was uptight and wired most of the time, but he didn't deserve this."

Jack paused as he listened to the sincerity in Dale's voice. "Thanks, Dale. I know you two didn't see eye to eye, but you being here means a lot. I've been meaning to call you, but the situation at work really has me preoccupied."

Jack and Dale slipped out to the church courtyard and sat down on one of the benches. Dale already knew what Jack wanted to talk about. "Don't worry, Jack. We're doing everything possible to find that maniac."

Jack had heard that so many times, and having it come from Dale didn't make it any easier to accept. "Listen, Dale, I wanted to run something by you. I was at the airport the other night picking Ben up and I was going over the accident with Bria. Now, this is just a theory so hear me out before you shoot me down. What if this bitch is challenging people to race and then purposely trying to kill them?"

Dale stood up and motioned for Jack to walk with him. "This Plymouth has caused so many accidents over the past couple of months that people are afraid to drive at night. Our accident investigation team has been working around the clock to try to piece together some kind of profile on this woman, but I gotta tell you, we're not coming up with much. Do you believe we even have half-assed psychics calling in and telling us she's some kind of demon out for revenge? Our team has several working theories. One of them being her purposely trying to cause these accidents, but we don't have a motive. We don't have a motive because we can't find any information on her or the car. We keep checking all the junkyards. We've gone through just about every garage in and around New York.

Hell, we've even raided some chop shops thinking we could get some kind of lead. Even those guys switched to stealing cars during the day. They don't want to drive at night."

Jack listened as Dale gave him everything he had, which wasn't much. "I'm sorry, Dale. I know the police are working hard, but it's just so frustrating. That stupid bitch came up on me last night while I was on my way to get Bria."

Dale stopped to listen to Jack, thinking there was more to the story. "So, what happened?"

Jack just shook his head. "Don't get too happy; nothing happened. I pulled to the side of the road. I wasn't about to take a chance on losing *Fringe* again. She actually pulled over ahead of me and sat there for a minute. I guess she realized I wasn't interested and drove off."

As usual, Dale had questions. "Did you get a good look at the car? Were there any kind of markings we could check? Was there a license plate? Anything?"

Jack had nothing. "Sorry, Dale. I didn't even see any damage. So that means she has to be repairing the car somewhere, which means she has to be ordering parts."

With a disappointing look, all Dale could do was try to keep from letting his frustrations out on Jack. "Don't worry, Jack, we'll come up with something eventually. I did want to bounce an idea off of you. It involves you and *Fringe*."

Jack listened with interest. "Go on. What are you thinking?"

Just then, the church doors opened and the congregation started to exit. Dale didn't really have any time to give Jack the details of the plan, so they agreed to meet later on in the week. Dale wasn't going to the cemetery so he said his goodbyes and left. Jack located Bria and they made their way to the car. On the way to the cemetery, Jack called Ben to check in, and Ben advised him not to worry. Everything was set to go for the next day. Although saddened by the death of his friend, Jack felt some relief knowing Ben had the situation at work well in hand.

When Ben hung up the phone with Jack, he called the company law firm to talk with Lawrence about the possible internal takeover of Kotter Industries. Lawrence was in and was anxious to talk with his old friend Ben. "Benjamin, it's been a long time."

Ben was happy to hear Lawrence's voice instead of an answering machine. "Larry, you old dog. Where the hell have you been?"

After a brief chuckle, Lawrence told him he was glad to hear from him. "Ben, you gotta come visit me at my new office. It's only thirty-two floors up."

Ben gasped then laughed. "You gotta be kidding. The only thing up that high are clouds and planes. No, thanks. I like it down here on the ground."

After a couple more exchanges, Lawrence got down to business. "So, Ben, you didn't sound very good when you left your message."

Ben paused to gather his thoughts. "Well, Larry, when I called you before, I had somewhat of a problem. Some of our executive board is trying to muscle Kotter Industries. Don't ask me how I know, but they've gone as far as hiring a law firm to start legal proceedings."

Lawrence wasn't shocked that Ben knew beforehand about the lawsuit. He was never surprised by anything Ben knew about. "It sounds like you're not too worried now. Did something change over the past week?"

Ben ruffled through some paperwork as he was gathering his mental notes. "As a matter of fact, things have changed dramatically. I have a working plan in progress and it looks like I'm going to be able to swing the board around to my way of thinking. And as a bonus, get rid of a snake in the grass. I'll have Hellen fax over some papers for you to go over. I also want to have you on standby, just in case this whole situation blows up in my face."

Lawrence knew all too well about the kind of plans Ben came up with. "Alright, Ben, but if your plans involve SUV's with tinted windows and men with black suits, which they usually do, I don't want to hear about it. But I will be around if you need me. Hey, when you've cleaned up the mess, we need to get together and have dinner. Say hi to Jack for me."

Lawrence hung up the phone and Ben went back to ironing out some last minute details. Once again, he called on his old CIA friend Roy Dobbins. "Hey, Roy, I know you're semi-retired, but I have something you might be interested in. I just need some personnel and some equipment if you can spare me the time."

Although Roy was a good friend, he also knew Ben could be a

pain in the ass, especially when dealing with his half-baked plans. "Alright, Ben. I have a feeling the information I gave you in China paid off. So, what is it that you think I might be interested in and what is it that you need?"

Ben briefed Roy on his plan, and Roy had no problem supplying Ben with what he needed.

The next day, Jack arrived at work bright and early and ready to go. He thought he was the first one in the office, but of course, Ben was already there waiting. He walked into Ben's office and was surprised to see Robert and Ben having coffee together. As Jack stood in the doorway with his dumbfounded look, Ben slammed his cup down with conviction.

"Damn, Kotter, didn't we have a conversation about knocking? Don't just stand there like a hump. Grab some coffee, and while you're at it, bring me one of those chocolate donuts."

Feeling a somewhat belittled, Jack walked out and made himself a cup of coffee. He grabbed a doughnut for Ben and walked back into the office. As he sat down, he handed Ben his treat and didn't say a word. Ben had his secret folders out, along with the paperwork he brought back from China.

"Listen, kid, I set this meeting up with Robert because I thought he deserved the benefit of knowing what's going on with Nick. I also let him know that we thought it might be him who was trying to sell information." Jack sat quietly as he took a drink of his coffee.

Robert was reading what Ben had in his folder and was amused. "This is really good. I can't believe you tracked my trip to China. I knew something was going on, but obviously, I don't have the connections Ben has, so I didn't really find out anything. Back then, I figured certain events would eventually come to light, but nothing ever became of it, so I didn't bother saying anything to Ben or your father."

Once again, Jack sat quietly sipping his coffee. Ben finished off his doughnut and started to riffle through some papers. "So, kid, you ready for today?"

Jack didn't say anything. He finished his coffee and stood up to leave. Ben placed his paperwork down and watched as Jack walked out of the room. He excused himself from Robert and scurried out after Jack. "Wait a minute, kid, wait up." Ben finally caught up to him at the elevator. "What's wrong, kid?"

Jack was so disgusted he couldn't even think straight. "Sometimes I wonder who actually runs this company. I gotta tell you, Ben. It doesn't seem like I have any say so in what goes on around here. And then I'm always the last one to find out when decisions do get made. Why the hell couldn't you just call me and let me know about your little meeting? Here I am thinking we're on the same page and come to find out you're going rogue. I'm tired of all these secret back-door deals and meetings."

The elevator door opened and Jack didn't hesitate to get on. Ben paused for a second then stepped on with him. Neither one said anything until they walked out to the parking garage. Jack had never been genuinely upset at Ben and Ben didn't really know how to handle it. Before Jack could get to his car, Ben finally opened up. "Listen, kid, can you wait a minute? Please just give me a chance to explain."

Jack stopped and turned around, thinking Ben would apologize and that would be it. Ben had his hands in his pockets and was looking down at the ground. He almost looked like a little boy about to be scolded. He finally mustered up the words he was looking for. "Listen, kid. I've always been rough around the edges. Back in the day, you had to be rough and tough or you wouldn't survive. When you came along, you struck feelings inside me that I didn't know I had. People saw a change in me. Hell, I saw a change in me. As time went on, you became more dependent on me. Granted, it was usually the times when I had to pull some strings to get you out of trouble. Even now, sometimes I still look at you as a little boy always needing my help. Maybe I'm just afraid my time is gone and it's me that needs your help. Whatever it is, kid, I'm sorry. This company is yours and I promised your dad I would do everything in my power to help you keep the company strong. I don't blame you for being mad at me. You were right. I should have let you know about the meeting between Robert and me."

After all that, Jack couldn't stay mad. "In all my years, Ben, I've never seen you open up like that. Damn, I was expecting 'I'm sorry' and 'let's get back to work.' Listen, I know my dad died before both of you could really give me the proper knowledge I need to maneuver around the various industry land mines, but maybe you can give me the benefit of the doubt. I learned a lot from you and my dad. There might be times when I make mistakes, but that's all part of life. You have to give me the chance to make those mistakes so I can learn from them."

Ben thought about just walking away, but something inside wouldn't let him. He took a few steps towards Jack and gave him a hug. "I love you, kid."

Jack embraced Ben and apologized for making him come all the way downstairs after him. Afterwards, it was business as usual. Ben checked his watch then looked back at Jack. "Come on, kid, we have a fish to fry."

Jack smiled as both men walked back towards the elevator. "So listen, kid. What do you say we go upstairs and meet with Robert? We'll get all of our ducks in a row, and when the time comes, you take the meeting with no interference." Jack was definitely on board with that and agreed.

As Jack and Ben made their way back upstairs to Ben's office, members of the board started to arrive down the hall in the main conference room. First to arrive were Ethan and Fitzgerald. Although they had nothing in common, they eliminated the tension by making coffee and preparing the room for the meeting. Next to wander in were Stanley and Kathy. Kathy said nothing to anybody except good morning. She ignored Stanley all together. William walked in with donuts and pastries and placed them near the coffee. Jonathan, Anthony, Richard, and Lewis all arrived at the same time, talking about sports and who was going to beat who. As everyone lingered around the conference table, Linda walked in. Of course she had to make a grand entrance so everyone could see how gorgeous she looked. Her one mistake was thinking Jack was already there. When she realized he wasn't, the disappointment on her face was almost laughable.

Back in Ben's office, Robert spoke to Jack about why he thought it would be necessary to file a lawsuit. "As much as I admired your dad, I think he would have understood and respected my decision. Jack, don't take it personally. This is business and the objective is to stay on top."

Jack sat and listened and was respectful enough not to interrupt.

But when Robert was finished, Jack felt he had to stand up for himself, his dad, and the company. "Over the years, my dad and Ben taught me so much that it's almost like not having a choice. My dad started this business with ambition and one truck. Now it's up to me to keep this business going, not only for the money aspect of it or the lifestyle it provides, but because our employees rely on our good business sense to keep food on their tables. Now, I've listened to your reasoning and I understand your actions, but we need to start thinking long-term survival instead of short-term gain."

Robert gave Jack the same respect he was given and just sat and listened. He was very impressed with Jack and how he presented himself. It reminded him of Jack Sr. After listening to Jack's plans for the computer industry, Robert was even more impressed and agreed to support Jack all the way. Ben was equally impressed and decided to go along with Jack.

After waiting for what seemed like forever, Ben was just dying to tell Robert his plan for Nick. Robert listened knowing Ben liked to pull out all the stops when dealing harshly with someone. Once again, Robert was in agreement with the plan. After the meeting, the three men engaged in some lighthearted conversation then decided it was time to face the executive board members.

Ben opened the door with some authority and entered the boardroom followed by Jack and then Robert. The rest of the board sat about with lifeless expressions. Some played with their empty coffee cups, while others read whatever magazine was available, and some just stared out the window at the world going by. Ben looked at his watch and called the meeting to order. As everyone took their seats, Jack noticed Nick wasn't in the room. Just then, the door opened and in walked Nick grinning from ear to ear. He walked over to Jack and rapped his arm around him. "Hey, Jack, I got it. Bought it right off the showroom floor."

Jack would usually play into whatever Nick was leading up to, but not that day. Nick picked the wrong day to try to be friendly.

"Come on, Jack, you're not going to guess?"

Jack had a blank expression on his face and shrugged his shoulder signaling to Nick that he was uncomfortable with his arm around him. Nick took a step back in surprise. "Damn, Jack, you look like you're about to cry. Listen, I went and bought a new Corvette right off the showroom floor. You gotta see it. It's awesome. I just might give *Fringe* a run for her money."

Before Nick could say anything else, Ben barked out an order to sit down. "I'm so glad you could make it, Mr. Cummings. The meeting has already been called to order. Now sit down and shut up." Nick knew Ben didn't have any tolerance for lateness, so he quickly made his way to his seat without a word.

Ben stood up and looked around the table. "Over the past few years, we've argued and bickered over whether or not to enter into the computer race. Now, before we all start to argue and bicker some more, Jack and I have a little business to take care of."

Ben opened his briefcase and pulled out the photo that was taken of Nick in China. He also had all the documentation from China Steel and from his friend Roy Dobbins. "Now, most of you know the history of Kotter Industries. Hell, some of you got here off the sweat and tears of past relatives who were original members of the board. This brings me to the business at hand. Carroll Cummings was an original member of this board and a trusted friend of Jack Sr. and myself. He took the lead with many of our projects, including a possible deal back in the '70s with one of our biggest competitors, China Steel. Now, I know this information isn't in our 'welcome to Kotter Industries' brochure, so that's why I'm giving all of you some background. As you know, Carroll is no longer with us, but his son Nick has been a member of this council for quite some time now. I want to share with all of you some information that has recently come to light. While all of you have been crying over money and wondering where your next million-dollar home was going to be built, Jack and I, along with some friends of mine, have been working on a situation that, quite frankly, I find disturbing. I know all of this isn't making sense at this time, so what I'm going to do is show a photo."

Ben reached over and turned on a projector he had ready for the meeting. He placed the photo of Nick at China Steel on the projector's platform. Everyone just sat and stared for a minute. Finally, Nick stood up. "It's a photo of me talking to a Chinese man. Is this a joke? What's going on, Jack?"

Ben walked over to Nick with fury in his eyes. He really wanted to deal with him, but he'd promised Jack he would give Nick a chance to explain. "You're lucky Jack is a better friend to you than you are to him, you little punk."

Jack stood up and looked Nick in his eyes. "Tell me you have a good explanation for this, Nick. Tell me you had the good of the company in mind. Tell me you were trying to play some kind of sick joke that backfired. Tell me anything reasonable."

Nick just stood in front of Jack and said nothing. Suddenly, Jack let out an enormous scream. "Tell me something, Nick! You were my friend."

Nick turned and walked over to the window and stood looking out. He then turned around to address the board members, who still had no idea what was going on. The tone of is voice escalated with every word. "My father poured everything he had into this company." Everyone could see the anger on his face as he peered at Jack. "Without my father heading up projects, who knows where Kotter Industries would be right now. Just when he was about to make the deal of a lifetime, what happened? This company turned its back on him like he was nothing. Like he was a used up piece of trash you just threw out." Still aiming his anger towards Jack, Nick continued his rage while pointing his finger at Ben. "After all the time away from his family and all the blood, sweat, and tears that went into what he was trying to accomplish for your precious Kotter Industries, Old Man Kotter and the high and mighty Benjamin Marcus walked away smelling like roses, while my dad was left flapping in the wind."

Ben was leaning against the table listening, and he glanced over at Jack. "Well, first off, you're right. We trusted Carroll with many of our projects. As I said, he was a good friend and a great businessman. Those were hard times back then. The government got involved and threatened to shut us down. There was nothing we could do."

With a full head of steam, Ben marched over to Nick. He stood head-to-head, as if they were two competing rams. "It was your dad who decided to move his entire portfolio over to China. He got greedy and jumped the gun before anything was finalized. With that said, you're damn lucky Senior let him keep his position within this company, because I wouldn't have been so gracious."

Nick went off and pointed his finger in Ben's face. Then he became loud and belligerent. "You're an asshole, old man. My dad carried this company through tough times, and you could have done a hell of a lot more than just walk away."

Ben grabbed Nick's finger, and with his free hand, grabbed him around his throat. As Nick struggled to get free, Ben jammed him up against the wall. Jack and Fitzgerald jumped up from their chairs and pried them apart. Jack was already emotionally upset so it wasn't too hard to become physically upset. He finally pulled Nick away from Ben and pushed him to one side of the room, while Fitzgerald kept Ben from a second attack. "Calm down, Benjamin. You're not that young anymore."

Ben smiled and caught his breath as he rested his hand on Fitzgerald's shoulder. "You're right, old friend. I'm not that young anymore, but I can still whip that punk's ass seven days a week and twice on Sunday."

Nick fixed his jacket and tie as he regained his composure. "Don't worry, Jack. I'll make it easy for you. I never did like you. You and your little cronies running around town living it up like you were some kind of royalty. Little rich kids. Never wanting for nothing. Screw you. Screw your dad for stabbing my father in the back." Once again, Nick turned his anger towards Ben. "I hope you rot in hell, old man. The day will come when Satan is shoving a pitch fork up your ass."

By then, Jack was back to being his cool self. He knew the information was good, but deep down, he was hoping Nick had some kind of reasonable explanation for his actions. "You had me fooled, Nick. I really thought you were my friend. I even talked Ben into allowing you the opportunity to explain yourself."

Eventually, everyone around the room started whispering about the seriousness of what was going on. Of all people to make a statement, Anthony stood up to confront Nick. "I knew your father well, Nick. He was a good man. He was also an ambitious man. I remember when your father went to China. He was so excited. He had handled many projects before, but that one was his golden opportunity to finally step out of the shadow of Kotter Industries. Jack Sr. knew what Carroll wanted and he didn't try to hold him back. Even after your father jumped into bed with China Steel and lost out, Jack Sr. still stood by him and brought him back into the company. Listen, son, you have no right to be blaming anyone for your family's downfall."

Although Nick was listening, his anger kept him from hearing what Anthony was trying to say. "I'm not your son, you old goat. All of you think Jack Sr. was so great. The great Jack Kotter. The one and only Jack Kotter."

Just as Nick was about to make his exit, the door opened and in walked two very large men with black suits. They closed the door behind them as they fixed their eyes on Nick. Nick turned towards Jack. "So this is it? This is what you resort to? You're gonna have your goons take me somewhere and bust me up?"

Jack didn't say a word. He was so disgusted at that point, all he could do was calmly sit down in his chair and wait for Ben's plan to play itself out.

During Anthony's little speech, Ben had pulled some more papers out of his briefcase and had them waiting on the table. By then, Ben's blood pressure had dropped back down and most of the redness had left his face. He turned his attention towards Nick as he picked the papers up off the table. "Before you leave here today, tough guy, I have some paperwork for you to sign."

With a sense of distrust, Nick walked over, and Ben handed the papers to him. Nick took a moment to read to himself as he looked the paperwork over. After reading for a few minutes, Nick realized the paperwork consisted of him handing over his stock options to Kotter Industries. He looked at Ben then over to Jack in disgust. He laughed then slammed the papers down on the table. Nick turned towards the door then realized the two large men were still standing in front of it.

Ben picked the papers up and walked over to Nick. He sat on the end of the table and handed the papers back to him. "As you know, I'm good friends with the State's Attorney. The company law firm has already been in contact with their office. Now, you can either sign over your stock or face many years in a federal prison. You sign now and Kotter Industries won't press the issue. I think it's a pretty generous offer."

Once more, Nick looked the papers over. This time, he placed them down on the table and signed them. "This isn't over, Ben." He turned towards Jack as if to continue the argument, but didn't say a word. He just walked towards the door, brushing his leg against

Jack's arm. As the two men stepped aside, Nick walked out without saying a word to anyone.

Jack stood up and met Ben over at the window. Both men stared out over the parking lot as the two large men escorted Nick out the door. Just then, a black SUV with tinted windows pulled up and Roy Dobbins stepped out. Jack looked on as Nick was aggressively helped into the truck. Jack looked over at Ben with a bit of surprise. "I thought he was free to go."

Ben turned and walked back over to the table. "I never said he was free to go. I simply stated we wouldn't press the legal issue. I have no control over what the CIA does with him. Although, I have the feeling it's going to be a cold day in hell before we ever hear from that little punk again."

Whispering was still going on around the room as Robert and Ben attempted to quiet things down. Eventually, everyone took a seat in order to continue on with the day's business. Just as Ben was about to give the floor to Jack, Jack stood up and walked out. Ben paused for a moment then excused himself. He walked out of the conference room and down the hall to Jack's office. When he walked in, he found Jack at his desk with his head resting on his arms.

"Come on, kid, you knew it would come down to this. You knew the plan and you knew what the outcome would be. What's the problem, kid?"

Jack looked up with a somber expression. "You're asking me, what's the problem? For Christ's sake, Ben, the CIA just took one of my best friends away, probably never to be heard from again, not to mention I just found out our whole friendship was a lie in the first place. What's the problem, you ask? I thought I knew what I was doing. I thought I learned enough from you and my dad, and I thought I could take over this business, but obviously, I don't know anything. Hell, I can't even tell who my friends are anymore. And, by the way, didn't we have a conversation about knocking first?"

Ben gathered his thoughts and took a seat. "You're right, kid. Your father and I spent a lot of time trying to instill confidence in you so when the time was right, you wouldn't have any problem handling anything that came your way. Obviously, when you're dealing with a corporation that spans the globe, there's bound to be some things that just can't be solved by using traditional means. This is where using your resources comes into play. This is where you get down and dirty and learn the unconventional ways of doing business. Sometimes, that involves getting your hands dirty. Sometimes it involves making sacrifices we normally wouldn't make."

Knowing he thought better on his feet, Jack stood up and started pacing the room. "You don't understand, Ben. It's not the business end that has me doubting myself. It's all this cloak-and-dagger stuff and whatever goes along with it. I don't think I'm cut out for it."

Ben could almost feel a fatherly bond with Jack, but he knew Jack needed more than just the "everything is going to be alright" speech. "Listen, kid, I'm not going to tell you this stuff doesn't get to me sometimes. In fact, most of the time, I have the daunting task of being the coldhearted person who has to go for the jugular. We can't sit around hoping for the best. Unfortunately, that's not how this world works. If this company is going to survive, then we have to forge ahead, and that means we have to shoot for the moon instead of just chasing stars."

Jack stood in the middle of the room rubbing his face as the mental fatigue started to take its toll. "I don't know, Ben. I think, in a sense, Nick was right. Growing up, I never really paid attention to what was going on around me. I just enjoyed all the comforts my dad was providing for me. I never thought about how those comforts were being obtained."

Ben could feel his anger levels creeping back up. "Listen, kid, I don't have to sit here and defend myself to you, but I will tell you this: Your dad and I did some things in the past that may have been questionable, but we never did anything to anyone who wasn't trying to hurt us or this company first. Your dad and my brother built this company with the idea that the American dream was for anyone who was willing to work hard enough to take it. Now, you can keep sucking on your momma's tit or you can get out there and join the fight. Either way, I'm through with trying to baby you."

Ben stormed out of the office and made his way back to the conference room. As he walked in, everyone was doing their usual nothing. He poured himself a shot of Jack Daniels and didn't waste any time chugging it down. He then made himself a cup of coffee and took a seat at the table. Everyone could tell he was in no mood to talk, so they continued on with whatever conversations they were having before he came in.

Robert took the initiative and approached Ben in order to find out if the meeting was going to continue with or without Jack. Unfortunately, Ben didn't have an answer. He wanted to give Jack some time to make a decision, so he asked Robert to address the members to fill them in on what had transpired earlier.

Just as Robert finished addressing the board, the door opened and in walked Jack. Ben perked up as Jack walked over to him. He leaned over and whispered into Ben's ear. "By the way, my mother never breast fed me."

Ben smiled as he stood up. Just a few minutes earlier, he had the weight of the world on his shoulders, but after Jack's return, he felt nothing but relief. He brought the meeting to an order and gave the floor to Jack. Jack stood at the head of the table and surveyed the room. Everyone sat quietly waiting for his opening remarks.

"As you know by now, we had a situation with Nicholas, which has now been resolved. I believe this company will move forward as planned, and over time, we will forget all about Nick and his actions towards this company. As you also saw, Nick was given some options in which he chose to sign over his stock to Kotter Industries, which means to me.

"Now, I can honestly say it's been a real roller-coaster of a year. We've had several meetings about whether or not to expand into the growing computer industry, and we seem to be divided in our thinking. After I say my peace, we're going to take a final vote. Jack opened his briefcase and pulled out some paperwork that included a list of small-time manufacturers of computer parts. The businesses were owned by some fly-by-night companies struggling to stay afloat. He handed out the list so everyone could look it over and follow along.

"Now for a little Kotter Industries history. Some of you might already know, and the rest of you, well, here's an opportunity to get educated. Back in the early '60s, Kotter Industries entered the space race. That is, we bought most of the little ma-and-pa companies that were supplying materials to NASA. Those smart business decisions propelled Kotter Industries into a whole new tax bracket. Our stock went through the roof and our profit margins went even higher."

Jack took a strategic pause while he wallowed in his opening words. He felt confident that by the end of the meeting most, if not all, the board members would see things his way. He took a drink of water and continued. "Let me give you an analogy. Two bulls, one old and one young, are up on a hill overlooking a meadow filled with cows. The young bull says, 'Hey, let's run down there and get with one of those cows.' The older bull being much wiser says, 'Why don't we walk down there and get with all the cows?' This is my proposal. Why have one product and be a competitor when we can buy out some of these manufacturers and be a supplier to all?"

Jack handed out some more literature referencing projected profits over a five-year period. While the board members were busy trying to crunch numbers, Jack took a moment to speak with Ben. "What'ya think, Ben? You think I have their full attention?"

Ben stood up to stretch his legs and to refill his coffee. "You're asking me what I think? I think you have them by the balls, but they just don't know it yet. I can't wait until you tell them your plan for Robert. I gotta get a picture of their faces when you drop that bomb."

Jack and Ben walked out into the hallway while the rest of the members tried to find fault with Jack's proposal. Robert followed Jack and Ben out into the hall and congratulated Jack on a solid opening and even a better presentation.

While Jack and Ben stood in the hall talking to Robert, Anthony walked out to stretch his legs and take a break. He noticed Jack and Ben weren't arguing with Robert as usual. Instead, they were laughing and having a pleasant conversation. He paused then continued down the hall. Lewis also walked out looking for Jack. It didn't matter that Jack was already involved in a conversation. Whenever it was time to crunch numbers, Lewis had no qualms about stepping all over people.

"You just can't spring this on us like this, Jack." He turned to Robert for support. "Tell him, Robert. We need time to analyze these figures."

Just then, Anthony came walking up from behind. He heard what Lewis was saying. "You mean you need more time to find fault with Jack's plan. Do yourself a favor, Lewis. Try to be more supportive rather than trying to always undermine people. You might become a better person."

Anthony walked back into the conference room and sat down. Jack looked at Ben, who was staring at Robert, whose mouth was hanging open. All three men just stood there dumbfounded at what they'd just heard.

Right on cue, Linda walked out and wrapped her arms around Jack. "Hey, handsome, I need to go to the little girl's room. Care to walk and talk with me?"

Robert and Ben decided this would be a good time to retreat. Ben turned around just before he stepped in the room and laughed, "You're on your own, kid."

Jack took a step back. He didn't find it amusing. He was actually quite annoyed. "Why do you keep throwing yourself at me like a whore in heat?"

Linda smiled and took a step towards Jack in order to close the distance between them. "You know you want me, Jackie boy. I don't know why you keep fighting me. That little girlfriend you have can't do the things I want to do to you."

Jack took another step back and headed for the door. He looked back in order to get the last word in. "I'll give you this much. You're one of the sexiest women I've ever seen, but you're also just as sick in your twisted little mind."

Jack made himself a cup of coffee and wandered over to the window. He was still thinking about what Anthony had said. He wondered why and how the company changed after his father passed away. Ben was still around, along with several others who had been around for a while. The only thing he could think of was greed. The up-and-coming younger generation didn't think long-term. They only wanted the here and now. Jack turned around and took a good look at everyone in the room. He knew the meeting was going to go as planned, but he couldn't help but think about the future and what problems he would have to face with the generation gap and board members always in disagreement.

Linda finally graced the room with her presence. As usual, she couldn't help herself. She brushed her outer thigh against Jack and leaned into him. "There wasn't anyone in the ladies' room, Jack. I was really lonely. Just think about what kind of fun we could've had." Afterwards, she gave Jack her sinister grin and walked away.

As everyone took their seats in preparation, Ben stood up and walked over to Jack. "Come on, kid, concentrate. You can eat that pie later. Right now you have a more important agenda"

Jack had no words. He just shook his head and laughed. "I don't know how you do it, Ben, but the timing of your words are always perfect." Ben gave Jack a confident pat on the back as they walked back to their seats. As Ben sat down, Jack stood at the head of the table. "Alright, let's get started. I proposed my plans to you. I've given everyone the projected profits. You've all had time to review the paperwork. Now, before we take it to a vote, I will give the floor to Robert."

As Jack sat down, Robert stood up and addressed the board. "Everyone knows the problems we've had over the past few years. We've been bickering with each other over something that may or may not help this company. As some of you may know, I was planning to take legal action against Kotter Industries. That is no longer in the works. I've decided to lend my support to Jack because I think he has a solid plan for the future of this company. The bottom line is that it just makes sense. With that said, I give the floor back to Jack."

When Jack stood up, he could see the surprised looks on everyone's faces. It took everything he had not to laugh. "While all that sinks in, I would like to take this time to announce that Robert will be heading up the buyouts of those businesses on the list I handed out. I think he is the best person for the job and that is not up for debate." Jack paused for a minute because a low buzz started among the board members. Whispers were being traded as the opposing board members realized they no longer had a foothold.

"Let me say this, and afterwards I no longer want his name mentioned in this building. Although Nicholas originally voted with me, evidence suggests, and I believe, he was going to change his vote. As you are aware, Nicholas has chosen to relinquish his stock to me and is no longer with this company. This means, if nobody else has recently changed their opinions, we're no longer at a stalemate. With that said, we will take a fifteen minute break so everyone can rethink their position. When we reconvene, we will take a final vote."

Robert stood up and shook Jack's hand. "Great job, Jack. Your father would have been proud."

As Robert walked away, Ben was the next in line. Gleaming with pride, he shook Jack's hand. "Damn, kid! That was a work of art. Your father's probably looking down at you right now and clapping his hands." Ben's appreciation didn't last long. He asked Jack to meet him in his office for a brief talk. Ben patted Jack on the back and walked down the hall. As Jack looked around, he noticed some dissatisfied looks, but he knew he wasn't going to be able to please everyone.

As Jack collected his paperwork, he closed his briefcase with a profound sense of gratification. He smiled to himself and headed for the door. As he walked across the room, Fitzgerald met him at the door. "Good job, Jack. You're finally stepping into your father's shoes. I'm glad." As they walked out into the hall, Fitzgerald saw Linda waiting and decided to make an exit. "Sorry, Jack, gotta go. Good luck."

Linda was leaning up against the wall trying her hardest to be appealing. "So, Jack, what's it going to be? You going home tonight to the same old boring girl or to my house where you can boss me around and be the dominating bull?"

Jack turned somewhat red in the face, but he didn't care. He was confident and sitting on top of the world. For a change of pace, he took a step forward, towards Linda, and leaned in, up close and personal. "So, you liked my story about the cows?"

Linda became a little hot and bothered because Jack had never been that close to her before. She grabbed the knot of his tie and moved even closer, to a point where they could feel each other's breath on their faces. "Damn right I liked that story, baby. Come on, Jack, meet me at my house tonight where we can continue that storyline."

Just when Jack was so close, almost to a kiss, he pulled away. "Not if you were the only cow in the pasture."

As he smiled at Linda, her face turned several different shades of red. "You just wait, little boy. I'm going to make you beg on your hands and knees one day. You're going to want me so bad, you're gonna wish you had no pecker."

Jack walked away laughing to himself. He knew Linda wasn't one to let somebody get the best of her, but he figured he would enjoy the moment while it lasted. He stopped at Ben's office door, which happened to be closed. He thought about opening the door just to get a reaction out of him, but what the hell, why ruin a good day? Jack knocked several times until he heard Ben's crackly voice yell, "Come!" As Jack walked in, Ben had his back towards the door staring out of his office window. He told Jack to make himself a drink and to have a seat. This didn't sound too good to Jack. He thought Ben would have been in a happier mood. Jack made two drinks and gave one to Ben. He sat down and waited for Ben to explain why the sudden gloom.

Surprisingly, Ben turned around with a smile on his face. "Well, kid, how does it feel?"

Jack could see the pride glowing from his smile. "Honestly, I don't really feel anything. I feel that I did the best job I could and I feel good about the decisions I made."

Ben sat down and leaned back in his chair. "That's good. That's exactly how you should feel. Like it's an everyday thing, because that's what running a company this size should feel like. Natural. It's okay to feel like you've accomplished something, but you should never accept the feeling that you're finished."

Jack took a drink in order to let Ben's words sink in. "Thanks, Ben, for the vote of confidence, but I don't think this is what you asked me in here for."

Ben reached into his desk and pulled out a copy of the old lockbox key he'd already given Jack. "Listen, kid, take this key and do whatever the hell you're gonna do with it. I told you how I feel and I'm not gonna say any more."

Jack flicked his eyes from Ben to the key, then back to Ben. He wasn't sure why Ben was so uptight about something that may or may not be anything. Time was running short, though, and Jack had to finish out the meeting. He took the key and placed it in his pocket and walked towards the door. As he made his exit, he turned back to Ben. "What'ya say we go fry some fish?"

Ben was already halfway across his office as he whisked past Jack and continued down the hall. With a half-grin, Jack just closed the door and made his way back to the meeting.

As Jack entered the conference room, he noticed everyone was already seated and there wasn't a whisper to be heard. "Alright, everyone, let's not waste any more time. Let's just take our vote so we can move onto the next big problem. Anyone here opposed to my plan?"

Richard and Linda were the only two people to raise their hands. As they looked around the room then at each other, they quickly realized they'd made the wrong choice. As their arms slowly dropped to the table, Jack wasted no time collecting the prize. "Alright then, I will close this meeting by saying thank you for your time and patience. I know we've made the right choice and I'm anxious to get started. Obviously, there will be progress reports along with monthly financial reports sent out. If there is no other business, I declare this meeting adjourned."

The room was still quiet as everyone made their exit. No one was talking or even looking at one another as they walked down the hall. Jack noticed Ben had left without saying anything to anybody. He hung back just in case someone needed to speak to him privately. He watched as everyone but Robert walked out. Then he waited momentarily, as Robert was still going through some paperwork.

Just then, Anthony came back in. "Jack, I'm not going to take up much of your time. I just wanted to tell you what a great job you did. At times, I felt like I was watching your father in action."

Jack stood listening and was really surprised. "Thank you, Anthony. I have to admit, I thought you were going to fight me on this, and you really surprised me today."

Anthony hung his head then looked back up at Jack. "I'm sorry, Jack. Not just for the past few weeks, but for past years. I've done nothing but complain and bask in my own misery. I've also been oblivious to the needs of this company. Your father always treated me like family and I'm hoping you can forgive this grumpy old man."

Jack didn't know what to say at first. But as usual in situations like this, he thought about his dad. He reached out in friendship and shook Anthony's hand. "My dad thought enough of you to call you a friend so who am I to say any different." Just then, Jack noticed Robert had been standing behind Anthony. He stepped to the side as Anthony turned to face Robert. Jack didn't know how long Robert had been listening.

Robert stared at Anthony for a second then told Jack he needed someone to assist him with the list of software companies that were being targeted for potential buyouts. Jack was caught somewhat off guard, but told Robert to use his own discretion. Robert glanced at Anthony then shot Jack a smile. "I'm glad you said that, Jack, because I have just the person in mind."

Just when Anthony was about to excuse himself, Robert informed Jack he thought Anthony would be perfect for the job. Once again, Jack was caught off guard, but not as much as Anthony was. Robert turned to Anthony and awaited an answer. "What do you think, Anthony?"

Anthony was still trying to grasp the concept that Robert wanted to work directly with him. "After all these years of bickering and feuding, you want me to head up a project with you?"

Robert knew Anthony would be somewhat leery of him, but he also knew he could ease his mind. "I know in the past it seemed like we were never friends, but at the same time, I never considered you an enemy." Robert paused for a moment to collect his thoughts while Anthony pondered what was being said. "One of my hobbies over the past few years was studying the history of this company and its success. I've also looked through the archives and found out you, along with Ben, were involved in many of the buyouts of various small companies during the late '60s and all through the '70s. Honestly, I think there's a lot we can teach each other and maybe even come out as friends on the other side."

After hearing Robert talk so positively, Anthony perked up and was ready to enjoy a conversation for a change. Jack took the opportunity to excuse himself. He said his goodbyes and left to go meet up with Bria. Robert and Anthony walked over to the table and sat down like a couple of schoolyard pals. They ordered some takeout and settled in for a long afternoon of strategic thinking.

Before Jack left, he stopped at his office and tried to call Ben. There was no answer. On the way out, he stopped by Ben's office, but he had already left for the day. When Jack asked Hellen about it, she said Ben was in no mood to talk and for Jack not to try to call him. As usual, Jack didn't understand why Ben was the way he was, but he wasn't going to worry about it. He had a date with Bria and he was in a hurry to get there.

As Jack darted to his car, whatever problem Ben was having was going to have to wait. He started *Fringe* and, as always, she purred like a kitten. He left the parking lot in his usual manner, leaving nothing but tire tread and smoke. He was quickly making his way down Route 110 when he checked his watch and noticed he had some time to spare. Knowing Bria took forever to get ready, and God forbid if they should arrive at a night club before anyone else, he decided to get some payback.

After taking care of their legal problems, Jack knew Walley and Jimmy would be at the Wiley Roadster stirring up trouble. Even without their hotrods, they were showing off and chasing the women. As he pulled onto the lot, he noticed the Mopar brothers leaning up against a rental car. As Jack crept through the lot, he pulled up beside Walley and revved his engine. "Hey, Walley, that's a real nice rental you and Jimmy have." Jack shut his car off and stepped out laughing. "Yeah. Thought it was funny when the shoe was on the other foot. Now look at you." As Jack shared an embrace with the brothers, it was obvious something was bothering them. He took a step back and looked around the lot. He saw all the usual suspects, so he knew it couldn't have been anything serious. "So, what's up? Why the long faces?"

Jimmy tried to laugh it off in his own quirky kind of way. "Nothing, Jack. Nothing you should be worried about."

Jack turned to Walley because he knew Walley would never try to keep anything from him. Walley also tried to laugh it off, but with no success. "What? Why is it I have to be the one to say something?"

Now Jack was positive it wasn't serious, but was still concerned. "Come on. Let's have it. What's going on?"

By that time, Jimmy was about to burst at the seams. "Listen, Jack. Far be it from us to judge you, but we heard you had a chance at Lilith the other night and you backed down."

Now it was Jack trying to laugh it off. "Is that it? That's what you've been holding back? If you really want to know, that's exactly what I did. She came out of nowhere the other night. Scared the hell out of me. I wasn't going to mess with that stupid bitch again. Besides, I was on my way to meet Bria."

Jimmy and Walley looked at each other as if there was more to the story. Jack saw they had something else on their minds. "Tell me. What else are you not saying?"

This time Walley came out with it. "Listen, Jack. Everyone knows the damage this woman has caused, and we don't blame you for not wanting to go after her, but word has it she went into a rage after you turned her down. The police spotted her later that night and she wrecked three of their cars. There's a rumor going around she wants you dead."

Jack didn't know what to think, so as usual, he made a joke. "Wow! Talk about a woman scorned. Listen, guys. Don't worry about me. I'm not going to give that bitch another chance to wreck *Fringe*, and I'm certainly not going to risk my life trying to wreck her car. Anyway, Dale has some kind of wacked-out plan he wants to run by me to maybe catch that menace. Which reminds me, I have to give him a call. Listen, don't worry. I'll see you guys at the club." Jack started *Fringe* and off he went to meet Bria.

After Jack picked Bria up, they went to meet some friends who'd rented out the Palladium Nightclub. The building itself was built in 1927 and used for everything from a movie theater to a music hall. Then, in 1985, it was converted into a nightclub by Steve Rubell and Ian Schrager after they were forced to sell the infamous Studio 54.

When Jack and Bria arrived, the club was in full-swing. Everybody who was anybody was there having a good time. As Bria went her way, Jack went another. He wandered around for a while until he saw Dale ordering drinks at the bar. Before he could walk over to talk, Monica came up beside him. She had on a skirt that barely made it past her thighs, with black stockings hooked to a garter. She swung her long blonde hair around Jack's neck and pulled him close. "Hey there, fella. Haven't seen you around. Haven't seen Bria either. Are you two still taking a break?"

Jack could feel his knees starting to buckle. He tried to stay cool, but just couldn't resist sliding his hands around her waist. "Well, not really. She's here tonight with me, but she went off to talk to her friends."

Before Jack could say another word, Monica leaned forward and stuck her long, sensual tongue in his mouth. Jack's knees started to quiver as his motor functions failed. His libido took over and he slid his hands down Monica's waist to the lower side of her buttocks and back up to the small of her back. All thoughts of Bria were replaced with fantasies of Monica's incredibly nice ass.

As the long kiss came to an end, Jack stepped back to adjust himself. Monica smiled as Jack tried desperately to gather his composure. "Don't worry, Kotter, I would never try to take you away from Bria."

Jack was still bedazzled but could finally organize his words. "Are you sure? I mean, of course. I would never cheat on Bria, at least not that I know of."

Monica leaned forward and gave Jack a peck on the cheek, then wandered off into the crowd, leaving Jack to ponder his relationship with Bria.

By then, Dale had collected his drinks and made his way over to Ethan and the Mopar brothers. Jack bought himself a beer and decided to join them and, hopefully, stay out of trouble. As he greeted everyone, he slid into the booth next to Dale. "I've been wanting to talk to you about Lilith. You said you had a plan but you needed my help."

Dale didn't want to talk in front of everyone, so they grabbed their jackets and stepped outside. There were limos and high-priced sports cars crowding the streets and people still lining up to get in. As Dale lit up a cigarette, he motioned for Jack to stroll down the sidewalk with him.

"Listen, Jack, I have this plan that I've been trying to get the department to go along with, but it involves all kinds of liability on our part and yours."

Since Jack never had a chance to hear the plan when they were at Bobby's funeral, he had some curiosity. After hearing Dale's opening statement, he was really intrigued. "I don't understand. What is it you need me to do that you think is so dangerous?"

Dale stopped and took a puff of his cigarette. As he exhaled the smoke, he threw it to the ground and stepped on it. "I need you to chase down Lilith for me."

Jack smiled and just stared at him for a moment waiting for a punch line. "Okay, so what's the rest of the joke?"

It started getting cold, so Dale slipped his hands into his pockets. "There is no joke. You have the car to do the job, and I heard she really wants you bad."

Jack thought about it for a minute and tried to run various scenarios through his head. "So, what about the police? What are you going to be doing while I'm trying to catch her and keep myself from getting killed? And what makes you think she's going to run? We already know her motive isn't to win races."

As the two men turned to walk back to the club, Dale let Jack know the rest of the plan. "Listen, Jack, we know where she likes to do her dirty work and we know about what her time frames are. We also know she's been stalking you. We just don't have anything fast enough to keep up with her. We're probably only going to have one shot at this. The plan includes help from several different agencies, including state police and two helicopters. All you have to do is drive like you normally do."

As Jack and Dale made their way back to the Palladium, Jack was still running scenarios through his head. He thought about their first encounter. He also thought about Bobby and the Mopar brothers.

Dale could see Jack had reservations about the idea and he wasn't going to push him into something he felt uncomfortable doing. "I don't need an answer now. Think about it for a few days and let me know."

Jack knew if he said no, Dale wouldn't think any worse of him. "I don't know why you smoke. It's bad for you and you never finish a cigarette."

Dale wasn't expecting sarcasm, but that was okay. He knew Jack would be taking a huge risk if he said yes.

Jack didn't say anything else. He walked back into the club to look for Bria. He came across Bobby Jo and Dee from the diner. "Hey, my two favorite diner girls. How are you?"

After giving hugs, the two girls offered to buy Jack a drink. "Ben told us you were a really cool guy, but wow! You really know how to have a good time." After a brief conversation, Jack politely declined the drink and excused himself.

After talking to a few more friends, Jack was finally able to track down Bria, who was already half-past drunk. "What do you say we get out of here and go someplace quiet?"

Bria was having such a great time that she wasn't really paying attention to what Jack was saying. She downed the last of her drink just as one of her favorite dance songs came on. "Come on, Jack, let's go grind." She tugged on Jack's arm, but he wasn't budging. Normally, he would be all too pleased to go dance, but not that night. After several attempts to get Jack out on the dance floor, Bria finally gave up and joined some of her friends who were already dancing.

Stressed out and disappointed, Jack walked away and made his way to the front door. On the way out, he saw Ethan trying his best to sweet-talk a six-foot blonde. "Hey, Ethan, can you do me a favor? How long are you going to stay tonight?"

Ethan was excited because the blonde actually showed some interest in him. "I don't know, Jack. This chic is really hot and I think she likes me."

Jack thought he was joking at first, but quickly realized Ethan was serious. "Well, I don't really think she's your type. Besides, I need you to keep an eye on Bria for me and make sure she doesn't get herself into any trouble."

Although he was a friend and a business associate, Ethan could also be a bit sensitive. He took offense to Jack's comments. "What do you mean she's not my type? You always have women crawling all over you, and the one time I have someone interested in me, you want me to walk away and babysit your girlfriend."

Jack could hear the hurt in Ethan's voice and knew he lacked confidence when it came to women. "I'm sorry, Ethan. You're right. I'm being selfish. This is a great opportunity for you and here I am trying to steal your thunder."

Ethan couldn't tell if Jack was being sincere or if he was just apologizing to get his way, but in any case, he went along with it. "Alright, I'll make you a deal. Let me go talk to this girl for a few more minutes to see if I can get more than just her phone number."

As stressed out as Jack was, he couldn't help but laugh at Ethan. "Listen, Ethan, I wouldn't be a very good friend if I let you go over there."

Ethan became upset and was just about to lay into Jack when Jack pointed out the lump protruding out of the six-foot blonde's throat. "You see that, Ethan? Only guys have an Adam's apple, and if you bothered to look a little closer, you would have seen that clumped on makeup trying to cover the razor stubble."

As the blonde bombshell was dancing and winking at Ethan, he took a closer look. He then told Jack he would be glad to keep an eye on Bria and walked past him in shame.

Jack made a beeline for the door and found Dale outside smoking another cigarette. "Hey, Dale. I meant to ask you before, besides the fact she's pissed at me, I haven't really heard anything lately about Lilith."

Dale took one last puff then snuffed out his cigarette. "Yeah, she's been off the radar ever since you saw her the last time. Sightings by the local residents also stopped pouring in. That's why I said we may only get one shot at her if you decide to go through with the plan."

Jack was listening to what Dale was saying, but couldn't help thinking Lilith was just waiting for him. There had to be other reasons. "Let me know if you guys get any knew leads. I'll call you next week and let you know what I decide."

As Jack headed home, his mind wandered in several different directions. Obviously, he would be in harm's way if he decided to take on Lilith again, not to mention his car would most likely be damaged again. He was also concerned about his relationship with Bria. Ever since Jack took over Kotter Industries, it seemed their relationship had become more strained. And on top of everything else, he was worried about Ben. As Jack drove, he had to be aware of his surroundings in case Lilith decided to make an appearance. Just then, he took notice of Joe's Garage. It had been closed and boarded up for many years, but he noticed there had been some recent activity. He thought to himself, somebody may have finally bought the property.

Jack finally made it home, only to find Ethan and Bria already there waiting for him. As Jack pulled up the driveway, he could see the disgust on Bria's face. He could also see the fear in Ethan. As Jack pulled to a stop and stepped out, Ethan scurried over. "Sorry, Jack, I tried to tell her you left and you asked me to get her home safe, but she wouldn't listen."

Jack walked over to Bria to try to explain, and she suddenly slapped him across his face. "Who the hell do you think you are, Jack Kotter? You just left me there like I was nothing. And don't think I didn't see you hanging all that slut Monica with your tongue in her mouth, you bastard."

Jack noticed Ethan had already made his exit, which was a good thing. This way, he could deal with Bria. He grabbed her by the arm and pulled her into the house as she kicked and scratched the whole way. "You ever slap me again, you drunken bitch, I'll wear your little ass out." He then pushed her into the sofa. Bria immediately bounced back up just as Jack slapped her across her face.

She stood looking at him for a moment then jumped into his arms for a passionate kiss. She then ripped through the buttons on her blouse and flung it off to the side. As she raised her arms in the air signaling for Jack to take her, she stretched her arms around him again. "Come on, Jack. Right here. Let's do it right here on the table. I love when you take charge of me."

Jack picked Bria up and set her on the table. As he laid into her again and again, the table shook violently. Before it was all over, Bria pushed Jack off then grabbed hold of his manhood and finished him off with her lips.

With all of his stress gone for the moment, Jack carried Bria upstairs and laid her on his bed. The effects of the alcohol in her system began to take their toll, so she reached out for one last kiss before laying her head on the pillow and closing her eyes. With Bria fast asleep, Jack took the opportunity to enjoy a hot relaxing shower. Afterwards, he snuggled up to Bria and fell asleep.

Without any thoughts or stress, Jack's mind started to wander as he entered into a dream state. He was in a smoke-filled lounge looking at a man smoking a cigar and having a drink with some friends. The man seemed to be carefree. He also noticed it was the same man he had dreamed about before. Suddenly, there was a loud moan like a ship that was settling at the bottom of the ocean. The friends were now gone and the man was sitting alone. The cigar floated away as the man started to bleed from his head. There was another loud moan, then Jack woke up. He was soaked with sweat and shaking. He noticed Bria was still sleeping, so he eased out of bed and went down stairs.

It was still dark, but the sun was about to rise. Jack walked out onto his front porch and sat down. While a cool morning breeze blew by, he tried to figure out why he was having dreams about a man he'd never met. He also couldn't help but think about his last encounter with Ben. He was concerned because usually he understood Ben's anger, but after the episode in the office, he had no clue. Suddenly, the little light bulb in his head lit up. The last time Ben was over at the house, they sat on the porch discussing the box. When he was in

Ben's office, Ben was upset that he hadn't made a decision about the box. Jack remembered that Ben had tossed the key at him, but why be upset about it, and what did he do with the key?

As the sun started to rise, Bria emerged from the house with two cups of coffee. She handed one to Jack and snuggled up next to him. "Another bad dream?"

Jack took a sip of coffee as another cool breeze blew by. "I don't know why I'm having them. The man in the dream isn't familiar to me, and what really has me baffled is every dream is on *Titanic.* That's the really crazy part."

Bria sipped her coffee as the steam floated out of the cup. "Well, you told me about the high school project you were working on and how your dad became angry at you. Maybe all this stress you've been under has brought back some old memories."

Jack thought about it, and although he thought it was a stretch, it was the only thing that made sense. "It wasn't that my dad was angry at me; it was the project itself. I remember when he closed the book and laid it in front of me. The look he gave wasn't anger, but something else. I can't really put my finger on it. There was something else there. Anyway, I think I know why Ben is so upset."

Bria finished off her coffee and sat up to listen. "I don't know why you concern yourself with Ben's problems. He's old enough to take care of himself."

Jack smiled and gave her a little shoulder to shoulder nudge. "Yeah, I know, but this time the problem concerns me and that little box my dad left me. I think Ben would rather I not open it, but in thinking about the situation as a whole, I think Ben is upset at the fact my dad left me something personal and didn't do the same for him."

It was still early morning hours so Bria was still tired and didn't have any of her usual comebacks. "So, why don't you just take the box and open it up with Ben? That way you can share whatever is inside with him. I'm betting there's really nothing of any importance."

Jack knew Bria was good when it came to reasoning problems out, and this time was no different. He knew there wasn't anything in the box that couldn't be shared with Ben, knowing how close Ben was with his dad. Jack put his arm around Bria and pulled her close.

"You always have such good ideas. I knew there was a reason I keep you around."

Bria then stood up and opened up her robe. She straddled Jack and sat on his lap as she buried her breasts in his face. "Well then, Jack Kotter, how about this for an idea? How about we go back upstairs and you can give me some morning-time delight."

With Bria wrapped around him, Jack stood up, taking her with him. "I think that is a great idea. Maybe we can continue where we left off last night."

Bria was definitely up for that. As she climbed down from Jack's hips, she took him by the hand and led him into the house. "Well, this time, how about I start on you with my lips and you can finish me off with your explosion."

CHAPTER THIRTEEN

Later that morning, Jack was awake and feeling good. He called Ben and suggested they take the day off and spend it together. Ben wasn't exactly thrilled with the idea, so he countered with offering to buy Jack breakfast at the diner. When Jack arrived, he was surprised to see Ben was already there waiting. He was also surprised to see Dee getting out of his car. "Hey, Jack. Good times last night. You should have stayed a little longer."

As Dee walked into the diner, Ben stepped out of his car. "Well, kid, what's so important that you want to spend the day together?"

Jack could hear the tension in Ben's voice, but was determined to find out what the problem was. "Come on, Ben, you promised me breakfast. Let's go inside and talk."

Once in the diner, they saw Dee was already in full-swing. There weren't many people because of the rainy weather, so Dee asked them to seat themselves. The two men sat in their normal booth as Bobby Jo emerged from the kitchen. "Hey, fellas, how we doing this morning?"

Jack shot her a smile and asked for some menus. "So, you looked like you were enjoying yourself last night."

With her usual cracking of the gum, Bobby Jo placed the menus on the table. "Yeah, that was a great time. Dee and I danced all night long. By the way, who was the friend you were talking to? He was cute."

Jack thought for a second then laughed. "Are you kidding? I talked to a lot of people last night. What did he look like?"

As Bobby Jo was about to answer, Dee walked over. "Hey, Jack. What happen last night? You left too early."

Jack wasn't in the mood to air out his personal problems, so he used his go-to excuse of being tired. "Bobby Jo was about to tell me which one of my friends she was interested in."

But just when she was about to try again, Ben lashed out. "Are we gonna eat breakfast or did you bring me here to watch a God damn soap opera?"

After a brief silence, Bobby Jo took their orders and walked away. Dee was all too familiar with that tone, so she excused herself and went back to work. Jack was in high spirits, but Ben's outburst pushed him over the edge. "I love you like a father, Ben, but I'll be damned if you're going to make everyone's life miserable just because you're upset over some silly little box."

Just when Ben was about to bark back, Jack really laid into him. "You want to act like a little kid, then maybe you need to resign and go some place where you can be by yourself and wallow in your self-pity. I came here today with expectations of sharing with you whatever my dad left me. Now, we can sit like two civil men and talk this out, or I can get up and leave you to your own self-destruction. When you brought the box over to the house, I told you it was both of our responsibility."

Bobby Jo came to the table and put their food down. When she turned to walk away, Ben grabbed her hand. "I'm sorry, Bobby Jo. I've been trying to work my way through some personal feelings lately and haven't been doing a very good job."

Still cracking her gum, Bobby Jo leaned over and gave Ben a kiss on the cheek. "That's okay, sugar. I'll just expect a bigger tip than usual. Would you like to extend your apology to Dee?"

While Ben was asking for forgiveness, Jack started wolfing down breakfast. "So, Ben, does this mean you've come to your senses?"

While Bobby Jo went to get Dee, Ben turned his attentions to Jack. "Your father never spoke to me like that. What makes you think you're so privileged?"

Jack tried to keep from laughing while he finished chewing his food. "I don't think anyone has ever spoken to you like that, at least nobody that I know of. I just think you need to understand I think of you like a father, but you're not. You're my closest friend and business partner, and I can't think of anyone better to share whatever it is my dad left me."

As Dee slowly made her way to the table, Ben stood up and gave her a hug. She was reluctant but happy Ben's mood had improved. "Don't worry, Benjamin, I don't need a tip. You just give me some of what you gave me last night and then we can work on forgiveness." She gave Ben a peck on the lips and went back to work.

As Ben watched her shake as she walked away, he sat down and started in on his breakfast. "So you think you have this thing figured out?"

Jack took a drink of coffee and washed down some food. "As a matter of fact, I do. This whole thing with you started when you found that box. I think after you realized it might be something special, your feelings became hurt. Ever since then, you've been trying to talk me into discarding it. So when you realized I was waiting for the right time to open it, you became even more angry. There's only one thing I'm not really sure of. Are you more pissed off at my dad because he didn't include you in this one last cloak-and-dagger moment, or are you more pissed at me for not taking it seriously?"

Ben finished off his coffee and waved to Bobby Jo for a refill. "Listen, kid, I appreciate what you're trying to do and I commend you for having the balls to call me out. I'm not angry at either one of you, at least not anymore. Your father and I shared a lifelong friendship. We had some bad times and a multitude of good times. It was more of a disappointment when I found that box. After all your dad and I had been through. All the battles with competitors and trying to align ourselves with employees willing to sell information, or as you would call it, cloak-and-dagger moments. After all those years, your dad decided to leave you a mysterious gift that didn't include me. So yeah, I was hurt by that."

As Bobby Jo refilled the coffees, Jack gathered his thoughts. "I don't want you to think I was ignoring the box. It's just that we had so much going on with that whole China thing and then, on top of that, the board members being divided, and I just didn't want to open up a can of worms without first closing out some of the problems we were already working on. You taught me that."

Ben smiled because he knew Jack was right. "I'm proud of you, kid. You've shown me the patience it takes to run a company this size, and more importantly, you listened to your father and me and applied the knowledge we instilled in you. I know I offered to pay for breakfast, but you're the boss. You can afford it more then I. Now let's blow this popsicle stand and go to work."

Jack took one last drink of coffee as he wiped his mouth. "You're really something, Ben. Do you also need me to take care of Dee tonight?"

Reluctantly, Ben walked over to the counter where Dee was working the cash register. Smiling and shaking his head in disbelief, Jack slapped some money down on the table then waited by the door. After Bobby Jo cleared the table, she wasted no time continuing where she left off. "So, Jack, your friend with the glasses. Is he available?"

Jack had to think for a second and realized she was talking about Ethan. "Are you sure he had glasses? Maybe it was Dale. I was talking to him most of the night."

After a brief cringing of the face, Bobby Jo slapped Jack on the arm. "No, it wasn't Dale. I know Dale. He's a pig, just like all cops. Nothing but dirty dogs. I'm talking about that cute guy with glasses who left with Bria."

It's not that Jack didn't want to play matchmaker, but he just couldn't see the attraction. "That's my friend Ethan. He's also on my board of directors. Would you like to meet him?"

Almost immediately, the look on Bobby Jo went from cringe to Christmas. "Hell, no. Why don't the both of you come see me where I work down at Flashdancers. Then he can see me on stage, and afterwards, I can introduce myself."

Just then, Ben came walking over. "Okay, kid, let's go. Bobby Jo, we'll see you later."

As Ben walked out the door, Jack gave Bobby Jo a nod as he stood holding the door. "I'll talk to Ethan, but I have to warn you, he doesn't have a lot of experience with women."

Jack walked out to the parking lot where Ben was waiting. "Listen, Ben, I know you're anxious to get to work, but I brought the box with me. What do you say we go to your office and open this thing up? Maybe all these emotions we're having are for nothing."

Ben laughed because he knew Jack was right. "Okay, kid. Maybe we'll get a big laugh out of all this. I haven't had this many emotions since you were born."

As Ben drove away, Jack felt a sense of ease as if a huge weight was lifted. He felt good that Ben was going to be part of whatever was in the box. As he drove off the lot, Jack started to get that funny feeling that someone was watching him. He checked all of his mirrors and even his blind spot, but didn't see anything. He finally pulled into Kotter Industries with a sense of relief. After parking his car, Jack grabbed the box with enthusiasm and made a beeline for Ben's office. He was in such a hurry, he ran up four flights of steps instead of taking the elevator.

As Jack stepped onto the fifth floor, he received the usual warm welcome from the office workers. Normally, he would stop and make pleasant conversation, but that day was different. It was finally time to find out what his dad thought was so important to hide away until after his death. As he approached Ben's office, Hellen had a cup of coffee already waiting for him. He burst into Ben's office and found that Ben wasn't there. With some disappointment, he walked back out to speak with Hellen. "Where's Ben? He was supposed to be here waiting for me."

Hellen didn't say anything at first, but she knew Jack needed an answer. Just then, Hellen's phone rang. Instead of answering it, she shook her head in disgust and handed it to Jack. Jack hesitated, but then answered it. "Hello?"

It was Ben telling him to turn around. As he turned, Jack saw Ben sitting at his desk. "What the hell are you doing, Ben?"

Jack handed the phone back to Hellen and walked into the office. "I thought the plan was to meet here so we could open this box."

Ben laughed as he stepped out from behind his desk. "I'm sorry, kid. I just wanted to see the panic on your face when you saw I wasn't here."

Jack walked over and laid the box down on the desk. "Why did you do that? You're not really known for playing jokes like that."

Ben walked over to his wall safe and opened it up. "I wanted you to have an idea about the anxiety I've been feeling ever since I found that box in your dad's safe. I've been dying to know what was in it, but I didn't want you to know that. You see, kid, when your dad first told me about it, he gave me specific instructions. Although it's my recommendation to discard the damn thing, my curiosity has been killing me, and I'll tell you why. When I opened your dad's safe and saw the box, I saw that he left two keys to it. One for me and one for you. I guess when your dad thought up this plan, he wasn't quite sure how it would play out, so he wanted both of us to have a key just in case."

Jack pulled both keys from his pocket and studied them for a few seconds. "I knew my dad had total trust in you, but it must have driven you crazy knowing you could have opened it whenever you wanted. I'm really sorry, Ben."

Ben picked the box up and handed to Jack. "Don't be sorry, kid. I think you made the right choice. You made Kotter Industries your priority and handled your business. I'm proud of you. Now, let's see what your dad has in store for you."

Jack placed the box back down on Ben's desk and stared at it for a few seconds. "I'm glad my dad had sense enough to leave two keys because mine went missing for awhile. I found the damn thing in the laundry the other day."

Jack took a deep breath and looked at Ben. Ben smiled and nodded at Jack to encourage him to open the box. Jack looked at the key then pushed it into the keyhole. As he tried to turn it, there were a few brief squeals as the old mechanism began to tumble. Finally, the key stopped and the mechanism clicked. The lid to the box popped open and the smell of many years crept out and filled the area around Ben's desk. A few moments passed as Jack and Ben looked down at the contents.

Inside were some old papers that had turned yellow over the years and an old skeleton key. Ben reached down and grabbed the key and studied it up close. "I haven't seen a key like this since I don't know when. My God, it's probably been forty years or more."

Jack picked up one of the papers and unfolded it. It looked like part of a letter. He could tell it was his father's handwriting but didn't understand what it was about. "Hey, Ben, listen to this and see if it means anything to you.

"Suddenly, everyone became panic stricken. At first no one could move because they were in shock, but after the initial shock wore off, everyone started running. They ran in every direction. I don't know where they were running to. We were in the middle of the ocean.

"I remember my mom being in shock, with one hand covering her mouth, and she just kept looking around. It seemed like everyone was moving in slow motion, and at the same time, the many screams and loud crashes from furniture being knocked over didn't match what was going on. It was like the sound traveled behind the action.

"I could tell my mom was frightened because her other hand was wrapped around mine and she was squeezing really tight. I started to cry, not because of all the panic, but because my fingers were hurting. I briefly thought about pulling my hand away, but just then, she let go and quickly reached down and picked me up. She took a step in one direction but stopped. I don't think she was thinking clearly. She turned and headed out towards the deck. She tried her best to keep me from being bumped against, but it was impossible.

"Through all the yelling, I could hear a man's voice. 'Women and children only, women and children.' I laid my head on Mom's shoulder and I asked her where Dad was. I don't know if she ignored me or was just trying to pay attention to what was going on around us. I never saw my dad again."

Ben shook his head. "I don't know, kid. I've known your dad all my life. It sounds like he was part of some kind of disaster at sea, but your dad never liked deep water. Although, I did find it kind of strange when he would take his annual fishing trip. I don't even think he liked fishing. He never brought anything back. I don't know, kid. What's on the other papers?"

Jack unfolded another paper. "This one had a California address. Are we affiliated with anything in California?"

Ben looked at the address and once again, came up blank. "Not that I know of. Christ, this company has gotten so large over the years, I don't know half the stuff we control anymore. What else you have in that box?"

Jack pulled out another paper and unfolded it. "What the hell is this?" Jack handed the paper to Ben.

"These are coordinates. To what, I have no idea. We'll have to look them up and maybe the location can tell us something. Let's see that last paper."

Jack reached down and took out the last paper that was in the box. He unfolded it and started reading as the color left his face. He stopped and looked at Ben. "I think it's for you."

Ben took the letter and briefly skimmed it with his eyes. It was a personal letter from Jack Sr. written especially for Ben.

My dearest friend, Benjamin, I'm glad you are finally able to read this letter. I thought I would have more time, but as you can see, time never works in anyone's favor. I've known you all of your life, and it was a privilege to share with you all the joys life brought my way. This included my only child, whom you helped raise. Now I must ask of you one more favor. Both you and Jack are about to embark on an adventure which can only be described as impossible. But with your intelligence and the technologies that are available, I'm sure you will guide my son through difficult times and help him complete the tasks that are ahead of him.

My friend, thank you for all that you've meant to me. May God help you both through this journey and keep you safe. 1985.

With a single tear running down his face, Ben looked at Jack and handed him the letter. "I don't know what it means, kid. I don't know what the hell any of this means. Somehow your dad knew I would be around for you. I don't know what adventure he's talking about, but I gotta tell you, kid, I don't like the sound of it."

Jack gathered all the items and placed them back in the box. He closed it then sat it down. "Something isn't right, Ben. Obviously, there's more to the story, but I'm really worried."

Ben walked over and poured two drinks. As he made his way back to his desk, Ben swallowed one with one gulp and handed the other to Jack. "What the hell did we do, kid? I've had my fair share of being blindsided before, but I think this one definitely gets the booby prize."

Jack's mind was racing as he paced the floor. "My dad never talked about his parents. I know my grandfather died when my dad was young and my grandmother had to raise him herself. I never really had any interest in finding out any background information. I guess that's one of the downfalls when you grow up with money."

Ben kept going over all the times Jack Sr. went away on fishing trips just to return to talk about the big one that got away. "Can you think of anything, kid, anything at all that would tie all this together?"

Jack thought about it, but couldn't come up with anything. "I've never known my dad to be on anything bigger than a fishing boat, and like you said, he never wanted anything to do with deep water."

Ben stared at Jack for a moment contemplating whether or not to make the suggestion of locking the box and never opening it again. "It's not too late, kid. We can pretend we never opened this box and just walk away from it. I'll place it back in your dad's safe and we can forget all about it."

On one hand, Jack understood the reasoning behind Ben's words because Ben was a man who based his decisions on information he could readily comprehend. On the other hand, he couldn't believe Ben would turn down the last wishes of a lifelong friend. Jack walked over to the window and stared out into the morning sky. "My dad obviously had this planned out for a long time. That letter alone he wrote in 1985. There has to be some significance to that date. Did something happen with Kotter Industries during that year?"

Ben thought about it while he poured himself another drink. "Nothing unusual that I can remember. Your dad had his annual fishing trip, but funny thing, that was the one time your dad came back and didn't really talk about anything. As a matter of fact, that was the first time I had ever seen him bothered about anything."

Jack smiled because he thought about the time his dad had become upset over his school project. "Yeah, I know what you mean. I saw my dad get upset once and that was enough for me. Listen, Ben, I know you would rather see me walk away from this, but it's my dad. I don't think he would do something to hurt us or Kotter Industries. I'm asking you as a friend. Help me figure this thing out. I promise you, the minute I think this is some kind of disaster, we'll drop it like it never existed."

After taking a deep breath, Ben sighed and agreed. "One condition, kid. Whatever this is, your dad trusted me enough to see it through with you, so I call the shots up until we actually find out what the hell is going on. Got it?"

A big smile came onto Jack's face as he felt a huge relief. He was glad Ben was going to take the lead on wherever this secret was going to take them.

Ben opened the box back up and wrote down all the information they needed to get started, then he locked it and placed it in his safe. "Listen, kid, clear your schedule for the next week or two. We have some traveling to do. I'll have Hellen find out who your dad booked his fishing trips with. Hopefully they can answer a few questions about your dad and maybe give us some idea on these coordinates. I'll also see if Robert can help us out since he's an old navy guy. You have Bonnie book us a flight out to California and book a couple of hotel rooms. If you don't mind, I'm going to hang on to this skeleton key so it doesn't wind up in your laundry."

Jack turned and walked to the door laughing. "Yeah, I think you're right. I'll see you later." Jack walked down the hall to his office and told Bonnie to book the flights and reservations.

He was about to close his door when Ethan came in. "Hey, Jack, you feeling lucky tonight?"

Jack sat down and ruffled through the pile of mail on his desk. "What's so special about tonight?"

Ethan helped himself to a drink and sat down. "Nothing. Just thought we could go out and have some fun."

Jack stopped momentarily then continued flipping through the paperwork. "Well, now that you mention it. Yeah, let's go out. I know just the place we can go and I think you're going to have a great time"

Ethan kept his thoughts to himself, but he didn't like the way Jack was sounding like he was too sure of himself. "What are you up to, Jack? You normally don't tell me stuff like that."

Jack stopped with the mail and walked over to the minibar. "Don't worry, I didn't want a drink. Remember the other night at the club when you were eying up that guy?"

Ethan remembered, but was trying not to. "Don't remind me. That would've been such a disaster."

Jack finished off his shot as he walked back to his desk. "Well, as you were checking out that guy, a friend of mine was checking you out. She's a really nice girl, but she doesn't want me to introduce you two. She wants the opportunity to approach you on her own terms."

Ethan lit up like a Christmas tree, but still had reservations. "I don't know, Jack. It's not that I don't trust you, but at the same time, I don't like surprises. Is she hot looking?"

Jack shook his head with a smile as he started back with his mail. "She's incredibly hot. She works down at the diner on 110. She also works a second job at a club in Manhattan. So, are you interested?"

Like a jack-in-the-box, Ethan popped up from his chair. "Hell, yeah, I'm definitely in. You just better be right about her looks."

Jack leaned back in his chair as he maneuvered it back and forth. "It's not all about the looks, you know. She does have a nice personality, but I'm guessing that doesn't matter this early in the game."

Ethan wasn't really listening at that point. He was too busy thinking about preparations. "I gotta go, Jack. I gotta get ready."

As Ethan turned to walk, out Jack jumped up laughing. "Hold on, Casanova, it's only noon. Listen, go do your thing. I'll arrange for Casey to pick us up and take us out tonight."

Ethan was all too eager to agree. "Sounds great, but what about the hottie? Will she be working?"

Jack assured Ethan everything would be set. "Don't worry. I'll make sure she's working, but not all night. You, me, and Bria can have an early dinner then swing by the club. Afterwards, the four of us can go someplace a little more romantic and have some drinks."

Ethan agreed as he walked out. "You're the best, Jack. See you tonight."

Jack sat at his desk thinking about the contents of the box. Although he felt good about Ben helping, he couldn't help but think his dad was counting on him for something deeper in meaning than just trying to figure out some puzzle he had left behind.

Just then, Bonnie came in and confirmed their flight and hotel. "I've printed out your flight information. Your flight leaves in the morning."

Just as Jack walked out to go tell Ben, Ben was on his way up the hallway. "Come on, kid, we're going to your dad's office. Hellen didn't have the information I needed because, apparently, your dad made his own arrangements when it came to his trips." As Ben brushed pass Jack, he pulled out a set of keys and unlocked the office door.

"Listen, kid, I know you haven't been in here for a while, but I need you to concentrate."

As the door opened and Ben walked in, Jack paused for a moment before stepping in behind Ben. Ben walked over and hit the button that operated the drawer. "You okay, kid?"

Jack was standing just within the door. "Yeah, I'm good. It's been a long time. I was just remembering how my dad would let me play secret agent whenever he needed to go into his safe. He would always let me press the buttons." As the drawer popped out, Ben stood up straight and backed away from the desk. Well, come on over here, secret agent man, and press this other button for me. I'm getting too old to be bending down that far. Jack smiled like a little kid as he walked over and sat at his dad's desk. As Ben waited for the wall to open, Jack reached into the drawer and pressed the secret button for the wall safe. Jack sat reminiscing about his earlier years, as Ben opened the safe.

"Come on, kid, get with it. Check your dad's rolodex for a name or a phone number." Ben pulled some old files from the safe and sifted through them as Jack ran his fingers through the rolodex.

"Hey, Ben, check this out. *Just by Chance.* Sounds like the name of a boat or a horse to me, and there's a number."

Ben walked over and snatched the card from the rolodex. "What are you waiting for? Dial the damn number. Jesus, kid, you want me to do everything?"

Jack smiled as he dialed the number, but he heard that all too familiar phrase telling him the number had been disconnected. "Sorry, Ben, dead end."

Ben walked over and slammed the safe closed. "Will you get your head out of your ass. Look up the name of the boat. See if it was registered. Come on, kid, you gotta at least step up to the plate if you're gonna take a swing at this."

With grumbling and disgust, Ben walked out of the office leaving Jack to bask in his memories. Jack hung around for a little while longer thinking about times spent running around the office while his dad conducted business. After he realized how late it was getting, he phoned Bria to let her in on the plan for Ethan. Afterwards, he said his goodbyes for the day and went home to get ready for the evening.

Later in the evening, Casey pulled into Jack's driveway with the limousine. Jack emerged from his house looking sharp with a three-quarter length leather jacket. Casey was waiting with the door open. "You look great tonight, Jack."

Jack smiled as he climbed in. "Thanks, Casey. We're going to pick Bria up and then Ethan. I want you to take us to Delmonico's Restaurant for dinner." Opened in 1837, Delmonico's was one of New York's oldest restaurants. Casey shut the door and made his rounds picking up Bria, then Ethan. They had a few drinks as Casey drove them into Manhattan.

Ethan was still excited because Jack hadn't told him what nightclub Bobby Jo worked at. "Come on, Jack, just a hint. I won't say anything. Please, Bria, talk some sense into him for me."

As Casey pulled to the front of Delmonico's, Jack and Bria shook their heads laughing. As Casey opened the door, Jack stepped out and helped Bria out. "You're going to drive yourself crazy, or worse, you're going to drive Bria and me even crazier. Let's just have a nice dinner and enjoy the evening."

At dinner, Ethan kept throwing out subtle hints and trying to get Bria or Jack to slip up, but nothing worked. He finally gave up and decided to shift gears with the conversation and enjoy the food and wine. "So Jack, is the company still doing well with Y2K? Is our computer system still recognizing the new millennium?"

That was one problem Jack hadn't been too worried about, because his dad was one of few people who'd had the insight to look ahead. Although Jack Sr. died before the new millennium was even thought about by most, he had already hired a team of experts to study the problem and create a solution. "We were ready before it was even thought about as a problem. Those federal watchdog committees were breathing down everyone's neck and we were already in position to make an easy transition."

As everyone finished dinner, the waitress approached to ask if anyone wanted dessert. Ethan quickly declined as he glanced over at Jack hoping he would get the hint. Jack smiled and politely declined. "I think our dessert is going to come later tonight."

As Jack paid the bill, Ethan and Bria waited outside for Casey. Shortly after, Jack joined them just as Casey came pulling up. Ethan was so excited, he stepped in front of Bria when Casey opened the door. After a momentary pause, Jack and Bria stepped in and made themselves comfortable.

During the brief silence, Jack poured Bria a drink and grabbed two beers for himself and Ethan. "I'm glad to see your manners haven't been affected through all your excitement."

Ethan opened his beer and took a drink. "Sorry, Bria, I wasn't thinking. Come on, Jack, you can't keep it a secret much longer.

Jack took a nice long drink then reached over and pressed the intercom. "Hey, Casey, let's take a drive over to Flashdancers."

After realizing what Jack said, Ethan nearly dropped his beer. "What are you doing, Jack? This is no time for strippers. We're supposed to be going to see my date." Ethan looked to Bria for support. "I know you don't want to see strippers."

Bria couldn't help but feel sorry for Ethan, but she played along with Jack. She shrugged her shoulders with a smile. "Actually, I wouldn't mind seeing some strippers tonight. I might see some new moves I can try out on Jack."

As he rolled his eyes, Ethan took another drink. "Come on, Jack, don't do this to me. Let's skip the strippers for tonight."

After downing the last of his beer, Jack decided to let Ethan in on the plan. "This is why you're on my board of directors, Ethan. You don't let anything slip by you. I promised you dinner and I told you we would go visit your date where she works and have drinks."

Ethan sat for a minute and thought about it. Suddenly, the light in his brain started to flicker. His eyes grew big and his jaw dropped. "No way. Are you serious?" Ethan stared as Jack smiled and shook his head yes.

"What'ya say, Ethan? You still want to skip the strippers tonight?"

Ethan nearly leaped into Jack's lap as his excitement reached his libido. "No way, Jack. Are you jerking me around?" Ethan turned to Bria with a bewildered look. "Is he jerking me around, because I've been to that place and the women there are almost too gorgeous."

Bria handed Ethan another beer. "You'll be alright, Ethan. Just don't act like an idiot and you'll do just fine."

As Casey rounded the corner of Broadway, Flashdancers came into view. To Jack and Bria's surprise, Ethan was very calm, almost surreal. Casey pulled the limo to the front door, where they were met by a doorman. He opened the limo door so the trio could step out. Casey quickly made his way around to make sure the three made it out and to let Jack know he would be back later to pick them up. When Jack opened the club door, Bria walked in, then Ethan. The three stood within the door for a moment waiting for their eyes to adjust, then Jack spotted a table that was next to the main stage. As they took their seats, a waitress took their drink orders. She recognized Ethan almost immediately.

"Hey, Ethan, how are you? I see you brought some friends with you tonight."

Feeling somewhat embarrassed, Ethan blushed because he didn't want Jack and Bria to think bad of him for being a regular at a strip club. Jack stood up and introduced himself and Bria then let the waitress know they were there for somebody in particular.

After Jack whispered Bobby Jo's name in her ear, her expression became clear. "Oh, yeah, she told me you were coming by tonight. She'll be up in a little while. I'll get your drinks. Enjoy the show."

As Jack sat down, Bria leaned over into Ethan. "So, big boy, you know this place pretty well?"

Ethan might have been embarrassed, but he wasn't going to let Bria get to him. "I know many places, including the one I carried you out of the other night." Bria understood the point and decided to leave Ethan to his fantasies.

As the waitress set the drinks on the table, the music started and the lights dimmed. Then the announcer introduced the next girl. "Now on stage for your enjoyment, and making her New York debut, introducing Strawberry Delight."

Suddenly, appearing out of the smoke came a fair-skinned bombshell with legs up to her neck. She had strawberry colored hair and was wearing a schoolgirl uniform with stiletto heels. She grabbed one of the stage poles and swung around letting her long hair glide through the air. As Jack, Bria, and Ethan looked on, she mesmerized them with her erotic dance moves. Then, with a blink of an eye, off came the see-through blouse, letting her breasts jiggle and breathe.

As the routine heated up the stage, Jack ordered another round of drinks. "I can see why you come here, Ethan. Maybe we can set up one of our corporate parties here. I think everyone would have a blast."

Ethan thought about it then laughed. "Yeah, maybe we can get Linda up on stage. I'm sure she could get some of the old guys to pop off." Just when Jack and Ethan looked back towards the stage, off came the skirt showing everyone the real reason why her name was strawberry delight.

As Ethan and Jack were checking out the obvious, Bria was concentrating more on the outfit and moves. "What'ya think, Jack? Maybe we can get a pole installed in the bedroom." Jack didn't mind the idea but declined to comment. Ethan was too busy enjoying the show to even know what was being talked about.

As the smoke cleared and the music came to an end, the lights flickered back on and the beauty faded off stage. Ethan turned to Jack in order to get some kind of response, but with Bria there, that wasn't going to happen. "So, Jack, when am I supposed to meet this mystery girl? Is she a waitress here or one of the bartenders?"

Just then, the lights dimmed again as the announcer introduced yet another girl. "Hey, everyone, I hope you're enjoying your night, because we have a real treat for you. Making her way to the stage is one of Flashdancers' most popular performers. Get your Andrew Jacksons ready and give a big warm welcome to Bo Bo Bodacious."

Ethan lit up with a smile as he took a drink of his beer. "You gotta see this girl, Jack. She's incredible." The lights momentarily went black, and as they came back on, Bobby Jo was on stage wearing a 1950s-style housewife dress with an apron. She had a dust rag in one hand and a frying pan in the other with a rap around her hair.

Ethan leaned over the table to explain the scenario. "She has a few routines, but in this one, she's playing the bored housewife that cheats on her husband."

When the music started, three male dancers dressed in home improvement clothing stepped onto the stage. As they danced around Bobby Jo, she threw the dust rag and frying pan off to the side. With a provocative walk, she maneuvered around the stage brushing up against each guy as her hand glided across their manhoods. Jack and Bria watched Ethan as he lost himself in Bobby Jo's fantasy. As the next song started, one of the male dancers untied Bobby Jo's apron and tossed it to the side, while another unraveled the rap from her head and threw it into the crowd. As the third male dancer slipped in behind Bobby Jo, he lifted her dress as they both started to grind to the music. Suddenly, another male dancer ripped the dress from her body and Bobby Jo lit up the crowd with her 40DD breasts. The crowd stood on their feet, clapping as Bobby Jo grabbed the male dancer by the back of his head and buried his face in between her twin mountains.

While one grinded and the other enjoyed his view, the third stooped down and came up between her legs dancing and rubbing his cheeks on her inner thighs. As the four separated, Bobby Jo, broke out into a pole spinning dance, letting the crowd know she had been liberated. As the music started to die down, it was the male dancers' cue to make their exit. One by one, as they walked off stage, Bobby Jo slipped her tongue deep down their throats, giving the audience one last picture in their minds to fantasize about. When only Bobby Jo remained on stage, the lights went black as one last song started to play.

Because the table Ethan was sitting at was directly next to the stage, Bobby Jo was able to dance her way over and stand almost directly over top of him. As the strobe light came on, Bobby Jo started to twist, turn, and bend over as she placed herself as close as she could to Ethan. When the music died down, Bobby Jo sat on the edge of the stage and straddled her legs around Ethan's shoulders. As Ethan sat in awe, Bobby Jo leaned forward and placed her breasts in Ethan's face. She then slid her tongue across Ethan's lips then up the front of his face. The crowd was in silence and almost shocked as Bobby Jo stood up and gave Ethan a wink then walked off stage.

Jack and Bria knew Bobby Jo was going to do something special for the night, but even they were stunned over her performance. Ethan was so taken his jaw was still hanging as it dangled over his beer. "Did you see that, Jack? I've been coming here for awhile and I've never been part of anything like that. That was incredible."

As bold as Bria was, she didn't dare ruin Ethan's moment after all that. "Wow, Ethan. That was a real treat. I can't believe she picked you over everyone else. Maybe you can buy her a drink later."

Although Ethan was still on cloud nine, he didn't forget the original reason why he was there. "Probably not. I still have to meet

Jack's mystery woman. Which reminds me, it's getting kind of late, Jack. When is my date supposed to show up?"

Just then, the waitress walked over with another round of drinks and set them on the table. As she walked away, Bobby Jo, who had gotten dressed, sat down next to Ethan and introduced herself. "Hello, Ethan, I'm Bobby Jo. How are you?"

Ethan who always has problems talking to women was speechless. He just sat and stared until finally, Jack had to intervene. "Hey, Ethan, Bobby Jo works down at the 110 Diner. She was hoping you would buy her a drink tonight."

Still in awe, Ethan just didn't get it. "Um, sure. Whatever you want. I gotta tell you, that was an incredible performance tonight. I've been here a few times and have seen your acts, but I've never seen anything like that."

Bobby Jo was also nervous, but she did her best not to let on. She ordered her drink and continued with the conversation. "So Ethan, what do you do?"

Ethan finally calmed down to a point where he could talk and be himself. "Well, I'm one of the board members at Kotter Industries. Among other things, I help make decisions for the company."

Bobby Jo already knew that, but she needed a way to break the ice. Ethan was oblivious to the fact that it was Bobby Jo whom he was supposed to be meeting. "I gotta tell you, Bobby Jo, as much as I would love to sit here all night and talk, I was supposed to be meeting someone tonight."

Bobby Jo smiled and took it in stride. "I understand. It's getting pretty late, though. Are you sure she's coming?"

Ethan turned to Jack hoping he would have an answer. "Well, Ethan, she's actually been here for a while."

Just then, Bobby Jo stood up and reintroduced herself. She leaned over and gave Ethan a little peck on the cheek and apologized. "I had Jack bring you here tonight so maybe we could get to know each other. I'm really sorry for the deception. I thought it would be fun." At first, Ethan was intimidated, but he soon let go of any ill will when Bobby Jo took him by the hand and led him over to the bar for a more private conversation.

At Bria's request, they stuck around for a few more shows then called Casey to pick them up. Bria walked outside while Jack stopped and talked to Ethan. "Casey is on his way so we're going to get ready to leave."

Ethan and Bobby Jo had had a few drinks and were getting to know one another. "That's fine, Jack. I think we're going to hang out for a while longer then maybe get some breakfast."

Jack already knew what that meant, so he said his goodbyes. "Alright, I have to get up early for my flight, so enjoy and I'll talk to both of you later."

Jack walked out just when Casey was pulling up. After a good long laugh, Jack made sure Bria was taken home first because he knew if he let her talk him into staying at his house, he would never get any sleep, especially after what they saw that night.

CHAPTER FOURTEEN

Early the next morning, Casey drove Jack and Ben to the airport. The flight wasn't leaving until 9:00 a.m., so they sat and had some breakfast. Jack couldn't help but think about when Ben suggested he go see Bobby Jo and her act. "You should warn a guy first before you send him to see Bobby Jo. I think the show she did took everyone by surprise."

Ben was busy chewing his food and took a drink of his coffee in order to talk. "Listen, kid, all I can do is point you in the right direction. It's up to you to figure the rest out. I've seen a few of her shows. Which one did she do?"

Jack shook his head and smiled. "She did the one dressed as a housewife that cheats on her husband, with three guys on stage simulating sex acts. It was incredible. You should have seen the expression on Ethan's face when he found out we took him there as her date. Talk about priceless."

As Jack laughed it off, Ben just shook his head. "You gotta be kidding me. She's interested in Ethan? That boy doesn't know what he's dealing with."

After what Ben just said about pointing someone in the right direction, Jack looked at Ben and laughed. "Really? You just told me you have to let people find their own way and now you're being hypocritical of Ethan. I think their personalities will complement each other."

Ben stopped eating and wiped his lips then took a drink of coffee. "Listen, kid, before you brow beat me, I'm just stating my opinion. You place a piece of meat into a hungry tiger's cage, there's only one outcome."

Jack finished off his breakfast then drank the rest of his orange juice. "We'll just have to wait and see. I think you'll be surprised."

As the waitress placed the check on the table, Ben finished the rest of his coffee. "Listen, kid, I like Ethan. He's bright and full of energy. He's open-minded and stands up for himself. That's a great combination in the boardroom. I would hate to see his life get derailed because of a broken heart, not to mention the fact she's going to wear his ass out in the bedroom on a daily basis."

Jack looked at the check and pulled out his wallet. "I don't suppose you would like to pay this time?" Ben didn't say a word. His silence spoke for him. Jack already knew the answer. He just liked to poke fun at Ben, as usual.

As Ben was busy in the men's room, Jack took care of the check and walked to the departure gate. As he sat and waited, he thought about the contents of the box and what might be waiting for him in California. In the back of his mind, he was hoping it was nothing, but knowing his dad, it was probably something big.

When Ben finished, he joined Jack at the checkout gate. "Listen, kid, there was something that I wanted to talk to about at breakfast, but I didn't get the chance."

Jack knew when Ben started off with those words it was usually something bad. "Alright, Ben, come on. Let me have it."

Ben smiled, which was rare in itself, giving Jack a sense of relief. "Listen, kid, I had Hellen run down the address in California. It's the house your dad built for your mom right after he asked her to marry him."

Jack didn't know what to say. With a blank look on his face, he just stared at Ben. "Why did I not know that? I spent most of my childhood in that house."

Ben really didn't have an answer, nor was he worried about it. "I don't know, kid. Over time, we tend to forget things like that."

Jack stood up and looked out at some of the planes that were coming and going. "I haven't been out there since mom died. Wasn't it destroyed by an earthquake in eighty-nine?"

As Ben stood up and walked over to Jack, airport personnel announced that their flight would be boarding in five minutes. "The house was only partially destroyed. Since the house was built for your mom, your dad didn't see any point in having it rebuilt. Right after your dad passed, some kids got in there and set it on fire. Didn't do much damage, though."

Jack removed the boarding pass from his pocket to make sure everything was in order. "So, what kind of shape is the house in now?"

Ben motioned Jack towards the gate and pulled out his boarding pass. "Well, I'm not sure. I haven't been out there since the quake. I think the company hired someone to manage the property. I do know there's a separate out building on the property. Your dad had it built shortly after the death of your mom. My guess is that it's still there, if the quake didn't destroy it."

As Jack and Ben boarded the plane, they quickly found their seats. Of course, Ben didn't waste any time asking the stewardess for a drink. He reached over as the stewardess walked by and pinched her on the thigh. "I'll take a Jack and Coke when you get a chance, sweetie."

The stewardess turned to Ben with a smile as she quickly reprimanded him. "You touch me again, old man, and I'll twist your fingers off. You and your friend are going to have to wait until we're in the air for drinks."

As she walked away, Ben turned to Jack who was already laughing. "Listen, kid, if you want something, don't be afraid to go after it. Hot and sassy. Just the way I like'em. You watch, kid, I'll have her begging for me before the end of the flight."

Still laughing, Jack buckled his seatbelt and made himself comfortable. "I remember my dad telling me he drove down the coast with my mom from San Francisco. I'm guessing we're not doing that."

Ben stood up and took off his jacket then sat and buckled himself in. "No, kid. I like you but not enough to drive all the way down the coast with you. Bonnie has us flying into San Francisco then chartering a private jet to take us down to Pebble Beach. There should be a rental there waiting. It's not too far of a drive from there."

After takeoff, it wasn't too long before the stewardess came around taking orders for drinks and food. As she approached Ben, he apologized almost immediately. "I didn't mean to come off that strong, sweetie; I just think you're really beautiful."

Although Ben shot her puppy dog eyes, she knew he wasn't being sincere. Still, she decided since it was a long flight, she would let him off the hook. "Alright, dirty man, we'll let it go for now. Besides, there's a cuteness about you."

As the stewardess walked away, Ben watched her hips move from side to side. Jack nudged Ben's arm as he shook his head. "I can't believe you. How do you do that?"

Ben let out a quick laugh as he contemplated letting Jack in on his secret. "Listen, kid, most of you young studs have nothing to rely on but yourselves when it comes to your sex drive. On the other end of the spectrum is us old guys. We rely on modern chemistry, which is more reliable in bed. All the ladies know we're a sure thing. My secret formula is one ExtenZe mixed with half a Viagra and a couple of drinks. Just like the energizer bunny, I can go all night."

After lunch and a few drinks, Jack sat quietly watching the clouds float by. He was tired, but had too much on his mind to sleep. He found himself remembering his childhood in California with his mom and dad, and how happy everyone was. As he sat and stared aimlessly out the window, Ben took comfort in the fact the airline had the latest edition of The Wall Street Journal. "Listen, kid. It's the new millennium and the world is still here. All those idiots that predicted a global collapse are probably kicking themselves in the ass. Your dad and I started making investments after the Korean War, but we always shared the idea of investing more into our business and the people that worked for us. Are you hearing what I'm saying, kid?"

Just then, Jack pulled his face away from the window. "Is there a point to all this or are you having one of your moments?"

Ben's face became a little red, but he kept his cool knowing they were on a plane. "Yes, there's a point to all this. I'm sitting here looking at the paper and reading about how some of these companies are merging and buying each other out. If we were at work right now, I'd tell you to take out your pen and pad and take notes."

Jack smiled and took the paper from Ben. "We buy out companies all the time, so what's the difference?"

Ben snatched the paper back from Jack and folded it. "The difference is we make a good solid plan and then execute with reason. These buffoons nowadays buy out their competitors like they're buying a cup of coffee. They're always thinking bigger is better, and that's almost never the case. Your father taught that to me and he was right."

Jack went back to staring out the window while Ben was left feeling his business lesson for the day had gone by the wayside. "Listen, kid, if you see something interesting out the window, come and get me. In the meantime, I need to stretch my legs and find that cute stewardess."

As Ben stood up and walked to the rear of the plane, Jack slumped down in his chair and closed his eyes. As he fell asleep, the plane was forced to make maneuvers to avoid some bad weather. As the turbulence shook the passengers, the plane rose above the clouds. Unaware of the uncomfortable ride, Jack entered into his dream world. He could hear music playing as a band came out of a fog. They had on early century clothing and were playing ballroom music. Suddenly, the band started to lose their balance as the soothing music abruptly stopped. Out of nowhere, a tidal wave of water washed over the band silencing them forever.

Startled from his sleep, Jack opened his eyes and sat up in his chair. As he took a quick look around, he could still hear the music from his dream. When Jack turned to see where the music was coming from, he noticed an elderly couple sitting behind him listening to a portable CD player. "I don't mean to interrupt, but what is that music you're listing to?"

The elderly man smiled with pride as he turned the music off. "I'm sorry, young man, I hope we weren't disturbing you."

Jack paused then wiped the sleep from his eyes. "No, sir. Not at all. I was just wondering about the music."

The elderly man opened the CD player and took the disc out to show Jack. "I'm sorry, young man, you can't buy this in a store. My grandson made this for me. He took my collection of music and put them all together so I could enjoy them anytime."

Although Jack was feeling strained with the dream still fresh in his mind, he let out a brief, pleasant smile and continued pondering the music. "That was very nice of your grandson. Would you happen to know anything about that particular piece you were just listening to?"

Jack could tell the man was delighted that he was so interested in the music. "Oh, yes. It's called Bethany. You probably don't know it, but it comes from a hymn called "Nearer, My God, to Thee." The elderly man smiled as he rolled his eyes. "They just don't make music like this anymore. My wife and I like to listen because we don't like flying and it helps us stay focused on Jesus, Our Savior."

Just then, Ben came prancing down the aisle with a silly smirk on his face. "Hey, kid, I see you finally came out of your shell and decided to be sociable."

Jack took the joke in stride as he excused himself from the elderly couple. "Thank you for the conversation and thank you for the information about the music."

When Jack turned to sit, Ben plopped down in his seat with his usual subtleties. "So, what the hell was that all about?"

Jack slowly sank back into his seat as he glared at Ben. "What is your problem? Why do you have to be so rude all the time?"

Still with his smirk, Ben glared back at Jack. "That's two questions. Which one do you want the answer to?"

Still feeling the effects of the dream, Jack turned to continue looking out his window. "You really get on my nerves sometimes." Ben paused as he opened his Wall Street Journal. "Come on, kid, I'm only yanking your chain."

Jack thought about it for a moment and apologized. "You seem to have the ability to yank my chain at the wrong times."

Ben stopped reading as a look of concern crept on to his face. "What's the problem, kid? Did something happen while I was gone?"

Jack pulled his face from the window as he contemplated telling Ben about his dream. "Sometimes I think I'm going crazy. I don't know if it's the pressure at work or just the stress of life itself."

Ben crumpled his paper as he tried to figure out what Jack was talking about. "I don't understand your generation. You have everything you could ever ask for and then some, and you still complain about stress."

Once again, Jack took Ben's comments in stride. "I've been having these weird dreams periodically and I can't figure out why. I think they're connected, but I don't know how. It really bothers me that I can't figure it out."

Ben could see Jack was hurting, and just like a father, he felt bad because he didn't know how to help. "Listen, kid, I don't have an answer for you. Maybe it's all the strain you've been under. All this nonsense about whatever your dad was working on, along with trying to handle this company and keep Bria happy at the same time."

Ben reached over and placed his hand on Jack's shoulder. "Why don't you take some time off when we get back. Maybe take Bria someplace nice. Spend a few weeks together just you two."

Very few times in his life had Jack ever seen Ben sincere, and this was definitely one of those rare moments. "I think you're right, Ben. I thought I was tough enough to handle everything, but I guess I ran into some unexpected problems. The death of Bobby and now this whole secret box thing my dad had going on. Sometimes I feel like just letting it all go."

Ben could hear the sorrow in Jack's voice and offered him some words of wisdom. "Listen, kid, people like you and I go through life thinking nothing bad will ever happen, but you have to try to stay away from that kind of attitude. My brother and I and your dad worked our fingers to the bone all our lives to build this corporation, and now, as fate would have it, it's been dropped into your lap. Remember, Kotter Industries is pretty much self-sufficient. All you have to do is show up every now and then and guide it in the right direction. Personal problems are exactly that. They belong to you. They're personal."

Jack tried to keep up with Ben's words, but at times it could be difficult. "So, what you're saying is I shouldn't throw all of my problems into one pot and expect to solve them with one swipe of my magic wand."

Ben smiled as he opened up his paper. "You get the idea, kid."

While Ben read about what was going on in the business world, Jack sat quietly pondering Ben's latest words. He went back to thinking about growing up and walking around the office building with Ben as he conducted business and socialized with the secretaries. Most of the time, it was the latter. He thought about asking the elderly couple more about the type of music they were listening to, but when he turned to speak, he noticed they had both fallen asleep holding hands.

Ben finally finished reading his paper and decided to lounge back and close his eyes, but not before Jack posed some questions. "Where exactly did you go when I was talking to the couple behind us?"

With some irritation, Ben sat back up. "Come on, kid, wasn't it obvious?"

Jack thought for a moment, but had no answer. "I don't know. You were gone for too long to be in the restroom and stepping out for some fresh air is out of the question."

Ben looked behind him and saw the elderly couple asleep, then looked up and down the aisle. He leaned over and spoke softly into Jack's ear. "I was renewing my membership for the Mile High Club. I knew that stewardess liked me, but damn was she hot."

Jack couldn't help but laugh and it felt really good. Though it was just temporary, it felt like all of the stress had suddenly left his body. "Do you even know her name?"

Ben thought about it for a second then blurted out something that sounded like a guess. "Maggie, Margaret, whatever. It doesn't matter. We're supposed to get together in a couple of weeks when she's back in New York. I'll find out then. Now if you're done interrogating me, I would like to take a nap."

As Ben lounged back and closed his eyes, Jack took the opportunity to snatch The Wall Street Journal from his lap. With Ben sleeping and Jack reading the paper, the rest of the trip was relaxing and quiet.

A few hours later, they landed safely in San Francisco. With a slight jolt, the wheels hit the ground and woke Ben. As the plane approached the gate and came to a stop, the intercom came on with instructions. Jack and Ben readied themselves to disembark. When the aisle was clear, they made their way up the Jetway into San Francisco International Airport. As they emerged from the gate, Ben felt a tug on his arm. When he turned, the stewardess was there waiting for him. When Jack noticed Ben was no longer beside him, he turned to see him holding hands with her.

"Hey, Ben, I'm going to make a phone call to confirm our reservations, and then I'll pick up our luggage. You have fun with your lady friend." Ben barely heard what Jack said and really didn't care. As he trotted off in the opposite direction, Jack made his way down to baggage claim.

A little while later, Ben caught up to Jack, who was waiting at the taxi stand. Once again, Ben had that silly smirk on his face. "Hey, kid, glad you had the common decency to wait for me."

Jack was tired and didn't feel like playing into Ben's comment. He just smiled and shook his head. As the taxi driver loaded their bags, Ben and Jack climbed into the back seat. Jack knew Ben had something to say, but he was trying to avoid any conversation dealing with his sexploits.

Jack leaned forward and asked the driver to take them to the Hyatt Regency, but the driver didn't understand. Luckily, Jack had a brochure in his pocket and showed the driver. The driver gave a pleasant smile and shook his head yes then continued to exit the airport. As Ben watched, he couldn't help but add his charm to the situation. "Damn foreigners. How the hell can you get a job here and not be able to speak English? For that matter, how the hell do you get a damn driver's license?"

Jack was hoping for a quiet ride to the hotel, but quickly realized it wasn't going to happen. "Come on, Ben, you just can't give anyone a break, can you?"

Ben smiled then let out a rare laugh. "You want to know something, kid? You don't get to where I'm at by giving breaks."

As the taxi maneuvered in and out of traffic, Jack couldn't help but notice all the people who were crowding the sidewalks. "What about you? Didn't Sergis take a chance in hiring you when he and my dad bought their first steel mill? And what about all the workers who helped make Kotter Industries what it is today?"

As Ben thought for a moment, he smiled with pride. "You're absolutely right, kid. But it was a lot different back then. People were grateful for what they had and they worked hard to earn it. Nowadays it seems like half the population wants to stay at home and work in their pajamas. They don't get up until late afternoon, then they stay on the computer the rest of the day. Lazy bastards."

Jack knew Ben was frustrated with the younger generation, but he was having too much fun getting him all worked up. "So what does any of that have to do with this poor guy not speaking English?" Ben's face grew red and Jack knew he was about to explode.

"Listen, kid, don't try to slap me with your liberal attitude. I don't have a problem with people wanting to succeed no matter where they're from. My problem is this country isn't what it used to be. We're not the land of opportunity anymore. There's only so much to go around and it's rapidly disappearing. As our national debt grows more and more, our resources are being depleted."

Jack saw how upset he made Ben, so he didn't say any more. He figured if he didn't ask any more questions, Ben would just calm down and relax. But Ben wasn't finished. "I don't know, kid. This world is advancing faster than I can keep up. Maybe I need to retire so then I can sleep 'til the late afternoon."

Jack could hear the tone of Ben's voice start to wind down, not that he took him seriously about retiring. "You retire? I don't think so. You have too much fun tormenting the members of the board. Besides, who else am I going to fuss and fight with?"

As the taxi arrived at the Hyatt, Ben had a half-smile on his face. "Yeah, I guess you're right, kid. I live for all the hostile confrontations, and yes, I get off on tormenting those damn board members."

Jack and Ben stepped out of the taxi while the taxi driver unloaded their suitcases. "By the way, friends, my English is quite good. It's just that I'm deaf in one ear, and sometimes I can't hear the first words you speak."

Ben was stunned momentarily, but quickly apologized. "I'm sorry, son. Please don't take my words personally. Far be it from me to condemn someone from trying to better themselves."

Luckily, the driver was lighthearted and didn't take offense to Ben's comments. "That's okay, sir, I happen to agree with you. Times are a lot different now. Nobody wants to get their hands dirty anymore or work up a sweat. Computers are taking over and making everything too easy."

Jack decided to leave Ben to squirm in his embarrassment in order to go check in. Very seldom did Ben get caught off guard with someone, but the taxi driver did just that. "Tell me something, young man, you don't exactly fit the profile of a taxi driver. Not that there's anything wrong with it. Do you do any other work?"

The driver closed the trunk of his car then stepped back over to Ben. "Well, I have a master's degree in oceanography and I'm an amateur deep sea diver. I've applied to several universities, but I haven't received any responses yet."

Ben pulled a business card from his pocket and handed it to the driver, along with a Ben Franklin. "Listen, son, you keep doing what you're doing and I have no doubt you're going to be successful. In the meantime, if you ever find yourself in New York, look me up. I could really use a man of your character." With a mutual respect, the two men shook hands then parted ways.

Ben caught up to Jack, who was already in the lobby. He was reading a message left at the front desk. "Hellen says she finally had some luck locating the person my dad was dealing with on those fishing trips. Some old sea dog who goes by the name of Salty Crab."

Ben recognized the name almost immediately. "It's been many years since I heard that name. I would have thought he was dead by now."

Jack folded the paper and shoved it in his pocket. "So, who is this guy and what's the connection to you and my dad?"

Ben motioned Jack over to the lounge area and sat down. "Your mom's family was heavily vested in the shipbuilding industry when she married your father. We were touring one of the New Jersey facilities one day when we met this guy. He was a little older than me. We called him Old Salty Crab because he would always have crab pots strung out all along the piers. The company didn't mind because he would always supply the crabs for all their parties."

Jack sat back in his chair and listened as Ben told his story. "We spoke here and there, but it was your dad that kind of took to him. They even had a little side deal going on. Old Salty always wanted to own a couple of fishing boats, so your dad gave him some start-up money. I don't know what kind of deal they made, and at the time, I didn't think it was any of my business. Old Salty ran his fishing boats out of New Jersey and eventually got noticed by some bigger company. They wound up buying him out. I don't really know what happen to him after that. I always figured he went some place tropical and retired."

As the wheels in Jack's head started to turn, he stood up and started pacing. "So, my dad, for reasons unknown, hooks up with this guy, Salty, and fronts him cash for a fishing business. As far as we know, the only return my dad got was free trips out to go fishing, which he didn't even like to do. Not only that, you said my dad didn't like deep water. What the hell is going on, Ben?"

Ben stood up to try to comfort Jack, but didn't really have an answer for him. "I don't know, kid. This is ridiculous. It seems we raise more and more questions with each answer. Listen, kid, it was a long flight and we're tired. Why don't we go up to our rooms and relax for a while, and I'll meet you later tonight for a late dinner." Ben's plan sounded good, and besides, Jack was too tired to think straight.

CHAPTER FIFTEEN

As Ben entered his room, he flopped backwards onto his bed with relief and closed his eyes. He made a brief attempt to try to remember all the memories he had of his best friend Jack Sr. "What have you gotten me into, Jack?" After a few minutes he dozed off into a light sleep.

Jack went to his room and called Bria to let her know they'd landed safely. The bed looked so tempting, but he had too much on his mind to sleep, or so he thought. He popped open the minibar and pulled out several small bottles, along with some fruit juices. He made two drinks. One for himself to take the edge off and one to toast his dad. Without hesitation, the first drink went down smooth. He picked the second drink up and held it in the air. "Cheers to you, Dad, and whatever we find at the old house tomorrow." Jack laid back onto the bed and closed his eyes. It wasn't long before he fell asleep.

The next morning, Jack woke up and realized he had been sleeping all night. He and Ben were supposed to meet for a late dinner the night before, and knowing Ben's anger, Ben was going to explode all over him. Jack hurried as he showered and dressed. Afterwards, he walked quickly to Ben's room in order to take his brow beating. Jack reluctantly knocked on the door and waited. After a minute or two, he knocked again. When Ben opened the door, he was in his boxers and t-shirt. "Come on in, kid."

Surprisingly, Jack didn't detect any hostility in his voice. He walked in, only to find a young lady getting up out of bed. She had on a pair of orange laced panties and nothing else. Looking into his eyes, she brushed past Jack gently running her finger tips across his chest. Afterwards, she walked into the bathroom and closed the door. Ben sat on the bed scratching his head then his inner thigh. "Damn, kid, you're up early."

Jack walked the rest of the way in and sat down at a desk. "You gotta be kidding me. Here I am thinking you're going to tear my head off and you're in here screwing some eighteen-year-old chic. What happen to dinner last night?"

Ben stood up and opened his suitcase. "Hm! Hm! I think orange is my new favorite color. Listen, kid, I fell asleep and woke up around midnight. I wasn't going to bother you that late, so I went down to the bar. There wasn't much going on, so I sat and talked to Jamie. She's the barmaid and she's twenty-one, by the way. As you can see, we kind of hit it off."

Jack shook his head in disbelief. "Kind of? You are just unbelievable. You do know that, don't you?"

Ben smiled as he pulled out the clothes he planned on wearing for the day. "I told you, kid, modern chemistry. Can't go wrong with it. Listen, kid, I told Jamie we would hit the breakfast buffet. You're welcome to join us if you like."

Jack declined as he stood up to leave. "You both go have a blast. I'm going back to my room and ordering room service. Call me when you're ready to leave."

As Jack opened the door to leave, Jamie stepped out of the bathroom still wearing just her panties. As she lay back down on the bed, Ben walked over to show Jack out. "Okay, kid, but we might be awhile." Ben closed the door as Jack slowly walked back to his room.

As the morning progressed, Jack was overwhelmed with the feeling of excitement. Suddenly, he couldn't wait to get to the old homestead. It had been years since he was there, and as an added bonus, he would finally be able to find out his dad's big secret. Jack was sitting in the lobby waiting, trying to contain himself, when Ben finally showed up. "Hey, kid, been waiting long?"

With some spring in his step, Jack jumped up from the chair. "What are you doing? Let's go."

Ben stood looking at him as a father would, knowing the excitement Jack must be feeling. "Okay, kid, we'll get there. All of a sudden you want to expedite things."

As Ben took a seat, Jack sat back down on the edge of his chair. "So, why are we not going? You've had your sleep, you've had your sex and then more sex, and you've had your breakfast. What else is there?"

Ben sat back in his chair and just stared at Jack. "Tell me something, kid, what happens if you find something out about your dad you don't like?"

Jack could feel another one of Ben's talks coming on, but like a freight train, he just couldn't stop it. "I don't know. I haven't thought that far ahead. Besides, you knew my dad better than anyone. If he was doing something he shouldn't have been doing, you would have told me by now."

Ben smiled almost with pride. "You're right, kid. That was a good answer, not because of the words, but because you were honest. With that said, I did know your dad very well. I also knew enough not to question him every time he went away or when he made a decision that didn't make any sense, like that deal he made with Old Salty. I gotta tell you, kid, over the past few days, I've questioned myself over and over again, because until we opened up that box, I thought I knew everything about your dad. So I'm going to pose the question to you again. What's going to happen if you find out something about your dad you don't like?"

Jack slowly stood up because he really didn't have an answer for Ben. More importantly, he didn't have an answer to give himself.

Ben stood up and walked towards the lobby doors. He stopped short of the door and turned to Jack. "Well, you coming, kid?" Jack quickly caught up as they walked out to catch a cab.

On the way to the airport, Ben sat in silence as Jack thought about the question. "Why did you lay that on me like that?"

Ben glanced over and shot Jack a smile. "I had to, kid. You've been living in a fantasy world, reminiscing about the good old days. I had to somehow bring you back to reality. Come on, kid, think about the lessons learned over the years. Don't limit yourself to tunnel vision.

Keep an open mind no matter what you're doing. Think ahead. I'll tell you something, kid, I don't like the way this is going. You have your head buried in your ass and you're not thinking straight, which leads me to believe you're not going to be able to handle what we find out there."

Jack knew Ben was right. He knew Ben had always been there to clean up the mess, get him out of jams, and take care of anything he couldn't handle, and now the responsibilities had fallen back on to him.

It wasn't a long ride to the airport, so Jack sat quietly processing all the information he had. As the driver pulled to the curb, he quickly exited the cab and opened the door for Ben and Jack. They didn't have any heavy luggage because they had planned on only being at the house for a day.

As they boarded the sleek-looking jet, Jack noticed how extravagant it was. "I know it's not a big deal to you, but this is really nice."

Unexcited, Ben sat down and wasted no time asking for a drink. "Yeah, kid, you're right. It's not a big deal. Now have a seat."

As Jack picked out a seat, he looked around with awe. "How come Kotter Industries doesn't have its own jet? There's no doubt we would get plenty of use out of it."

Ben took a sip of his drink as he shook his head. "Sometimes I think you're one of the brightest people I know and filled with unlimited potential, and other times I think you must have hit your head too many times as a kid. Fundamentals, kid, fundamentals. You know how much these jets cost and how much money they burn up just to maintain? All these big corporations with their jets and helicopters and yachts. They're the ones you always hear about laying off employees or selling off inventory, getting bought out, or even going out of business. Your father and I decided a long time ago it would be best for the company to try to stay focused on business instead of going after all the perks."

As the jet taxied down the runway, it started to pick up speed. Jack couldn't help but think how smooth and fast it was. He turned to Ben to argue his point, but Ben had already closed his eyes and fallen asleep. No wonder after the night he must have had, not to mention the early morning delight. After a night of tossing and turning, Jack realized Ben had the right idea: Sleep on the way to Pebble Beach. So he reached over and drank what was left of Ben's drink and closed his eyes.

When the pilot announced they had arrived at Monterey Peninsula Airport, Jack and Ben perked up and quickly fastened their seatbelts for landing. As they made their exit, Ben could tell Jack was still trying to get over his fascination with the jet. "Let's go, kid. You can buy one of those things when I'm dead and buried."

There was a SUV with tinted windows and a driver waiting for them at the hanger to take them to Sanctuary Beach Resort. Neither Ben nor Jack was in any mood to talk so they just relaxed and enjoyed the scenery. It wasn't too long before they arrived. They only had one overnight bag each, so the driver wasted no time getting them settled. After tipping the driver handsomely, Ben informed Jack he wanted to freshen up, and afterwards, he would meet him in the lobby.

Jack took the opportunity to walk the grounds and gather his thoughts. The day had finally arrived to get a look at the secrets his dad left behind. Before Ben could make it to his room, he was stopped by the hotel concierge. He handed him a message from Robert. It simply said to call him immediately. Ben wasted no more time. He got to his room and threw his jacket on the bed. He called Hellen and told her to have Robert pick up on a secured line. When Robert picked up the phone, Ben could tell he was hesitant.

"Well, Ben, I don't know if I helped you or hurt you."

Ben wasn't sure what to make of the statement, but he had the feeling it wasn't good. "Just tell me what you found out and we'll go from there."

There was a silence, then Robert gave the information Ben wanted. "Those coordinates you wanted me to look up are in the middle of the Atlantic Ocean."

Ben thought momentarily about Jack Sr.'s fishing trips. "Alright, so what's out there, an island? Is there something other than cold water?"

Robert didn't respond right away. Instead, he took a deep breath. "Well, there's nothing there, per say. At least nothing on the surface."

Ben was not really known for patience, and he started getting irritated. "What the hell does that mean? Speak English."

Robert let out a small laugh because he knew he had Ben squirming on the hook. "Alright, Ben. There's nothing out there to see. No island, no tourist trap. Maybe an iceberg or two sometimes, and very cold water. But that's on the surface. The coordinates you had me look up happen to be some of the most famous coordinates of all time, because two miles down lay the remains of the *Titanic*."

Ben didn't say anything, but Robert could hear him breathing. "You okay, Ben? I don't know what you and Jack are doing, but I hope that helped you out."

Ben thanked Robert for the information and told him he would be back in town as soon as possible. As he hung up the phone, he sat on the edge of the bed thinking out loud. "I don't think you were taking fishing trips at all. What the hell were you doing, old friend?" Ben looked at his watch and realized he was supposed to be meeting Jack. He quickly changed his clothes and gathered himself together. As he made his way to the lobby, Jack was there waiting with a rental car. When Ben climbed in, Jack noticed the look on Ben's face and knew he had something to tell him.

"Come on with it, Ben. I don't want to be halfway there and you lay a bombshell on me."

Ben sat and stared out the window because he didn't know what to say. The only thing he could come up with was his twisted humor. "Well, kid, you want to take in some sights or go straight to the old house?"

Jack smiled and felt somewhat better knowing Ben was making jokes. "So, what's the problem? You look like you have something to say."

Ben finally gathered his thoughts then took a deep breath. "Well, kid, I had Robert check out those coordinates that were in the box. It turns out those coordinates are out in the Atlantic Ocean."

Jack sat and listened, but had no clue about what Ben was trying to say. "So, what's out there? An island getaway?" Jack thought about his dad and smiled. "Was that what my dad was doing all this time? Going on vacation without my mom?"

Ben didn't say anything and just stared at Jack for the moment. Jack knew Ben always had some kind of smart comeback, but this time, there was silence. "I'm sorry, Ben. I shouldn't kid around like that."

Ben shook his head and took a breath. "That's alright, kid, don't worry about it. There's nothing out there but water. There is something else, though. Robert told me those coordinates are also where the remains of the *Titanic* are located."

As soon as Jack heard the word *Titanic,* he completely shut down. Suddenly, all those dreams he'd been having flashed through his mind, along with thoughts of his dad's anger about his school project. Ben noticed all the color had gone from his face. "What is it, kid?"

Jack could barely breathe. He could feel his chest thumping from the beating of his heart. As he spoke, his words were almost broken. "Nineteen eight-five. That was the year *Titanic* was discovered. I only know that because of a book I read back in school."

Ben just stared at Jack trying to piece everything together, but he just wasn't getting it. "You and Robert have the same problem. Neither one of you speak English. What the hell are you talking about?"

Jack's mind was racing with information, but he couldn't get it out fast enough. "The letter in the box. It was written in 1985. That's when *Titanic* was discovered. The coordinates are to the *Titanic.* That's where my dad was going each year. Damn, we really have to find that old fisherman you and my dad knew."

Ben took a breath and just stared out into space. "I don't know, kid. Why would your dad want anything to do with a ship that sank decades ago? I'm trying to think about how old your dad was or if he was even born yet. This just doesn't make any sense."

The wheels in Jack's head started to turn as he was connecting the puzzle pieces together. "Remember when I told you I was having those weird dreams and I couldn't figure out why?"

Ben thought for a minute. "Yeah, you never said what they were about."

Suddenly, Jack started getting a sick feeling. "They were about the *Titanic.* All of them. Seeing the people running and dying. Watching the water coming up over the ship. Let's just stop and think a minute. The contents of the box. The letter to you from my dad, written in 1985. *Titanic* was found during that same year. The diary letter which points towards some kind of disaster at sea. Obviously, we can place *Titanic* in that category. The California address is our old house. What's out there, we don't know yet. Then there's the coordinates that are the same as the location of *Titanic,* and last is the old key. We don't know what that goes to yet."

Ben heard what Jack was saying, but was still leery of what it all meant. "What's going on, kid? You sound like you're getting excited about all this."

Jack smiled because in the back of his mind, he was excited. "Don't you see, Ben? It's like a puzzle. We just have to put all the pieces in the right place. Then we'll be able to see the whole picture. Want to know what I think?"

Ben rolled his eyes then scoffed. "Not really, but I'm sure you're gonna tell me anyway."

By that time, Jack was overwhelmed with excitement. "You're damn right I am. I think the last couple of pieces to the puzzle are at the old house. So, what do you say we go find them and figure out what the hell my dad was working on?"

Ben smiled, not because Jack was on a mission to solve some unknown mystery, but because he took pride in seeing Jack go head-to-head with a problem without fear of failure. "Okay, kid, we'll head up to the house and see if we can put an end to your mystery."

It wasn't long before they pulled into what was left of the driveway. The beautiful handcrafted gate that once spawned across the driveway was gone. It had been constructed of wrought iron and decorated with copper tips and was no doubt stolen after the 1989 earthquake. The brick wall that once surrounded the property was falling down in most areas. As they pulled in front of the house, Jack noticed the area where his bedroom had been was completely collapsed. It looked like someone looted most of the windows, and the ones that remained were shattered. The roof of the house had been all slate and had also been taken away. There were no contents in the house because they had been packed up and shipped to New York years before.

Ben knew it had to be hard for Jack coming back there, especially under mysterious circumstances, so he decided to just give him some time to soak it all in.

Jack stepped out of the car and stood staring at the house. Childhood memories filled his thoughts, along with memories of his parents laughing and living life to the fullest. "Hey, Ben, remember when Connie and I were riding our bikes and he dared me to try to jump my mom's garden? Man, I wiped out and nearly split my head doing it."

Ben stepped out of the car with a smile. "Yeah, kid. I don't know what you were thinking. You tore your mom's flowers all to hell that day."

Jack shook his head and laughed. "Yeah, I thought my mom would flip out, but she didn't. She came running out to see if I was alright and then laughed at me. On the other hand, my dad didn't think it was too funny. He went out and bought all new flowers and made me plant all of them." Jack walked over to where the garden once prominently shined. All that was left was twelve years' worth of weeds. "Yeah, he told me later the money he used to buy the flowers was my allowance for that month. Man, that really sucked. Little did he know Connie was hooking me up whenever I needed to buy something."

With a big smile, Ben walked over to Jack and let out a healthy laugh. "Little did you know your dad knew about Connie's generosity and let it slide."

Suddenly, the feeling Jack had when he was able to get away with something left and so did his smile. "No way. There's no way he could have known."

Ben looked down at the ground as he kicked around a few loose stones. "Your dad knew many things, especially when they involved you."

Jack didn't say anything because he was hoping Ben would elaborate on his comments. Ben knew he'd sparked something inside of Jack, because up until then, Jack thought he had been able to get away with a lot of things growing up. "Listen, kid, I don't mean to burst your bubble, but your dad knew everything you ever did. All the trouble you thought you were hiding. All the pranks you pulled in high school. All the times you wrecked your car. Even all the times you wrecked your friends' cars. Everything."

Jack thought about all the things Ben was saying and even some that he'd forgotten. "What about that time I called you from the police station after that drunken barroom fight and you came down there and spoke to the captain and smoothed everything over? You promised me you would take that to the grave."

Ben could see the look in Jack's eyes like he had just been betrayed. "Come on, kid, I made you a promise and I kept it. What you didn't know was your dad was good friends with most of the police force. That same captain was on the phone as soon as we walked out the door."

With all that Ben was saying, Jack started to get the general idea. "So, you're saying my dad constantly spied on me but never said anything about all the trouble I got into?"

Ben smiled as he walked over and put his arm around Jack. "No, I'm saying your dad loved you very much, so he gave you space to grow. Most parents reprimand their children for every little thing, and all that does is limit their ability to learn and think for themselves. Your dad wanted to make sure you could get out of any bad situation you got yourself into. Now look at you. Head of one of the largest corporations in the world. Not too bad, kid. Not too bad."

Just then, the caretaker drove up the driveway. As he stepped out of the car, Ben walked over to greet him. The elderly gentleman held out his hand as a friendly gesture. "Hello, my name is Walter. You must be Mr. Benjamin Marcus."

As Ben shook his hand, he introduced Jack. "This is Jack Kotter Jr. I'm guessing my secretary Hellen called to let you know we were coming?"

Walter scratched his head and motioned Ben towards the house. "Yes, she called. Didn't really tell me much, though. Was kind of curious if you were coming down here to sell the property."

Before Ben could answer, Jack asked about the house. "So, Walter, how often do you ride out here to tend to the property?"

Once again, Walter scratched his head then looked Jack up and down. "I know it's been some years, but I would have figured you'd remember me."

Jack stared at the aging man for a moment, but nothing was coming to mind. "I'm sorry, sir, I don't think we've ever met."

Ben looked at the man with curiosity but also didn't know him. Walter walked over to the old flower bed and pointed. "Your father was very proud of the flowers he picked out for your mom, and it took me two days to figure out the arrangement of where they were going to go. Then you and that punk kid, Connie, came along and messed them up."

Jack smiled because it just hit him like a brick wall. "Oh my God, you were the groundskeeper back then. I remember you now."

Walter smiled and gave Jack a hug. "You've really grown into a handsome man."

Ben stood quiet for a moment as he thought back to try to remember Walter. "Didn't you once threaten to flatten my tires after I parked on the grass one night?"

Walter walked over to Ben with a big grin on his face. "It worked, didn't it? Afterwards, you never parked on my grass again."

Ben shot him a smile and shook his hand again. "You old dog, how the hell have you been?"

Walter stepped back to take a better look at Ben. "I have no complaints. God's been good to me over the years."

As Ben and Walter continued to talk and catch up on old times, Jack walked to the side of the house to take a look at the six-car garage that was built with the house. Unfortunately, the only things left standing were a few walls. Everything had been destroyed by the earthquake. He walked around to the rear of the house and saw where the fire had done damage to the deck off the kitchen. Jack stood looking around as Ben and Walter made their way around to the back. Walter could see Jack was upset at the way the house looked.

"I'm sorry you had to see the house this way. I'm sure you never thought it would ever look like this."

With a sad look, Jack didn't say anything. His eyes kept scanning the property looking at all the damage. "I'm guessing it's not a coincidence Kotter Industries hired you to maintain the property."

Walter reached into his pocket and pulled out a business card and handed it to Jack. "Well, it kind of is. I just happen to own the company that Kotter Industries hired. I usually let most of the younger guys come out on these jobs, but your dad was a good man. He always had kind words for me and always treated me like a friend instead of an employee. So I come out here three to four times a week to make sure nothing else happens to the property. Besides, your dad had that storage unit built a couple years before the house was destroyed. Don't know what's in it and I like to make sure nobody else does either."

Ben looked around, but didn't see the storage unit Walter was talking about. "Senior told me about the storage unit before he died. So, where is this shed?"

Walter looked at Ben with some hesitation. "Listen, Benjamin, I don't mean to sound rude, but I'm really not at liberty to say."

Ben was somewhat surprised because that wasn't the answer he was hoping for. "What does that mean? I thought Hellen spoke to you about why we were flying out here."

Walter shrugged his shoulders and began to explain what the problem was. "Listen, I know this is going to sound funny, but after Jack Sr. died, I received a letter from some lawyer's office. It basically said there would be only one person who would be able to open the shed and not to divulge any information to anyone but that one person. It was some real James Bond-type stuff, if you know what I mean. The letter didn't have the name of this person, but it said I would be able to identify them by a certain key he would have. I'm guessing it opens that weird looking lock that's attached to the door."

Jack and Ben looked at each other and realized another piece of the puzzle had just been solved. Ben pulled out his wallet and pulled out a card from Schonfeld and Weinstein. He held it up for Walter to see. "Is this the lawyer's office the letter came from?"

Walter briefly looked at the card and recognized the name right away. "Yep, it sure is."

Ben then reached into his pocket and pulled out the old skeleton key that was inside the box. "Is this the key that fits the lock?"

Walter took the key from Ben and looked at it for a few seconds. "I don't know. The letter didn't say exactly what the key would look like. It did say it would be a key from the old days and that the person would be able to describe the locking mechanism."

Just then, Ben thought back about the times Jack Sr. would use those types of keys for their company lockboxes. There was one box in particular his brother Sergis had specially designed. Ben smiled because he was about ninety percent sure he could give the right answer. He looked around and saw an old beat up bench that had been overturned. He fixed it upright and sat down. Memories of Sergis came rushing back as he sat and thought about the times Sergis would show off the one-of-a-kind locks and boxes he created. He remembered one in particular that Jack Sr. was very fond of. He stood up and walked over to Walter and took the key back. He held it in his hand and just stared at it.

Jack knew Ben had the answer. "So, what about it, Ben?"

Ben folded his fingers over and held the key tight. "Alright, Walter. The locking mechanism has the face of a lion. This key should fit inside the mouth of the lion. You then turn the key counterclockwise until you hear a click. The face of the lion should then detach itself from the mechanism turning it into a doorknob. Afterwards, you turn the key counterclockwise again, which allows you to turn the detached lion head clockwise and open the lock."

Walter stood in awe looking at Jack, while Jack was completely astounded at what Ben just described. "Are you serious? You guys would actually go through all that just for lockboxes? Unbelievable! It sounds like you guys had too much time on your hands back then."

After getting no response from Ben, Jack turned to Walter. "Well, what do you think? Is that the million-dollar answer you've been waiting for?"

Walter looked like he had the weight of the world lifted off his shoulders. "Absolutely. You don't know how long I've been waiting for this day to come." Walter looked at Ben and smiled. "I can't believe after all these years it would be you that has the key to that old spooky-looking lock. Well, I guess the only thing left is to show you the location of the shed."

Still clenching the key in his hand, Ben sat back down on the bench. Jack could see something was really bothering him, so he took a seat next to him. "What's wrong, Ben? This was why we came here. Don't you want to see what the mystery is all about?"

With a sad look on his face, Ben handed the key to Jack. "My brother took a lot of pride in making various types of locks and boxes. He and your dad. It started as a security precaution and turned into a hobby. I really miss those days, kid."

Jack handed the key back to Ben. "Well, we can't go back. We can only go forward. Besides, according to my dad, you're supposed to be helping me. So come on. Let's go pull back the curtain and see what the wizard looks like."

Ben stood up and shook off the old memories. "Okay, Walter, let's go."

But Walter stood fast. "Sorry, guys. I can't. The letter was very specific. I'm only to show the person with the key and anyone with him where to go." He then turned around and pointed at a break in the tree line. "There's an old pathway that runs through that break. If you walk down the path, you'll come to a fork. Stay to the left and the shed will be on the left hand side."

Jack took a few steps towards the pathway and stopped. "I remember that path. Connie and I use to ride our bikes back there. I remember my dad would tell us old ghost stories about it just to scare us into not going back there. As usual, though, we never listened. I can't believe it still exists."

As Jack and Ben readied themselves, Walter said his goodbyes and left. Jack took one last look at the house then turned towards the path and started walking. It wasn't too long before Ben started telling Jack to slow down. "Hey, kid, I don't exactly have my hiking outfit on, so slow your roll."

Jack apologized, but the excitement had started to build back up. As they approached the woods, the pathway came into sight. Memories of Connie and all the fun they had came rushing back as Jack took the lead. Stepping over branches and pushing through overgrown shrubs wasn't too pleasant, but Jack didn't care. "Unless something has changed over the years, this trail should go around in circle." Finally, the fork in the path Walter had told them about was in sight. Jack pushed on, going left as Ben followed behind. They were both hoping the shed would come into sight soon, but it didn't.

After what seemed like forever, they managed to walk the entire length of the trail and wound up back at the fork. With his hands on his hips and breathing heavily, Ben looked around in frustration. "I knew we should have had Walter tag along. Now what, Mr. Mountain Man?"

Jack's breathing was also somewhat strained. "I don't know. Nothing has really changed since Connie and I trampled through these woods years ago. Except for the overgrowth, the landscape isn't any different. Maybe my dad had a sense of humor and we're just not seeing it. Did you see anything out of the ordinary?"

Ben was in no laughing mood and was ready to call it a day when he noticed some thick vine that had grown downward from the side of the hill. "Hey, kid, what about all that vine? Do you remember it being that thick when you and Connie were running around back here?"

As he looked up the hill, Jack took a few minutes and walked over to the vine. "I remember we used to pretend it was rope and we would climb up and down on it all day, but it wasn't this thick." Jack picked a fallen branch up from the ground and took a few steps up the hill. As he began poking at the vines, he suddenly hit something solid. "Sorry, Ben, I think we walked that trail for no reason." Jack pulled out a small pocket knife and started cutting away some of the overgrowth. As the vine started to fall, he could see an old door slowly start to reveal itself.

As Ben watched, that eerie feeling he had about the box started creeping in. "Hey, kid, I'm not saying I'm scared, but I'm really not feeling this."

Jack laughed as he stopped and turned around. "Are you kidding, Ben? This is awesome. I feel like I'm uncovering buried treasure. Although, I could really use a bigger knife right about now." Jack cut away a few more vines and pushed away some of the loose dirt. "I'm guessing the earthquake did most of this. All the dirt must have tumbled down the hill, and over the years, this vine grew over top of it. Listen, I'll go up to the house and see if there's something to dig this out. Why don't you just sit on that log and relax."

Ben didn't really like the idea of staying there by himself, but he was still tired from the hike around the trail. "Don't be all day, kid. I would like to get back to some kind of civilization sometime today."

Jack smiled as he turned and walked back towards the break in the trees. Ben sat down on the log and stared at the hill. He tried to picture what the shed may have looked like when it was first built. He thought about his friend Jack Sr., who apparently held some kind of secret for many years, wondering the whole time what could be so important to go through all the trouble. Just as he finally caught his breath, Jack came running back down the trail with an old shovel head without the handle.

"Hey, Ben, this was all I could find, but I should be able to dig out the door." Jack immediately went to work digging out dirt and chopping more vines. Finally, the dirt started to collapse, revealing the top of a wooden door. Jack stopped for a moment as Ben stood up and walked over. He took a step back and they both stood in awe at the size of the door.

"Holy shit, kid. I was expecting a little backyard storage shed. This door must be at least 12 feet wide and maybe nine feet high. We can't dig this out with this broken shovel."

Jack stared with disappointment, but he was determined to end the mystery. "If you want to leave, I understand, but I'm staying. I don't care if it takes me all night." Just then, more dirt trickled down revealing some of the hinges.

Ben took a few steps up the hill to try to get a better look. "You might be in luck, kid. This door rises up like a garage door. If we can take enough pressure off the door, we can just raise it up."

Jack's happy feeling came back, but it wasn't long before it was gone again. "We still need to deal with whatever locking mechanism that key goes to."

Ben reached into his pocket and pulled out the key. "Well, since I was right about the lock, then it can only be in one place. That particular lock was made to work evenly by placing it in the center of the door. So, if we can figure out the dimensions of the door, we can then figure out exactly where the lock is located. It might be a little more digging than we thought, but it's still better than digging out this whole mess."

Jack stepped further back as he reminisced about days gone by when he would dare Connie to jump down after climbing up the hill. Even with the overgrowth and the excess dirt, he could still remember where the ground met the hill. "Okay, it looks like the door is eight feet high. Now looking at the top, you can tell it's 12 feet wide because there are 12 panels equaling a foot each."

It wasn't long before Jack was once again hard at work digging. He managed to dig out a portion of the hill he thought would be directly in line with the center of the door. He stopped to rest for a few minutes as he returned to the old log for relief.

Ben could see Jack was exhausted, but he also knew he was determined. He took a seat next to Jack. "Well, kid, I'm really sorry about all this."

With a confused look, Jack glared over at Ben. "What are you talking about? You didn't do any of this." Ben took a quick breath and let it out, then he stood up and walked towards the hill. "Well, when you opened the box and I saw that key, I should have known there would be something intricate involved."

Ben studied the top of the door then walked back over to Jack. "I know I told you my brother and your father would build these weird locks and lockboxes, but I failed to tell you just how hard they were to figure out. I gotta tell you, kid, we wouldn't even be here right now if it wasn't for the fact I remembered how much your dad admired the locking system that's now buried under that dirt. I'm only hoping your father didn't add anymore tricks to this adventure."

Jack could feel his second wind coming on and stood up. He walked past Ben and stopped at the foot of the hill. "That box sat in my dad's safe for a very long time. Then it sat at my house after that. I could have taken your advice and just let it go, but I didn't. I think sometimes you forget that I'm grown now. I can make decisions for myself."

Ben stepped over to the hill and put his arm around Jack. "I know coming back here couldn't have been easy for you, kid, but as long as you're making the decisions, why don't you make the decision to start digging again."

Jack laughed because it was good to see Ben's sense of humor was still intact. "No problem, old man. Why don't you go sit back down and I'll have this dug out in no time."

After about an hour of digging, Jack dug out a small walkway almost to the door. As he dug, more and more dirt broke loose and fell to his feet. Finally, he hit something that sounded like steel. When he did, Ben stood up and walked over. "I think you may have found it, kid."

Suddenly, Jack had some newfound energy. He started digging out the area around where he thought he'd hit something, and pretty soon, he had the entire mechanism exposed. Jack stepped back so Ben could take a look at it.

"I can't believe it, kid. It's just like I remember it. The last time I saw this lock was back during World War II. I was really young when Sergis hired me. Kotter Industries hadn't even been formed yet. The company was still called Up and Down Hauling. When your dad and Sergis started to expand, Sergis had the idea of using old time lockboxes to carry payroll, paperwork, and other valuables to the factory workers using our trucking company. To make sure nothing was tampered with, they created these weird mechanisms to protect against theft. Eventually, as time went on, the war came to an end and the banking systems became more advanced. These lockboxes and locks were packed away in some warehouse and forgotten about." Ben took out a handkerchief and started brushing away some of the loose dirt from the lock. He used his fingers to clear the chunks of dirt out of the lion's mouth. When he did, he could finally see the keyhole.

Jack leaned over Ben's shoulder to take a better look at the lock. "I can't believe the size of that thing. How big was the box it was used for?"

Ben remembered the box almost immediately. "Well, to give you some kind of idea, we had to use a forklift to load it onto one of our trucks."

Jack thought about Ben's words for a moment while he caught his breath. "You think I should try to dig that out more?"

Ben looked at the top of the door then looked at the positioning of the lock. "No, kid. I think I'm right about the door. I think once I unlock it, it should lift straight up like a garage door." Jack was all too happy to throw the shovel to the ground as Ben pulled the key from his pocket.

"Well, kid, here we go." Ben reached inside the mouth of the lion and placed the key into the hole. He paused for a second as he turned and looked at Jack. Jack nodded his head, giving Ben the okay to go ahead. Ben then turned the key counterclockwise until he heard a click. He could hear the inner workings of the mechanism squealing, then suddenly, the head of the lion snapped and started to push away from the lock. When it stopped, Ben once again turned the key counterclockwise. This allowed him to turn the lion's head clockwise like a door knob.

Jack stood back as he listened to the mechanism unlocking the bars that were inside the door. Then there was silence. Jack could feel his adrenaline flowing as he stood in awe of what he'd just seen. "Unbelievable, Ben. You guys really took your security pretty seriously back then."

Ben smiled with pride while he took a few seconds to calm his nerves. "Yeah, kid. We were all scared back then. It was the beginning of the war and no one really knew who was going to win. So, what'ya say we lift this door up and bring this so-called adventure to an end?"

Jack felt nothing but relief and was ready to finally see what all the secrecy was about. "Hell, yeah, I'm ready. Let's do this thing."

Jack climbed to one end of the door while Ben stayed in the middle with the lock. "You ready, kid?" Jack grabbed a hold of one of the decorative ridges in the door and gave Ben the signal to start trying to push the door up. Ben slid his hands under the locking mechanism and started to try to lift while Jack did the same. It was a no-go. The door didn't budge. Jack turned to Ben and told him to push on the door at the same time they tried to lift. After a second try, it was still no-go. Jack climbed down from the hill as Ben walked over to the log and sat down.

"Well, kid, I thought if we could unlock the door, we would be able to just raise it up, but I guess there's too much pressure against it from the remaining dirt."

Jack wasn't about to give up, though. In his mind, they'd come too far to stop. "Listen, Ben, I have an idea. Just sit tight and let me dig out some more dirt."

Ben shook his head in frustration. "I'm telling you, kid, you're probably going to get the same results, but you go ahead. I'll be sitting here rooting for you." Jack grabbed the shovel and quickly went to work. It wasn't long before he'd shoveled out a space just big enough to lie down in. When he was finished, he threw the shovel to the side and sat down to catch his breath.

"I promise, Ben, if this doesn't work, we'll call it quits for today and come back tomorrow."

By then, the afternoon had come and gone, and Ben was getting grumpier by the minute. "I gotta tell you, kid, I love you like a son, but if I don't get something in my stomach soon, I'm going to rip off one of your limbs and eat it in front of you."

Jack's energy was also starting to fade out because of hunger, but he was sure his plan was going to work; besides, he knew he could outrun Ben.

Jack walked over to the space he dug out and lay down on his back. He started pushing and kicking on the door in order to loosen it up. After a few minutes, he wedged his legs up under the lock and started pushing upwards. After a few good shoves, the door finally gave way and raised up out of the hill revealing an old twelve by eight by forty shed. With his heart beating a mile a minute, Jack jumped up and raised his arms in triumph. "Yeah! I told you, Ben. You just have no confidence."

Ben stood up and walked over to the hole in the side of the hill. "That's not true, kid. I don't have a problem with confidence. I'm having a problem with a lack of food."

Both men stood at the foot of the hole looking down. There was just enough late afternoon light shining through the trees to see that the shed was still intact. Once again, Ben had some concern about going forward. "Alright, kid. You did it. Now what?"

Without Jack realizing it, all the excitement of just getting to that moment had left his body, only to be replaced with doubt and nervousness. "Well, I guess this is one of those defining moments you're always preaching to me about. You once told me I have to step up to the plate if I want to take a swing, so here goes nothing." With that said, Jack stepped down into the shed then turned around to help Ben down. The drop-off was only a few feet so neither Jack nor Ben had any problem.

They stood side by side as their eyes adjusted to the dark. Some of the remaining daylight made it into the shed, making it a little easier for them. The first thing they both noticed was a large desk congested with paperwork. As they walked over to it, Jack noticed an old black and white picture of a man in a small decorative frame. As he picked it up to get a closer look, his heart sank. "This is the man in my dreams I was telling you about."

Ben took the picture from him and looked at it. "What are you talking about, kid? Do you know who this is?"

Jack's heart was still pounding. He thought for a second trying to remember if he had ever met the man. "Except for my dreams, I've never seen him before. Who is he?"

Ben looked at the picture again because there was something familiar about it. "Well, he kinda looks like your dad, but I don't know who he is. Jack never talked about his family much. Could he be a relative of yours?"

Jack thought about it, but drew a blank. "No, you're right. Dad never spoke about his family. It was my mom's side that always came over for holidays or get-togethers. I never really thought to ask my dad about it."

Ben placed the picture back down on the desk and started rummaging through some of the paperwork. There was a lot of dust to brush away, but once he did, he could see there was some kind of overseas financial records. Jack started looking through some of the desk drawers to check for anything else that would give them some answers. As he pulled open the first drawer, he pulled out a list of names. Some were scratched out and others had circles drawn around them. As he looked down the list, he didn't recognize any of the names. He handed the list to Ben to look at, but Ben was still scanning through the financial records he had found.

"Here, kid, take a look at these." Jack sifted through the papers as Ben checked the list of names. "Sorry, kid, I don't know any of these people."

Jack finished looking through the papers and handed them back to Ben. "I don't even know what the hell I'm looking at."

Ben smiled as he folded the papers and placed them in his pocket. "They're financial records from overseas. I don't recognize any of the banks so I'll have our financial department take a look and see if they can decipher them."

Ben pulled open another drawer and found an old book on *Titanic*. He glanced at the cover and handed to Jack. Jack knew almost immediately what it was. "This is my book." He flipped the cover over to find he was the last person to check it out of the library. "I can't believe this."

Ben just stared with confusion. "What's wrong, kid? It's just a book."

Jack held the book up for Ben to see it was a library book with Jack's name inside. "This is my book that I checked out of the library when I was in school. My dad came home and saw it and went berserk. I can't believe he went and got it after I took it back. Why would he keep it all these years?" Ben didn't have an answer, but he knew Jack was just thinking out loud.

As Jack was trying to get over his shock about the book, Ben reached into the drawer and pulled out another old photograph. It was another black and white photo of the same man, a woman, and a child. He recognized the child because Jack Sr. once showed him a picture of himself when he was very young. After a few seconds, Ben determined the man and woman were probably Jack Sr.'s parents. He reached over and picked up the other photograph and held them side by side. "Hey, kid, I think I know who the man is in this picture." He set the two photos down on the desk so Jack could also see them side by side. "That's your dad when he was about four years old. The reason I know that is because he showed me a picture of himself when we were working late one night. I'm guessing the two people with him are his parents."

Jack took a moment and studied the photos then noticed something in the background. As the color in his face disappeared, he felt his legs become weak. Ben could see the sickly look on Jack's face and pushed the desk chair over for him to sit. "Damn, kid, what's wrong?"

Jack fell back into the chair as the tears started to form in his eyes. "I never knew my grandparents. My dad never talked about them. This is definitely the man in my dreams, but I don't understand why. I didn't know him and I never saw a photo of him."

After a few minutes, Jack caught his composure and stood up. He handed the photos to Ben and took a step back from the desk. "Look at the photo again. Notice anything in the background?"

Ben took another look at the photo and noticed a life preserver hanging on a wall alongside of some early century lounge chairs. The word on the life preserver read "*Titanic.*"

Ben was astounded. "Jesus Christ, kid, that letter from the box about some kind of disaster. Your dad and grandparents were on the *Titanic*. Holy shit, I think I need a seat now."

Ben felt sick, but it wasn't from any of the information they just discovered. "Kid, it's been a long day and we haven't eaten since breakfast. We're also starting to lose daylight."

Jack was numb and really couldn't think straight, but with hesitation, he agreed. "Alright, Ben. As usual, you're right. We're going to have to come back tomorrow. If we have to, we'll pack food and lighting."

Using the last bit of energy he had, Ben stood up with delight. "Now you're talking, kid. I'm going to take these financial records and fax them to our financial guys in New York."

Jack grabbed both photographs and the library book and climbed up out of the shed. After helping Ben up, they hurried to the car and drove straight to the nearest restaurant. Both were dusty and dirty, but neither one cared.

There was no conversation during dinner. Afterwards, they drove back to the hotel in silence. As Jack pulled into a parking space, he finally broke his silence. "I don't even know my grandparents' names."

Ben looked at Jack with sadness because he knew this wasn't exactly the adventure Jack had thought it was going to be. "Listen, kid, I'm not sure if this means anything. Your dad and I, along with your mom, were coming back from one of the recycle plants we had just built when your dad wanted to make a small detour. We stopped at this small flower cart along the side of the road and your dad bought a bunch of flowers. I assumed they were for your mom, but a little while later, we made another stop at the Cemetery of the Holy

Rood. Your dad walked over to a couple of graves while Bianca and I stayed in the car. I don't know what it was, but it seemed like one of those surreal moments. Your mom didn't say anything and I didn't feel it was my place to ask. Anyway, your dad laid the flowers on a couple of graves and walked back to the car. Now here's the weird part. Although I couldn't read it, I could see there was a name on the first gravestone, but on the second, there was nothing written. If you want, I can call to see if I can get some more information."

Jack appreciated the story, but he was exhausted. "That's fine, Ben. Whatever you can find out. Just let me know." Jack stepped out of the car and headed straight for his room.

As desperate as he was to take a shower, Ben just sat in the car thinking for a few minutes. "Well, old friend, I don't know what tomorrow is going to bring, but I sure hope it's better than today." With his thoughts on hold and his belly satisfied, Ben stepped out of the car and headed for his room.

CHAPTER SIXTEEN

THE NEXT MORNING, JACK WAS UP BRIGHT AND EARLY STUDYING THE two photographs. Thinking to himself, his grandmother wouldn't have wasted time retrieving photos, Jack guessed his father must have tracked down the original photographer and had copies made. He had already picked the photos apart, but he kept trying to understand why his dad kept such a huge secret. All he could come up with was maybe the answers were in the storage shed.

After breakfast, Jack met Ben at the car. "Well, kid, how do you feel?" This time, they were both wearing appropriate clothing.

"Well, I'm surprised. I slept really good. Probably because of all the digging I did yesterday. Of course, I still have a lot of questions, but I think today is going to be a good day for getting answers."

After a quick stop to pick up supplies, they were once again on their way to Jack's childhood home. This time, they had everything they needed to make a day of it. Once there, Jack drove straight onto the property and down to the path. As Ben unloaded the car, Jack took one of the shovels he had bought and dug out a slope so they could walk in and out of the shed without any problems. Ben used his industrial knowledge and ran some cable along the ceiling of the shed then hung some temporary lighting. Just then, Jack noticed something big in the rear of the shed. Whatever it was, it had a large canvas over the top of it. Jack and Ben stood in front of it staring, but both were too nervous to take the canvas off. Ben turned to Jack and just smiled. "Well, kid, it's your show. You can have the honors."

Jack took a deep breath then pulled the canvas away revealing a Cracker Jack surprise, and what a surprise it was. As Ben stood staring in awe, Jack's eyes lit up like a Christmas tree. "You gotta be kidding! What the hell is this?"

Ben already knew the answer but was completely blown away that it was actually here. "It's a Ferrari, kid. To be exact, it's a 1959 Ferrari 250 GT Spyder convertible. The car your father had when he proposed to your mom right down the hill from here. But what the hell is it doing here?"

Jack was too excited to even think. "Who cares why it's here. It's mine now. I can't believe my dad was even this cool. Would you look at this thing? It's in mint condition."

Ben opened up the glove box to check the registration. It still had the rental company name. He checked the mileage and saw it still had the original miles after Jack Sr. was supposed to return it to its owner. "I remember your dad borrowed the car for a week to drive Bianca down the coast just so he could propose to her. I thought he returned the car, but I guess not. He must have contacted the rental company and bought it. I just can't believe he never said anything. I'm also guessing your mom didn't know anything about it because your dad told me she fell in love with this car when she first laid eyes on it. There's no way she would've let him keep it from her."

As Jack was still admiring the car from behind the steering wheel, Ben looked around and saw another surprise waiting for him. Shoved into one of the dark corners was a table with an old hand-carved lockbox complete with custom lock. Carved into the box were the names Sergis and Benjamin. As Ben stood staring at it: he remembered the significance of the box.

Jack noticed Ben had found something, so he tore himself away from the car to find out what it was. "Hey, Ben, that's one of those old lockboxes you were telling me about. Judging from that lock and the fact that it has your name on it, I'm guessing there's a trick to getting it open."

Ben stood quietly for a few seconds then reached out to slide his hand across the top of the box. "This was a gift from Sergis when he first hired me. We actually used it a couple of times, way back when. I almost forgot it existed. I packed it away in one of our warehouses when Sergis died. I didn't even know your dad knew where it was."

Jack stood admiring the craftsmanship. "Do you still remember how to open it?"

Ben smiled, not because of the question Jack posed, but because he remembered what Sergis taught him. "My brother always said, 'just because something looks difficult, doesn't mean it is.' That's a good lesson for you, kid."

Jack looked at Ben then at the box. "So, now it's your turn to open a box. How does this thing work?"

Ben paused for a second then smiled with pride. "If you were a thief, how would you try to open it?"

Jack stepped closer to the box and studied it for a few seconds. "Well, I guess I would try to figure out what kind of key opens it, and if that didn't work, maybe try to somehow pick the lock."

Ben chuckled as he stepped in front of Jack. "Look, kid, what did I just say? Things that look difficult usually aren't."

Ben reached his hand around the back and pushed a little button at the bottom corner. "This was Sergis' idea of breaking me into the habit of keeping things simple. He also wanted to show me that keeping things simple would fool even the most experienced thief." Ben didn't waste any more time with lessons. He opened the box only to find another letter from Jack Sr.

My dearest friend Benjamin,

I apologize for all the secrecy. I can only guess my son is standing next to you. I figured you would get a kick out of seeing this old box after all these years. Below is a list of passwords which go to the overseas bank accounts you found on the desk. Don't worry, they're all perfectly legal. I know I'm asking a lot and it goes against everything we stood for, but I wouldn't ask if it wasn't something extremely important to me.

My friend, once you put everything together and realize what I'm asking you to do, use the money in these accounts to take care of the expenses. I know I'm asking the impossible, but I'm sure you and Jack together will shine as a team and complete the task.

If by some chance you decide not to continue, as your friend, I would understand. I leave the decision completely in your hands. Your friend, Jack.

After Ben finished reading, Jack took the letter from him and reread it. "I don't know, Ben. I'm just not getting it. It seems my dad gave us the means to get whatever he had planned for us done. I wonder how much money is in those accounts."

Ben stood staring at the box then closed the lid. "I don't know, kid. Hopefully, our guys will be calling me with that information sometime today or tomorrow. In the meantime, let's finish going through the desk. There's gotta be more information."

Jack handed the letter back to Ben and walked over to the desk. He pulled out the bottom drawer and found some old files. In one of the files was another list of names in a binder. There were too many to read, so he set it aside. In another file were records of various types of equipment. Cranes, barges, and a record of various types of ships and boats. "Hey, Ben, check this out."

Ben looked at the records, but didn't see any significance. He laid them down and pulled out the final drawer. Inside were more photos of *Titanic* docked, and many more photos from when the wreckage was discovered. There were also records of expeditions paid for by Jack Sr.

"Look at this, kid. Your dad financed expeditions out into the Atlantic. Now I'm starting to realize your dad wasn't going on fishing trips. But I'm still not connecting the dots."

Jack took a break and leaned on the desk. He picked up the thick binder and glanced through it. Suddenly, he had the idea to compare the other list he had found the previous day. He saw that the names matched what was in the binder. "Check this out, Ben. The names we found yesterday are in this binder."

Ben grabbed the binder and looked at the names. He saw they were in alphabetical order. He flipped the pages over to "K" and realized what he was holding. "Here, kid. Take a look." Ben held the binder up so Jack could see what he was talking about. "This is all the passengers who were on *Titanic*. You can see your father and your grandparents names listed. Check out your grandfather's name. Victor Carnelius Kotter."

When Jack saw the name, he was surprised. His dad had given him his grandfather's middle name, Carnelius. It just reaffirmed what they had already discovered. "I just can't believe all this is happening. A few days ago, I was so excited about coming here and finding something really great, but now I'm not really sure how I feel about all this. What'ya say we take a break and eat something, and at the same time, have an old-fashion sit-down and try to put this puzzle together?"

Ben was definitely on board with that idea. Jack walked over to a cooler of food and drinks he brought along and set up two chairs. After lunch, he sat back in his chair with some paper and a pen. "Alright, let's write down what we have so far. A mysterious box my dad left for me. Inside is a letter to you, an old diary letter of a tragedy at sea, the address to this house, coordinates that we now know are the coordinates to *Titanic*, and the key that opened this shed. Now, we get here just to find a desk with a photo of my grandfather, along with another photo of my dad as a little boy with people we now know are my grandparents standing on the *Titanic*. We found overseas accounts my dad left for us to utilize for whatever he had planned out. We found the names of all the passengers on *Titanic*, along with a library book about *Titanic* I had when I was in school. We also know my dad financed expeditions out to the *Titanic*, and we also have files on heavy equipment used at sea. Over in the corner is your old lockbox, which was given to you by your brother, with a letter from my dad to you giving you the passwords to the accounts. There are also pictures of the wreckage of *Titanic*, and last but not least, we have my dad's car, which doesn't really tie into anything. Have I missed anything?"

Ben took a drink of his iced tea while he thought about it. Jack could see he had already figured out some of the puzzle, if not all of it. "Alright, Ben, I know you have something, so what is it?" Ben had a distraught look, and that was something rarely seen by Jack. "Come on, Ben, you have me worried now. What's going on inside that thick skull of yours?"

Ben stood up and walked over to the desk. He started sifting through some of the loose paperwork that was spread around on the desktop. He picked up some papers he'd looked at the day before but didn't think anything of. Listed on the paperwork were various museums from around the globe and some names of cemeteries. Fairview Lawn, Mount Olivet, and Baron de Hirsch cemeteries. They were all names of cemeteries in Halifax, Nova Scotia in the eastern part of Canada. Although these papers didn't mean anything the day before, they now confirmed what Ben already knew. "Hey, kid, give me a few minutes. I want to call some friends of mine to verify a few things."

Jack's patience was growing thin, but he knew enough to give Ben space when he asked for it. As Ben stepped out of the shed and headed for the clearing, Jack was all too happy to go back and continue to check out the Ferrari. Of course, first thing was first. Check out the engine. When Jack popped the hood, he was shocked to even think his dad, as stuffy as he was, drove that kind of car. That particular car was fitted with a V-12 competition engine with an aluminum block. It also had three Weber 40 DCL/6 carburetors and probably tapped out at about 140 mph. Pretty fast for an old-school ride. He checked to see if there was any oil left in the engine, but it was bone dry. He checked all the fluids then realized his dad must have drained them all for storage purposes. Jack tampered with the car for a while longer before Ben came walking back in. He walked over to the desk and looked through the paperwork again as though he was looking for something specific.

By then, Jack's fascination with the Ferrari had subsided, so he took a chance at trying to pick Ben's brain. "Listen, Ben, you want to let me in on whatever you're trying to do? I might be able to help." Jack could see the frustration in Ben's face, but still decided to press him. "Come on, Ben, my dad wanted you to help me. Not the other way around."

Ben stopped shuffling papers then took a deep breath. "I'm sorry, kid. You're right, I need to tell you some things and I just don't know how to do it. Have a seat, kid. Let's talk."

Jack didn't like the sound of that, but he knew if he shook a bee's nest long enough, he would eventually get stung. As he sat down, all he could think about was extremely bad news. Ben grabbed two iced teas from the cooler and handed one to Jack as he sat down. "Listen, kid, let me ask you a question. Do you remember how devastated you were when your father died?"

Although Jack Sr. had been older, Jack remembered back when his father died and remembered how much he hurt. "What does my father's death have to do with anything?"

Ben hesitated because he knew he was stepping on shaky ground. "Listen, kid, how do you think you would feel if instead of your dad dying in old age, he died when you were a little boy, or even worse, he disappeared, never to be found."

Jack sat and stared at Ben because he just didn't understand what Ben was trying to get at. "But my dad died late in his life. So I don't know how I would feel. I guess I would be just as devastated."

With some reserve, Ben took a deep breath. "Alright, kid, stay with me. Take a look at the list you made of things we know so far. Tell me what you think."

Jack reached over and grabbed the list off the cooler. He studied it for a few minutes but just couldn't come up with anything. "Well, it seems my dad and grandparents were on *Titanic*. Judging from all the memorabilia, he was fascinated with the sinking."

With disappointment, Ben stood up scratching his head. "Come on, kid, think. Your dad was on *Titanic* when he was four years old. He made it off along with your grandmother. Think about it, kid. I'm going to ask you one more time. How would you feel if your father disappeared never to be found or heard from again?"

Jack's heart suddenly became very heavy. "If it was me, I wouldn't stop until I found him or found out what happened to him."

With half a smile on his face, Ben sat back down. "Exactly, kid. You get to go to the head of the class. Now look around you, kid. What do you see? Look at your list. Think about the diary letter with the bank accounts. Come on, kid, you're almost there."

Jack thought he knew what Ben was getting at, but wasn't sure because it sounded too bizarre. "I can't imagine the hurt my dad must of felt knowing how his dad died, but if you're suggesting my dad was going to somehow find Victor and recover his body after all these years, then you're as loony as that idea sounds."

Ben let out a deep sigh as he tried to think of a way to bring Jack up to speed. "Well, kid, you're kind of on the right track, so let me try to fill in the missing pieces. While you were playing with that car, I phoned some friends who specialize in historical facts. Those papers I was looking at had names of cemeteries on them. They're the cemeteries where they took a lot of the remains from *Titanic*. All the graves are marked by numbers in order from the way they found the bodies. We also know your dad was funding expeditions in the Atlantic. I think your dad was looking for more than just a body. Judging from the files we found with all the equipment listings and the files with the bank accounts, he was looking for *Titanic*."

All that information over just a couple of days was a lot for one person to handle, but Jack was hanging tough. "Okay, so he wanted to find *Titanic* because his dad died during the sinking. Someone else beat him to the punch. I remember seeing it on the news when *Titanic* was found. I don't remember my dad getting too excited over it. Actually, I don't remember him paying any attention to it at all. But I do understand, after all these years, why he was so upset over my school project."

This was a lot for even Ben to comprehend, but he also knew he had to help Jack get through it. "Listen, kid, I also called our financial guys back in New York to see if they found anything out about those mystery accounts. They were able to pull some strings and put together some rough figures for me. It seems your dad had been sending money to these accounts for a very long time."

As Jack sat on the edge of his seat waiting for Ben to reveal an amount, Ben thought about it then changed his mind about telling Jack exactly how much money was in the accounts. "I also found out your dad placed four names on the accounts, I'm guessing for your protection."

Jack felt deflated like a balloon when Ben didn't tell him the amount of money involved. He stood up in a rage and tried to bully Ben for the information. "Come on, Ben. Being the head of Kotter Industries, I think I have the right to know everything you know, so what kind of money are we talking about?"

As Jack stood there with his hands on his hips pouting, Ben couldn't help but laugh at him. "I'm sorry, kid, you just don't know how funny you look right now." Ben stood up and walked over to the desk. "Listen, kid, you're absolutely right. When it comes to Kotter Industries, you have the right to know everything about a situation.

Unfortunately for you, your dad kept all this separate from the company, so you can forget the whole idea of being in control. Getting back to those accounts, as I said, there are four names on them. Your dad's name was first. Then your mom's. My name was third, and last but not least, your name is fourth. Now, these accounts were set up specifically for one purpose and they came with very strict guidelines."

As Ben continued to explain, Jack's frustration started to ease. "Alright, so now what? What do we do with the money in the account?"

Ben started shuffling through the papers on the desk again, looking for something. Jack stood beside him watching and wondering. "You were looking through these papers earlier. What are you looking for?"

Ben looked for a few more seconds then slammed the papers down in frustration. "Damn!"

Jack could see the anger in Ben's eyes, but knew he had to somehow press him to get information. "Please, Ben, if you just let me help you, maybe we can figure this out."

With his anger still at its peak, Ben walked over to the car to try to calm his nerves. "That's the problem, kid. I've already figured it out. As soon as I saw those damned accounts, I knew what your dad had planned."

Jack walked over and stood next to Ben, then he turned his head to briefly look at the car. "Yeah, I kinda figured you knew what was going on, and I can take an educated guess that you don't like it. Judging by your frustration, you were hoping to find something in those papers that would bypass whatever it is that we're supposed to be doing."

With disbelief, Ben just stared at Jack. "You gotta be kidding me. Sometimes, kid, you can be so on and other times, just ignorant to intelligence. Listen, kid, I guess I still look at you as a small child, and that's not your fault. I find myself trying to protect you at all cost, but I have to stop doing that. All these years you've grown up in front of me and that kind of snuck up on me. Listen, kid, I'm really tired. I'm getting old and I just can't for the life of me figure out why your dad would leave this godforsaken problem behind for us to deal with."

Jack didn't respond because he figured the strain was taking its toll on Ben, so he decided to give him some breathing room in order to get him to finally tell him what he thought was going on. Instead, he decided to lighten the conversation. Jack turned around and stared at the car. "So, was my dad actually this cool or do you think this car was a one-time thing?"

Ben took his mind off his thoughts momentarily and turned to look at the car. "Well, kid, I don't think. I know your dad was cool. Not because of this car, but because of the kind of person he was. He was a lot more than cool. Ben placed his arm around Jack and walked him over to the desk. Listen, kid, this is what I'm thinking. For whatever reason, your dad was on the *Titanic* with his parents, Victor and Elizabeth. I think the letter that was in the box described what happened probably an hour or so before the ship finally sank. I can't fathom the horror of seeing something like that as a child. I'm guessing somehow Victor got separated from Elizabeth, so she did the only thing she could. She picked Jack up and ran for a lifeboat."

As Jack listened, Ben leaned back and sat on the edge of the desk and folded his arms. He shook his head a few times as he tried to picture the event in his head. "I can only imagine what your dad was thinking. Listen, kid, your dad was a very heartfelt kind of guy. He was a humanitarian in every sense of the word. You were kind of right about him trying to find Victor, but you were thinking in the wrong way. I think your dad wanted to find Victor in spirit, along with every other poor soul that perished during that awful tragedy and bring them home."

Jack listened but was waiting for Ben to make a little more sense. "I'm sorry, Ben. I'm trying to follow what you're saying, but you lost me with the spirit thing."

Ben turned around and picked up the papers that had the cemeteries listed on them. "Look, kid, your dad had the right idea about researching these cemeteries, but I'm guessing he found out the same information I found out when I called those history buffs. All those people who were buried in those graves had numbers placed on them instead of names, which means they weren't prominent people. Those were the people that were found days, even weeks later that couldn't be identified because most were second and third class passengers. I think your dad may have thought Victor went down with the ship and probably remained there in spirit. When I spoke to our financial guys a little while ago, they confirmed what I already thought." Jack was on pins and needles and stared intensely while Ben paused.

In his mind, Ben still couldn't believe the magnitude of what was happening. "Over the years, with interest rates on the rise, your dad accumulated millions of dollars in those accounts. There's only one conclusion that I keep coming up with. You dad wanted to raise the *Titanic*."

Jack heard what Ben said, but was blown away that he even suggested it. "What! I don't believe you, Ben. You've come up with some crazy stuff in the past, but nothing compares to this. Do you seriously think my dad would waste away a lifetime chasing a delusional dream like you're suggesting?"

Ben didn't feel any shame in what he was saying, but he knew it sounded pretty far-fetched. "What do you want me to say, kid? Nothing else makes sense. Your dad wasn't delusional. I just think he was on a quest to find some closure. Look at what we have. Millions of dollars sitting in secret accounts, expeditions to *Titanic*, and research on deep sea salvage equipment. Not to mention all the information your dad had about *Titanic*."

Jack walked over to a chair and sat down. His mind was racing and he was worn out and worn down. "Alright, Ben, let's say for the time being that you're right. Now what?"

Ben really didn't know what to say, but he had an idea of what he wanted to do. "Listen, kid, forget about this. Your father led a good life. Let him go. What'ya say we pack all this stuff away and move on with our lives."

Jack thought about it probably longer than what he should have. "What if it was your father? Would you still feel the same way?" When Ben hesitated to answer, Jack knew right then he couldn't just walk away. "I have an idea. It's been a long day and we're both really tired. Why don't we have all this shipped back to New York so we can at least think about what our next step will be?"

Ben had no argument. He was ready to put California behind him. "Alright, kid. You're right. We'll go back to New York first thing in the morning. When we get back, we'll sit down and figure something out."

CHAPTER SEVENTEEN

When Jack made it back to his room, he made some phone calls and had a local company ship everything to a storage facility in New York. Afterwards, they didn't waste any time flying back to San Francisco, where they stayed the night. The next morning, they were up early and on their way to the airport. During the cab ride, Jack noticed Ben was quiet and still looking rundown. "What's the matter, Ben? Don't tell me you couldn't sleep as tired as you were."

Ben glanced at Jack with the naughty look he usually had after he just had sex. "Listen, kid, if I tell you I slept fine, will you leave me alone?"

Jack smiled as he thought about opening that proverbial can of worms. "Nope. You would just be lying. So what gives?"

Without hesitation, Ben rubbed his eyes as he blurted out the previous night's sexploits. "Okay, kid. So I hooked up with that barmaid, Jamie, again. After going through all that information we found yesterday, I needed a nice stiff drink or four. I gotta tell you, kid, the things that girl can do with her mouth are unbelievable, and I never knew a female could have so many orgasms. She wore me out like an old ragdoll."

Jack didn't say anything else. He'd asked for it and Ben gave it to him. Instead, he started to concentrate more on his dad and thinking about growing up and the times they had spent together. Just like

Ben, Jack couldn't figure out why his dad would leave behind such an impossible task.

Ben slept on the plane during the flight back to New York, which gave Jack time to thoroughly think about the past few days. When their flight finally landed, Casey was there waiting with the limo doors open. Although, there was nothing of significance going on at Kotter Industries, Jack and Ben agreed to stop by and take care of any mail or messages that were piling up in their absence. When they arrived, everyone was gone for the day except Hellen and Bonnie. Bonnie knew Jack would be back in town, but was surprised to see him walking off the elevator. Hellen, on the other hand, also knew Ben would be back in town and she wasn't a bit surprised to see him prancing down the hallway. "You old goat. You just couldn't stay away, could you?"

Before he entered his office, Ben stopped and smiled. "It's nice to see you too, Hellen."

While in his office, Ben quickly discarded all the junk mail and listened to the few messages he had on his phone. Of course it was time for a drink, and of course he made two. One to gulp down and one to sip and enjoy while he kicked his feet up and rested at his desk.

Jack, on the other hand, had plenty to do. After taking care of messages and mail, he called his friend Dale. "Hey, Dale, I'm back in town. What'ya say we get together one day this week and have dinner."

Dale was all too happy to hear Jack's voice because he needed to tell Jack to forget the whole Lilith idea he had. "Hey, Jack, sounds great. Just let me know something soon so I can take the night off."

After talking to Dale, Jack walked down the hall to Ben's office. Bonnie and Hellen had gone for the night, so he opened the door and peeked his head in. "You ready to go, Ben?"

Ben opened his eyes and shot Jack the look of death. "I know your arms can't be that tired."

Jack just stared for a moment, not knowing what Ben was talking about. Then it hit him. He'd forgotten to knock. "Sorry, Ben. Old habits are too hard to break. Jack smiled as he closed the door. I'll be waiting for you at the elevator."

Ben finally pulled himself together and made his way to the elevator. "So, kid, what'ya think about all this?"

Jack didn't really have a lot to say. Mainly because he was all thought out. "Well, I think we both have some decisions to make."

As the elevator descended to the lobby, Ben thought about what Jack said. "We don't have anything to decide. You have to decide whether or not you're going to let this pipe dream go."

When the elevator doors opened, Ben stepped out without hesitation and walked towards the lobby doors. Jack knew what Ben was trying to do. In the past, he would bait him into an argument so he would eventually back down just to appease him. But that was then and this was now. Jack was older and had some pretty big shoes to fill. He picked up the pace because he wanted to resolve the argument before Ben made it to the limo. "Wait a minute, Ben. I can't believe you're trying to pull this old bullshit with me."

Ben could hear the tone of Jack's voice and wasn't in the mood for it. "No, you wait a minute. I don't give a rat's ass about some broken down ship at the bottom of the ocean and neither should you. You need to let this nonsense go for the good of Kotter Industries. Ben didn't give Jack a chance to respond." He stepped into the limo and shut the door. Casey understood the hint and stepped around to the other side of the limo. He stood by the door waiting for Jack, but Jack was still stunned by what Ben had just said.

"I thought we agreed on talking about this?"

Ben slid across the seat and peered out at Jack. "I thought we agreed to drop anything that resembled a disaster?"

As Jack heart sank in disappointment, he glanced over at Casey, who was still waiting with the door open. "That's okay, Casey, I'll find another way home."

Casey almost said something, but he caught himself because he didn't want to step between two friends. So he climbed into the driver seat and drove off.

It was getting late so Jack called Bria, but she didn't answer. He figured she was out with friends at the clubs, so he called Dale back. "Hey, Dale, if you're not busy, I need a ride home."

Luckily, Dale wasn't working, so he agreed to pick Jack up and have a late dinner. Jack walked to the front of the building where the company had set up some benches so employees could sit and have lunch. As he sat thinking about the conversation with Ben, he thought about his dad and all the times they had together. Jack remembered the incident with the box and how upset Ben was about it. Maybe it was the same with *Titanic.* Maybe Ben was just really hurt that after all the years together with Jack Sr., he wasn't part of what was going on. Nevertheless, it didn't give Ben the right to explode the way he did.

When Dale finally pulled up, he could tell Jack was feeling really down. He was a little hesitant to ask about California, but he decided to anyway. "So I'm guessing your trip didn't go very well."

Jack glanced over and smiled. "You think?"

Afterwards, neither person said anything, but Dale knew just the place to go. The Wiley Roadster. After all, it was Jack's favorite place to be, and the food was good. As they pulled onto the parking lot, there seemed to be a lot of new faces and cars spread about. Dale pulled alongside a '56 Dodge truck. It had potential, but was still in rough condition. Jack glanced over and noticed it was the Mopar brothers, Walley and Jimmy. "Hey, guys, nice truck. Where did you steal it?"

Walley stepped out and walked around to give Jack a handshake and a hug. After all the pleasantries were exchanged, Dale walked over and ordered some food and drinks. Of course the main subject Jack wanted to know about was Lilith. "So, come on. You guys know I've been out of town. What's going on with that bitch?"

All Walley could do was shake his head in disgust. "Well, you see all these new guys spread out across the parking lot? It seems that her reputation has spread. All these new guys you see are from Upstate. Some drove all the way from Massachusetts and Boston."

Jack looked around at all the new cars. Some were nice and some looked deceiving, but none were prepared to handle anything like Lilith. "I'm wondering what these guys are thinking."

Finally, Jimmy stepped out of the truck to express his dismay. "These clowns come down here to our turf and set up shop at the Wiley Roadster. It really pisses me off."

At the risk of starting a fight with his brother, Walley laughed. "You're an idiot, Jimmy. This isn't the '50s and '60s, and this isn't our turf, so shut your face."

Just then, Dale came walking over and handed Jack his dinner. "Let me guess. You're talking about that Plymouth."

As Jack gobbled down some fries, he prepared himself for any information he could get from Dale. "Damn right I am. What's the deal with these guys from Upstate."

As he prepared to give Jack an answer, Dale set his food down on the hood of his car. "Well, I'm not sure what Jimmy and Walley told you so far, but all these clowns want a shot at Lilith. They don't care about the deaths and the people she's hurt. All they see is a trophy."

As Jack ate his food, he looked around at all the cars lining up to prowl the strip. "Can't you do anything about this?"

Dale laughed as he started wolfing down his burger. "Do what? What do you want me to do? Unless they're doing something wrong, my hands are tied. Your favorite cop, Sergeant Lactgan, is out there right now waiting for some of these knuckleheads to let loose so he can catch them in the act. Other than that, all we can do is clean up the aftermath."

Jack leaned back on the car and thought about what Dale was saying. He also thought about the plan they'd discussed. "So, has anybody actually seen her since she wrecked those three police cars?"

Without hesitation, Walley jumped right in. "It's been awhile, and everyone thought she was gone for good, but she's recently been seen sneaking around the area."

As Dale finished eating, he crumpled up his trash and placed it back into the bag. "That's not all. Right before all these knuckleheads showed up this week, two guys from the Bronx went looking for her."

Jack listened closely because he knew what the ending was going to be. "I'm guessing they found what they were looking for."

With a somber look on his face, Dale continued with the story. "Yeah, you can say that. Lactgan chased all three, but they must have been hauling ass because he couldn't even get close. Later on, we got the call for an accident and possibly a pedestrian struck. When we got there, it looked like one of the guys may have flipped his car. He's still in the hospital. Doctors say it's not looking too good. With the other guy, we're not really sure what happened. His car was at the scene and didn't have a scratch on it. He was found about twenty feet away mangled beyond recognition. Our traffic team put together a scenario that I think is probably pretty accurate."

Walley and Jimmy already knew the story so they decided to

walk over and talk to some women friends who had just pulled onto the parking lot. "Listen, Jack, come see us before you leave."

Jack gave a half smile and head nod. "Alright, I'll be over in a minute." As he turned his attention back to Dale, Jack noticed the parking lot had started to clear. "Well, there they go."

Dale watched as one by one the cars roared as they left the lot. "I don't know whether to curse them or feel sorry for them. Anyway, getting back to that poor soul I was telling you about. After an extensive investigation, our traffic guys came up with a pretty good idea of what happened. They think the Plymouth may have somehow flipped the first car. From there, his friend made the mistake of thinking it was over and got out of his car to check on his friend. This is where it gets interesting. We followed the tread marks and it looks like Lilith circled back around and ran the guy down, dragging him away from the scene. Now check this out. This bitch went from being dangerous to being psycho. It looks like she not only ran this poor guy down, but she backed up and ran him over several times. I don't know, Jack. I know I spoke to you about my plan, but now I don't think it's a good idea and neither does the department anymore."

Jack didn't say anything. With a distraught look, he rubbed his neck and walked out to the middle of the parking lot. He could see the Mopar brothers laughing and playing with a couple of barely legal women, and as he looked around, he remembered his friend Bobby and what Lilith did to him. He took a few minutes to himself then walked back over to Dale. "Do you have anything to go on?"

Dale could hear the shakiness in Jack's voice and knew how he felt about Lilith. "Well, our forensics team is working on some things and our traffic team is still trying to put together a profile. Homicide has now been given the green light to work as much overtime as they want, as long as they're working this case."

With the weak tone of his voice and the look in his eye, Dale didn't sound too convincing. Jack smiled as he kicked some rocks around. "You don't have anything, do you?"

Dale wasn't surprised that Jack had guessed it. "I'm sorry, Jack. Not only do we have nothing, we have absolutely nothing. She's so damn fast our new traffic cameras can't even keep up with her."

It was getting late and Jack wanted to get home. "I think I've had enough of this day. Let's get out of here."

As they drove by the Mopar brothers, Jack could see they were still trying hard to hook up with the young women, so he yelled, "See'ya later," and waved goodbye.

When Dale finally dropped Jack off, he was almost too tired to walk into his house. As he did, he noticed some things were thrown about. As he stood looking around, Bria emerged from the kitchen area dressed in a very skimpy maid's outfit. She started role playing and attempting to speak with a French accent. "Oh, Monsieur Kotter, I wasn't expecting you home this early. Please forgive me for the mess. I will do anything to make it up to you."

Jack couldn't help but laugh. He was so tired and was expecting to just crash once he made it home. "So, what should I be calling you?"

With her usual devious smile and stiletto heels, Bria walked over to Jack. With her best fake accent, she whispered into his ear. "I am your new maid, Corine." Before Jack could say anything else, Bria turned and walked up the steps. As she neared the top of the steps, she unbuttoned the first three buttons of her outfit. She then kicked her stilettos down the steps and walked into the bedroom.

As he slowly walked upstairs, Jack knew he was in for a long night. As he entered the room, Bria was there to greet him. "So, Monsieur Kotter, what shall I do to make up for my disobedience?"

Jack smiled as he pulled the rest of Bria's buttons, letting her outfit fall to the floor. When Bria pulled Jack's zipper down, she dropped to her knees as he shut the bedroom door.

CHAPTER EIGHTEEN

During the early morning hours, Jack and Bria lay sleeping, but Jack's thoughts became restless and he started to toss and turn. He suddenly found himself riding in the passenger seat of a car. The car was going very fast, but he couldn't see the driver. He couldn't make out a face because it was cloaked in a dark shadow. Suddenly the mysterious figure spoke. "I'm going to kill you, Jack Kotter." He recognized the voice immediately. It was Lilith. As he pulled the door handle to jump out, it wouldn't open. Without warning, the car plunged off a bridge and into the dark murky water below. Lilith was gone and in her place was Victor, his grandfather, the man he'd been dreaming about on *Titanic*.

As fast as the dream began, it was gone. Jack woke up in a sweat and screaming, with Bria wide awake and looking at him in horror. "What's wrong, Jack? You were tossing and turning, then all of the sudden, you screamed."

Jack jumped out of bed and hurried into the bathroom. He threw some cold water on his face as he glared at himself in the mirror. Bria walked in to find Jack dripping with sweat. She quickly grabbed a towel and started drying him off. "What happened, Jack?"

Jack took the towel from Bria as he stood up straight and finished drying himself off. "I can't do this anymore. I just can't do this."

Bria wasn't sure what he was talking about, so she gave him a few minutes to stop shaking so he could calm himself down. She led Jack back to the bedroom and sat him down on the edge of the bed. As she knelt down between his legs, she looked Jack in the eyes. She could see the emotion was drained from his face, so she just sat quietly until he was ready to talk.

As Jack stood up, he threw the towel around his neck and took a few minutes to regain his composure. He turned to Bria and told her everything that had happened in California. He also reminded her about the dreams he'd been having.

Bria could hardly believe what Jack was saying. It sounded like something straight out of Alfred Hitchcock. "I can't believe this is happening, Jack. Your grandfather whom you've never met died on *Titanic* and is now in your dreams. Now you think your dad had plans to salvage the *Titanic*? Even if that were true, I don't think it's possible."

Jack knew he was really testing the boundaries of possibilities. "Well, my dad always said if you have determination and resources, anything is possible."

Jack and Bria sat up talking until sunrise. Afterwards, Jack prepared for a full day. He knew he had to call Dale. He also had to take a trip to Jersey with Ben to go see Old Salty Crab, and he would probably be confronted by Ben about the contents of the shed. As he left the house, he tried to call Dale, but had to leave a message.

On the way to work, Jack went over the dream in his mind over and over again. At least he now knew he wasn't going crazy, but that didn't mean it was any less difficult to have to deal with. At that point in his life, he was used to dealing with company problems, but this was more personal and he kept coming up with the same conclusion: Try to fulfill his dad's last wish, which meant taking on Ben and doing the impossible. Raising the *Titanic.*

As he pulled into the parking lot at work, Ben was there waiting for him. "For once in your life, kid, can you be on time for work?"

Jack pulled *Fringe* into a parking space and stepped out laughing. "Come on, Ben, I didn't know the owner of a company had a specific time to be at work."

Ben didn't find that to be funny and gave Jack a tongue lashing. "You lead by example, Jack. If you come off looking like a playboy then nobody will take you seriously. If nobody takes you seriously, then how the hell are you supposed to run this company? Domino effect. One leads to another. In the end, you're just a poor little rich kid who nobody wants to know. Now let's go. Casey has the limo waiting."

Ben never called Jack by his name, so Jack knew Ben was serious, which meant it was going to be a long ride to Jersey.

As they left New York, Jack was hesitant to mention anything about what he'd been thinking about, especially since Ben was upset, but he knew it was better to take the plunge instead of waiting like he had with the box. "Listen, Ben, I know you're upset right now, but I really feel we need to talk."

Ben reached over to the minibar and grabbed two beers. He popped one open and handed the other to Jack. "I've said what I had to say and that's it. Don't worry, kid, I'm not going to hound you about it anymore. I just think your dad and I taught you better."

Jack was relieved. For a minute he thought Ben was talking about California. "Thanks, Ben. You're right about leading by example. That's why I need to talk to you about what I've been thinking about."

Ben knew what Jack wanted to talk about so he took a nice hefty drink as he prepared himself for battle.

Jack set his beer down and gathered his thoughts. "You do realize it's only nine o'clock in the morning and we're drinking beer?"

Ben smiled as he finished off the rest of his beer. "Hell, yeah, it's a nice feeling to be able to drink while you're at work."

Jack could only shake his head and laugh. "And you just got done calling me irresponsible."

Ben set his empty bottle down and geared up for another lesson. "Listen, kid, being at the top has its perks, but it also has its responsibilities. Both are important when you're constantly under duress. But that's enough of that. Let's get down to what you've been wanting to talk about. Let me begin by telling you I had Hellen check into those tombstones your dad visited. I was right. One was Elizabeth Kotter and the other was blank and had instructions at the cemetery office. It was to be engraved when her husband, Victor Kotter, arrived. I can't believe your dad and mom are buried so close and I didn't think to check those graves. I guess at the time my mind was elsewhere."

Jack was actually relieved that Ben told him that. "So you see where my dad was going with this, and you think because he's dead it should just be dropped."

Ben promised himself he wouldn't get upset or yell simply because of the delicate nature of the discussion. "Listen, kid, before we even left California, I knew what you were thinking. It's honorable and I respect you for it, but it's just not practical. You have no idea how much damage taking on such a massive project like that would do to this company. I understand your argument about your dad's last wish and I know he wanted me to help, but there's a reason why my name is on those accounts, and I'm not willing to risk all that we built simply for the sake of a shipwreck and somebody's spirit, which may or may not still be down there. It's just not going to happen."

Jack sat back in his seat and wound up for another pitch. "Listen, Ben, when you drive onto that parking lot every morning, what name do you see on that building? You see the Kotter name. When you walk into my office and look at that name plate, what do you see? Jack Kotter Jr., president of the company and, may I add, majority shareholder."

With a sadness in his heart, Ben just stared at Jack. "So, kid, is that the way you want to play this? Alright. I've been trying to humor you this whole time, but maybe I should have been more direct." Ben saw the pitch and was ready for it. One swing was all it took. Home run out of the park. "You might control Kotter Industries, but those bank accounts are under the direction of my authority. And that's that. After we see what Old Salty has to say, we'll be done with this."

Jack felt about as small as he could feel after being scolded by Ben, but Ben was right. His dad placed Ben's name on those accounts for a reason.

From there on out, it was a quiet ride all the way to Jersey. After what seemed like forever, Casey finally pulled into the Clark Landing Boat and Yacht Club. It was one of the oldest yacht clubs in Jersey and was named after Rodderick Clark, the man who'd founded it in 1872. Jack didn't waste any time jumping out of the limo. He was still pretty hurt from Ben's words. He didn't even wait for Ben to step out. Instead, he made a beeline for the office. Ben knew Jack was upset so he let him go while he took a stroll out onto the pier. As he looked around, he saw two young men about Jack's age loading up for what looked like a fishing trip. Then he noticed the name of the yacht. *Just by Chance*. Suddenly, an elderly man walked out of the cabin. Ben stared for a moment then made his way over to the yacht, but by that time, the elderly man had disappeared.

As Ben approached, he called out to the young men. "Hello, I couldn't help but notice the name on your boat."

The two young men stopped what they were doing and stepped off the yacht to talk with Ben. "Sorry, mister, we're booked for today."

Ben smiled and introduced himself. "My name is Benjamin Marcus. Maybe you can help me out. I'm looking for an old friend of mine. Maybe you know him."

Before Ben could say anything else, one of the men cut him off. "Sorry, mister, I don't think you have any old friends around here."

Ben noticed the hostility right away but decided not to provoke a fight. Suddenly, the elderly man, looking raggedy and worn, appeared on deck again. "I would know that old sour face anywhere. Benjamin Marcus, you old sea hound."

As the elderly man stepped onto the pier, Ben extended his hand in friendship. "Old Salty Crab. It's been a long time."

When Salty finished shaking hands, he turned to the two workers and barked out some orders to get back to work. "Sorry about that, Ben. Those are my two grandsons. They're very protective of me. They're always thinking I'm gonna sell the family business out from under them. You dressed in that thousand-dollar business suit didn't help any. Anyway, Jack always said you would show up one day. Come on, let me give you the five-dollar tour. We have a lot to talk about."

As Old Salty gave a tour of his yacht, Ben listened to what he had to say. "Jack told me you would have questions, so I'll do my best to answer them." Salty took Ben into a lounge area so they could have a drink and talk. "So, after all these years, I probably have just as many questions as you do, but you can go first."

Ben started right in, but not about the trips Jack Sr. took. Instead, he asked about the relationship between the two men. "Tell me something, Salty. I've always wondered why Jack gave you start up money for your fishing business."

Old Salty smiled because he could hear the jealousy in Ben's voice. "Well, that Jack was a crafty one. He got in contact with me about a week after us three had met. He knew about a fishing boat

I wanted to buy, so he made me a deal I couldn't refuse. He would supply me with the startup cost for several fishing boats if once a year I would take him on a fishing trip out into the Atlantic. Now, here's the funny part. He never liked to fish. He would always bring along charts and portable sonar equipment. I used to ask him what he was looking for, but he would always somehow change the subject, so I stopped asking questions."

Ben sat listening while Salty stood up and poured more drinks. While mixing the drinks, he noticed someone creeping around outside the yacht. "Hey, Ben, you expecting somebody else?"

Ben stood up and walked over to the window. He saw Jack checking out the yacht. "That would be Jack Jr. I guess he finally decided to join the party."

Old Salty walked out to greet Jack and to welcome him onto the yacht. "You're a good looking boy. I should have known you were Jack Kotter's son."

As Jack walked into the lounge area and saw Ben, it made him even more angry. "What the hell is going on, Ben? Why didn't you come and get me?"

Just then, Old Salty handed Jack a drink and invited him to sit down. "I'm guessing you have questions about your dad?"

Jack graciously accepted Salty's invite and sat down. "I'm here because apparently my dad was living some kind of double life and I thought you might know something about what he was doing."

After a brief pause, Salty looked at Ben, and Ben gave him the okay head-nod to tell them everything he knew. Salty took a sip of his drink and sat down. "Well, I already told Ben about the agreement between your dad and me. He gave me startup money for a fishing business, and in return, I took him out into the Atlantic Ocean once a year. He never brought any fishing gear. Instead, he brought sonar equipment. Real fancy state of the art stuff. He wanted to crisscross certain areas, and much of his time was spent writing in his little book he kept with him. After doing the same thing year after year, sometime back in the mid-eighties, I remember he showed up one time without any equipment. He handed me some coordinates and asked me to take him there. By then, I knew enough not to ask questions, so we headed out. When we arrived, there were a couple of vessels already there. They looked like research vessels. I finally got up enough nerve to ask your dad what he was looking for all those years. I'll never forget the look on his face. He turned white as a ghost and he says, 'My dad is down there.' I just kind of stared at him for a minute then he says, 'These are the coordinates for the *Titanic.* They finally located her.'"

By that time, Jack and Ben had finished their drinks. Ben didn't say anything. He stood up and walked out to the deck. Jack sat quietly and waited to see if Salty was going to say any more. "Did you and my dad ever really talk about anything besides what he was doing out there?"

Salty paused for a moment then refilled their glasses. "I knew your dad for a very long time. Your mom too. They were so happy together. It was only by chance that we met. Thus the name of this yacht. Your dad was checking out the shipyard I worked at when he saw me crabbing off the piers. He walked over and introduced himself to me and you know the rest."

Jack stood up and walked over to the window. He noticed Ben standing on the deck looking out over the water. "Did my dad ever mention anything more about *Titanic* or what his plan was after it was found?"

Salty walked over to Jack and stood next to him. "Your dad was a very private man. All those years of going out into the Atlantic with his sonar equipment, and he never once said anything to me about what he was doing. And I had enough respect for him not to ask. Our last trip together, when he finally told me about those coordinates, he told me the story about being on *Titanic* during that God-awful night. He told me God took his dad away and that he was going to do everything in his power to get him back, and I believed him."

Jack could feel himself getting choked up, so he quickly turned away and excused himself to use the facilities. After showing Jack the restroom, Salty walked out to talk with Ben. "So, Ben, you've done well for yourself over the years."

Ben was still thinking about the story Salty had told. "Yeah, I can't complain. I'm curious, though. Why would a large fishing corporation be interested in someone such as yourself who only had a couple of small fishing boats?"

Old Salty knew where Ben was trying to go and he had no problem calling him out. "Come on, Ben. I think you already know the answer and you're just trying to put together the final puzzle pieces."

Ben smiled because Salty was right. "Okay, let me take a stab at it then. Jack Sr. has a dilemma but doesn't quite know how to go about handling it without arousing suspicion. By pure chance, he meets you and finds out you one day want to have your own fishing business. Now, suddenly, he sees an opportunity he can't pass up. So he offers you a deal. He gives you the startup money and you take him on these make believe fishing trips once a year, which is a perfect cover for what he's really doing. Now, here's where it gets interesting. He doesn't like deep water to begin with and I'm guessing being out in the Atlantic can get pretty rough in a modest fishing boat."

Salty asked Ben to hold that thought while he retrieved two more drinks. After he handed Ben his glass, he held up his drink and made a toast. "To Jack Kotter Sr., may he rest in peace soon. Now let me continue what you started. You're right about Jack. There were times he got so sick I thought his insides were going to fall out. I didn't find out 'til much later. Apparently, Jack knew the owner of the company that bought me out. I knew there were reasons why they offered me so much money, but who am I to look a gift horse in the mouth? After the deal went down, Jack told me there was a lot of money to be made if I took my new found fortune and invested it in a couple of party yachts. He told me there were a lot of rich people who liked to have fun and that I could pretty much name my price when renting these yachts out. So I did exactly that. It just so happened, from then on out, Jack had a much better time on his trips. Now my two grandsons run the show. They sometimes take me out fishing and crabbing once in a while, just to keep me happy." With a sneaky smile on his face, Salty leaned over and got up close to Ben. "Besides, they can't take ownership of the company until I'm gone. I gotta tell you, that Jack really knew how to manipulate a deal."

Salty could tell Ben was visibly upset. "Listen, Ben, I don't believe in chance. There was something bigger going on than two old goats like us could comprehend when Jack and I met. I don't believe that man is going to rest until what he wanted is complete. Now it's fallen upon his son to complete what the father started. I only hope you have enough sense not to stand in that boy's way."

Ben looked around the room then looked at Old Salty. "Well, old friend, looks like we've both done well over the years." Once more, Ben held out his hand in friendship. "Take care of yourself, Salty. I'll see myself out."

Just then, Jack walked out to the deck area and noticed Ben was leaving. "What happened? Why is he leaving?"

Old Salty smiled as he walked over to Jack. "Well, son, I guess he got what he came here for. Listen, young man. Your dad was on a quest to retrieve someone who was taken from him. Only you can decide to continue his dream. So, how 'bout it? Did you get all that you came here for?"

Jack appreciated all the help from Salty. He shook his hand and said goodbye. Afterwards, he caught up to Ben who was waiting at the bar inside the main house. "So, what do you think about Old Salty?"

Ben had taken the liberty of ordering some food for him and Jack and was waiting on two beers. "What do you mean? He's an old fisherman who hit the jackpot when he met your dad. You heard what he said, so are you satisfied?"

Jack was hoping Ben would be more receptive after talking with Old Salty, but he'd thought wrong. "No, I'm not satisfied. You keep blowing me off like I'm some kind of little kid and I'm sick and tired of it. I just don't understand your reasoning for not wanting to talk about this."

By then the food was being served, which was right on time because Ben wasn't in any mood to argue. "Listen, kid, let's just eat our food and go back to New York. I'm tired and this discussion is getting old."

After drinking all morning, Jack wasn't feeling any pain, so he decided to place the argument on hold and eat some food. Afterwards, it was a long, quiet ride back to New York.

Ben couldn't wait to get back to work bothering people and just being a general nuisance around the office. Jack, on the other hand, had plenty going on. He started to do some backdoor investigations into the overseas accounts his dad had set up. He hired a legal team that specialized in retrieving funds and other valuables and set up a meeting away from the office. After giving as much information as possible without revealing the nature of the project, he decided to head back to work.

Jack finished out the day by shuffling paperwork and sending out emails. Towards the end of the day, he decided to call to find out when his father's belongings from California would arrive. He couldn't take his mind off the Ferrari. He was so excited and couldn't wait to get it on the road. Unfortunately, it was coming in by freight train and it was going to be another day before it arrived.

When Jack finally decided to leave for the day, as usual, everyone else was gone, including Ben. Most of the time, he called Jack to say goodnight, but that day he hadn't. That was okay, though. Jack was headed to the local shopping mall to see an old friend and to pick up some flowers for Bria. When he arrived, he saw his friend Riley, the shoe shine guy, standing in line at the flower shop and walked over to say hello. Riley had a couple of shoe shine chairs he'd inherited from his father, who had inherited them from his father. He also had a small portion of stock in Kotter Industries. He was financially well off, enough not to have to work, but he chose to, out of respect for his father and grandfather. Jack and Riley had known each other a long time and often conversed about business and investments.

"Hey, Riley, how are you?"

Riley just finished paying for his flowers and turned to greet Jack. "Hey, Jack, where the hell have you been?"

After Jack handpicked a couple of red roses, both men walked back to Riley's stand. "Well, I've been around. Just not here. Got a new project I'm trying to put together and I'm getting hammered from all sides, including Ben."

Jack climbed up into one of the chairs and placed his feet on the stand while Riley grabbed his towel and some paste. "Well, Ben is Ben, and he'll never change." Riley stopped and smiled. "Do you know that old man came here one time and tried to haggle me down for a shine? I think we came to an understanding when I wouldn't back down. Don't know what he was thinking, but we see eye to eye now."

Jack laughed because he knew Ben could be difficult at best when it came to spending money. "Yeah, I remember that day. You must have really gotten the best of him because he came in the office that day mad as hell. All he kept doing all day was bitchin' and complaining about you, but you definitely gained his respect."

Riley smiled as he shined Jack's shoes. "Yeah, we get along great now. He even asked my opinion once about tax dollars being spent on frivolous government projects."

Jack had a newspaper in his hand and usually read it as he talked, but this time, he was more interested in talking with his friend. Riley was almost finished when he stopped and looked up at Jack. "So, what about this project you want to do?"

Jack leaned forward a little. "It's an excavation project out in the Atlantic Ocean. That's all I can say about it right now. The bill is pretty hefty and Kotter Industries could take a huge hit if something went wrong. That's why Ben is dead set against it."

Riley started back with the shine. "Well, you've never seemed too worried about money before, so why now?"

Jack slouched back and took a breath. "Well, that's another big problem. It's a personal project that could end up with me using company resources. That would pretty much leave me wide open for the board to take legal action and take Kotter Industries from me."

As Riley finished, he stood up and then hopped up into the chair beside Jack. "I can see your problem, but let me ask you something. Is that personal project worth everything your dad worked for and built?"

Jack thought to himself and smiled. "How ironic you should ask me that. It's my dad who started the project and he left me with the burden of trying to complete it."

Riley looked around and saw the other shopkeepers closing, so he climbed down off the chair and started to clean his area. "Well, Jack, I hope you don't think I'm being insensitive to your problem, but I've been wanting to talk to you about something."

As the two made their way out to the parking lot, Jack wondered what Riley could be so concerned about. "Listen, Riley, if I thought for one minute Kotter stock was going to drop, don't you think I would let you know?"

Riley smiled as he bumped Jack on the shoulder. "No, stupid. My concern is about you. I keep hearing stories about this Lilith character and how she's out to get you. Now before you say anything, I happened to be watching the news the night she wrecked your car.

I've also seen the havoc she's been creating on the streets. This isn't a game, Jack. You could really get yourself hurt messing around with that maniac."

Jack found it touching that Riley offered his concern, but it fell on deaf ears. "Riley, I appreciate what you're saying, but that bitch made it personal. I don't think I have a say so one way or the other. Besides, I have faith that the police will eventually get to her before she gets to me. Don't worry, you have many more years of putting up with me."

Riley didn't really feel relieved, but he knew Jack was just like his dad. Headstrong and stubborn. "All right, Mr. Invincible Jack Kotter. Tell Bria I said hi." Jack said his goodbyes and left to go meet Bria.

After all that had happened, Jack had plans to spend a quiet evening alone with Bria. As he left the mall, there was a fresh layer of powdered snow on the ground and the flurries were still falling. It was such a beautiful time of year, but Jack was too preoccupied to enjoy it. He thought about the conversation with Riley and the question he'd posed. Why should he risk it all for some project that was impossible to begin with? Not to mention all the people who relied on him for their livelihood. Jack started to feel all the stress of the past week, so he stopped alongside of the road and leaned his head back in deep thought. As he glanced over, he noticed old Joe's garage was coming along pretty well. Since the recent purchase of the property, the building looked in very good shape, but he noticed the old rusted sign was still hanging out front. It was barely readable, but Jack knew what it said. Jack saw two men working and thought how nice it was someone finally took interest after all those years,.

Jack remembered the story his dad told him about the original owner, Joe Jarred. Mr. Jarred opened the garage in the late '20s and was doing very well, but as automobiles started to advance, his business started to decline, because he couldn't keep up with the technology. His son was born in the '40s, but he took no interest in carrying on with the family business. Joe Jr. was only interested in one thing: racing. He was about to turn pro when his daughter was born with special needs. Eventually, old Joe died and his son let the business go under. Joe Jr. was out one night when two young teens challenged him to a race. Joe Jr. couldn't resist. He was the best and nobody was going to tell him any different. It wasn't long before Joe was in the lead, but then one of the boys tapped his rear corner panel and spun him off the road. His car flipped several times before it came to a stop upside down. The accident snapped Joe Jr.'s neck and his spinal cord, killing him instantly. With no other family left to help, his wife felt she had no choice but to place their daughter in an institution where she could have proper care.

Jack remembered the story because his dad used it as a learning tool. He and Ben always talked about the domino effect, where one event led to another, then that led to another, and so on. Jack took a moment and laughed to himself. Like father, like Ben. Both always had the same advice. Suddenly, Jack found himself wanting to talk with the two men. Due to decades of neglect, the parking lot wasn't suitable for cars to drive on, so Jack climbed out and bundled up in his coat. As he exhaled, he watched his breath and walked towards the garage.

The man on the roof kept working as the man in the car bay saw Jack and walked out to greet him. Jack stretched out his arm to shake hands. "Hello, my name is Jack Kotter."

The man shook his hand then introduced himself. "I'm Oliver. Can I help you with something?"

With the quiet tone of Oliver's voice, Jack suspected him to be of grace, so he gave a polite smile. "I've been coming past here for years. I always thought this building would eventually be torn down."

Oliver took a deep breath then pointed to the man on the roof. "Yeah, my brother and I grew up right over on Whispers Grove Road."

Jack looked towards the roof as Oliver's brother stopped working momentarily. After a brief pause, he continued on, fixing the roof. With the brisk air, Oliver cleared his throat. "We always wanted to have a business together, so we finally decided to do it. We've been working on this building day and night." Suddenly, Oliver recognized the name. "Jack Kotter. Aren't you ... "

Before Oliver could say anything else, Jack affirmed his suspicion. "Yep, that's me."

Oliver became a little apprehensive. "Sorry, Mr. Kotter. If you're about to make an offer, we're not interested."

Still feeling the stress, Jack gave Oliver a half-smile. "Oh, no. You don't understand. I was just driving past when I noticed the two of you working. It's cold and late, and I don't get to meet many people as dedicated as the both of you."

After a brief uneasy pause, Jack was about to speak when Oliver's brother came walking over. Out of curiosity, he climbed down to make sure Oliver was alright. Oliver smiled with pride. "This is my older brother, Paul." Paul reached out and shook Jack's hand.

Once again, Jack gave a polite smile as he shook hands. "Hi, Paul, I'm Jack."

As the flurries came to a stop, Jack took in the fresh air. "Well, fellas, it's cold, so I won't keep you any longer. It was very nice meeting both of you. I wish you the best of luck with your venture."

Jack shook both of their hands again then turned to walk away. As he made it halfway to his car, he stopped and turned around to admire their determination. He watched for a few minutes as both brothers picked up their tools and continued working. Jack stood remembering the stories told to him by his father and Ben. All the hard work and determination they had, and how together as a team they built Kotter Industries. Jack stepped back into his car and waited a few minutes until the car warmed up. As the warmth started to filter in from the vents, he began to reflect on some of the values instilled in him as a child. Work hard, never give up, and follow your dreams. Most of all, never let anyone discourage you. Jack Sr. knew discouragement was like a disease. Once it made its way into the heart, it would eventually destroy a person.

When *Fringe* was finally warm and ready, Jack left the area and continued home. He thought about Ben and the arguments they had. He wasn't feeling discouraged, rather, he knew there was a lot more involved than just the project.

When Jack arrived home, Bria had a late night candle lit and dinner waiting. He was happy just to spend some time together and handed Bria her roses. Unfortunately, as Jack ate dinner, his mind was somewhere else. Bria sat quietly watching as Jack stared off into space. "Come on, Jack. This was supposed to be a night just for us."

Jack was so far gone he didn't even hear what Bria said. Bria threw her fork down and stood up. She stormed into the kitchen with her plate and threw it in the sink. She then whisked past Jack and ran upstairs. Jack wiped his mouth and quietly followed. He walked upstairs to find Bria crying on the bed. "What are you doing? I don't know why you're getting so upset."

Bria sat up on the edge of the bed. "Look at me, Jack. I had dinner all planned and I even sat at the table with my brand new lingerie on. You didn't even notice."

Jack had no defense, because she was right. He didn't notice the black lace panties with the garter and see through lace top. "I'm sorry, Bria. I just have too much going on right now."

But Bria wasn't as forgiving as Jack would have liked. "I'm sorry too, Jack. I'm sorry your life is so tied up that you don't have time for me. We don't go out anymore. We don't have any fun together, and all you seem to do is bend over backwards to kiss Ben's ass. Don't you think I get tired of waiting around for you? I'm always there for you, listening to your problems, but it seems like you can't set aside one night for me."

Jack really didn't feel like arguing, but he knew once Bria started, it was hard to get her to stop. "What do you want me to say, Bria? I'm sorry I inherited a huge corporation. I'm sorry my dad dropped this bomb in my lap. I just can't ignore the things I have to do when it comes to Kotter Industries."

Bria was tired of listening to Jack throw excuses at her. She went into the bathroom and changed. She washed the tears off her face and walked out of the bedroom. "The next time you have a nightmare, get your friend Ben to console you, because I won't be around."

Jack ran downstairs just as Bria was walking out the front door. "Come on, Bria, don't be like this. What do you want from me?"

Bria stopped short of her car and turned around. "I want a man who's going to marry me and not his company, like his father did. That's what I want." Before Jack could say anything, Bria jumped in her car and drove off.

CHAPTER NINETEEN

THE NEXT DAY, JACK WAS BACK TO HIS BUSY SELF. HE'D SEEN BRIA GET upset plenty of times and he knew after a few days, she'd find a way to surprise him with sex. As usual, Jack had everything but the kitchen sink on his mind. He especially wanted to get down to the storage facility where his father's belongings had finally arrived. As he rolled the steel door up, he saw all the boxes of paperwork, along with Ben's box and the desk. He looked to the rear of the room and saw the Ferrari covered with the old canvas. With some excitement, he pulled the sheet off and there she was. All he could think about was what he could do with a car like that. But in the meantime, he just settled into the driver's seat and fantasized. He thought about beefing up the engine and transmission, then he dreamed about what kind of paint job to put on that beautiful body. He'd shine up whatever chrome was on the car and then replace the exhaust system with an up-to-date monster. Finally, he'd finish it off with the best-looking rims he could find.

Just when his thoughts couldn't get any better, his phone rang and pulled him back into the real world. It was Ethan. Before Jack could say hello, Ethan was screaming in his ear. "Why didn't you call me to let me know you were back in town? I have so much to tell you."

Jack laughed as he held the phone to his ear with one hand and placed the other on the steering wheel. "Calm down, Ethan. I didn't know I had to report to you every day, and besides. I figured you were still rolling around in the sack with Bobby Jo."

Ethan finally calmed himself enough to talk civilly. "Come on, Jack. Rolling around is an understatement. You have no idea what this girl is capable of doing. This girl is a beast. I've never even heard of some of the things she likes to do in the bedroom, and you know me, all I watch is porn. I can't thank you enough, my friend, for hooking me up with Bobby Jo. I think I'm in love."

Jack chuckled as he pretended to be driving, moving his hand around the steering wheel. "So, how many times this year have you told me you're in love?"

Ethan knew Jack was joking, but he was right. "Yeah, yeah, I know, but this is different, Jack. This girl is very smart and funny, and the sex is just incredible. I don't know what else to say. I'm in love, Jack, and I have you to thank for it."

Jack stepped out of the car and walked over to the boxes. "Well, you're welcome. I hope it works out, because both you and Bobby Jo are very good people. Maybe in a few days Bria and I can hook up with you guys and we can do the town." Ethan was all too happy to agree.

Jack opened up the boxes and pulled out some of the paperwork from California. He took a few minutes to sift through some of it, but realized time was on his side. He didn't really need to deal with it right that moment, nor did he want to. He placed the paperwork back into the box and locked the door. He wasn't sure if he wanted to go to work because he knew Ben was there, and he hadn't talked to him since they'd come back from New Jersey. He called his legal team to find out if there was any progress with the accounts his dad had set up, but they didn't have any good news. All they could say was his dad did everything right. Everything was air tight and legal. There was no way to get the money without Ben's approval. Jack knew it was a long shot, but he'd had to try.

After realizing there was nothing to do if he played hooky from work, Jack decided to go and risk a confrontation with Ben. When he made it to work, there was an unusual quiet about the place. All the normal people said hello, but it seemed different. As he made it to his office, Bonnie informed him Ben wanted to see him ASAP. Just then, Jack realized why everyone had such a long face. When Ben was upset about something or somebody, his normal routine was to make everyone else miserable.

At Ben's office, he stopped and said hello to Hellen, but she gave Jack the look of death. Jack knew if Hellen was feeling the effects, it had to be bad, because she didn't take crap from anyone. That made Jack rethink his approach. He decided to be courteous and knock before entering Ben's office. As he walked in, he saw Ben sitting at his desk in a very calm state of mind. "Come on in, kid, have a seat."

His tone didn't match everyone else's fears, so Jack sat down with caution. Just as Jack slouched back in the chair, Ben stood up and walked over to the bar and made some drinks. When he came back, he handed one to Jack and sat back down. "So, kid, any new developments on that dead-end project?"

This didn't make any sense to Jack at all. He was expecting some kind of explosion when he walked in, but all he was getting was a calm conversation. "Well, to be honest with you, Ben, I would really like to discuss some options when you get some time."

As Ben finished off his drink, he shot Jack a suspicious smile. He stood up and walked around to Jack and stood over top of him. "So, you want to talk options do you?" Suddenly, out came a burst of anger. "Who the hell do you think you are, you little prick? You try to backdoor me with your petty little legal team and think I won't find out? I know everyone in this God damn town. An alley cat can't even take a piss without someone telling me about it. Your little bitches couldn't figure out a way to get the money, so you come to me groveling and talking about options. You have no options, and if you did, they're gone now."

After screaming at the top of his voice, Ben finally stopped and walked back around to his chair. He was still upset, but now his voice had dramatically lowered. "Listen, kid, don't ever make the mistake of thinking you can outsmart me. Many men have tried and wound up losing everything. Next time you try to backdoor me, I'll rip your head off and shit down your neck. Now get the hell out of my office."

Right about then, Jack didn't feel like the owner of Kotter Industries, but he knew enough to just leave Ben alone. He felt like a dog that had just had its tail whipped, so he stood up and scurried out the door. As he left, he couldn't even bring himself to look at Hellen. He hurried to his office and locked the door behind him. As he walked across the room, he noticed the title plate on his desk that read "President." He picked it up and broke it in half then threw it across the room. He saw that he had some messages on his answering machine and decided to take a break, hoping one of them would be Bria. Ethan had left a message to try to set up some time to go out, but until Jack heard from Bria, that wasn't going to happen. Dale had also left a message trying to set up a time to talk about some information he'd found out about Lilith. Jack also decided to put that on hold.

After taking the tongue lashing from Ben, Jack needed to get out and go. He thought it would be a great idea to go check out the graves Ben told him about, so he warmed up *Fringe* and decided to take a nice long drive up to Westbury, New York to the Cemetery of the Holy Rood. While he was there, he found exactly what Ben described: his grandmother Elizabeth's grave site along with a blank gravestone next to it, only 20 feet from where his parents were buried. There was a small bench nearby, probably placed there by his dad some time in his final years. Jack sat quietly wondering about what his dad must have been thinking about when he sat there all those years. So much history and Jack was oblivious to all of it. With the peace that surrounded the graveyard, Jack was finally able to gather up all his thoughts and put them in perspective.

In contrast, Ben was back in his element, enjoying the hectic life of running a corporation. He had his cleaning delivered to his office so he would have a selection of suits to change into during the week. When Hellen hung the clothing in the closet, she handed him some paperwork he had left in one of his jackets. Ben looked through the papers and noticed it was the financial records he found in the storage shed in California. With all the arguing and fighting going on with Jack, he had forgotten all about them.

Although he denied Jack access to the funds, Ben still had to figure out what he was going to do with the accounts and all the money. When he first found the records, he'd faxed them to his accountants back at Kotter Industries. He really didn't take the time to look through them in detail, so he thought he would take the opportunity to do it then. The numbers were staggering. Ben couldn't believe his best friend had accumulated such a large amount of funds without him knowing. As he scanned the last page, he noticed it wasn't anything to do with overseas banks. Instead, it was a financial record of funds paid to several private investigators going all the way back to the forties. As he checked the payment history, he noticed a handwritten list of names. Ben recognized some of the names as being those on the lists found in the shed. Most were scratched out, except two, Mr. Charles Joughin and Ms. Winnifred Quick. Although, Ben was trying to put all the nonsense behind him, it didn't keep his curiosity from being peaked. He was never a fan of computers, but even he knew they were a good tool to utilize for gathering information, so he fired up the internet and looked up the names. The more he read, the more interested he became.

Although their stories were intriguing, there had to be other reasons why Jack Sr. wanted to find those people. As he read the story of Charles Joughin, Ben noticed he had passed away back in 1956, but Ms. Quick, who was married, was one of the remaining still living *Titanic* survivors. In spite of the fight he and Jack had, Ben decided to humble himself and give Jack a call. When Jack answered his cell phone, the reception was terrible.

"Hold on, Ben, let me move to another area."

Ben waited a few seconds. "Where the hell are you, kid?"

As the reception became a little better, Jack was finally able to talk. "I'm at the Cemetery of the Holy Rood."

Ben wasn't really surprised. "Did you find what you were looking for?"

Jack paused for a minute. "I did. You were right about the gravestones."

As awkward as the conversation was, neither Ben nor Jack held a grudge. "Listen, kid. I found something that you might be interested in. I would rather explain it in person, so get your ass back here as soon as possible. I'll wait for you." Jack agreed, and after paying respects to his parents, he collected his thoughts and left.

By the time Jack made it back to Kotter Industries, the day had already passed and dusk was starting to settle in. Most of the employees were gone for the day, except Hellen, of course. As Jack arrived, she was leaving to go home. Jack was still feeling the sting of the argument from earlier, so he wasn't in a really big hurry to get upstairs to talk to Ben. As he stepped off the elevator, he made his way down the quiet hall to Ben's office. He wasn't really in the mood to fight or argue, so, of course, he knocked first before entering. When Jack walked in, Ben was standing by the window looking out over the property. "Grab a drink, kid, and have a seat. I found something interesting you might want to look into."

Jack wasn't in the mood to drink, so he just sat down and waited for Ben to explain. "Listen, Ben. I wanted to apologize to you about what I did, but you didn't leave me any choice."

Ben sat down and listened for a moment. "Forget about that, kid. I already have. Listen, not that I'm coming around to your way of thinking, but I found something earlier when I was looking through those financial records we found in your father's storage shed." Ben reached across the desk and handed the paperwork to Jack. "Check out the last page. It's a record of transactions your dad had with some private investigators he must have been using."

Jack scanned the list and noticed the same thing Ben did. At the bottom of the page was a list of people from *Titanic*. All were crossed out but two. "So, what is it you wanted to talk to me about?"

Ben stood up and walked around his desk. He took the papers from Jack and walked over to his window. "Listen, kid, I know the last few weeks have been hard on you, but I still stand by my decision not to pursue your father's dream. I understand he needed closure and he wanted to do it on a grand scale. On that same token, you feel the need to complete what your dad started. Listen, your dad, for whatever reason, felt the need to hire private investigators to find all these people, so he must have gotten something out of it. Don't you want to know what your dad found out? I have time and energy tied up in this mess, so I would like to know."

Jack wasn't sure what to think. Maybe Ben felt guilty about turning him down. Maybe he felt bad about the ass chewing that morning. Or maybe he was just being a good friend. Either way, it gave Jack more opportunity to work on getting Ben to see things his way. "Alright, Ben. Let's go see what these people told my dad."

It was getting late, so traveling arrangements would have to wait until the next day. "Listen, kid, I did some checking on my own. Charles Joughin died back in 1956, but Winnifred Quick is still alive. Go home and get some sleep because we're leaving early tomorrow."

On the way home, Jack drove by the old garage to see its progress.

It looked really good, but the brothers weren't working on it. Jack was tired and didn't think much of it, though, so he kept driving. He thought about Bria and the fact she still hadn't tried to call or surprise him with some wild idea. Suddenly, out of nowhere, three police cars and an ambulance came rushing down the road. Thinking about Lilith, it sent chills up Jack's spine. He finally made it home and was hoping he would open the door and see Bria, but that didn't happen. The only thing waiting for him was a dark, quiet house.

CHAPTER TWENTY

THE NEXT MORNING, JACK WAS UP EARLY, DUE TO THE FACT BEN WAS banging on his door and ringing the doorbell. "What did I tell you last night, kid? We were leaving early."

Jack barely had one eye open. "I heard what you said, but I didn't think you meant predawn. Give me a minute and I'll get ready."

Jack managed to shave, shower, and get dressed in twenty minutes, but Ben wasn't impressed. "Let's go, kid. We have a private jet waiting for us at the airport."

Fighting off a yawn, Jack climbed into the limo. "What do you mean, private jet?"

Ben had Casey stock the limo with coffee just for occasions such as that. Ben made two cups and handed one to Jack. "Yeah, kid, you heard right. Private jet. I called a friend of mine who was gracious enough to let me use it. I usually don't ask for favors this big, but I figured what you're going through is a little more important than my humility."

With the speed of the jet, the flight only took one hour. Jack slept most of the time. He awoke when the plane touched down in Michigan. Ben had already made arrangements to have an SUV waiting. From University Airpark to East Lansing, it was a short drive. When they arrived, they were greeted by a visiting friend of Mrs. Quick's.

They were graciously welcomed into the home, where Mrs. Quick was sitting quietly, waiting. "Come in gentlemen. Please, sit down."

As Ben and Jack sat, they glanced around at the warmth and comfort of the house. Ben didn't feel uncomfortable, but he didn't exactly feel at home. He took the initiative to speak up and present the reason for the visit. Ben stood up and walked over to Winnifred and shook her hand. "Mrs. Quick, my name is Benjamin Marcus and this is my friend Jack Kotter. We appreciate you seeing us on such short notice."

As Ben walked back to his seat, Winnifred gave a pleasant smile. "My name is Mrs. Van Tongerloo, but if it makes it easier, you may call me Mrs. Quick or Winnifred." She turned her attention to Jack and gave another pleasant smile. "Jack Kotter? You look like the man who came to see me years ago, and he was also a handsome man with the same name, but much older than you. You must be his son."

Jack stood up and shook Mrs. Quick hand. "Yes, ma'am. My father passed away and left me with somewhat of a problem." Jack sat back down and started to explain. "My father was working on something related to the *Titanic* and some of the notes he left behind led us to believe he may have come and spoke to you."

After offering some refreshments, Winnifred was ready to talk about *Titanic* and her conversation with Jack's father. "I'm sorry for your loss, young man. Your father was a very kind soul. I imagine he got that trait from your grandfather."

As Jack sat on the edge of his chair, Ben was more somber and relaxed. "Mrs. Quick, why exactly did Jack Sr. come to see you?"

Winnifred thought for a second as she took a calming drink of her warm tea. "Well, I imagine it was because of what Mr. Joughin must have told him. That kind man passed away back in the '50s. We corresponded a few times before his passing. Such a delightful man."

Winnifred was always so delighted to have company that sometimes her excitement would get the best of her. Although Jack could barely keep from jumping out of his skin, Ben on the other hand was surprisingly patient. "Mrs. Quick, you were saying about why Jack Sr. came to see you?"

Winnifred caught herself being playful and continued with her story. "I'm sorry, Mr. Marcus. Sometimes, I get carried away. Anyway,

I think Mr. Kotter must have found out something interesting when he spoke with Mr. Joughin, because Mr. Joughin told a story that not very many people know about. Mr. Kotter was very interested in that story, and when he came to see me, he was even more excited when I reaffirmed what Mr. Joughin had said."

Now Ben was on the edge of his seat waiting to hear what Winnifred had to say. "Go on, Mrs. Quick. What was the story?"

Winnifred took another sip of tea as she prepared to tell what happen to her during the last moments on *Titanic*. "It was 14 April 1912, and I was eight years old on *Titanic*. Listed as a second class passenger, I was sleeping in my cabin, along with my mother and my sister, Phyllis. Our mother woke me up after a woman passenger knocked on our cabin door. Phyllis was still asleep. She was always a heavy sleeper. At the time, I was very sleepy and I didn't understand why my mother was trying to dress me in the middle of the night. Then a steward banged on the door and started yelling at our mother to stop dressing and to get our lifebelts on. He told us the ship had struck an iceberg and that it was sinking. Our mother threw a coat over me and picked Phyllis up out of bed. She wrapped Phyllis with a shawl and grabbed my hand. I remember being so sleepy but still having to walk up five flights of steps. We finally came out onto one of the decks. There were a lot of people scurrying around. Mother walked over to the rail and leaned over. That's when she realized just how serious the accident was. We needed to get up an iron ladder that led to A Deck, but with two young girls in her arms, it was going to be more than difficult. That's when Mr. Joughin realized we needed help and extended his kindness. He was carrying three bottles of whiskey and placed them at his feet. That's when Mother handed Phyllis to Mr. Joughin while she placed her lifebelt on."

Winnifred glanced over at Jack and continued telling her story. "Then another gentleman, whom your father favored very much, came along and placed a lifebelt on me; that's when it happened."

Still on the edge of their chairs, Jack and Ben stared as though they were watching a horror story. With her pause, Winnifred took a sip of tea to sooth the dryness that came from talking. She then continued with her story.

"That's when three young men came and wanted to take our

lifebelts. Mr. Joughin still had Phyllis in his arms. I had become hysterical and was crying because I thought since I had a lifebelt on, I was going to have to jump into the water. Mr. Joughin waited patiently while mother ascended the ladder and the other gentleman pushed the three men away and rebuked them harshly. I remember standing there crying as they started to fight. When Mother reached the top of the ladder, Mr. Joughin lifted Phyllis up to her. He then somehow got me up the ladder. Just before I reached the top, I turned to see the gentleman get struck in the head with one of Mr. Joughin's whiskey bottles. One of the boys must have picked it up during the struggle. By the time Mr. Joughin was able to help, it was too late. The gentleman was lying on the deck bleeding profusely."

Once again, Winnifred paused, but not to take a drink. Jack and Ben could tell the story started to become difficult to tell. After a few brief moments, Winnifred continued on. "It was calm up on A Deck. There was no confusion at all. Men were standing around making sure the lifeboats were being loaded properly. I was still shaking when Mother, who was still holding Phyllis, grabbed my hand and led me over to lifeboat 11. I remember becoming very frightened when the sailor in charge told mother there was only room for the children. Mother was very upset. She told the man 'no' and said, 'Either we go together or we stay together.' I was so happy to hear mother say that, because I didn't want any of us to be separated. Just then, that kind gentleman who'd defended us came walking up. His clothing was covered with blood and it was dripping down his face and neck. He demanded the sailor let us, including Mother, board the lifeboat. I could tell the sailor was very frightened, but he was also very rude. He reluctantly agreed and tossed me and my sister into the lifeboat like we were trash. I was very upset, because in the process, I lost my slippers. Mother then climbed in afterwards. The last I saw of that kind soul who helped us was the look in his eyes. It was a very weak look. I could tell he was slowly losing his composure. I don't imagine he made it off that ship.

"As we were lowered into the water, another crewman yelled down to row fast because the suction might pull us down. Phyllis was still asleep in Mother's arms, and I was now crying because my feet were cold. My slippers were gone and the water in the bottom of the boat was very cold. As we rowed away, I could hear the band playing music. After getting a distance away from the ship I saw the lights go out. Afterwards, I heard a loud explosion. One of the sailors in the boat said one of her boilers had exploded. I then saw something I wish I had never witnessed. The stern of the ship rose up and I could see it silhouetted against the night sky. I heard a loud cracking along with a thunderous crash. Then it vanished into the ocean. That's when all the screams and cries could be heard across the water. All those people in the freezing water where *Titanic* vanished. It's something I can't forget. Eventually, all the cries gradually faded away. I had finally stopped crying and I told mother I wasn't afraid anymore. I'd asked God and he'd said we're going to be saved. There was a German lady sitting beside me and she wrapped a coat around me. With her arms around me, I was so calm and relaxed, I fell asleep. When I awoke, it was morning and people were yelling and cheering because a rescue ship could be seen on the horizon. We eventually were picked up by the *Carpathia*.

"I often wondered about Mr. Joughin and the other kind gentleman, until one day I received a correspondence from Mr. Joughin. He told me he helped the unknown man to his feet and made sure he was alright. He said the gentleman asked about us, so he directed him up to A Deck. That Mr. Joughin was such a crafty fellow. He wound up drinking the other two bottles of whiskey, which helped him keep warm in that freezing water for three hours, before being rescued."

Once again, Winnifred glanced over at Jack. "Mr. Joughin wrote to me shortly after the visit from your father. I never saw or heard from that unknown gentleman again, but your father was very intrigued with the story. Especially when I told him he looked just like the kind soul who'd helped us during that fateful night."

Jack was speechless. And for once, Ben had nothing to say. There wasn't any more Winnifred could tell them, so Jack and Ben thanked her for her kindness and said their goodbyes.

On the way back to the airpark, Jack felt an even stronger urge to finish what his father started. "Sorry, Ben, I know that wasn't what you wanted to hear. What a fantastic story, though. I can't imagine what my dad thought about it, but by the sound of it, I think in his mind it had to be Victor Mrs. Quick was describing."

Ben was still trying to absorb what was just told to him. "I think your father was systematically going through and talking with all the survivors he could find. When he came across Charles Joughin, he knew he'd stumbled onto something. Then when he visited Mrs. Quick, it was the final piece of the puzzle he was looking for. Well, kid, it seems Victor never made it back to his family because he stopped to help some people in need. You're right. That's not something I wanted to hear."

With that said, Jack saw another opportunity to try to get his argument in. "Come on, Ben. My dad laid it all out for you, because he knew if anyone could help me pull this off, it would be you. Besides, this company wouldn't exist if it wasn't for my dad, and your life wouldn't exist without my dad."

Ben could feel his blood pressure coming to a slow boil, but he knew Jack didn't mean what he was saying. "Listen, kid, I loved your dad, but if I remember correctly, my brother had something to do with the success of this company. Why can't you just dedicate a plaque and have it placed on the ship? I've heard it's been done before."

Jack took a second to sulk. "You're right, Ben. I'm sorry for saying that. As for a plaque, it isn't enough. If it was that simple, my dad would have done it and we wouldn't be having this argument."

Ben smiled and chuckled. "What argument? There's nothing to argue about. I'm not going to buckle under your pressure just because somebody tells me some fantastic story that may or may not be true, and that's the end of it."

Although the plane ride to Michigan was short, the trip back seemed like it took forever. Ben just sat staring out the window. Jack could tell all the arguing was starting to affect him, and with the stress on Ben's face, it showed. Jack decided he wouldn't press the issue, because he knew there would be another opportunity to try again. Instead, he had the idea to call on his old friend Connie. By then, Connie had established his own business conducting deep sea fishing trips, along with scuba diving and deep sea exploration. He was accredited for several dives on notable shipwrecks, such as the *Andrea Doria* and the *Edmund Fitzgerald*. He would also have the knowledge of what it would take to raise a vessel up from the bottom of the ocean. Jack also decided to do some research on his own. Utilizing his laptop, he decided to take advantage of Ben's silence. He used the time to bookmark some notable expeditions.

After reading up on some of the wrecks that were raised, Jack couldn't wait to get home and really dig into the research needed to start such a project, but first, he needed to tie up some loose ends. He knew he was gaining ground with Ben, but he needed to back away some so everything could sink in, especially the information Winnifred provided.

When the plane finally landed at the airport, he told Ben to go on ahead. Since there was no conversation on the plane, Jack felt a little uneasy being around him. He called Dale to see if he was available to pick him up. Luckily, Dale was just getting off work. When he finally arrived, Jack could hardly contain himself. "Listen, Dale, I've been thinking about that plan you told me about."

Before Jack could say anything more, Dale jumped in with a disappointing attitude. "Forget about the plan, Jack. That bitch has caused several more accidents and there's no sign of her letting up. Our teams can't seem to come up with any working theories. That plan I had is no longer on the table. It's just way too dangerous."

Jack was aware of the consequences, but he was willing to take the risk. "Please, Dale, just hear me out. I've been thinking on this ever since you pulled me aside that night at the club. You already know that bitch is out to get me. I don't understand why she's so fixated on me, and right about now, I don't really care. I have a lot going on and I can't afford to be looking over my shoulder for some maniac that's out to kill me. So I'm asking you as a friend to reconsider."

Dale could hear the passion in Jack's voice, but unfortunately, the decision wasn't up to him. "I'm sorry, Jack. It's out of my hands. My superiors were all for it at first until everything started getting too far out of control. If you remember correctly, I told you I needed an answer. Now the window of opportunity is gone."

Jack wasn't angry with Dale, but lately, everyone had been turning him down, and that just made him more determined. "Listen, Dale, it's gonna come down to her and me going head-to-head, so why not have a plan in place? Just hear me out and I won't ask you about it anymore."

Dale thought about it and he knew Jack was right. Eventually Lilith was going to catch up to him. Dale knew that when it happened,

Jack wouldn't stand a chance. "Alright, Jack. I'll give you the courtesy of listening to whatever half-ass plan you have."

Jack laughed because it felt good to finally be taken seriously, or in this case, somewhat seriously. "You know the old 110 Garage?"

Dale thought momentarily then nodded his head. "Yeah, old man Joe's place. That old place has been there forever. It's been boarded up for several decades."

Jack's plan included a trip to the 110 Garage to talk to the new owners, Paul and Oliver. As they made their way to the garage, Dale asked about Bria. "I saw Bria downtown the other night dancing and having a good ole time. I tried to talk to her, but she seemed distant."

Jack didn't want to get into details, so he told Dale they decided to take a break from each other. Dale respectfully didn't ask any other questions, but it was pretty plain to see there was a problem. The remainder of the drive, Jack kept Dale busy telling him about Ethan and Bobby Jo. They laughed and joked about it as the old garage came into sight.

As Dale pulled his car along the shoulder, Jack glanced over and saw that somebody was there. When they approached the garage, Oliver opened the door and greeted them. "Hello, Mr. Kotter."

Jack shook hands then introduced Dale. "Where's Paul at tonight?"

Oliver invited them in and explained Paul was taking care of business elsewhere. Dale looked around because he'd been told the same story Jack was told about the garage. He took notice of the broken padlock that was on the front door. "Tell me something, Oliver. I see your lock was broken off. This area usually doesn't experience much crime."

Oliver didn't seem to be too disappointed. "Yeah, when my brother and I bought the place, we found a bunch of old tools, along with some old clothes and a few old pictures hanging on the walls. The pictures were from back in the day. I'm guessing they belonged to the original owner. The tools were pretty old, so they were probably from when the garage was still in operation. The clothes we kind of thought belonged to some homeless people using this place as shelter. The weird part about the break-in was nothing was taken except all the old junk that was already here. The pictures, old tools, and the clothing. All of our new tools and personal items were left untouched."

Dale thought about it, and although it was unusual, he was glad nothing else was taken. "Well, maybe it was an honest homeless person."

Oliver pulled some cold drinks from a cooler and invited Jack and Dale to have a seat. "So, what brings New York's finest to my humble garage?"

Jack popped the lid on his drink and took a sip. "Well, I don't know if you've been watching the news or if maybe you've seen something along Route 110, but there's an old Plymouth Road Runner racing around creating accidents and killing people."

As he took a drink, Oliver shook his head yes. "I've seen both. That car is constantly racing up and down this road creating havoc. Both my brother and I have seen it on the news and the accidents that it's caused. My brother Paul seems to think it's some kind of demon named Lilith that was around when time began, but that's just him. He's always been into the supernatural. I don't buy into that stuff. By the way, I did see that little episode that involved you wrecking your Pontiac. Too bad. That was a beautiful car you had."

Jack couldn't do anything but smile. "Yeah, that was a big mistake in more ways than one. I got the car repaired and I had to take some punishment from my girl, but all is well now. We came here tonight because Dale came up with a plan to catch whatever or whoever it is running around out there, but the problem is the police department won't endorse the plan anymore. The original plan was to use my Pontiac as a bait car and to get her into a race then try to corral her. The problem with that plan is she's not trying to win races, which makes having a fast car a moot point."

Dale sat listening while he finished his drink. "So, if you don't use *Fringe*, what else is there to use?"

Oliver stood up and motioned over to the rear bay doors. "I have a couple of old junkers out back, but nothing that could compete with that Plymouth."

Dale stood up and threw away his empty bottle. "I agree, Jack. That bitch isn't exactly 'Driving Miss Daisy.' She's driving a damn battleship and it's fast as hell. Whatever her plans are, she picked a perfect car to execute them in."

With some reservations, Jack stood up and paced the floor. "You're absolutely right. She definitely knew what she was doing when she chose a Road Runner, but that's the beauty of my plan. She's sporting speed, power, and torque. The one thing she doesn't have in maneuverability. Those cars have no turning radius, nor do they have the ability to make turns on a dime. That's the only mistake she's made so far. She's been relying on everyone trying to out run her. All I want to do is piss her off enough to chase me right into the arms of the police."

Dale shook his head in disbelief. "Damn, Jack, you're even more convoluted then I thought. Why would you want to risk everything just to get back at this lunatic?"

Jack knew in his heart it wasn't about revenge. Ben always said to stay focused and not to let anything hinder what was trying to be accomplished. Jack knew if he didn't take care of this problem soon, not only would many more people get hurt, but with all the constant worry, it would hinder what he was trying to accomplish for his father. "Listen, Dale, I can't really get into details, but it's not about me verses her or revenge for what she did. I need to do this so I can move on with my life. Like I said, I don't want to have to look over my shoulder every time I drive down the street."

Dale didn't like it, but he understood what Jack was saying. "Alright, Einstein, do you have some kind of fast maneuverable car hiding up your sleeve, or does your plan consist of you running alongside Lilith as she tries to run you down?"

Suddenly, Jack smiled from ear to ear. He couldn't wait to tell Dale and Oliver about the Ferrari. "Well, fellas, as luck would have it, I do have a car up my sleeve. I recently took a trip to California and found that my dad left me a 1959 Ferrari 250 GT Spyder."

Oliver took a deep breath and smiled. "Wow! All my dad ever left me was debt. That's a really nice car. I've only seen one in my time, and that was at a car show." All three men sat back down as Jack started to lay out his plan. "The car has been sitting in storage since my dad bought it back in '59, so although it still looks nice, it probably needs some work done to it." He glanced over at Oliver and nodded. "That's where you and Paul come into play. I want you guys to work on getting her ready for action. Maybe even beef up the engine and possibly replace the suspension."

As the wheels in his mind started to turn, Oliver sat up on the edge of his chair. "Mr. Kotter, I would give my right arm to work on a car like that, but as you can see, this garage is far from being operational."

As Jack looked around, it was apparent the work needed couldn't be done in the garage's present condition. "I see what you mean. The last time we spoke, you guys were pretty hard at work. I figured you would've had a lot more done by now. What's taking so long?"

With some irritation, Oliver suddenly spoke with some attitude. "Look, Mr. Kotter, my brother and I don't have it like that. Our credit is maxed out and so is our cash flow. The reason we've been working day and night is because we're all we've got. The banks won't lend us any more money and we already have too many credit cards."

Sometimes Jack forgot not everyone had a blessed life such as he did. "I'm sorry, Oliver. I didn't know things were so hard for you. I know you look at me as if I have the world by the tail, but that's definitely not me. My world also consists of rules and regulations, and I'm also bound by credit scores and debts. Please accept my apologies. I didn't mean to upset you."

Oliver could hear the sincerity in Jack's voice and he appreciated the kind words. "There are plenty of garages in the area. I would be glad to recommend one if you need the work right away."

Jack thought about it, and though he did need the work done immediately, he wasn't willing to go elsewhere to have it done. "Listen, Oliver, the night I stopped to talk to you and your brother, I wasn't kidding when I told you I admired both of you for working as hard as you were. It was late, cold, and snowing, and you guys were still plugging away at this old garage. I don't want anyone else to do the work. I need someone I can trust to do it right."

As Jack sat thinking about the setback, Dale came up with an alternative idea. "What about your fleet of trucks, Jack? You have several terminals where your trucks get repairs done."

Jack thought about it and remembered one of their terminals up in New Hampshire was shut down. All the equipment was still there, so it would be perfect. "Would you and your brother be willing to place your garage on hold for a few weeks and relocate?"

Oliver didn't really have to think about it because he knew Paul wouldn't go for the idea. Paul was too headstrong in regards to getting their garage up and running. "Sorry, Mr. Kotter, my brother and I need to concentrate all our efforts on our investment."

Just then, Oliver's cell phone rang. It was Paul with bad news. Paul was out of state trying to secure loans to finish the repairs on the garage and to buy much needed equipment. Unfortunately, the brothers were tapped out and their luck had run out. After Oliver hung up, Jack could see the disappointment in his face. He was also all too familiar with the pride that went along with it. Jack wasn't going to try to press the issue, so he decided to get himself ready to leave.

Just as Jack and Dale were about to say goodbye, Dale blurted out another idea. "What about this, Jack? Your equipment is just sitting in a vacant building. So what if you have it brought down to this garage? That way, Oliver and Paul can gain business and utilize the funds to invest back into their garage."

Jack just stared at Dale for a moment. "Sometimes I wonder why you work for the police department and not me. That's an excellent idea, but what say you, Oliver?"

Oliver thought for a moment and agreed it would be possible, but he had to consult with Paul before any decision could be made. Dealing with Ben constantly, Jack was definitely on board with that concept. "Alright then, Oliver, I look forward to hearing from you soon. By the way, you gotta stop calling me Mr. Kotter. That was my dad's name. Please, just call me Jack."

Oliver smiled big and agreed. "Alright, Jack."

When Jack finally arrived home, he was exhausted. He had too much to do with too little time. He checked for messages, but Bria hadn't left any. Even with being as tired as he was, Jack became worried. It was already late, so he had the idea of taking the following day off and surprising her with a day trip. When morning arrived, Jack was up bright and early planning a nice day for him and Bria. A day at the metropolitan museum of art then an overnight stay at The Hamptons. Perfect. Jack was very excited and couldn't wait. He left home in his usual way. Laying rubber to concrete.

The way Jack drove, it didn't take him long before he pulled to the front of Bria's house. He waited as he knocked on the door a few times. He thought she might be sleeping since it was still early. In any case, he had a key to let himself in. As he crept through the door, the house was dark and quiet. He thought about waiting, but he knew if things were reversed, Bria would definitely pounce on him. He wasn't going to startle her, but the plan was to crawl into bed and lay beside her until she awoke.

Once he made it to the top of the steps, Bria came walking out of the bedroom, but she wasn't exactly glad to see him. "What the hell are you doing in my house, Jack?"

Jack kind of smiled jokingly. "Hi, honey, I'm home."

Bria wasn't laughing nor was she happy about Jack letting himself in unannounced. "I don't have anything to say to you, Jack, so I would appreciate it if you would leave."

Jack knew she was upset, but he didn't realize just how serious it was until then. "Come on, Bria, I've already apologized. Don't you think you're being a little too hard on me?"

Bria brushed past Jack and sat down on the steps. "No, Jack. I don't think it's too much to ask for the person you love to spend some time with you. I don't think it's too much to ask the person you want to spend your life with to think about something other than himself or his company. I wanted to have a life with you, Jack. I wanted us to be happy together. I was hoping we could start our own family, but I've come to the realization it's not going to be a fairytale ending for us."

This was definitely more than Jack had planned. He always figured on marrying Bria one day and starting a family, but he suddenly realized he was just like his dad. Everything else just seemed to get in the way. Feeling as low as low could be, Jack placed his hands in his pockets and walked past Bria as he made his way down the steps. "I'm sorry. I really am. I keep thinking if I can just take care of whatever current problem I'm having, then maybe we could be happy together, but it seems like as soon as one problem is resolved, two others pop up in its place. I just can't seem to catch a break. I never figured on having these kinds of problems."

Jack walked out the door without even saying goodbye. When he got to his car, he sat for a moment thinking about all the events that led to his life being in its current state. He was trying so hard to fill his father's shoes by keeping Ben happy, keeping the board members in line, and solving everyone's problems. He was also trying have a personal life, and on top of everything else, trying not to get killed by some psycho bitch. Just before he drove off, Jack thought to himself, *How the hell did my life get so out of control?*

Jack drove for a while, feeling sorry for himself, then found himself pulling into the mall parking lot where his friend Riley worked. He decided to walk in and see if his friend could offer up any good advice. Once inside, Jack saw that both of Riley's' chairs were empty. "Hey, Riley, how are you?" Jack climbed up into one of the chairs and smiled.

Riley was surprised and didn't know what to think. "What are you doing here, Jack? You're usually in here during evening hours."

Riley was right, but Jack wasn't there for a shoe shine. "I was driving around and found myself pulling into the lot, so I thought I would come in and say hello and maybe ask for some advice."

Coming from Jack Kotter, Riley thought it was a little strange. "What do I look like, a bartender? What kind of advice could I possibly give to a guy like you?"

Jack didn't say anything at first, but Riley knew he just wanted to vent, so he climbed up into the other chair so he could lend his ear. "Let me guess. Ben is getting on your last nerve?"

Jack chuckled as he gathered his thoughts. "Ben always gets on my last nerve, but that's just part of it. Remember when I spoke to you last time, I told you about a project my dad was working on? I can't convince Ben to go along with it, and on top of that, I'm still looking over my shoulder for this Lilith character."

Riley heard what Jack was saying, but he wasn't buying it. "Listen, Jack, I know all about the pressures of having to take over the family business and that it usually works itself out. I'm guessing there's something more going on, like maybe something with Bria? I've seen her out and about for the past week or so. She doesn't seem to be herself lately."

Jack's long face pretty much answered Riley's question. Jack climbed down from the chair and stood looking around the mall. He watched the husbands and wives and girlfriends and boyfriends. He saw how they were holding hands and enjoying their time together. "Look at them, Riley. Look how they're laughing and smiling, and look how they're happy just being together. Bria and I don't have that anymore. I'm always too damn busy trying to please everyone else. I can't blame her for wanting to call it quits."

Riley climbed down from his chair, but he didn't really have anything promising to say. "I'm sorry, Jack. Please don't take this the wrong way, but maybe you're just not cut out to run Kotter Industries. I remember your dad and the way he was. It seemed like he always had everything under control."

Jack thought about it, but he didn't take offense. "I think I would be okay if it wasn't for this project my dad left behind. I just can't ignore it. At this point in time, I'm too deep into it. If it wasn't for Ben running interference, I probably wouldn't be in this position right now. Listen, Riley, I appreciate the talk. I'll catch up to you later."

Jack left the mall with a new perspective and with new direction. He knew his dad was a very important businessman in New York. Not only was he involved with several charities that helped support the city's economy, but he also knew most of the heavy hitters who were on the board of directors for all the large banks. Jack had the idea of riding his dad's coattails to possibly secure loans to complete the project. It would mean dealing with some of New York's biggest banking institutions. Since the day was shot, he decided to make an appearance at work, hoping he wouldn't run into Ben. When he arrived, he had Bonnie make an appointment with the Bank of New York. That was where Kotter Industries did most of its business. There were no board meetings that day, so Jack decided to lay low in his father's office. Just when he sat down to relax, his cell phone rang. It was Oliver.

"Hello, Jack. I just wanted to let you know I spoke to Paul and he's alright with the idea, but he wanted to meet so we could go over some details of the agreement."

Contrary to what he thought the outcome of he and Lilith's confrontation would be, this was great news. Jack was happy the brothers decided to do the work and agreed to meet later in the day.

Once again, Jack found himself sitting in his dad's office wondering why his father pursued such an outrageous project. The fact that Victor gave his life helping others was understood, but just the idea of raising the *Titanic* would have such historical significance. While Jack was looking through some old paperwork, his cell phone rang again. This time, it was his old friend Connie. "Hey, Connie, I can't believe it's you. You're harder to get ahold of than the president. How the hell are you?"

Connie laughed for a few seconds then told Jack he'd just come back into town. "Hey, Jack, it's great to hear your voice. It's been too long."

Jack was ecstatic to hear Connie was in town. "What'ya say we get together and have some dinner? There's so much I want to talk to you about, plus we need to catch up."

Connie agreed, but their dinner plans would have to wait. He had some personal obligations to attend to and also some business to dispose of. After a few more minutes of talk, Jack told Connie he would call him in a few days.

Jack checked his watch and saw the day was going by pretty quickly, so he decided to stop by and talk to Oliver and Paul. As he was pulling up to the garage, he had that all too familiar feeling somebody was watching him. He hadn't seen Lilith in a long while, but that didn't mean she wasn't around. Just as he exited his car, Paul came out to greet him. "Come on in, Mr. Kotter. I just made a pot of coffee. Oliver told me about your situation and I gotta tell you, I don't envy you. I've seen that Plymouth racing up and down the highway and I've seen the damage it's caused. He also told me you have an old '59 Ferrari. Are you sure you want to go up against Lilith with a classic like that?"

Jack accepted the offer of coffee and made himself comfortable. "I know what you're thinking. How can I take down all that power? Her driving is very good, but she has limits with maneuverability. I want to use that against her and hope she makes a mistake."

Paul made himself some coffee and sat down. "Well, it's your choice to make, but we need to talk about your idea of moving equipment in here."

As he took a sip of his coffee, Jack let out a sigh. "I wanted to have Dale here with me when we talked, but he's busy chasing down criminals. Anyway, Kotter Industries shut down a terminal recently because it was no longer useful. We opened a new facility with updated equipment closer to home so we wouldn't have to travel out of our way to get our vehicles serviced. The old terminal still has all the old equipment in the building. We're not doing anything with it, so Dale had the idea of lending it to you and your brother so you can open your shop for business. And I was hoping you could help me get the Ferrari road-ready."

As Paul thought about it, he made two more cups of coffee and handed one to Jack. "You have to understand something, Mr. Kotter. It's not that I'm being ungrateful, but my brother and I had the idea of fixing up this old garage and reopening it utilizing just our skills. We weren't counting on anyone's help and we certainly don't want any handouts."

Jack could hear the pride in Paul's voice and was ready to counter with an offer. Jack stood up and looked around. He saw Oliver hard at work patching some holes that were in the floor. "I know what it feels like to want to do something on your own, only to have someone else either take over or just plain tell you it can't be done. So, why don't we look at this as being beneficial for both of us? You need heavy machinery and equipment in order to reopen this shop. Oliver told me you guys are tapped and the banks won't help. I have the equipment and don't really need it, so I will lease it to you with the option to buy it. If you want, I'll have my lawyer draw up a contract so you'll have something in writing, and I would be honored to be your first customer."

Before Paul could say anything, Oliver came walking in, wiping his hands and face. "Well, the floor is done. It will take a day to dry, but it'll look good."

As Paul poured some coffee for Oliver, he smiled at the good news. The offer made Paul look at the situation in a whole new light. "Okay, Mr. Kotter, I think we can do business together." Paul shook Jack's hand and agreed to the terms. "Have your lawyer draw up the paperwork and my brother and I will sign it."

It was a great feeling for Jack, because it was nice to be making business decisions without Ben looking over his shoulder. "I'll have the equipment picked up in the next few days and delivered to you."

Just as Jack was about to leave, Oliver asked about the Ferrari. "I don't mean to burst your bubble, Jack, but that Ferrari of yours is going to need some work that requires some delicate equipment. A car of that quality isn't exactly rough and tough. They're all about speed and finesse. I'm guessing most of what you have is for heavy road vehicles."

Jack thought about it and came up with a great idea. "I think I know who to call. I'm very good friends with the owner of the Wiley Roadster. He happens to be a car enthusiast and has everything you'll need. I'll stop by tomorrow and talk to him about it. By the way, once everything is in place, how long do you think it will be before the Ferrari is ready to go?"

Paul laughed as he walked Jack out. "All you multi-millionaires are the same. You want everything at the drop of a dime. We have to take a look at the car to see what all she needs, then we'll determine what we can do to try to give you every advantage possible. After that, we'll order parts if needed then do the work. Depending on how fast we can get set up and rolling, you're probably looking at a few weeks." That was disappointing for Jack to hear, but at least the ball was rolling.

Jack left the garage feeling relieved about finally moving forward. Ever since he came back from California, he'd felt as if he was just spinning wheels. On the way home, he called Dale and updated him on the situation. Dale was good to go because he had thought of a plan to disguise the fact there was a plan. "Listen, Jack, I brought in a couple of my friends and told them about our plans for Lilith. They're on board with it. I have a helicopter and at least four other officers involved, so if this thing goes south, we're all going to lose big time."

Jack appreciated what Dale was doing, but as usual, Jack was being Jack. "Well, I guess we better not let Lilith get the best of us."

After hanging up with Dale, Jack finally made it home. For the first time, he felt it would be a waste of time to check his messages because he was positive Bria hadn't called. He was tired and had a very important meeting in the morning with the bank. He was hoping the success he'd had earlier in the evening would carry over into the morning. A storm was brewing, which reminded him of Bria and the nights they would spend together just lying in bed listening to the rain fall. With his father's project depending on the meeting at the bank and thoughts of Bria, it didn't make it easy for him to sleep.

CHAPTER TWENTY-ONE

In the morning, Jack was tired and frustrated. He woke up late and was rushing to get ready. He had no time for breakfast and he was out of coffee. He really hadn't thought about what he was going to tell the bank the loan was for, so he had to come up with something quick before he arrived. As he arrived, he threw his tie on in a hurry and rushed to beat the clock. Jack checked his watch as he entered the bank. He made it with very little time to spare, so he wasted no time hitting the men's room to freshen up. In order to calm his nerves, he splashed some water on his face. He stared at himself in the mirror, wondering if Ben's reaction would be positive if he was able to get the bank to go along. *Oh well,* he thought. *I'll deal with that problem later if it comes to that.*

As he walked out into the waiting area, he wiped his brow and buttoned his jacket. He approached the receptionist and announced who he was, and she kindly asked him to have a seat. As he sat waiting, he watched other people come and go and saw others as they filled out various forms and documents. Jack had never had to deal with a bank before, so he pondered what would be required of him in order to make his plan work.

In the current banking system and with the rollercoaster economy, even Kotter Industries had to play by the rules. Though Kotter Industries had grown into an international success, it was still limited in the amount of funds it could borrow. Jack knew this all too well when the idea came to him. This was the institution Kotter Industries had most of its accounts with, so he knew if he couldn't close the deal there, no other bank would even listen to what he had to say.

During the night, Jack couldn't think of anything but the up and coming meeting. He knew he needed to present his A-game. When the time came, Jack was ready and waiting on the accounts manager, Mr. Rupersberg. As Jack sat quietly in the waiting area, Mr. Rupersberg entered the bank. He was tall and thin with a distinguished but young look. He greeted all the employees with a smile. As he made his way to his office, Jack's anxiety took over and he jumped up and met him at his door.

Before the banker could open his office door, Jack introduced himself. "Hello, Mr. Rupersberg, my name is Jack Kotter."

The receptionist, Ms. Baines, stood up and apologized for the incident. "I'm sorry, Mr. Rupersberg, Mr. Kotter has a ten o'clock appointment with you." Afterwards, her facial expression turned angry. "He seems to be a bit impatient."

Mr. Rupersberg had a newspaper under one arm and his daily Starbucks coffee in his hand. "It's alright, Ms. Baines. Mr. Kotter is welcome any time. Please, come in and make yourself comfortable."

Jack breathed a sigh of relief. "Thank you, Mr. Rupersberg." He followed the banker into his office and sat down.

Mr. Rupersberg placed his coffee and paper down on his desk and hung his jacket on the coat rack, then he made his way around to his chair and sat down. He took a moment and looked at Jack. "I apologize for staring, but I don't think you're Mr. Kotter."

Jack took a breath and gained his composure. "No, Mr. Rupersberg, I'm not. I'm Jack Kotter Jr. I know you're used to doing business with my dad, but obviously, he's not available."

Mr. Rupersberg's face showed no emotion. "May I call you Jack?"

Jack tried not to grind his teeth and forced out a small grin. A knot started to form in his stomach and he knew the meeting was going to be an uphill battle. "Sure, Jack would be fine."

Mr. Rupersberg grabbed his coffee and leaned back in his chair. "So, Jack, I was looking forward to meeting with you. I met your father once when I was up and coming. It's fascinating to meet a self-made man."

Jack knew it was a cheap shot aimed at him. He had big shoes to fill. He also had to patronize the idiot sitting across from him. "Yes, it's nice when your parents give you everything. It saves a lot of the ass kissing one has to do when trying to get ahead in life." Jack knew he shouldn't have, but he just couldn't help it.

Mr. Rupersberg smiled and placed his coffee back on his desk. "How rude of me, Jack. May I offer you some coffee or juice? Our bank carries a variety of refreshments."

Jack graciously declined and attempted to jump-start the reason for the meeting. "Mr. Rupersberg, I wanted to meet with you because I'm undertaking a personal project that's going to utilize much of Kotter Industries available resources. I'm here to try to alleviate some of the financial burden my company will have to endure over the next few years."

With a look of interest, Rupersberg smiled. "You have my attention, Jack. Do you have any details or financial projections or even a timeline of when the loan will come to a conclusion?"

Jack knew these questions were going to be asked and he had no real answers. "Well, I can't give details on the project. It's personal. I can't really predict the financial gain if there is any, and as for the loan itself, that could be worked out between my accountants and this institution."

Rupersberg finished his coffee then contemplated what he was going to say next. He knew Kotter Industries was a long-standing customer and was worth billions. "Jack, help me understand. Is this a personal loan for you or a business loan for Kotter Industries?"

Jack had to come up with something better than what he had presented so far. "It's kind of both. It's a business loan for Kotter Industries that's for a personal project I'm overseeing."

Rupersberg tapped his fingers on his desk with a look of confusion. It was obvious that giving out a loan without details was out of the question, but he wanted to give Jack every opportunity to beg. "Look, Jack, let's talk about exactly what you need and we'll try to come up with a plan to accommodate you."

Jack felt his window of opportunity slipping away and he could give no grounds for trying to salvage the meeting. "Mr. Rupersberg, this project will employee a number of people and will generate well-needed salaries for a lot of workers. I can't give you details because it's a project very close to my heart and I need to keep it out of the media for now."

With a sense of satisfaction, Rupersberg kept dangling his line. "So, what are we talking about? Give me a bottom line number."

Jack wasn't naive. He knew the meeting wasn't going the way he wanted, but he was desperate, so he kept at it. "Rough estimate, I would say two hundred million, and maybe an additional fifty million if needed."

Rupersberg looked at his watch and decided to put an end to the cat and mouse game. "I'm sorry, Jack. I know our relationship with Kotter Industries has grown over the years. Largely due to the fact your father was one hell of a businessman, and Benjamin, he's a legend within the banking industry. The deals those two men put together over the years have become mandatory textbook reading for guys like me. That being said, times have changed. We no longer work off of handshakes and goodwill. If this institution gave out money like that to anyone with a personal adventure, we would be out of business. So, as much as it saddens me, I must turn you down, Jack. Now, if you'll excuse me, I have other obligations I must attend to."

Jack wasn't surprised. He knew it was a slim chance, but he had to try. He stood up and reached his hand across the desk. "Thank you for your time, Mr. Rupersberg."

The banker stood up and shook Jack's hand. "It was very nice to meet you, Jack. I wish you the best of luck on your adventure, and please let me know how it turns out."

Jack could feel his blood boiling but kept his composure in check. He turned and walked towards the door. As he opened the door, he turned and paused. "When you get some free time, you should check the bank's archives. You'll find this institution financed a small business in 1927 called Up and Down Hauling. That was my dad's first business venture. Since then, Kotter Industries has always honored its obligations to this institution." Jack walked out the door with his chin up. He didn't feel any worse, just more determined. A quick thought to himself: *So much for riding coattails.*

As he made his way back to the main lobby, he noticed the two brothers Oliver and Paul sitting with one of the loan officers. He could tell they were upset, so he wanted to wait and find out why. Jack could see the loan officer shaking his head and shrugging his shoulders. He had the feeling they were getting the same treatment he received.

Jack grabbed a bank slip and a pen and pretended to be writing. As the brothers stood up to leave, he noticed they avoided shaking the loan officer's hand. He kind of chuckled and thought to himself, *good move.* Jack made sure he turned away as Oliver and Paul passed him and walked out the door.

After the brothers were out of sight, he walked over to the loan officer who was filing paperwork, probably in the denied drawer. With the encounter with Mr. Rupersberg still fresh in his mind, Jack approached the loan officer's desk. Before he could say anything, the man jumped up and greeted Jack with excitement. "Hello, Mr. Kotter, so glad to finally meet you." With a bit of surprise, Jack reached out and shook the man's hand. The loan officer introduced himself as Mr. Hunsford and offered Jack a seat. "So, what do I owe the pleasure of your visit today, Mr. Kotter?"

Jack felt bad that he was going to take his frustrations out on this unsuspecting employee, but he had just about all he could take in one day. As it was, Jack was in no mood for niceties, but he tried to be as pleasant as possible.

"The two men who were at your desk earlier, what business did they have with you?"

Mr. Hunsford paused for a few seconds. "As you probably know, Mr. Kotter, that's confidential, and our ethics policy here doesn't allow for us to divulge other customers' information."

Jack knew Mr. Hunsford was right, so he had to try another approach. "Mr. Hunsford, you obviously know who I am, and far be it from me to attack your ethics code, but I'm guessing those two gentlemen were attempting to become customers but came up short. And I'm also guessing you'll never see them again."

Jack saw the intimidation in Mr. Hunsford's face and decided to keep going. "Now, what if I were to tell you I know those two men and that they would be bringing their future business needs to you?"

With his frustration starting to build, Mr. Hunsford leaned back in his chair. "Mr. Kotter, I don't like where this is going. I know Kotter Industries is one of our main accounts, so I'm going to extend this courtesy to you just once. They were trying to acquire a business loan, but I couldn't help them."

Jack already knew this information, but had to play along to get more. He sat on the edge of his chair and tried to keep his composure. "Why not?"

Mr. Hunsford, now sitting firm on the edge of his chair, attempted to be just as intimidating. "We don't give business loans to people without proper collateral." Now, with rules and regulations on his side, Mr. Hunsford felt comfortable enough to try to bully Jack. "You of all people should know that basic concept, Mr. Kotter. I'm sure your father understood the rules of business and banking."

For the second time that day, Jack was on the losing end of an argument. He surely didn't appreciate Mr. Hunsford bringing up his father, but he remained calm and decided to continue on. "They have a nice garage. It also sits on a pretty nice piece of property. I've seen it. It's a prime location and I'm sure the profit margin will be more than enough to cover whatever loan they need."

Mr. Hunsford dropped his shoulders with a long sigh. "We've already evaluated the property. The problem is the real estate market. It's too unstable, so we're trying to get away from using property as collateral."

Jack was getting more and more frustrated as time went by. "So, without a thriving business that's already making money, you don't exactly roll out the red carpet for the middle class people."

Mr. Hunsford grew tired of the argument and attempted to end it as pleasantly as possible. He stood up to try to let Jack know he was ready for him to leave. "I'm sorry, Mr. Kotter, but I have other obligations to attend to, so if you'll excuse me."

Jack had just had his last nerve plucked. "Incredible. You're the second banker that's said that to me this morning. What is that? A mandatory phrase they test you on in school? Let me just say this, it's men like my father and those two brothers with their dreams and hard work who built this country. The arrogance and ignorance of banking institutions do nothing but mock them. By the way, I won't be excusing you."

Mr. Hunsford admired Jack for his candidness and sat back down. "So, now what, Mr. Kotter? Are you going to ask for my supervisor? I do believe you already met him earlier, when you nearly knocked him down trying to introduce yourself. Judging by the mood you're in, I don't think things went too well with him either."

Jack knew all about mind games. They were usually played when individuals were trying to obtain information or attempting to gain the upper hand in some kind of contest. This conversation didn't pertain to either.

"Look, Mr. Hunsford, the afternoon hasn't even arrived yet and I'm already mentally worn out. I don't want to argue. I'm not here to threaten you and I certainly don't want to piss you off. This is what I want to happen and you let me know if it's workable for you."

Mr. Hunsford gave a smug smile and sat up to listen. "Okay, Mr. Kotter. You have my attention. Give it to me."

That's all Jack needed to hear. Just like a Trojan horse, he looked harmless on the outside, but was gearing up for one last battle from within. "This is what we're gonna do. Tomorrow, you're going to call those two men back and apologize to them for the inconvenience you've caused. Then you're going to tell them you have reconsidered their loan application and will be recommending approval."

Trying to keep a straight face, Mr. Hunsford let out a small laugh. He placed his hand over his mouth to try to cover it, but was unsuccessful. "I'm sorry, Mr. Kotter. Why am I going to do that?"

Poor Mr. Hunsford. He just didn't realize the wrath Jack was about to poor out. Jack took one last healthy breath and leaned across the desk. "First, if you don't, Kotter Industries will withdraw all of its accounts and will no longer do business with this institution, causing millions in lost revenue. Second, those potential customers you turned away this morning will be receiving a service contract from Kotter Industries to maintain our fleet of vehicles here in New York. The contract has an estimated worth of five million a year."

Looking like a school boy who'd just been scolded, Mr. Hunsford's bag of tricks was empty and his ethics rule book didn't apply to this situation. All he could do was sit and listen. Jack could tell he had the upper hand, but he just wasn't the kind of person to kick someone when they were down. "So, Mr. Hunsford, you have an opportunity to climb your corporate ladder as a hero or you can spiral downwards as a zero. Either way, by the end of the week, you're the one who's going to be in Mr. Rupersberg office."

Mr. Hunsford stood up slowly and placed his hands in his pockets. With a worried look, he walked to the side and sat on the corner of his desk. He was well aware of the history of Kotter Industries. "Well, Mr. Kotter, you definitely know how to drive a point home. You would do this and jeopardize a 73-year working relationship for two men you may or may not know?"

Once again, Jack knew his window of opportunity was beginning to close. He had one last business trick his dad taught him. Always be sincere in your delivery of an idea. Jack looked down at the name plate on the desk. Michael P. Hunsford. "Look, Mr. Hunsford. Mike. May I call you Mike?"

Still with the worried look, Mr. Hunsford paused. "Sure. Mike would be fine."

Jack gave a half smile and continued with his reasoning. "Mike, I'm going to level with you. I just met Oliver and Paul the other night. I saw them working on their garage and decided to stop and talk. As the conversation went on, I happened to notice the potential of the property and how the location was ideal for their business. I was telling the truth about the contract. Kotter Industries has been unhappy with the service of our vehicles and we've been waiting for the contract to run out. When I was talking to Oliver, I noticed their facility would be big enough to handle the account, but small enough to get the personal service we're looking for. This is a win-win situation for you and me, and definitely a win for Oliver and Paul, but this whole scenario rests on your shoulders."

Mr. Hunsford sat back down in his chair. With his hands folded, he leaned forward on his desk. Jack could tell the thought process was in motion and decided to let his reasoning stand on its own merits.

With his hands still folded, Mr. Hunsford placed them on top of his head and leaned back in his chair. Jack sat quietly as he listened to the leather from Mr. Hunsford's chair rub against his suit. As he gathered his thoughts, Mr. Hunsford stood up once again. This time he had some reasoning of his own. He let out a pleasant smile as he spoke. "Mr. Kotter, Jack. May I call you Jack?"

Still feeling the effects of their mind game, Jack sat on the edge of his chair with a smile. "Sure, Jack would be fine."

With a perplexed look and his arms crossed, Mr. Hunsford leaned on the side of his desk. "This is what I'm going to do for all parties involved. I'm not going to make that phone call like you want, but what I am going to do is pull their application out of my files and place it back on my desk. There it's going to stay, let's say, for one week. Now, if somehow within that week your accountants crunch numbers, gather last year's maintenance records, and put together a new contract, and somehow all that makes it to my desk within that week, only then will I be making that phone call. What do you think, Jack? Is this an acceptable plan for you?"

With satisfaction in his heart and one big smile on his face, Jack stood up and agreed to the terms. He thanked Mr. Hunsford as they shook hands. As Mr. Hunsford sat back down, Jack decided to throw in one last thought. "You know, Mike, I was told this morning this institution doesn't work off handshakes and goodwill. Go figure."

Mr. Hunsford smiled and could only imagine what went on during Jack's meeting with Mr. Rupersberg. "Good day, Jack. I'm looking forward to reviewing that paperwork."

Jack walked out of the bank feeling the satisfaction of winning at least one of his battles. He also felt good about the solid business decision of offering Oliver and Paul the service contract. On the way to work, he stopped by the garage to speak to the brothers. When he arrived, he could see the brothers were arguing. Jack didn't want to say anything about his little meeting with Mr. Hunsford. His plan was to let the situation take care of itself. As Jack walked to the door, Paul and Oliver stopped bickering and greeted him. Oliver politely excused himself as Paul and Jack walked into the office.

"I'm glad you stopped by, Mr. Kotter. I was really excited about our deal when you presented it to me, but now after sleeping on it, I'm starting to have second thoughts."

Jack definitely wasn't expecting that from Paul, but he understood why. "Listen, Paul, I wanted to talk to you about another business proposition I have. Kotter Industries has a small fleet of company vehicles that are used by our top executives and most of our managers. These vehicles aren't leased, so we need to maintain them on a regular basis. It just so happens the current contract we have is about to expire and I thought maybe I could offer it to you and Oliver. There's not a lot involved, just oil changes and tire rotation and, of course, regular maintenance, such as brakes and other fluids."

Paul took a minute and looked around the garage. He saw all the work that still had to be done. "I'm sorry, Mr. Kotter. I know you're only trying to help out and I appreciate your efforts, but even with the equipment you're willing to give us, my brother and I can't conduct business until the building inspector signs off on this property. I was at the bank this morning trying to secure a loan so we could expedite the repairs, but I got shot down. I wasn't really surprised, but I had to try."

Jack was feeling a little like Ben. Trying to manipulate a situation to benefit himself. Although he knew it would also greatly help the brothers, it still didn't change the fact he was pulling all the strings. "I understand, Paul. I was really hoping to be able to do business together."

Jack decided to leave knowing all the plans depended on Mr. Hunsford keeping his end of the bargain and approving Paul and Oliver for a loan, so he wasted no time getting to work and faxing over all the necessary documentation concerning a service contract offered to the brothers from Kotter Industries. Afterwards, he walked down to his father's office to try to make some sense of everything going on.

After a few minutes of meditation, Ben came bursting through the door. "Thought I would find you here, kid. Anything new going on?"

Jack didn't answer right away. He could tell Ben had something to say and was trying to bait Jack into an argument. "I don't know. You tell me."

Ben shut the door and sat down. "Come on, kid, you've been avoiding me for days. What's going on?"

Jack still wasn't going for the bait. Instead, he tried to avoid any conflict with Ben. "I'm telling it like it is, Ben. There's nothing going on."

Ben stared for a few seconds because he knew Jack would start to squirm. Jack wouldn't even look at him. He tried to avoid the eye contact Ben was trying to make. Ben could see Jack wasn't going to be suckered in, so he decided to come right out and put Jack on the spot. "Come on, kid. Did you really think you could bypass me and try to take a business loan out for that godforsaken project? Did we not just have a conversation about going behind my back?" Jack's heart sank knowing Ben was about to rip into him. "After that little stunt you pulled with your makeshift legal team trying to figure out how to get to that money, it was only natural you would try to approach the banks. Unfortunately for you, I play golf with all the top executives of those banks. I warned them you would be coming. Rupersberg called me right after you left there this morning. He's a real weasel, but he knows enough not to cross me. You have a lot of fight in you, kid. I can't deny that, but in the end, you lost."

As his blood started to boil, Jack had just about all he could take of Ben's arrogance. "I don't know what you're trying to pull, Ben, but whatever it is, I'm not giving up. I don't care if I have to take down both you and Kotter Industries. I'm going to finish what my father started."

Ben stood up and walked over to a portrait of Jack Sr. hanging on the wall. "And then what, kid? Why stop there? Why not raise the *Olympic* or the *Britannic*? Hell, let's go after all the lost ships."

Jack loaded both barrels as he stood up to face off against Ben. "My grandfather isn't on any of those ships, you sorry bastard, and I can't believe you would even try to make a joke out of it."

Ben was surprisingly calm as he tried to put a little space between himself and Jack. "Listen, kid, I'm not trying to be disrespectful of your family, but I know you're not thinking with a clear head. Do you remember the promise you made? No more new projects after that long drawn out battle we had with the board over the computer industry. Then when we opened that box, you also made the promise we would drop it if things became too difficult. Well, raising the *Titanic* seems a little difficult to me."

Still feeling the sting of Ben's joking nature, Jack loaded up for another go round. "Damn it, Ben, I thought you were my friend. I thought you were my dad's best friend. He reached out from beyond the grave to ask for your help. Doesn't that mean anything to you, or was my father just your meal ticket for your sorry ass to make it to the top?"

Normally, Ben would be yelling at the top of his voice right about then, but he was trying to give Jack some leeway. "Listen, kid, you keep throwing your father in my face, trying to make me feel guilty, but it's not going to work. Now, I know you think you have to step into your dad's shoes and be the patriarch for the company, but that comes with a hefty price. You can't just think about yourself anymore. You now have thousands of employees around the world who depend on the paycheck they get each week. Most of those people live from paycheck to paycheck. If some rogue project goes wrong for you, you get to walk away and still have money in your pocket. Your employees might not be as fortunate as you. By the way, did you forget about your board of directors? Do you really think they would back you on some half-ass idea that may or may not benefit the company?"

Ben started to walk out the door then turned back around. "Think about that, you sorry bastard." Ben slammed the door and walked back to his office.

Jack sat back down and ran through the argument in his head. Just then, his cell phone rang. It was Ethan. Still angry at what just happened, he was reluctant to answer, but he did anyway. "Hey, Ethan. I'm really sorry. I forgot all about our double date."

Ethan wasn't upset, because he had heard about the break up between Jack and Bria. "Hey, Jack, don't worry about it. I saw Bria last night and she told me everything. I'm really sorry, man. How about you and I get together tonight and we do the town?"

Jack thought about it and knew if he didn't do something, he would just explode. "Alright, you talked me into it. How about I meet you at the Katwalk Bar on 35th Street around 10:00?" Ethan gladly agreed and was looking forward to it.

When Jack hung up with Ethan, he could feel a sort of restlessness building up. He wasn't quite sure what it was until he went to walk back to his office and saw Linda coming from one of the conference rooms. He waited and watched her walk down the hall. She was wearing a skirt tight enough to choke a horse, but it looked really good. She also had on a blouse that was somewhat see through. Jack walked up behind her and nudged her from behind. "Hi, Linda, it's been a while. Can I talk to you privately in my office?" Jack opened the door as Linda followed him in. When the door closed, Jack grabbed her by the waist and swung her around against the wall. Linda was surprised at first, but quickly caught on to Jack's naughty plan. As Jack moved in for a passionate kiss, Linda slapped his face.

"Hold on, Jackie boy. I hope you're not mistaking me for one of your little whores."

Jack was stunned at first, but came right back and started to undo Linda's blouse. "What's wrong, Linda? Are you all talk, or do you have any action in you?"

Linda reached down and started to undo Jack's pants. As they shared their first passionate kiss, she reached down inside Jack's pants and found what she wanted. With Linda's blouse already unbuttoned, Jack unzipped her skirt and it fell to the floor. His hands found their way down her back to her black silk panties. As the kissing continued, Jack picked her up and walked her over to his desk. He placed her on the edge of the desk and pushed everything aside. He leaned into Linda as miscellaneous paperwork and other items fell to the floor. Just then, Linda kicked Jack backwards making him fall to the floor. "Remember what I told you, Jackie boy? I told you one day I would make you beg for me. So if you want me like I know you do, you're gonna have to crawl back to me on your hands and knees."

Jack did just that. He bent down on all fours and crawled over to Linda who was now standing up. As Jack made his way over to her, Linda slipped her panties off and stood waiting. When he made it back to her, she placed her hand on his head stopping him from moving any further. "Hold on, Jackie boy. After how you've treated me in the past, you need to show me just how bad you want me." She picked her foot up and inserted a few of toes her into Jack's mouth. "That's right, Jackie boy, suck on them. Make me want you as bad as you want me."

Afterwards, Jack ran his tongue up Linda's inner thigh, then once again picked her up and laid her on the desk. He stood between her long legs and ran his hands up until he reached her hips. With authority, he pulled her into him as he inserted himself into her. Linda smiled and moaned as she felt Jack's manhood create friction inside her.

After a few minutes, sweat started to form on Jack's brow. As he started to move faster and faster, Linda's moans became more intense. After several orgasms, Linda pushed Jack away and stood up. She spun him around and pushed him back onto his desk. She then climbed on top of him and gently lowered herself onto his manhood. It wasn't long before things started to heat up again. Linda slowly moved her hips as she hovered over Jack bracing her hands against his chest. "Come on, Jackie boy, let me hear you beg some more. Tell me how much you want me. Come on, Jackie boy, use that tool and make me feel like your dirty little bitch. That's right, Jackie boy, how bad do you want it?"

As Linda continued to move slowly, Jack became more anxious. Just then, Linda slapped him across the face. Afterwards, she began to move a little faster. "Hold it, Jackie boy, not yet." Once again, she slapped him across his face. Then she moved just a little faster. "Don't let me down, Jackie boy. Hold it as long as you can." Linda could see the look in Jack's eyes like he was about to erupt, so she came to an abrupt stop and climbed off.

To Jack's surprise, Linda grabbed him by his hands and stood him up. She then dropped to her knees and wrapped her mouth around him. Now it was Jack's turn to moan. Linda momentarily stopped and looked up at Jack. "Okay, Jackie boy, let's see how long you can hold it now." It wasn't long before Linda had Jack at her mercy again. Then it happened. In a moment's time, all the anxiety, restlessness, and stress came rushing out of Jack.

After a few more minutes of enjoyment, Linda and Jack caught their breath and got dressed. Realizing he'd probably made a huge mistake, Jack tried to play it off like it was no big deal. "Linda, I hope you don't think this means anything. I just thought it would be nice to get our sexual tensions out of the way so we could be better friends."

With Jack's tie in her hand, Linda walked over and wrapped it around him. She then pulled him closer and kissed him. "I hope you don't think you can just have your way then throw me away like a piece of trash. I could be your best friend, Jackie boy, or I can be your worst nightmare."

Jack backed away in order to create some space between them. "Don't try to threaten me, Linda. As far as I'm concerned, you're just part of everything else that's gone wrong today. Now, get the hell out of my office."

Linda laughed as she headed for the door. "Don't think this is over, Jack Kotter."

After picking everything up from the floor, Jack sat at his desk thinking about how he went from sitting on top of the world to rolling around at the bottom with Linda. After he made some phone calls and finished up some business, he decided to take a break and leave for the day. Before he did, he called to see if Connie could meet with him.

When Jack picked Connie up, he was all smiles. "Damn, Connie, how long has it been?"

Connie was just as happy to see Jack and was excited to be back in New York. "I don't know. If you remember, I moved to Africa for a while. I was doing some research off the coast of Africa, in the Indian Ocean. Sorry I didn't write, but our resources were very limited over there."

Jack laughed because Connie always talked about traveling around and living by the seat of his pants. "Well, I'm glad you're back, even if it's just for a little while."

Jack decided to pay a visit to the Wiley Roadster knowing Walley and Jimmy would be there. Surprisingly, when he pulled up, the two brothers were nowhere to be found. He asked one of the waitresses, who told him they both had found temporary employment. Jack was stunned for a moment and then laughed. "Wow, are you kidding? Mom and pop must have finally cut them off." The waitress went back to work as Jack pulled *Fringe* into a parking space.

Jack and Connie sat quietly for a few minutes enjoying the breeze and the girls prancing across the parking lot. Connie turned to take a look around and was happy to see Jack still had his dream car. "Not that I thought you would ever get rid of her, but I'm glad to see you still have *Fringe*. She's beautiful just like I remember her."

Jack smiled with pride. "Yeah, I almost lost her. I wrecked during some stupid race I got caught up in. Luckily, there wasn't any serious damage."

After a half hour of catching up on each other's exploits and some Wiley Roadster greasy food, Jack was ready to talk about *Titanic*. "Listen, Connie, your timing couldn't be more perfect. Before my dad died, he was working on a project that was very personal to him. Unfortunately, he didn't get to complete it, so he left it up to me and Ben to decide whether or not to finish the project. Ben is dead set against it because he's not really connected to the project in anyway except as my dad's best friend. On the other hand, I have a personal connection to it like my father did, so Ben and I have been going head to head over it. Because of your expertise with underwater exploration, I wanted to get your input so I can try to convince Ben to change his mind."

Connie was used to Jack always trying to set him up for a joke, but he could hear the seriousness in his voice. "Well, I'll do my best, but how do you know what I have to say will benefit you and not Ben?"

Connie made a good point and Jack knew it. "Well, I guess I just have to take that chance. After I tell you what I want to do and you tell me it's impossible or too risky, then I'll accept that, but if there's a chance of success, then I hope you'll support my decision to go forward."

Listening to Jack, Connie became very intrigued. "What are you up to, Jack Kotter? You really have my curiosity peaked." Connie could tell it was something big, but he wasn't prepared for what Jack was about to say.

Just in case Connie didn't have good feedback, Jack braced himself for the worst. "I want to raise the *Titanic*."

Connie just stared for a few seconds thinking there was a punch line coming, but there was none. "You're stupid, Jack. Here I thought you had something serious going on and it turns out to be nothing but a joke." Connie smiled as he shook his head laughing. "Same old Jack Kotter. Nothing ever is serious with you." A few seconds went by before Connie realized Jack wasn't laughing. "Jack, please tell me you're not serious." Connie could see the serious look on Jack's face. "You're not kidding, are you?"

Jack had already prepared himself for Connie's reaction and was ready to explain himself. "Listen, Connie. Before you rip me a new ass, let me explain my reasons why."

Although Connie was already thinking it couldn't be done, he wanted to listen to his best friends reasoning. "Alright, Jack, I can't believe you want to take on the holy grail of shipwrecks, but go ahead, tell me what'cha got."

Jack took a breath and began to tell his story. He told Connie about the mysterious box his dad left behind and how it led them to California. Then he told Connie about finding out his dad and his parents, Victor and Elizabeth, were on *Titanic* when it sank. Connie sat listening in awe as Jack continued on. "Well, after coming back from California, Ben and I argued like cats and dogs, mostly over the money my dad had set aside for the project. Ben won't let me anywhere near it.

"During that awful night, Victor gave my dad a smile and was never seen again. Apparently, through the course of his life, my dad hired private investigator to find survivors so he could interview them. He finally came across a survivor named Charles Joughin who told a story that intrigued my father, and that led him to Mrs. Winnifred Van Tongerloo. Recently, Ben and I took a trip to Michigan, where we spoke to Mrs. Van Tongerloo. She told us how Victor gave his life to help her family during the sinking. I can't even begin to imagine how my dad felt after hearing that story. Through his years, my dad searched for *Titanic* with every intention of raising her up and transporting her remains back to New York Harbor. It wasn't the ship he cared about, it was bringing Victor home and having some closure in his life."

After hearing Jack's story, Connie was floored. He wasn't laughing anymore, nor was he looking at Jack like he was crazy. He stepped out of the car into the brisk, cool air. After a few seconds, Jack stepped out and walked around the car. "So, what'ya think, Connie? Can it be done?"

Connie lit up a cigarette and blew out some smoke. "Damn you, Jack. I hear what you're saying, but it's not exactly a yes or no answer. There's a lot involved with bringing any vessel up from the ocean, let alone something like the *Titanic*. You can't just go out there and hook chains to it and haul it up."

Jack knew it was a lot to lay on somebody, but he was determined to finish his dad's work. "Connie, I wouldn't have asked you if I thought there wasn't a chance, but you haven't told me no yet, which leaves me to believe it can be done."

Connie took a nice, long drag of his cigarette then threw it to the ground. He looked at Jack and smiled. "I can't believe you had everyone fooled when we were kids. Everyone thought I was the troubled kid. Damn it, Jack, anything can be done when you have the resources. God knows I heard that phrase many times from your father and Ben when we were kids. It can be done, but I can't go along with you on this one. Don't you understand? It's a shrine. It's looked upon as a mass grave site. You can't desecrate that."

Jack was silent for a moment, then looked Connie in the eyes. "So, when did you start smoking?"

Connie laughed. "Sucker me into another question so I forget about the problem. Sorry, Jack, that worked when we were kids, but not now. But if you must know, I started about two years ago, but I was on the road to quitting up until a few minutes ago. Thanks a lot. And I'm still upset, so the answer is still no. I can't back you on this."

Jack understood why Connie was against the idea, but he still needed the information. "Alright, Connie, I wouldn't want you to do something you don't believe in, but I still value your opinion and expertise. I still need to know what it would take to pull this off."

Connie glanced at Jack then shook his head. "You wouldn't happen to have the right hand of God in your back pocket, because I'll tell you what, anything short of that and you're looking at failure."

Jack and Connie climbed back into the car and just sat staring at the nice cars coming in and out of the parking lot. Jack was running out of ideas and patients. He needed to appeal to Connie's friendship. "After Sergis died, Ben and my dad became really close. They were the best of friends right up until my dad passed away. My dad asked Ben to look after me. Inside that box I told you about was a letter to Ben asking him to help me through the difficulties I would have with this project. That didn't really work out the way I had hoped. I'm asking you as my friend, Connie; help me with this. I'm not asking you to square off against Ben. Just use your connections to get me the information I need."

Connie didn't say anything. He just sat staring out the window at the hot rods going by. "So, what kind of time does *Fringe* get in the quarter mile?"

Jack burst out laughing. "Sucker me into another question so I forget about the problem. You are too funny. I've actually had her running between nines and tens. So, does this mean you'll help me?"

As he pushed his hair back in grief, Connie smiled. "Yeah, I guess it won't hurt to supply you with information. I still don't think it's going to do you any good."

After wolfing down some of the Wiley Roadster's finest greasy food, Jack drove Connie home and left to meet with Ethan. It was still early, so he decided to stop by the storage unit and tinker with the Ferrari. After spacing out behind the wheel for a few hours, it was time to leave and meet Ethan for dinner. When Jack arrived, Ethan already had a table waiting. "It's about time, Jack. No wonder Ben is always on you about being late."

Jack sat down and ordered some drinks. "So, Ethan, once again, you're in love."

Ethan smiled from ear to ear. "Hell, yeah. I'm not kidding, Jack. She's really into me, and without saying too much, she can't keep her hands off me."

Surprisingly, Ethan didn't talk too much about Bobby Jo during dinner, which was just fine with Jack. Instead, they talked more about work related issues and the latest battles going on in the boardroom. After dinner, they sat at the bar and had some drinks. That was when it happened. Ethan blurted out his future plan with Bobby Jo. "I know it's been a short time, Jack, but I'm going to ask Bobby Jo to marry me."

When Jack heard that, he nearly dropped his drink. "Are you serious? What for? I mean, why not wait until you see what the future holds?"

Ethan smiled as he downed what was left of his beer. "I thought about that, but we're very happy together, and we're already making plans to buy a house together. I think she knows I'm going to ask, and that's the great part about it. She wants me as much as I want her."

Jack had no argument to offer so he offered his congrats instead. "Alright, Casanova. You're a good friend, so I wish you all the happiness in the world. Jack raised his glass for a toast. To friends and their wild ideas."

Ethan was happy but was expecting Jack to put up more of an argument then he did. "Well, I'm glad you're not going to try to talk me down, but maybe you're right. Maybe I'll wait a little while longer."

After a few more drinks and laughs, Jack left to go home. He was tired and beat down from all the arguments with Ben over everything that was going on. It was kind of late, so he was tired and ready to just go to sleep. As he pulled to the front of his house, he noticed a car parked out front. He didn't recognize the car until he climbed out and saw Linda sitting on his porch. "Hey, Jackie boy, I'm guessing you didn't think you would see me so soon after our little disagreement."

Jack stepped onto his porch and stood in front of Linda. "What are you doing here? I thought I made it clear there was nothing between us."

Linda smiled and stood up as she massaged Jack's groin area. "Come on, Jackie boy, let's just have some fun, and then I'll leave."

Jack could smell the liquor as Linda swayed back and forth. "Come on, Linda, what are you doing? You're drunk and you shouldn't have come here."

Linda sat back down as she started to undo Jack's zipper. "Come on, Jackie boy, just a little taste. I promise you won't regret it."

Jack was tired, but like most men, he followed what his libido said. When Linda realized Jack wasn't trying to back away, she leaned forward and began her seduction. It wasn't long before they were in Jack's bed moaning and groaning their way to satisfaction. After a couple of hours of pleasuring each other, they both fell asleep.

CHAPTER TWENTY-TWO

JACK WOKE UP EARLY AND SAW LINDA WAS GONE. SHE LEFT A NOTE FOR him on his night stand. *I told you it wasn't over, Jack Kotter. See you soon.*

Once again, Jack realized he was playing with fire. After a few minutes of regrets, he ate breakfast and went to work. On the way to work, he noticed a crew of firefighters cleaning up an accident scene. He didn't think too much of it. It was rush hour traffic and there were always daily commuters that just couldn't drive.

When Jack arrived at work, there was a message waiting for him to call Dale ASAP. Thinking he had some good news about Lilith, Jack didn't hesitate to call. "Hey, Dale, I got your message. What's going on?"

It took a second for Dale to swallow the lump in his throat. "One of your board members was involved in an accident in the early morning hours. She died on the scene."

Just then, Ben stormed through the door and was about to say something when Jack put his hand up to stop him. Ben realized Jack was probably talking to Dale, so he just sat quietly.

After Jack didn't say anything, Dale continued. "Linda Roth was the victim of a hit and run. Evidence is leaning towards Lilith. As the medics were working on her, she tried to describe the car that hit her, but all she said was the car was old and black. The medics said she went into shock and then died."

Jack didn't know what to say or how to react. "Ben's sitting in my office. I'm guessing you've already called him."

Dale let out a sigh, "Sorry, Jack. I tried to call you earlier, but you didn't answer. Ben was the only other person I knew to call. I'm really sorry, Jack."

When Jack hung up the phone, he still couldn't believe it. He sat down at his desk and stared out the window. Ben asked if a drink would help, but Jack just shook his head no. With a sick feeling in his stomach, he finally put together some words. "Dale thinks it might have been Lilith who caused the accident. Why can't anyone find out who this person is? Why is there no record of the car? I don't understand, Ben. What the hell is going on?"

Ben could see Jack was really upset. "Listen, kid. I wasn't a big fan of Linda. She was as tough as they came and ruthless right down to her core. I might have let her sink her claws into me if she wasn't such a bitch. I don't have the answers you're looking for, but we're going to get through this."

Jack sat quietly for a moment then decided to add fuel to the fire. "She was at my house last night."

Those words ran through Ben's veins like ice water. "What? What was she doing there?" Jack looked at Ben, and before he could say another word, Ben had already figured it out. "No, kid. Please tell me you didn't."

Jack had the look like he just swallowed the canary. "She was sitting on my front porch when I came home. She was drunk. What was I supposed to do?"

Ben stood up. He was furious. "There's a new invention out there now. Maybe you've heard of it. It's called taxi cabs. You couldn't dial a damn number and sent her ass home? What the hell is wrong with you, kid?"

Jack knew he had no argument to defend himself, so he decided to tell all. "I'm sorry, Ben. I guess it's partially my fault. With all this nonsense going on with my dad and then Bria leaving me, I was feeling restless. I saw Linda coming out of one of the conference rooms and she was looking so nice. I invited her into my office and we went at it like a couple of rabbits."

Ben could almost feel the smoke coming out of his ears before he could blast out some words. "Are you out of your f**king mind? With all the battles that go on inside these board meetings, you decide to sleep with the enemy. Well, I can tell your head wasn't in the clouds this time. That means it must have been up your ass. Christ, kid, are there any more secrets I need to know about, or are you saving some for another disaster?"

Once again, Jack just stood in front of Ben like a little child with no answers. Surprisingly, Ben didn't continue his verbal assault. "Alright, kid, I'm guessing nobody else knows about this, so let's keep it that way. I have to go and make some arrangements. Apparently, Linda had no next of kin, so she listed me as an emergency contact. Why she did that is anyone's guess."

Just as Ben was about to walk out, Jack remembered about the garage and asked Ben for his help. "Hey, Ben, before you leave, I have a favor to ask. One of our service contracts is about to expire and I have a place in mind I want to offer it to, but the building isn't quite up to code. I need you to work your magic with the building inspectors."

Ben knew with a snap of his fingers he could have such minor problems taken care of. "Damn, kid, now you're talking my language. Glad to see you thinking about the company. Write the address down and I'll call you back within the hour."

After Ben left, Jack sat for a moment thinking about Linda. He had so many questions running through his thought process. Was Linda just a random car Lilith saw on the road? Did Lilith see Linda coming from his house? Maybe Lilith thought Linda was a girlfriend and did it out of spite. Jack didn't have any of the answers, but he wasn't taking any chances. He called Bria hoping she would answer the phone. He was glad to hear her voice when she did. After a few minutes of conversation, Jack asked if she could meet for lunch, but Bria turned him down. She then agreed to let him come over her house if it was really that important to talk with her. Jack happily agreed.

He let Bonnie know he would be gone for the rest of the morning then snuck down the back staircase so Ben wouldn't see him leave.

He hurried to his car and drove to Bria's house. As he pulled to the front of the house, he suddenly became very nervous. After all the turmoil between them, now he had to tell her about Linda. He tried to rehearse what he was going to say as he walked to the door, but when he thought about it, planned speeches rarely went as planned. When Bria came to the door, Jack was almost at a loss for words. Even though she had on a pair of sweatpants and a t-shirt, she looked as beautiful as ever, and he could smell a hint of her perfume mixed with her soft skin. "Hey, Bria, sorry for the short notice, but I really needed to talk to you about something."

Bria was hesitant, but after a few seconds, invited him in. "Alright, Jack, what's the big emergency you couldn't tell me about on the phone?"

As they sat in the living room, Jack collected his thoughts then tried to be as subtle as possible. "I'm not sure if you saw the morning news, but there was an accident earlier this morning. Linda Roth was involved. She died at the scene. The police think Lilith was the cause."

Knowing Linda always had a thing for Jack, Bria had never liked her. "Wow, that's too bad. Why are we sitting in my house talking about Linda Roth?"

Jack understood why the two couldn't stand one another, but he couldn't believe the lack of emotion Bria had. "Listen, Bria, I know the two of you never saw eye to eye, but I just didn't come here to tell you about her death."

With some frustration, Bria stood up and walked towards the door. "Listen, Jack, I told you before, the next time you had some sort of sob story, you could go tell it to your pal Ben."

As she opened the door to motion Jack out, he grabbed her from behind and pushed her back. He slammed the door shut and finally blurted out what he was trying so hard not to say. "She was coming from my house when the accident happened."

Bria stood silent for a second then slowly started to smile. "So, she finally got her hooks into you. Figures. For all I know, you were probably spending all your time with her instead of me."

Jack could feel his anger starting to build, but he wasn't there to argue. "Why would you even think like that? I never gave you any cause to think I was cheating on you. Especially with Linda. You're probably not interested, but I'll tell you anyway. She was on my front porch when I got home last night. I could smell the alcohol on her breath and she could barely keep her balance. I couldn't let her leave like that. I don't want to get into details, but unfortunately, one thing led to another."

Bria shook her head then smacked Jack across the face. "You're a lying sack of shit, Jack. You're telling me that bitch just showed up on your door step out of the blue?"

Jack saw Bria was just about at the end of her patience, so he opened the door and stood in the doorway. He looked Bria in the eyes and told her the truth. "You're right, it was my fault. There was one incident before that probably led to her showing up at my house. I came here to tell you because I don't know if that accident was random or if Lilith is targeting people I'm associated with to try to get to me. Please be careful."

Jack closed the door and walked to his car. Before he could get to the end of the walkway, Bria came running up from behind. "Wait a minute, Jack Kotter." When Jack turned around, she grabbed his tie. "You have some nerve coming here, Jack Kotter." Once again, she slapped Jack across his face. "That's for sleeping with that bitch." She then gently tugged on his tie while she stood on her tippy toes and gave him a passionate kiss. "That's for loving me enough to come here and tell me the truth." Still with Jack's tie in her hand, she led him back into the house.

After making love into the afternoon, Jack was left questioning their relationship. "So, what exactly does this mean for you and me?"

Bria climbed out of bed and threw on her sweatpants and t-shirt. "I don't know. I guess it means we still have a chance."

As Jack dressed, he was almost hesitant to try to pressure Bria into any commitment. "Alright, I guess we'll take it slow, one day at a time?"

Bria wrapped her arms around Jack and gave him a kiss. "I wasn't going to say anything, but I really missed you, Jack Kotter. One day at a time sounds like a good plan."

It had been a long time since Jack felt good about their relationship, so he counted his blessings and asked Bria if she wanted to get together for dinner. Bria gladly accepted. After they said their goodbyes, Jack left to go back to work. As he was driving, his phone rang. It was Paul.

"Hello, Paul, how are you?"

Jack could tell Paul was excited about something, because he couldn't get the words out fast enough. "I can't believe it, Mr. Kotter. Everything is happening all at once."

Jack had an idea about what was going on, so he pulled to the side to try to help Paul through it. "Alright, Paul, just calm down and tell me what you're talking about."

Paul took a deep breath then gathered his thoughts. "Okay, remember I told you about the building inspector? Well, he showed up this morning out of the blue and signed off on the property. I can't believe it. We're not even done with half the things I thought we had to do."

Jack smiled and offered his congrats and told Paul he would stop by to see him. He was just around the corner, so it wasn't long before he was pulling up in front of the garage. As he walked into the office, Paul and Oliver were having a celebration beer. Oliver quickly popped one open and handed it to Jack. "Well, Jack, here's to success."

It was nice to see the brothers smiling after all the problems they'd had. "So does this mean you're reconsidering my offer?"

Paul smiled with excitement. "Tell you what, Mr. Kotter, why don't you drop off the Ferrari and we'll see what we can do."

Knowing the car might be destroyed when the time came to go up against Lilith, Jack was still happy to know it was going to be repaired and brought back to showroom condition. "What do you think about our discussion about my fleet cars? Is that something the two of you would be interested in?"

Without hesitation, Oliver stepped up to the plate. "Hell, yeah. That contract alone would keep us in the black."

After a few happy handshakes, Jack finished off his beer. "Alright, then. I'll have a courier drop off some documents and the contract for you tomorrow. Look them over and let me know what you think. In the meantime, I'll make arrangements to have the Ferrari and the equipment dropped off, and hopefully, you can give me some good news."

After Jack left, he was feeling great. He felt that his relationship with Bria was back on track and he'd managed to manipulate several deals in order to get rid of Lilith. As he drove back to the office, he was hoping to slip back in without Ben knowing he was gone. As he parked his car, he made his way to the back staircase. Just as he opened the door, Ben came walking out. "Whoa, kid, you scared the hell out of me. What are you doing down here?"

Jack felt like a deer in headlights but he kept his composure. "Honestly, I use this staircase sometimes to sneak out of work"

Ben laughed for a moment then smiled. "Wow, I thought I was the only one who knew about this staircase. Well, kid, good for you. Let's keep this to ourselves. This is how I get by Hellen when I need to go out and get a little ... Well, you know."

Jack was relieved but not surprised at Ben's extracurricular activity. "Sounds good to me. By the way, thanks for taking care of that problem with the building inspector. I wasn't expecting it to be that quick."

As he started to walk away, Ben shook his head. "Come on, kid, you know I don't play around when it comes to business."

When Jack made it back to his office, he called Connie to see if he had any good information to offer. Connie didn't have any good news, but he didn't have any bad news either. "I gotta tell you, Jack, this might take a while. There's a lot of research I have to do before I can give you any definitive answers."

Jack was okay with that and was grateful he had such a good friend helping. Before they hung up, Connie did have news of another sort. "Hey, you'll never guess who called me earlier today. Warner Jenks. She just got back into town and she wants to get together."

Jack almost fell over. "Really? Of course she called you first. She always did have a thing for you. I have an idea. Bria and I are kind of talking things out and we're supposed to have dinner tonight. What'ya say we all get together?"

Connie was definitely for that. "Sounds great. You pick the place and we'll meet you there, on one condition. No *Titanic* talk." Jack laughed as he reluctantly agreed.

That afternoon, Jack decided to take advantage of some free time. There were no meetings to attend and Ben was off on one of his sexploits, so he decided to start researching sunken ships and the cost of raising them up from the ocean floor. Looking online, he focused on three wrecks he had previously bookmarked. The *H. L. Hunley*, which was a Confederate Civil War submarine discovered in 1995 and raised in 2000. The *Vasa*, a Swedish warship built in the year 1628, which, like the *Titanic*, sank on its maiden voyage. It was discovered in 1956 and raised in 1961. The *Mary Rose* was built in the year 1510 for the English navy and was a favorite of King Henry VIII. It was discovered in 1971 and raised in 1982. It was the most expensive salvage in the history of maritime archeology, costing $4.5 Million. Jack wasn't too impressed. He knew the size of *Titanic* combined with modern day salvage prices would sky rocket the cost of his project.

Jack sat back in his chair and thought about it. The research didn't really mean anything without Connie's insight, and meant absolutely nothing without Ben on board. Jack decided not to get too involved until he heard from Connie. Still feeling the sting of Linda's death, he left work for the day and went back to the 110 Garage. As he pulled up to the front, he saw that the Ferrari had already been delivered. He saw the brothers were hard at work giving it a once over before tearing it down. Even though it had been sitting in storage for 42 years, it still looked bad ass to Jack's eyes.

The brothers saw Jack pull up and stopped slobbering over the car just long enough to say hello. "Well, Jack, we were just admiring the car before we get into tearing it down and rebuilding her. When you told us it wasn't in that bad of shape, that was an understatement. She's gorgeous. We could probably just do a tune up, change her belts, and put some nice tires on her, but I'm guessing you don't want that."

Jack smiled as he ran his fingers down the side of the car. "It's a damn shame. Aside from beefing up the suspension, that's exactly what I want. I don't want you to do anything extra. She was fitted with a V-12 engine and designed for competition. Once you get her back to her original splendor, she'll go as fast as I need her to."

Oliver went back to tinkering with the engine as Paul stood watching Jack admire the car. "I know I've asked quite a few times, Jack, but are you really sure you wanna go up against that maniac in this car?"

Jack just stood staring at the car for a minute. He tried to picture his mom and dad cruising down the California coast. "I'm sure I have to do something, but I guess I won't know if I'm right until one of us gets the other. How long do you think it'll take to get her on the road?"

Paul glanced over at the car and thought about it. "Well, if everything goes alright, maybe by next week."

Jack was pleasantly surprised at Paul's timeframe. "Good. I'll call Dale so he can start lining everything up."

After talking with the brothers for a few more minutes and going over the details, Jack left to go home and get ready for his dinner date. He was exited that Connie would finally meet Bria. Although they didn't correspond a lot, Jack was able to tell Connie about Bria before he wound up living in Africa. After he pulled to the front of the house and turned the car off, he made his way up to his porch and sat down. He thought his way through the day's events and then he thought about Linda. Although she wasn't exactly his favorite person, Jack still couldn't help but feel angry about Linda being killed by Lilith. Whether or not Lilith knew who she was or where she was coming from was irrelevant. Hopefully, it would be over soon.

After a few minutes of thinking about Lilith, Jack became frustrated and went into the house. He decided to lie down and take a nap before getting ready for dinner. As he lay sleeping, he still had Lilith fresh on his mind. As he slept, he found himself sitting in his father's Ferrari driving his mom down the California coast. Suddenly, out of nowhere, Lilith appeared beside him. As his mom started to scream, Jack lost control and drove off a cliff. Immediately, Jack was thrown clear as the car tumbled down the hill with his mom in it. He watched in horror as the car reached the bottom and exploded. Afterwards, waves washed over the car and carried it out to sea.

Jack woke up screaming and jumped up out of bed. He was frantic and dripping wet with sweat. He stood in the middle of the room trying to gather his composure, but he just couldn't. He knelt down and started to cry. He was so used to Bria being there, but unfortunately, it was just him. All he had for comfort was his loneliness. Between dreaming about *Titanic* and Lilith, losing Bria, and trying to stay on top of Kotter Industries, Jack couldn't help but think he was losing his mind.

When he finally calmed down enough, he checked the time and readied himself for the night. When he picked Bria up, she could tell something was wrong, but Jack just played it off. It was a quiet drive to Benjamin's Steakhouse. Located on 41st Street in Manhattan, Benjamin's was one of those places that had a friendly atmosphere for quaint business meetings, and at the same time, had excellent food if someone was just having dinner. It was one of Jack's favorite places to go for both pleasure and business. When they arrived, Connie and Warner were already at the door waiting. When Jack saw Warner, he forgot all about his frustrations. After embracing and shedding a few happy tears, Jack introduced Bria and the four went inside to start their evening.

Once inside, Jack looked around and saw Sarah was the hostess for the night. Sarah had always had her eye on Jack and wasn't afraid to show it. As Bria and Warner were talking and giggling, Sarah approached Jack. "Well, well, Jack Kotter, it's been awhile. You haven't been avoiding me have you?"

Connie quickly caught on and tried to stand between Sarah and Bria, hoping Bria didn't notice the friction. But it was too late. Bria stepped out from behind Connie and stepped between Jack and Sarah. "Yeah, he usually doesn't eat at places where they have cheap labor."

Sarah paused for a moment and smiled. "I see you have some friends with you tonight. Would you like the first floor or balcony seating?"

Jack liked to sit in the balcony because it gave an overview of what was going on in the restaurant. "I think we're all in agreement. We would like balcony seating."

As Sarah turned to walk towards the steps, she turned her attention towards Bria. "Follow me and watch your step. I see you're wearing some Gucci knockoffs tonight. I wouldn't want you to take a tumble and lose your wig." As Jack and his party were seated, they ordered some drinks and told the waitress to wait on dinner.

Although her parents had pushed themselves through many years of schooling in order to have professional careers, Warner chose to dedicate her life to helping others through the Peace Corps. She was full of energy and couldn't wait to tell about her adventures around the world. During the conversation, she reached over and intertwined her hand with Connie's. Eventually, everyone ordered dinner and, of course, more drinks. The girls conveniently excused themselves to the ladies' room while Jack and Connie talked. Jack couldn't help but notice Connie was smiling from ear to ear. "I seem to remember that look. You had that same look back in high school after you and Warner snuck outside to kiss for the first time."

Connie could barely let his smile subside long enough to answer. "Well, I know it's been a long time, but I still feel the same way when I'm with Warner and I think she feels the same. We were holding hands under the table like a couple of school kids. It felt really good, Jack."

With a slight grin, Jack downed his beer. "Well, I'm betting, at this very moment, the girls are in the ladies' room talking about the same thing. Connie, you know you're my best friend. I saw how broken you were after we graduated when Warner told you she was leaving. I just hope she doesn't do it to you again."

After the girls finally decided to come back, the two couples had a nice dinner and a few more drinks. Stemming from his conversation with Connie, Jack gracefully asked Warner about her future plans. Warner wasn't naive. She knew what Jack was getting at, but she was okay with it. "Well, during my time in the Corps, I became interested in how various cultures over time influenced the world in many ways, so I managed to get my doctorate degree in sociology. My plan is to start an international research foundation so we can teach our future generations how to work and learn from each other, so we can grow together as a people. My research has a lot to do with how past cultures traded goods and introduced various types of traditions by way of cargo ships. Connie has already agreed to help me get started with excavating a couple of known sites near the island of Cyprus."

Jack glanced over at Connie and smiled, then he turned his attention back to Warner. "My mom was from the Greek islands, Crete, to be exact. I've always wanted to go, but it seems like time is always against me. So, when is this trip to the Mediterranean Sea supposed to take place?"

While Connie and Bria sat listening to the conversation, the crowded restaurant slowly started to give in to the late-night hours. With Jack and Warner still deep into their conversation, Connie looked across at Bria, who had been yawning for the past ten minutes, then looked down at the first floor and saw the employees cleaning up. "I hate to cut you off, Jack, but I think it's time to go."

As the girls walked outside, Jack and Connie took care of paying the bill. Before they could walk out to the parking lot, Connie stopped and confronted Jack. "What the hell was that all about?"

Jack could hear the dismay in Connie's voice. "What are you talking about?"

Connie huffed and puffed as he felt his temperature rise. "We've known each other since we were kids. Don't try to play me, Jack. You haven't seen Warner in years and all you did tonight was interrogate her for information. I can't believe you. Now I can see why you and Bria are having problems." As soon as those words came out, Connie knew he stepped over the line. "I'm sorry, Jack. I shouldn't have said that."

Jack knew Connie was right. Not only about Warner, but about the situation with Bria. This was also one of those times he couldn't separate the business from his personal life. "You're right, Connie. Maybe I shouldn't have come off like an idiot tonight. I guess I'm just worried about this venture you two have planned. The big question is, if it doesn't work out, is Warner going to hang around or give you the same goodbye speech she gave you last time?"

Connie stared at Jack for a second then laughed. "Yeah, okay, Jack. Look me in the eyes and tell me this has nothing to do with me running off to the Mediterranean Sea and deserting your little *Titanic* project."

Jack smiled. "Little? Is there anything little about the name *Titanic*?"

Before Connie could come up with another sarcastic remark, Jack motioned him towards the door. As they walked out to meet the girls, Jack finally admitted his real concern. "You're right, Connie. I am worried about Warner breaking your heart, but I just can't get it out of my head that maybe Ben will eventually give in and help me with this massive problem my dad left behind. If he does, I'm hoping you'll be around to guide me through."

Hearing Jack admit to his real agenda didn't make Connie feel any better. "You're my best friend, Jack, but you know how I feel about Warner. You're placing me in a really bad position. I'm still working on that information you wanted, so let's just play it by ear for now." Jack didn't say anything, but he was okay with that.

CHAPTER TWENTY-THREE

THE NEXT DAY, JACK AWOKE FEELING GOOD. HE WENT TO WORK BRIGHT and early and even caught the attention of Ben, who was coming out of the main conference room. As Ben checked his watch, he couldn't believe it. "Damn, kid, you usually don't show up until noon."

Jack smiled because Ben liked to exaggerate. "Ha, ha, Ben. Funny guy. What's on the agenda for today?"

As they stepped into Ben's office, Jack made himself a cup of coffee. Ben shuffled through some papers then handed Jack a folder. "I know this is a little insensitive, but we need to vote in a board member to replace Linda. We have several candidates in mind."

Linda wasn't exactly anyone's favorite person, but this didn't sit well with Jack. "Please tell me you're kidding. There hasn't even been a funeral yet."

Jack wasn't surprised when Ben didn't show any emotion at all. "Don't worry about that, kid. She's being cremated as we speak." As Jack stared with a blank look, Ben almost broke a smile. "Come on, kid, you don't really think anybody would have attended her funeral, do you?"

Jack didn't know what to say, so he said nothing. Ben stood up from his chair and sat on the edge of his desk. "Listen, kid, she's gone. This might sound cruel, but this company is better off without her. If

I had the balls, I would flush her ashes down the toilet, but knowing that bitch, she would come back to haunt me. When we got rid of that weasel Nick, we were finally able to get back to having an odd number of votes. Now with Linda gone, we're back with the same problem. Sometimes I feel like this company is going in reverse. Now, take a day or so and look at that list of names, and tell me what you think."

As Jack walked to his office, he glanced over the list. He recognized a few of the names, but wasn't really interested in seeing any of them as a board member. When he made it to his office, he sat down and took a deep breath. He thought about the Ferrari as he threw the folder on his desk. He took another deep breath and realized it was going to be a long, drawn out week. Patience wasn't one of Jack's strong suits, but he had enough going on to where he could keep himself busy.

As Jack sat in his office creating an agenda for the week, Ben had plans to meet with Robert. He checked his watch then made his way to the conference room. Although Ben was usually upbeat and confident about any meeting he attended, he wasn't looking forward to this particular meeting. When he arrived, Robert was already waiting with coffee in hand, notepad on table, and briefcase open. "Grab some coffee, Ben, and have a seat. You and Jack have been jetting all over the country the past few weeks, so I figured eventually you would want to have a sit-down with me."

Ben controlled most of what went on with Kotter Industries, but this was unfamiliar territory. As he made a cup of coffee, he tried to figure out a way to start the meeting on a positive note. "Good to see you too, Robert. Sometimes, I think you're worse than me. Always thinking somebody is trying to pull one over on you."

After a few minutes of official business, Robert looked at Ben and smiled. "So, what is it you're going to try to talk me into this time?"

Ben knew he had to start someplace, so he started from the very beginning. He told Robert the story of Jack Sr. and what he left behind. Then, from there, he gave Robert all the details, including the secret bank accounts. Robert sat quietly in awe as Ben told his story, never once interrupting him. When Ben was finally finished, Robert still had no words.

After making a couple of stiff drinks, Ben stood staring at Robert. "So, what do you think?"

Robert gulped down his drink like it was nothing then made himself another. After taking care of that one in record time, he was finally able to put together some coherent thoughts. "What am I supposed to think? You just told me one of the most fantastic stories I've ever heard. I don't even think Hollywood could make something up like that. There's one thing you haven't told me yet. Why did Senior have these secret bank accounts?"

Ben didn't say anything right away. He made Robert a third drink and asked him to sit down. "Do you remember when we use to sit around during those boring board meetings and make jokes about Senior and his infamous fishing trips?"

Robert took a sip of his drink and smiled. "Yeah, I don't think he cared though. He would just laugh it off then try to change the subject."

Ben placed his drink on the table then took a deep breath and sat down. "All those years of going out into the Atlantic, but he wasn't fishing. He was looking for his father."

With a bewildered look on his face, Robert sat staring at Ben. "What do you mean? I thought you said Victor was lost when *Titanic* went down."

Ben sat up and leaned across the table. "Jack had it in his head that if he could somehow locate the *Titanic*, he could use the money to put together an expedition."

Still with the bewildered look, Robert just sat staring. "I'm an intelligent man, Ben, but you're really talking in riddles. What was he going to do, drop some kind of memorial down and hope that it landed on the *Titanic*'s deck?"

Ben smiled then let out a small laugh. "No, I wish it would have been that simple. He wanted to use the money to salvage the ship. My guess is that it would have given him some kind of closure. Not just for him but for all the people that lost family members during that disaster."

As he tried to swallow the lump in his throat, Robert's heart began to sink. "You're scaring the hell out of me now, Ben. You're telling me you and Junior have been crisscrossing the nation trying to chase down some fairytale that our eccentric friend left behind. And now what? This company was his life's work and now he's dead and gone. Why didn't you let this nonsense die with him?"

Ben wasn't angry at Robert's reaction. He understood all too well. "I use to think this company was Jack's life's work, but now I'm not too sure. I think his life revolved around finding his father. Kotter Industries was just a stepping stone to get to what he really wanted."

Robert stood up and paced the room. "I guess it's in our favor that *Titanic* was found to be in pieces. This could have turned out to be a public relations nightmare."

Ben easily related to everything Robert was saying, but nevertheless, he still had to face the fact there was more to tell. "Listen, Robert, I'm with you. Everything going through your mind has been bouncing around in my head ever since this whole nightmare started. Brace yourself, because there's more. The kid feels obligated to continue where big daddy left off."

Without hesitation, Robert smiled then let out a sincere laugh. "I've never known you to be a funny man, Ben, but that was a good one." Suddenly, Robert saw the serious look on Ben's face. With remnants of laughter still on his breath, that lump in his throat started to form again. "Come on, Benjamin, you can't be serious. This is cancer. Do you know what something like that would do to this company? Do you realize the ramifications at all?"

Up to that point, Ben knew there would be some frustrations from Robert, but enough was enough. "Listen, you pompous ass, there isn't a damn thing that goes on within this company that I don't know what the outcome would be, so don't you come at me with your high and mighty attitude. I've tried to talk sense into the kid, but he's not budging. To be honest with you, I guess I can't blame him. There are a lot of moral issues involved."

Robert stood up and slammed his glass down on the table. "Moral issues, my ass. As much as I respected and loved Jack Kotter, it sounds to me that he was playing with one card short of a full deck. Now his juvenile son wants to ride daddy's coattails and make a name for himself at the expense of this company. Well, I'm not going to let that happen. You want to talk moral issues? That's considered a mass grave site. How about that for moral issues? Besides, we have more important things that money could be used for."

Both Ben and Robert could be hard-asses at times, but they'd always had a good friendship and they had a tremendous amount of respect for each other. Nevertheless, they were usually head-to-head without being able to reach an agreement. Surprisingly, Ben took the initiative to try to reason with Robert.

"Look, about those bank accounts. Besides himself, Senior had several other names on those accounts. Bianca, then me, and the kid last. Specifically in that order so there would be no dispute. With Bianca gone, the decision of how to utilize the funds falls to me."

Like an undeterred bull, Robert took a breath and came running in with both horns. "You listen to me, Benjamin. I can see what this is leading up to, and I'm telling you it's not going to happen. You even think about bullying the board members into going along with this idea, I'll rain hell down on you and your little snot-nose sidekick. As for that money, you and Junior can go buy yourselves a lifetime of whores and booze for all I care."

Up until then, Ben was against the entire idea, but in his heart, he was walking a thin line between honoring a lifelong friend and giving in to the corporate grind. He found Robert's threat humorous at best, but that still didn't change the fact he needed him to help sell the idea to the board. "Old friend, call it what you will. Old age or maybe I'm just longing for the old days and growing soft. In any case, the kid isn't going to stop. He's like a pit bull with a piece of meat. Like his old man, he's got that deep down determination for success, and whether or not he realizes it, he has time on his side. He has the youth and energy to wait us out. You know as well as I do, once we're gone, there's nobody to stop him from running this company into the ground. Don't you think it better not to let that happen while you and I still have all of our marbles?"

Robert stood staring out the window. His thoughts were running rampant as he tried to think of an upside to all the craziness. "Don't think I don't know your tactics, Ben. Verbal Judo 101. I remember that class. Tell you what, though, I'll make a deal with you. If you can tell me how this company can somehow put a positive spin on this project, one that makes sense, then I'll do everything in my power to convince the board to support it. And I'm not just thinking about success. I'm also thinking about if we fail. One more thing. I can care less about Junior. Your reputation, along with your influence over this company, is on the line."

Despite the last remark, that's all Ben needed to hear. "Thank you, Robert. It's not much, but I'll take it. Give me 'til next week to research some things and I'll get back to you." As Ben stood up and walked towards the door, he stopped and turned his attention back to Robert. "Who knows, all this nonsense might be for nothing. It might not even be possible, but either way, I'll let you know. By the way, don't say anything to the kid. He doesn't know about our little meeting." Ben walked out with a sense of satisfaction. With Robert's support, he felt he had already made significant progress.

While Ben went back to his office to make some phone calls, Jack was just finishing up his to do list for the week. He had a few errands, but decided to stop by Ben's office to let him know how displeased he was about the list of candidates for the board. When he walked in, Ben was startled and quickly closed out the maritime laws he was reviewing on his computer. "Damn it, kid, I thought we came to an agreement. Are you ever going to get into the habit of knocking?"

Normally, Jack would have some kind of smart comeback, but he was in no mood. With some frustration, he took a seat. "Listen, Ben, this idea of yours to replace Linda isn't a problem, but this list you gave me to look at is."

Ben was still uptight about the lack of knocking, but he could see Jack was attempting to have a serious conversation. "Okay, kid, give me some input and let's talk about it."

Jack let out a sigh and stood up. Still frustrated, he handed the folder back to Ben. "Give me until later today. I have an idea, but I need to work out the details."

Ben took a second then reluctantly agreed. "Okay, kid, but we need to get this done. We have some important meetings this month and we can't risk a deadlock if any voting occurs." Jack didn't have any response. He simply walked out and quietly shut the door behind him.

While Ben went back to his research, Jack drove over to the mall to visit Riley. As usual, Riley was busy shining shoes and having fun doing it. Jack waited for the customers to leave then hopped up into one of the chairs. Riley glanced at Jack's shoes and smiled. "Doesn't look like you need a shine, so what do I owe the pleasure of Jack Kotter's company?"

Jack laughed while Riley cleaned up and prepared for the next customer. "We've been friends a long time now, Riley."

Not liking the way Jack started the conversation, Riley stopped what he was doing. "This doesn't sound good. I get the idea you want something?"

Jack smiled then climbed down from the chair. "Listen, Riley, you've heard by now about Linda."

Riley knew Linda wasn't anyone's favorite person, but he still gave Jack condolences. "Yeah, I'm sorry, Jack. She wasn't a likable person, but I don't think she deserved what happened to her."

Riley's words were true to heart and Jack appreciated it. "Thanks, Riley, that's why I'm here. You know Ben, all business. He wants to fill Linda's spot as soon as possible, so he gave me a list of names to review. To be honest, I'm not really impressed with any of them."

Riley could see Jack was getting anxious and leading up to something. "Hold on, Jack. Don't even think about it."

With a look of play-like shock, Jack raised his hands in disbelief. "Come on, Riley, I'm offering you a really good chance to expand your horizons."

Riley heard Jack, but just shook his head no. "What if I don't want my horizons to expand?"

Jack paused then dropped his arms in disappointment. "Why would you not want to get more out of life than just working at the mall shining shoes?"

Riley smiled because even though what Jack said came out the wrong way, he knew Jack didn't mean anything by it. "Listen, Jack, I'm happy with what I'm doing. What I have here belongs to me and people see the pride I have in my work. If I was in your boardroom, I would just be another pawn with no direction or satisfaction. Don't get me wrong, I appreciate the offer, but I can't accept it. Besides, I would have to be voted in and I don't think Ben would allow that to happen. Sorry, Jack."

Jack wasn't going to press the issue. Somehow, he knew Riley wouldn't accept, but he'd had to try. Same old Riley. Just a simple man. Just then, one of Riley's regular customers came walking up.

"Okay, Jack, duty calls. I'll catch you later."

Jack said his goodbyes and drove back to work. When he arrived at his office, Ben was there waiting. "So, any luck trying to get Riley to accept your offer?"

With a surprised look on his face, Jack slowly closed the door and walked to his desk. As he sat down, he noticed the folder with the list of names. "How did you know I spoke to Riley?"

Ben smiled with arrogance. "Come on, kid, that was a given. When you weren't happy with the list and asked for time, I knew there was only one person you could have in mind. If it's any consolation, kid, I already know Riley turned you down."

Jack just stared with amazement. "One of these days, you're gonna have to tell me how you do that."

Still feeling his own pride rush through himself, Ben leaned forward and pushed the folder towards Jack. "Listen, kid, Riley isn't the kind of person who's cut out for the corporate boardroom. To be honest, I think he's intelligent enough, but some birds just aren't meant to be caged."

Jack smiled as he briefly looked through the list of names. "That's funny, because he thought just the opposite. So you tell me. What am I looking for, because I gotta tell you, none of these names really stands out."

Ben walked around the desk and pointed out a few things about the people on the list, then he came to the conclusion that he was only interested in one. Mr. Mckinnley Wilmington III. "Sounds old-ish and out of date, but he's in his forties and has been with the company for many years. Mostly overseeing facilities overseas." Ben walked back around the desk and sat back down. "I think you'll like him, kid. He's very smart, but down to earth. He's finagled some pretty impressive deals over the years that really helped this company through some sticky situations. So, what'ya say, kid? Will you back me on this one?"

Jack took one last glance through the folder and handed it back to Ben. "Give me some time to read through his resume so I'm not going into this blind."

Ben agreed. With a smile on his face, Ben stood up and made his way to the door. "You're starting to get the hang of this whole millionaire businessman thing, aren't you, kid?"

CHAPTER TWENTY-FOUR

After a few days of boring business deals, late nights with Bria, and constantly looking out for Lilith, the end of the week finally arrived. Mckinnley Wilmington was voted in and all was well with the board. It was Friday afternoon and Jack was looking forward to just going home and relaxing, when Ben came rushing in. Jack was just finishing one of his many yawns of the day and was preparing to leave. Ben didn't say anything at first, but Jack could tell there was something on his mind. "Hey, Ben, it's Friday. Why do you look like you're on a mission?"

Ben made a couple of drinks and handed one to Jack. "I know it's Friday, kid, but that doesn't mean we get to stop working."

Jack was tired, but he couldn't resist the temptation of getting on Ben's last nerve. "I thought we already had this conversation. I run this company, and I think I'm entitled to a weekend."

Ben knew Jack was trying to push his buttons, so he came right back at him. "Shut up and listen, kid. You're right. We did already discuss this. You're entitled to whatever I tell you you're entitled to and that's that. Now drink up. I don't have time for your nonsense. We have more important things to do."

Jack decided not to press the issue and downed his drink. As the whiskey warmed his stomach, it brought back just enough energy for him to sit up and listen. "Okay, what's so important that it can't wait 'til Monday?"

With a look that could cut through steel, Ben drank the last of his drink and slammed the glass down on Jack's desk. "Listen, kid, sometimes I think you forget I have sources all over. Or maybe you think I'm just getting old and don't pay as much attention to details as I used to. In any case, I don't really care what you think."

Jack suddenly found himself wishing he'd left earlier, but it was too late. He would have to hunker down for a tongue lashing. "Ben, I'm not going to argue with you, because I really don't know where all this hostility is coming from."

Ben stood up and walked over to the window. He looked out at the parking lot, which was now empty. "This isn't hostile, kid. If I was hostile, you would have tucked your tail between your legs and ran out of here a long time ago. You need to keep in mind the history of this company. If you remember correctly, your mom's family was in the shipping business. We still have connections and contacts in the industry."

Jack wasn't in the mood for a history lesson, but he didn't want Ben to blow up again. "You're right, Ben, and I'm not trying to be a smart ass, but I still don't know where this conversation is going."

Ben knew if he let his temper get away from him he wouldn't be able to accomplish what he was trying to do, so he took a deep breath and sat back down. "Listen, kid, I had some of those contacts I just told you about call me earlier today. Seems that your friend Connie has been poking around, inquiring about *Titanic*."

Jack was stunned. He couldn't even look Ben in the face so he stood up and walked over to the minibar. Not wanting to let Jack wiggle off the hook too soon, Ben stood up and followed. He noticed Jack's hand was shaking as he tried to pour a drink. "Here, kid, why don't you let me do that for you."

As Ben poured two more drinks, Jack tried to catch his composure. "I don't know what to say, Ben. You knew how I felt, and yet you've done everything in your power to keep me from doing what I feel is right."

Ben handed the drink to Jack and told him to have a seat. "Listen, kid, time and time again you've tried to go behind my back or, in some way, tried to bypass me. After treating you like you were my own son and helping you grow as a person, I think I've earned enough respect I shouldn't have to be concerned about you stabbing me in my back. Now, before you try to weasel your way out of a situation you shouldn't be in, I wanted to sit and have a sensible conversation with you."

Rarely did Jack see this side of Ben. It always seemed to be his way or the highway. "Alright, Ben, I'm tired and I have a lot on my mind, but you've got my full attention."

Ben didn't know where to begin, because he didn't want to make it look like he was backtracking. "Listen, kid, you know I've been dead set against this whole plan you have to finish your dad's work, so after you hear what I have to say, don't be a smart ass. Now try to stay focused. I just wanted you to know I respect what you're trying to do for your dad. I tried to take that away from you thinking you would eventually back down, but I can see that's not going to happen. So, after doing a lot of soul searching, I've come to the conclusion it would be better to try to help you, because I know after I'm gone, you're going to do whatever you want."

Jack suddenly felt like a little kid at Christmas. It took all he had not to leap out of his chair. "I don't know what to say, Ben. This was the last thing I expected to hear."

Ben wasn't exactly smiling, because of course, there was always more. "Don't get too excited, kid. We have a lot of work to do and obstacles to get over. I recently had a conversation with Robert and I told him everything. Needless to say, he wasn't very happy, but I managed to convince him to help us. If we're going to pull this off, he definitely needs to be on our side."

Jack was overwhelmed with gratitude so he wanted to be careful about the kinds of questions he had. "So, besides me getting on your last nerve, what else was it that changed your mind?"

Ben thought about it and realized just how softhearted he was. "Like I said, kid, I've been thinking about it for a while. I don't really think it was any one thing, but I gotta tell you, the story Winnifred Quick told us really struck a chord inside me. With that said, this is something that can very easily blow up in our faces. So we have to bring our A-game if we're going to be successful."

Jack knew if anyone could make it work, Ben could. The sudden rush of excitement he felt when they first found the storage shed had come back. "Thanks, Ben, for backing me on this. My dad is probably smiling down on us right now. I know it's not going to be easy, and if it fails, I'll take full responsibility and accept whatever consequences come from it."

Ben could hear the sincerity in Jack's voice, but it didn't matter. "Listen, kid, there's something else I wanted to talk to you about. I told you I found out about Connie snooping around, but what I didn't tell you is that he found the information you wanted almost immediately and I'm wondering why he didn't tell you."

Jack didn't have an answer, and knowing left him wondering the same thing. "I don't know. I know he wasn't happy when I told him what the plan was, but I didn't think he would try to keep the information from me. He knows how important it is."

Ben could see the worry in Jack's face, but he couldn't help but laugh. "Well, kid, seems like you have everyone against you on this. Don't worry, though. I know Connie has nothing but respect for the ocean and all its secrets. He probably thinks you're going to desecrate a site that should be left alone."

Jack tried to put Connie out of his mind for the time being because he wanted to concentrate on what Ben was going to do. "So, contrary to what you might think, I really don't have a solid plan yet. I asked Connie to look up what we needed to do in order to put together an expedition and eventually bring the ship to the surface. I can't believe he held on to the information."

It was getting late, so Ben suggested an informal meeting on Tuesday with the other board members to try to get an idea of how everyone felt. "Listen, kid, before Tuesday rolls around, why don't we meet with Connie and compare notes. This way, I'll have some kind of idea of whether or not raising the *Titanic* is even possible. Come Tuesday, we might not even have to present the idea."

Jack agreed and made plans to call Connie later that night. Just before Ben was about to walk out, he threw out one last suggestion. "Hey, kid, just a thought. I think it best you not attend the meeting Tuesday if there is one. Before you go off, let me explain. You're too emotionally attached, so maybe you should just take the day off and

I'll meet with you afterwards." Jack understood Ben's concerns and was actually relieved that he would handle the board.

As Jack made his way down to his car, his cell phone rang. It was Paul. Thinking there might be a delay with the Ferrari, Jack answered expecting the worse. "Hey, Paul, how are you?"

Without sounding anxious, Paul gave Jack some good news. "Well, Jack, if you don't have any plans this evening, maybe you can stop by and see you're fresh-off-the-showroom-floor Ferrari."

Jack was pleasantly stunned. "Are you kidding? I thought it wasn't going to be ready 'til next week."

With pride in his voice, Paul was all too glad to explain. "Well, I have a friend who deals in exotic cars, historical and new, and he was able to cut me some really good deals. As a thank you for all that you've done, Oliver and I worked day and night putting her back together. I'm sure I'll see you within the hour."

Paul was definitely right. Jack couldn't wait to get to the garage. "Put on some coffee and I'll be right there."

Without hesitation, Jack started *Fringe* and screamed off the parking lot. He called Dale and asked him to meet at the garage. Luckily, Dale was on duty and was just around the corner. When Jack arrived, he could see Dale already admiring the car. The parking lot for the garage had finally been completed, so Jack was able to drive up and park. Like a, kid on Christmas morning, he stood with eyes wide, watching the light bounce off the perfect curves of his 1959 Ferrari 250 GT Spyder.

"I don't have any words. She's beyond beautiful." Jack's eyes grew even wider when he glanced over at Paul and Oliver. "Incredible. You guys did an incredible job."

Now the two brothers, along with Dale, were staring at Jack thinking the same thing. Did he really want to risk his life and the car to try to take down Lilith? Jack couldn't restrain himself any longer. He jumped in and started it up. The engine purred as he gripped the steering wheel. He tried to imagine what his father felt while driving along the west coast. After gunning the engine a few times, off he went. In a few short seconds, Jack disappeared in a cloud of dust that rose up from the newly paved parking lot.

Dale glanced over at the brothers and shook his head laughing.

"So tell me, Paul. You guys have any more trouble with break-ins or trespassers?"

Paul shrugged his shoulders and shook his head no. "Not at all. The warehouse district is right down the road and there's nothing around here but specialized businesses. After everything is closed for the day, this place is like a ghost town."

Not really looking for anything specific, Dale looked around the lot then shifted his eyes towards the garage. "You guys see that Road Runner very often?"

Suddenly, Oliver didn't like the line of questioning. "What exactly are you trying to get at? It sounds like you have us down as suspects."

Thinking Oliver was about to go off, Paul gently pulled his brother to the side. "Hold on. I'm sure that's not Dale's intentions. Give him a chance to explain himself."

Just then, Jack came barreling onto the lot just as fast as he left. Coming to a screeching halt, he stepped out of the Ferrari exhilarated. "I can't believe the way this thing drives. It's picture perfect." Jack noticed the long faces on the brothers and tried to curve his enthusiasm. "So, what's going on?"

Dale took a breath and apologized to the brothers. "I'm sorry, guys. I didn't mean to come off like that." With some worry on his face, Dale turned to Jack. "I think we might have a lead on Lilith, but I'm not sure yet. I don't want to say too much then be wrong. The department is still checking into it. I was asking Paul and Oliver some questions about Lilith, but they may have come out the wrong way. It seems to be that Lilith does most of her damage in this area, so we started concentrating on trying to figure out why."

Paul walked into the garage and brought back four beers. "Okay. So, let's drink to a job well done. Now, Jack, the million-dollar question. What are you going to do?"

Before Jack could answer, Dale cut in. "I'm not too sure about this anymore, Jack. If this lead pans out, we'll have some other options to consider."

Jack popped the lid off his beer and took a drink. We can't take that chance. "I saw the news the other night. She ran a family of three off the road. Luckily, they weren't hurt. I think we should go ahead as planned. It's me she wants. Like I said before, she's not going to stop until she gets me or I get her. I say we spring our trap late Monday night. There won't be anyone on the streets."

Paul glanced at the Ferrari and raised his beer. He shook his head in frustration as he blurted out a toast. "Here's to Jack and hoping he changes his mind before Monday."

Afterwards, Dale left to go back to work and make some arrangements. Jack stood looking at the car knowing it would probably be gone come Monday night. He handed Oliver the keys so he could store it in one of the garage bays. After talking some business about the garage, Jack finished his beer and left.

Jack was happy the Ferrari was finished, but as usual, he had ninety-nine other things going on at the same time. He called Connie to tell him about the meeting with Ben. Connie suggested a meeting over dinner so it wouldn't seem like work. Jack agreed, but he knew all too well when Ben was involved, it was nothing but work.

When he arrived home, Jack walked in and found Bria waiting for him with nothing on but a bow. "Well, well, Jack Kotter, welcome home. Now let's go upstairs so you can unwrap me."

As Bria slowly walked up the steps, Jack followed closely behind. "You didn't leave me much to unwrap, but I'm not going to complain." After some foreplay at the top of the steps, Bria took Jack by the hand and lead him into the bedroom.

CHAPTER TWENTY-FIVE

THE NEXT MORNING, JACK CAME DOWN STAIRS WITH A SMILE LEFTOVER from the previous night. He could smell breakfast cooking and wasted no time making his way to the kitchen. He thought he would find Bria with one of her sexy surprises, but instead, she was sitting comfortably at the table with her cup of coffee. "Good morning, Jack Kotter. Can I interest you in some coffee?"

Jack sat down then stretched across the table for a good morning kiss. "Sure. If you don't mind, I'll have what you're having."

As Bria was making a plate for Jack, he watched her tush move from side to side. "I can definitely get used to this if you let me. Which reminds me, ever since I can remember, you've called me by my first and last name. Why is that?"

With a smile on her face, Bria set the plate down in front of Jack. "Well, I like the way it sounds and I'm still hoping I will become Mrs. Jack Kotter someday soon."

Jack also liked the way it sounded, but he knew he would have to bring some things to a close before he made any other commitments, personal or business. "Ben and I are meeting with Connie tonight over dinner. Interested?"

Bria walked the dishes over to the sink. "Sure, I'm definitely interested." With a seductive smile, she undid the buttons on her flannel shirt. "How about you, Jack Kotter? Interested?"

After a long but pleasant morning, Jack took the opportunity to go for a nice enjoyable drive to clear his head. Eventually, he found himself back at the Cemetery of the Holy Rood. He sat for a while thinking about the various outcomes he would have to deal with come Monday. As his mind wandered through different thoughts, he speculated on his future with Bria. He also pondered what life would be like after the *Titanic* project. He glanced at Victor's gravestone and closed his eyes. He tried to imagine the last moments before *Titanic* sunk beneath the surface of the cold Atlantic and the terror people must have felt. He soon realized it wasn't a good idea and opened his eyes in fear.

The drive didn't do Jack any good. His thoughts were still scattered and there were too many variables to consider for all the problems in his life. Without feeling any satisfaction, he drove back home. He changed and prepared to pick Bria up. It was late in the day, but still too early for the meeting, so he decided to stop by and see the Ferrari. As Paul and Oliver rolled it out of the garage, Jack stood staring with a surreal feeling. He climbed in and placed his hands on the steering wheel, but had no intentions of driving it. The brothers could see Jack's thoughts were elsewhere, so they left him alone in his thinking.

A little later while Oliver took care of closing for the day, Paul walked out to check on Jack. He saw that Jack had left so he pushed the Ferrari back into the garage bay and locked the door.

Still feeling somewhat distraught, Jack was on his way to pick up Bria. Afterwards, it was a quiet drive to Gotham Bar and Grill on East 12th Street. With sophisticated cuisine, it was Ben's favorite place to entertain clients and fellow businessmen. When Jack and Bria walked in, they saw that Ben was already sitting at his regular table situated in a quaint little corner on the landing. As usual, Bria made a beeline to the ladies' room while Jack sat down. "So this is the spot you're always telling me about. This is nice."

Ben didn't say anything. He poured two glasses of wine and handed one to Jack. He placed the other where Bria would be sitting. "I assumed this was going to be a private meeting with you and Connie." Just then Connie and Warner came walking up. With some frustration, Ben poured two more glasses of wine. "Just great, the whole gang is together again."

As Connie sat down, he picked up his glass of wine. "Good to see you to, Ben. I see you haven't changed much over the years."

As Warner excused herself to the ladies' room, Ben wasted no time getting down to business. "Now, gentleman, before we start, I know Bria knows what's going on, but does Warner?"

Connie shook his head no. "I told her Jack was planning something big and I was doing some research for him, but that's all."

Since none of them were experts on *Titanic,* Ben thought it best everyone was on the same page. That way, if someone had an idea, they could contribute to the meeting. "Alright, when the girls get back, try to explain the situation, and hopefully, she'll be able to grasp the magnitude of it and still remain calm."

When the girls came back giggling, they noticed the long faces at the table. As Bria took her seat next to Jack, Warner sat next to Connie and quietly took a sip of her wine. She was always intimidated by Ben. With a look of stone, Ben sat across from her staring. "So, little girl, if I remember correctly, you used to get these boys in a lot of trouble." This was Ben's version of saying hello, long time no see.

Although, still somewhat intimidated, Warner was all grown up. At least she'd reached an age where she could handle herself. "That was then, Mr. Marcus, and this is now. People change. I would appreciate it if you called me Warner or Ms. Jenks."

Ben smiled because he liked her spunk. "Alright, Warner. It's good to see you've grown into a strong woman. Now, I know Connie has told you about a project of Jack's, but there's a lot more to it, so, if you would please, just listen."

The entire time Ben and Warner were exchanging pleasantries, Jack was trying to figure out how to start his story. He told her about the mysterious box then went on from there. By the time he was finished, Warner was absolutely floored. Sometime during Jack's story, her jaw had dropped as she tried to hang on Jack's every word. Jack didn't finish his story with an upbeat attitude, because at that point, he had to deal with whatever information Connie and Ben had.

After ordering dinner and more drinks, Jack attempted to be upbeat. "So, Connie, I'm guessing you found some useful information?"

Connie and Jack had been friends for a long time and he could tell Jack already knew the answer. With no joy in his voice, Connie gave in. "Yeah, Jack. I did some checking and called a few of my friends in the business."

By the arrogant look on Ben's face, he probably had the same information. Ben didn't even flinch. As usual, he had all his ducks in a row. After wetting his whistle, he gave Jack the news. "Without getting into all the mumbo jumbo, I'll just break down the basics. *Titanic* was originally owned by the British shipping company called White Star Line. In 1927 the company was purchased by Royal Mail Steam Packet Company. The company was then liquidated in 1932 and simply called Royal Mail Lines. Then in 1933, Cunard lines merged with the company and eventually, by 1947, was buying up shares. By 1949 Cunard Line owned everything.

"Now, hearing that little history lesson, the company has nothing to do with *Titanic.* After the sinking, there were enough inquiries and lawsuits to go around, but after everything was settled, the ship was virtually forgotten about. It wasn't until the rediscovery in 1985 that *Titanic* became a worldwide phenomenon. Since then, there have been numerous arguments and new lawsuits emerging. Arguments on whether or not to retrieve the ship and arguments over salvage rights. As of now, a New York company called RMS Titanic, Incorporated has the sole salvage rights to the wreck. It's pretty much everyone's conclusion that it's a mass grave site and it should be left alone. Now, here's the interesting part. They've already made several expeditions down to the site to retrieve various items, but they can only salvage the areas around the ship. They can't go inside or take anything from the ship itself. Currently, there's some litigation going on over tourists being able to go down to the sight. The bottom line right now, kid, is that until all the lawsuits are settled and we can get some kind of clear understanding on what we can and can't do, the *Titanic* is off limits."

Jack felt like he was just sucker punched in the gut. He was so disgusted he couldn't even look Connie in the face. Without saying a word, he stood up from the table and navigated his way to the front door. After a few moments, Bria and Warner stood up and excused themselves. Connie sat quietly eating his food. He finally found the words that had eluded him. "I was right, wasn't I? You haven't changed one bit. You love kicking people while they're down. Even when it's Jack, you just can't help yourself."

Without feeling any regret, Ben just laughed. "Listen to you sitting up on your high horse. I only did what you didn't have the guts to do. No use in trying to sugarcoat the damn situation."

Still feeling disgusted, Connie threw his napkin down and placed his silverware on his plate. "I would appreciate it if you let Warner know I stepped out to get some air."

Ben smiled as he shoved some food into his mouth. "Sure, let me put that at the top of my to do list."

When Connie walked outside, he saw Jack leaning against the wall. "Hey, Jack, I figured I would find you out here."

Fresh air does a soul good and Jack desperately needed some air. "Why didn't you tell me any of this when you found out?"

Connie lit up a cigarette and leaned against the wall with Jack. "Because I knew how important it was to you, and just like how I felt when Warner left me after high school, I didn't want to see you hurt like that. I guess I wasn't thinking you would eventually find out."

With a smile on his face, Jack laughed. "Really? Whenever Ben is involved, nothing gets by that man. Anyway, I hate to say it, but I'm feeling relieved. Ever since I opened that box, the stress in my life has skyrocketed."

After stomping out his cigarette, Connie shivered then shook off the cold. "Hey, it's getting cold out here. What'ya say we go back in?"

Jack shook his head and laughed. "Same old Connie. Is there anything else I need to know before I go listen to Ben tell me 'I told you so'?"

Connie didn't say anything at first and just looked down at the ground. "Well, there is something Ben failed to mention. With all his connections, it's hard to believe he doesn't know."

Like an emotional rollercoaster, Jack stood waiting for Connie to answer. "Come on, Connie, what is it?"

Connie didn't have exact details, but he told Jack what he knew. "Ben was right about everything he said, but there was more. There's some kind of litigation between several countries to come up with specific laws concerning the *Titanic*. It might take a couple of years for something to officially be on paper, but depending on what they come up with, there might be some loopholes you can exploit."

It sounded sketchy, so Jack wasn't really jumping for joy. "Well, let's go back inside and see what Ben has to say about it."

Just then, Warner and Bria came walking out. "Hey, guys, Ben said you two were out here." Warner was already feeling the effects of the cold, so Connie rapped his arm around her. "Listen, Jack, I think Warner and I are going to call it a night, but tell Ben thanks for dinner."

Bria was also tired of Ben's company, so she decided to catch a ride with Connie. After all the goodbyes were said, Jack walked back in and sat down. "Way to go, Ben. You've succeeded in scaring everyone away."

Ben was chewing on the last bite of his dinner and took a drink of wine to wash it down. "So, Connie weaseled his way out of paying for his dinner."

Jack was already upset and really wasn't in the mood to do battle, but Connie was his best friend. "Come on, Ben, what can you possibly have against Connie?"

Ben cracked a smile as he poured another glass of wine. "I like Connie. Maybe I've just come to the conclusion that, for the first time, I'm disappointed in you."

Jack was completely caught off guard and a little hurt. "What are you talking about? I've worked my ass off, and I think I've done quite well handling Kotter Industries thus far."

For the first time that night, Ben showed emotion and looked at Jack with sadness. "Yeah, kid, if you think so."

By then, Jack was totally disgusted and somewhat offended. "I know my dad wanted you to look after me and protect me, but come on, Ben, when does there come a time when you're not on my back about something?"

With his sadness turning to anger, Ben shoved his plate away as his voice grew louder. "You listen to me, little man. Your dad and I schooled you with all of our knowledge and then some, but I don't remember ever teaching you how to be a backstabber or a self-centered little prick."

Now Jack found himself getting loud. "What the hell are you talking about? You taught me to go after what I want and to utilize whatever resources I had to get it. Did you not tell me that, or have

I been dreaming the past few years and now I'm suddenly going to wake the hell up? I thought you were on board with all this."

Before Ben could respond, the manager approached the table. "I'm sorry, Mr. Marcus, but some of our guests are starting to complain about the noise."

As the manager walked away, Ben stood up and looked around at everyone staring. "Yeah, kid, I was on board, but remember I told you there were obstacles to get over. Well, we didn't even make it past the first one. If this nonsense leaks out to the news, Kotter Industries will look like fools. Your project is dead, so maybe you do need to wake the hell up."

As Ben walked out of the restaurant, Jack was left sitting at the table pondering his sanity. "Damn it. He stuck me with the check again."

Jack left the restaurant with mixed feelings. On one hand, he was relieved at the news Connie and Ben gave, but on the other, disappointed he wouldn't be able to complete his father's lifelong dream. When he arrived home, Jack thought Bria would be there waiting, but she wasn't, so he sat on his porch for a few minutes enjoying the cool crisp air. Afterwards, the exhaustion finally beat him down, so he made his way to his bedroom and fell asleep.

CHAPTER TWENTY-SIX

When Monday finally arrived, Jack awoke feeling no different than any other day. He thought he would feel anxious or nervous, but he didn't, so he went to work like any other Monday. When he arrived, he noticed Ben's office door was closed, which wasn't out of the ordinary, but then he noticed Hellen wasn't there either and that was. Usually, Ben let Jack know if he wasn't working, but maybe he was still pissed about the meeting. In any case, Jack made his way to his office and started his long, boring quest through endless paperwork and phone calls. As work progressed throughout the day, Jack thought about calling Ben, but didn't because he didn't want to risk a confrontation.

Finally, the end of day came and the final business was wrapped up. Jack watched out of his office window as the last of the employees left to go home, but still no Ben. As the sun started to set, the cleaning crew made their rounds, so Jack decided to make his exit. On his way over to the 110 Garage, he gave Dale a call to make sure everything was in place. Dale didn't have any good news. All the help he thought he had backed out at the last minute because the plan wasn't approved through the department. Dale did get a friend who happened to be a helicopter pilot and who happened he owe Dale a favor. Dale was also waiting on the lead he had spoken about with

Jack, so he tried one last time to talk Jack into postponing the plan. "I have a bad feeling, Jack. We don't have the personnel to pull this off."

As Jack pulled onto the 110 Garage lot, he saw the bay door partially open and Oliver tinkering with the Ferrari. By that point, he was thinking it was now or never. "I appreciate your concern, Dale, but I just need to do this."

Dale thought for a second then finally came to terms. "Okay, Jack. We'll stick with the original plan just to prevent you from going off on your own and doing something crazy. You need to get her over to the old abandoned warehouse district so we can lay our trap. But since everyone bailed, I'm going to have to rely on state police and Huntington police to do their jobs and respond quickly. Until you make it to that industrial park Jack, you're on your own."

Jack knew the dangers and was willing to risk it all. After hanging up with Dale, he watched the traffic go by for a few minutes while he ran through some last minute thoughts. Just then, Paul tapped on the window. Jack stepped out into the cool, brisk air and shook hands. "So, is she ready?"

Paul smiled. "I still can't believe you're gonna do this."

They walked into the garage just as Oliver closed the hood. The Ferrari was already waxed and ready to go, but Oliver couldn't resist running the cotton cloth across her hood one more time. "Well, Jack, what'ya think?"

Even though Jack had been around the car quite a bit, just staring at her didn't get old. "Fantastic job, Oliver. She looks better than new."

After having some coffee and talking awhile, it started to get late. As the clouds made way for the night-time stars, rush hour traffic started to die down.

Jack finished the last drink of his coffee and started the Ferrari. Paul opened the bay door as Jack drifted out to the parking lot. As the Ferrari came to a stop, Jack put the top up. "No use in sticking around. I'm sure you'll see something on the morning news." He shot Paul and Oliver a smile then drove off. As Paul and Oliver watched Jack pull off the lot, his taillights disappeared into the crowd of cars.

Jack drove down a ways and met Dale on the side of the road. Dale gave him a radio so they could stay in constant contact. By that time, late night had settled in and traffic gave way to silence. It was cold and Jack started feeling the effects of his nerves. "Hey, Dale, let me apologize to you ahead of time just in case this all goes to hell."

Dale shook Jack's hand and smiled. "Just get her over to the industrial park and I'll take care of the rest."

As Jack drove off, he thought about what Dale said about everyone bailing out. He didn't know what Dale had planned, but that was the least of his worries. Now, he was on the lookout for Lilith. The Ferrari didn't have any heat, but that was okay because the cold kept Jack alert. Slicing through the darkness, a helicopter flew overhead and Jack felt some relief knowing Dale was watching over him. The radio which Dale gave him suddenly came alive. "Come in, Jack. I need to make sure you copy."

For the moment, Jack felt like a little kid. "Hey, Dale, I copy you loud and clear. I'm glad you're up there. Keep an eye out for me."

Jack tried to stay within a few miles of the old decrepit industrial park, but it wasn't easy. An old Ferrari screaming up and down the highway with very little to no traffic in a desolate area didn't exactly blend in. Jack enjoyed the drive, but his nerves started to get the best of him. After an hour of just cruising, the quiet started to feel haunting. Just past midnight, a car came from behind blowing his horn and flashing his lights. Jack's eyes were heavy and the sound of the horn startled him.

As he glanced over, a slurred voice called out. "Nice car, wanna go?"

Jack's heart was pounding because he was so busy trying to stay calm that he never saw the car come up from behind. When he saw it was just some fool who'd had too much to drink, he gracefully pulled to the side and let the car pass.

With some relief, Jack stepped out to stretch his legs. As he breathed in the crisp clean air, he looked around at absolutely nothing. It was dark and cold and the stars were out, and besides the drunken fool who blew by a few minutes earlier, there was nobody else around.

When he stepped back into his car, the crackling of the radio broke through the silence. "You there, Jack? Everything okay?"

Jack took a deep breath and picked up the radio. "Yeah, just working through a case of the jitters. I guess I never realized how dark and quiet it can get out here."

Dale laughed, because many nights, he worked the graveyard

shift. "Yeah, I know all too well. Listen up; I have some news. I've been waiting on some information and it just came through. You're not gonna believe this one."

Jack shook his head and smiled. "With everything going on in my life, I can believe just about anything. But go ahead, give it your best shot."

After a brief pause, Dale gave the sad truth. "After you introduced me to Paul and Oliver, and I saw their garage had been broken in to, it didn't make any sense that none of their property was taken. So I started to do some digging. I know you remember the story of old Joe Jarred. Well, his son Joe Jr. made a name for himself racing up and down Route 110." Jack was already familiar with the story, but let Dale continue hoping to hear something new. Dale finally came to a question. "Did you know that Joe Jr. had a daughter?"

As Jack refreshed his memory, he remembered the story of the daughter. "Wasn't she mentally ill?"

Dale responded almost immediately. "Yeah, she was. When Joe died in that accident, the mom admitted her to the Hope for Angels institution. Apparently she was beaten and raped repeatedly over the years."

Jack sat listening as the night gave way to the early morning hours. As tragic as the story was, he couldn't help his sarcasm. "Wow, sounds like a great place to ditch your loved ones."

Although Jack was joking, Dale wasn't laughing. Instead, he kept his serious tone and told Jack more than what he was ready for. "Alright, funny man, would you care to try to guess the name of the daughter?"

Jack had no clue and it didn't sound like Dale was joking. "Well, I'm guessing it's not Rumpelstiltskin."

Dale still wasn't laughing. "Listen up, Jack, because this isn't funny. Joe's daughter name was Lilly, aka Lilith. She managed to swipe a doctor's coat with the identification hooked to the pocket and escaped by walking right out the front door. The institution tried to keep it hush-hush, but the story broke a few days ago about all the abuse. I'll spare you the guessing game of what kind of car her father drove. It was a 1969 Plymouth Road Runner, complete with red pinstripe."

As Jack tried to process the information, he started to feel a bit more uneasy about the situation he'd placed himself in. "This isn't good, Dale. It's been almost a year since she started her reign of terror. No wonder the police couldn't figure out who she was. She's been institutionalized since she was a little girl. Christ, she really is a crazy bitch. So, why all the death and destruction?"

Without hesitation, Dale already had the answer. "Think about it, Jack. The only family she had was destroyed by a couple of stupid kids who killed her father. The grandfather had already passed away and her mom abandoned her. From then, it's been nothing but abuse. The girl isn't in her right mind and she's not going to stop until she feels avenged. She was probably using her grandfather's old garage to hide and do whatever repairs were needed on her car. Besides the institution, the garage was the only other place familiar to her. After the brothers bought it, she broke in and took anything that meant something to her."

As frost started to form on his windshield, Jack tried to piece together the story. "Well, that would explain why she disappeared for a while. After the garage was bought, she needed to find someplace else to set up shop."

Jack noticed that he was starting to shiver. He wasn't sure if it was the cold or the story he'd just heard. Nevertheless, he was ready to go home. "Alright, Dale, now what?"

Once again, Dale didn't hesitate. "Now you get the hell out of there and hightail it back to the garage. Now that we know who she is, we can put together a better plan to catch her."

Jack was definitely on board with the idea, but before he could put his car into gear, he glanced at his rearview mirror and saw Lilith sitting behind him. Still feeling shaky, Jack grabbed the radio. "I think it's a little too late, Dale. Are you anywhere close?"

As the radio snapped crackled and popped, Dale's voice came over. "What's wrong, Jack? What's the problem?"

By then, Jack's voice was also starting to shake. "Sometime during our enlightening conversation, Lilith crept up on me. She must have turned off her lights and engine and drifted in behind me. God only knows how long she's been sitting there."

Now feeling pressed, Dale came back over the radio. "The pilot is turning around now Jack. We'll be there in five minutes. You need to get out of there."

Jack placed the Ferrari in gear and started to slowly move forward. "Sorry, Dale, she's not gonna let me out of her sight."

Once again, an anxious Dale came back over the radio. "Don't do anything stupid, Jack. Let me call for some back up."

As Jack slowly made his way off the shoulder and back onto the highway, Lilith followed behind, keeping pace. "Hey, Dale, looks like Lilith has a different plan."

Jack drove slowly to the red light and came to a stop as Lilith pulled beside him. With her usual format, she lowered her passenger side window down just enough for Jack to see her eyes. "Well, well, Jack Kotter. Nice car. Where's your friend, Ben? Maybe we can make it a threesome."

Jack was waiting for his anger to get the best of him, but instead, all he felt was sorrow and grief. "Listen, Lilly, I know who you are and so do the police. Why don't you stop all this nonsense and let somebody help you?"

Lilith let out a small laugh just loud enough for Jack to hear. "Now, now, Jack, why ruin a good thing?"

As the light turned green then back to red, the two cars didn't move. Jack could see that Lilith felt no remorse, so his sorrow and grief quickly turn to anger. "You stupid bitch, you hurt a lot of people and you wrecked my car."

As Lilith revved her engine, Jack could hear another subtle laugh. "Come on, Jack, you knew the rules."

As his anger reached full speed, Jack watched as the light flickered green then back to red again. "Rules? There were no rules."

Lilith glared over at Jack as the '69 Road Runner roared. "Exactly! There are no rules. People do what they want with no consequences, so why not be the victimizer instead of the victim?"

Just then, Dale came over the radio. "I have eyes on you, Jack. What's going on down there?"

Without taking his eyes off of Lilith, Jack reached down and clicked the radio to where Dale could hear the conversation. "So, what is it that you want, Lilly? I mean what is it that you really want? Obviously it has to be something more than just me."

Lilith continuously stroked her engine, until she finally blurted out her answer. "You're right, Jack. Not to hurt your ego, but it is bigger than you. You're just an appetizer. But if you must know, I want the boys who killed my father. I want all the men who hurt me over the years to pay for what they did. I want my mother to hold me again and tell me how much she loves me. I want all the wrong in this world to be right, but that isn't going to happen, is it, Jack?" Before Jack could say anything, Lilith yelled at him. "It isn't going to happen, is it, Jack! So why don't we just get this over with so we can see which one of us is going home tonight."

Lilith rolled up her window leaving Jack feeling more uneasy than ever. He quickly grabbed the radio. "Did you get all that, Dale?"

The radio crackled as Dale came back. "This isn't good, Jack. You really pissed her off. If you don't move, then she'll have no choice but to drive away. The state police are responding, but they're gonna be a few minutes."

Jack knew Lilith wasn't going away. Especially now that he pushed the wrong buttons. "Sorry, Dale, if I try to sit this out, she's liable to ram me."

As Dale hovered in the air, he felt absolutely helpless. "Alright, Jack, if something goes wrong, then we all go down."

Like a couple of lions, the two cars roared as they waited for the green light. Jack could hear sirens off in the distance, but his mind was already made up. The light hit green and Jack's body jolted as he shifted through his gears. It wasn't long before the two cars hit top speed. After the smoke cleared, Dale tried to keep up, but the helicopter could barely stay in range, so he made sure Jack didn't forget the plan. "Listen, Jack, don't worry about answering me. Don't lose sight of the objective. Just get her over to the old industrial park."

After racing side by side for a few minutes, Lilith decided to let Jack take the lead. Jack wasn't surprised. He knew his car couldn't outrun the Road Runner and Lilith made it no secret what her intentions were. Jack needed to go along with the cat and mouse game long enough for Dale to spring whatever trap he had planned. After a few more minutes, the chase turned into a bump and run contest. Lilith tapped Jack's rear bumper a couple of times just as a reminder that she was in control. Jack was able to out maneuver Lilith as the two cars twisted and screamed around every turn. It wasn't long before the industrial park came into site. It was decrepit and abandoned, and most of the buildings were leftover from the early 1900s. Some had given way to time and partially collapsed, creating even more twists and turns within the private roads of the park.

A couple more bumps from Lilith accelerated Jack into an old security gate ripping a hole in the passenger door and breaking the window. Afterwards, Jack was able to create some distance by cornering the tight turns that Lilith had to slow down for, but it didn't take long for Lilith to be right back at it. She took advantage of the straightaways by overpowering Jack and pulling alongside the Ferrari. As she tried to push Jack into the weather-beaten buildings, Jack desperately tried to push back. Finally, with one last clash of the fenders, Lilith was able to bump Jack's rear corner panel causing him to spin several times out of control. The Ferrari stalled as it came to an abrupt stop.

Before Jack could shake off the dizziness, Lilith had already positioned her car for one last attack. When his car failed to start after several attempts, Jack knew he was trapped. If he attempted to get out of his car, Lilith would easily run him down. If he stayed in the car, Lilith would most definitely ram him at full speed, crushing him within the car. Suddenly, Jack felt at ease. No fear. No sorrow. Nothing at all but peace. As Lilith prepared for her attack, she revved her engine. With a sigh of relief, Jack took a deep breath and picked up the radio. "I'm sorry, Dale. I tried my best. I hope God has a spot waiting for me."

When Lilith hit the gas, her wheels screamed violently. One last glance from Jack as he closed his eyes and laid his head back. The Road Runner didn't take long to pick up speed. Lilith gripped her steering wheel as she prepared for the final collision. Just as she zeroed in on Jack, a new Lamborghini Diablo came out of nowhere. It side swiped Lilith, pushing her past Jack and into a pile of rubble. There wasn't much damage, so Lilith wasted no time shifting into reverse and attempting to flee. Realizing Lilith missed his car, Jack opened his eyes and saw the Diablo just before it left to chase Lilith.

Jack quickly grabbed his radio. "Is that you, Ben?"

After a few seconds of static, a familiar raspy old voice came back. "Of course it's me. You didn't think I was gonna let you have all the fun, did you, kid? What'ya say? You getting back into the game or what?"

Suddenly, out of nowhere, another two cars came roaring by. They were two old beat up police cruisers that had been spray painted various colors. The radio flickered as another familiar voice came over. The Mopar brothers. It was Walley. "Hey, Jack, let's go get this bitch."

Jack's energy was in full-swing, so he anxiously jumped out of his car and popped the hood open. It was his battery cable. It must have come loose during one of the encounters with Lilith. He quickly reattached it and the Ferrari started right up. Jack wasted no time shifting through his gears and catching up.

By the time he had Lilith in sight, it looked like she had tangled with Ben a few times. Ben had damage on both sides and the rear of his car was severely damaged. The Mopar brothers had Lilith on the run and were bumping her from both sides. As the twists and turns came quick, Jack managed to cut through some buildings and come out on the other side ahead of Lilith. Just a single thought entered his mind. *Now we play, bitch.*

When Jack tried to slow down, Lilith would bump him from behind, but now, she had the Mopar brothers on both sides and Ben behind her. She tried to force herself free by pushing Jack, but it wasn't working. She then struck Jimmy on the passenger side, pushing him into an old rusted water tower that was half-collapsed. Walley checked his rearview mirror and saw the "I'm okay" wave, so he continued on. Without Jimmy, Lilith was no longer contained. She broke out and set her sights on Walley as her next target. Jack and Ben tried to keep her from getting too nasty, but with all the damage their cars had sustained, it was next to impossible to keep her battleship in check. Lilith continued to hammer Walley until, finally, he lost control and veered off into a pile of scrap iron, blowing his air bag and three of his tires. He jumped out of the car waving his fists in the air and yelling, "Get that stupid whore, Jack."

This left Jack and Ben to try to deal with Lilith. Luckily, she'd taken on some damage as she was desperately trying to get away. It was enough to allow Ben to maneuver his car to one side as Jack slowed down to take the other. The problem was neither one of their cars had enough weight to compete with Lilith. Their cars just bounced off her like pinballs. Without warning, Ben's car started shaking and knocking as he fell behind. Jack heard his voice come over the radio. "Sorry, kid, I've done all I can do."

This was Lilith's chance to make her move. She headed for the exit, but quickly saw that it was blocked by the state police. She decided to make her way back to the entrance, but still had Jack to deal with. Jack grabbed his radio. "Hey, Dale, she's headed back towards the entrance. If she gets out, we'll never catch her."

As the speeds increased, the buildings became a blur. It wasn't long before Lilith approached the entrance where they'd come in. Fortunately for Jack, it was also blocked by the Huntington police department. Back when the industrial age first began, industrial parks were built like prisons and for good reason. Competitors would often try to gain an advantage by stealing information. This particular park had only one entrance and one exit, and it was surrounded by a twelve foot brick security wall.

With the entrance and exit blocked, Dale up above in the helicopter, and Jack close behind, Lilith realized she needed to find an alternative way out. Luckily for her, the age of the facility and the weather had taken its toll on the century-old walls. There were several places where the wall had collapsed on itself. She knew Jack's car was heavily damaged and there was no chance of him catching her, so she quickly made a beeline to the nearest hole. The facility had long been shut down and abandoned, so over the years, some of the kids and teens from the surrounding neighborhoods would use the facility as their own personal playground. In some places, they had various obstacles set up for dirt bikes and homemade ramps built to conduct their stunts, dares, and contests. Lilith just had to find the one place that would provide her with the opportunity to escape.

As Jack desperately tried to keep up, Lilith pulled further and further away. Dale came over the radio and Jack could hear the fear in his voice. "She's headed for that break in the wall, Jack. There's no police anywhere close. You have to somehow cut her off."

Dale was right. There was a large hole in the wall with a ramp made out of some old wood and broken up bricks. To Lilith, this was manna from heaven, but in order to get out, she had to slow down enough to align her car with the old wooden planks. This gave Jack one last opportunity to try to stop her. As Lilith shifted down, Jack pushed the Ferrari with everything he had. Right before Lilith made it to the ramp, the two cars collided pushing Lilith faster than she wanted to go. As Jack lost control and veered off into a pile of bricks, only one of Lilith's tires made it onto the ramp. This caused her car to go airborne and flip several times end over end.

As the '69 Road Runner settled upright, there was an eerie calm and then silence. Nobody rushed towards the car. As the helicopter landed off in the distance, Jack slowly rolled out of the Ferrari. As he stood up, he glanced over at the Road Runner to see if there was any movement. The state police and Huntington police converged on the scene, but nobody took the initiative to check on Lilith. Finally, a sound broke through the silence. Lilith's passenger side door creaked slowly open. With caution, Jack walked over to confront the person who had marked him for death and nearly killed him. As he slowly approached, Dale came running up from behind. "Wait up, Jack. Take it easy. She might have a weapon."

Jack stopped momentarily and turned to Dale. "I'm thinking that car was her weapon and probably her safe haven, and now she has nothing." Jack could hear the medics approaching the park, but he needed to see for himself the person who had been terrorizing the suburbs of New York.

The car door was only partially open, so as Dale yanked on it, Jack stooped down to look inside. Lilith was sprawled across the front seat. She had a gash in her head that was leaking blood into her eyes, and her left leg was broken. Somehow, she was still able to crack a smile. "Well, Jack, have you come to gawk at me, or maybe to claim your trophy?" Jack had no words. As the medics approached, he stood silently.

Just then, sergeant Lactgan came running up. "You're done, Kotter. I have you now. You too, Dale. You can kiss your career goodbye, asshole. As for your little pals, Kotter, I'm gonna make sure their time in jail is hard time."

Jack could see Lactgan's lips moving, but he couldn't hear. He was so sick about the whole situation that somehow his mind was blocking out sound. He watched as the medics tended to Lilith. He then glanced over at his father's Ferrari and saw that a thing of beauty had been replaced by destruction. The car was completely destroyed. Jack finally came out of his coma just when Lactgan was finishing his attack. "And another thing, Kotter, all your clout isn't going to be worth a damn by the time I'm through with you."

Before the medics could load Lilith into the ambulance, Jack felt the need to talk to her one last time, so he walked over to the gurney. "I'm sorry, Lilly. I never meant for things to turn out this way, but you didn't leave us any choice."

By then, the medics had wiped the blood from her face and wrapped her head with a bandage. "Life is filled with choices, Jack. Unfortunately, most people make the wrong ones." Lilith's eyes started to flutter as she tried to keep from passing out. "Don't worry, Jack. I'm coming back one day, and when I do, I will have my satisfaction." As Lilith lost her battle to stay conscious, a tiny picture dropped from her hand. When the medics lifted the gurney and pushed her in the rear of the ambulance, Jack bent down and picked it up. It was a photo of Lilly, her parents, and her grandfather.

It was early morning and the sun was due to rise in a few hours. Jack was tired, but he was also concerned about Dale. As the state police vacated the area, and the Huntington police right behind them, the early morning grew silent once again. As usual, the Mopar brothers didn't have a care in the world. They slapped hands and congratulated each other several times and already started to exaggerate their stories. For once, Ben stood in silence, shaking his head at the second Lamborghini Lilith had destroyed. "This makes two half-million-dollar cars that bitch owes me."

While Ben continued to inspect all the damage and the Mopar brothers were off exploring, Jack turned his attention to Dale. "I can't believe you got those guys involved in this."

Dale smiled because it wasn't his idea. "Well, I couldn't keep them away. Somehow, Ben already knew, so he got the brothers to join in the fun. I just can't figure out how he finds out about stuff. He's like a mega super spy or something."

Jack was in total agreement. "Yeah, you're not too far off when you say that. So, from a scale from one to ten, how serious is this whole thing?"

Dale didn't answer right away. He took a deep breath and let it out. When he finally did give Jack an answer, it was very bleak. "Well, Jack, I would say the situation has climbed way past a ten. Everything Lactgan said was basically true. My career is probably finished, and you, Ben, and the Mopar brothers will probably spend some time in jail. There's really nothing more to do right now but to go home and wait. I'll have one of the midnight officers drive everybody home. I'm sorry, Jack."

Jack wasn't too worried about himself or Ben, but Dale took a huge chance and put everything on the line. "I should be apologizing to you, Dale. I'm the one who talked you into going through with this. I should be taking the fall, not you."

Dale cracked half a smile knowing Jack was genuine and sincere. "It doesn't matter what you did or didn't do, Jack. Ultimately, it was my idea and my decision to go through with it."

When a midnight shift officer arrived, Ben and the Mopar brothers wasted no time fighting over the seating arrangements. While they were busy bickering, Jack and Dale shook hands and agreed that it was just a bad situation for everyone involved. After Ben won the battle for the front seat, the brothers and Jack climbed into the back. Trying to see things in a positive light, Dale walked over to give Jack one last thing to think about. "I guess you'll have to wait to see God another time." Jack smiled as the patrol car pulled off.

As Jack walked through his front door, the morning sunrise finally made an appearance. He stopped for a few minutes and briefly reviewed the events of the night. The thoughts that ran through his mind when Lilith had him cornered were already starting to haunt him. All the arguments he and Bria had about their future and family had finally come to a head. She was right. He had become his father. Always feeling the need to solve everyone's problems. Already past the point of fatigue, Jack slowly climbed the staircase longing for his bed. When he opened the bedroom door, he saw Bria curled up under the blankets, sound asleep. He gently climbed into bed and wrapped his arm around her and closed his eyes.

Later that morning, Jack awoke and saw that Bria was already gone. He checked the time and noticed the afternoon was quickly approaching. Still feeling the fatigue from the night before, he jumped out of bed and took a quick shower. Before he left for work, he wanted to see the news. He expected to see the Lilith story on every channel, but instead, what he saw was mass destruction and confusion.

CHAPTER TWENTY-SEVEN

On 11 September 2001, terrorists hijacked four jet airliners. Two collided with the Twin Towers of the World Trade Center, one was directed into the Pentagon, and the fourth never made it to its destination. It crashed in a field near Shanksville, Pennsylvania. After the initial shock, Jack wasted no time calling Ben. The phone barely rang once then Ben picked up. "Where the hell have you been, kid? Get your ass in here." Without giving Jack a chance to respond, Ben hung up. With his heart pounding, Jack ran out the door.

He arrived at work only to find an empty parking lot and an empty building. When he made it to Ben's office, he was on a conference call, shuffling papers, and trying to write notes all at the same time.

"Grab some coffee and have a seat, kid."

As Ben ended the call, Jack made two cups of coffee and handed one to Ben. "What the hell is going on?"

As he took a sip of coffee, Ben turned the television on. "Well, kid, for the first time in my life, I have no idea. They're calling this a terrorist attack, but I've been on the phone all morning with my contacts from the CIA, FBI, NSA and every other initialed agency you can think of. Nobody is saying anything, which leads me to believe there's something more to this than what's being said. It's going to be a long day, kid. Have you checked on Bria yet?"

Jack checked his phone and saw that Bria had called several times. "Jesus Christ, Ben, when you can't get any information, that's when I start to worry. I'll be back. I'm going to my office to give Bria a call."

When Jack made it to his office, he called Bria only to find she was highly pissed off. "Where the hell have you been, Kotter? I've been trying to call you all morning."

Jack wasn't expecting an argument, but nevertheless, there were too many things going on at the time to try to pillow talk Bria. "I'm sorry you weren't my first priority, but in case you weren't aware, the United States has been attacked and Kotter Industries has offices within those buildings that collapsed. We have friends and business partners that we're not sure got out in time, not to mention sensitive information we're not sure hasn't been compromised."

Jack's tone of voice only angered Bria more. "You know what, Kotter? I'm tired of constantly chasing you, and I'm tired of playing second fiddle to Ben. By the way, I'm okay if you were wondering." The next thing Jack heard was the clicking of the phone as Bria hung up.

After a few moments of going over the argument in his head, Jack was comfortable with how he handled the situation. He walked back to Ben's office, where, once again, Ben was on a conference call. While Ben took care of business, Jack watched the television to see if there were any new developments. When Ben hung up the phone, he walked over to the bar and made some drinks. "Listen, kid, it's going to be a very long week. I've shut down everything we have across the country and even our overseas operations. I've also set up an emergency board meeting for later today, so do what you have to do and make sure you're at the meeting. Oh, and one more thing. I'm proud of you for what you did last night. You placed your own life on hold in order to save others. For a brief time, you reminded me of your father, kid. Great job."

With Bria upset, Jack didn't really have anything else to do, so he stayed at work and made phone calls to his friends. He wanted to call Dale to get an update on Lilith, but obviously, Dale was busy with police duties. As the afternoon rolled on, the board members started to show up one by one. The meeting went surprisingly well, and by the end of the day, Kotter Industries stood strong in the aftermath of disaster, as it always had. When Jack finally arrived at home, Bria was there waiting on the porch. "So, Jack Kotter, tell me one thing. When you got up this morning and saw everything that was going on, who did you call first?"

Jack took a deep breath and sat down. "Come on, Bria, how many times do we have to fight about this? I called Ben, but that was only because I'm responsible for the company. This means everything Kotter Industries owns."

Bria didn't say anything. She stood up and straddled Jack's lap. "I would be very upset with you, Jack Kotter, if it wasn't for the fact that I got up this morning and went to the Wiley Roadster for some breakfast. I ran into the Mopar brothers and they told me what happened. You just never cease to amaze me, Jack Kotter."

In the wake of 9/11, the weeks that followed weren't exactly business as usual for Kotter Industries. There were more board meetings than usual, and funerals to attend, and beefed up security at various factories, but those were things that had to be done.

Jack was finally able to meet with Dale to get an update on what they'd done. "So, I see you're still working and Lactgan hasn't showed up on my front door step with an arrest warrant."

Dale laughed for a moment. "Not that I think it's funny, but call it luck or fate or whatever you want. My guess is that 9/11 saved all of us. If it wasn't for the fact this country is now looking for heroes, Lactgan would have made good on his promises. Instead, for the service that you, Ben, and the Mopar brothers provided, the police department decided not to press charges. As for Lactgan, he ran his mouth one too many times and wound up getting himself demoted. He's now walking a very lonely foot post. As for me, the deputy chief wants me to head up a special task force that deals with hunting down violent criminals."

Jack breathed a sigh of relief. "Wow. I don't know what I'm going to do now. I have to get back to living normal without looking over my shoulder every time I drive down 110. By the way, Bria found out about what happened. She's okay with it though. What'ya think about getting together tonight? We're hooking up with Ethan and Bobby Jo at the Village Underground."

Dale didn't even hesitate. Because of 9/11, he had been working loads of overtime and needed a break. "Yeah, sounds great. I remember hearing about that place as a kid. It used to be Gerde's Folk City." Jack was glad Dale was going and offered to buy the rounds all night.

Later that night, Jack and Bria arrived at the club and saw Ethan sitting at a table enjoying the music. Of course, Bria was looking for Bobby Jo. After the hugs and kisses, Bria went straight to work. "So, where's Bobby Jo?" Ethan smiled and pointed to the ladies' room. As Bria made a beeline for the ladies' room, Jack ordered some drinks. He could tell Ethan was about to burst at the seams, so he asked what his problem was.

Ethan took a healthy gulp of his drink then made some funny faces as it burned his throat going down. "Well, I did it."

Jack took a swig of his beer as he waited for more information to follow. "Okay. Did what?"

Ethan was still feeling the effects of his drink but finally said it. "I popped the question to Bobby Jo."

Although Jack knew this wasn't going to sit well with Bria, he was still happy for his friends. Just then, Dale came walking over and sat down. He could tell immediately there was something going on. "Okay, is it business or something personal?"

Jack laughed as he handed Dale a beer. "No, nothing like that. Ethan and Bobby Jo are getting married."

Dale was happy for Ethan, but he also knew marriage was a bad subject for Jack and Bria. After a few more drinks, Bria and Bobby Jo finally made their appearance. Bobby Jo yanked on Ethan's hand pulling him out to the dance floor. Dale could see the look on Bria's face, so he quickly excused himself to the bar. Bria snuggled up to Jack and gave him a small kiss on the lips. "So, Ethan asked Bobby Jo to marry him. Isn't that nice?"

Although Bria was talking nicely, Jack could hear the tone with which her words were being delivered. "I know, I know. We've been together way longer than they have, but we've been through this argument more than enough times. What'ya say we give it a break and just be happy for our friends?"

Bria started to pout as she scooted away. "Come on, Jack Kotter. I've accepted the fact that you're just like your dad, but even your dad married the woman he loved."

Jack knew he was on thin ice. All the excuses he used before were useless. "Honestly, Bria, I love you. I always have, from the moment we met. I guess I'm just trying to find that perfect time to make it special. I was thinking about a trip similar to what my dad did, but I'm not sure. With the Ferrari beyond repair, I'm just not sure what I want to do now."

Jack and Bria finished out the evening without arguing then went back to Jack's house. The next morning, Bria made breakfast as Jack sat quietly at the table. Jack normally wolfed down anything made by Bria, but that morning, he just sat staring at his plate. Bria stretched across the table and gave him a kiss on the cheek. "Listen, Jack Kotter, I know you're having a hard time trying to run your company and find time for me, but it'll work itself out. You'll see."

Jack tried to think positively, but it wasn't going to happen. "Sorry, Bria, but it's just not that simple. The past few years have been one thing after another. My dad died and I inherited the company. Nick, one of my best friends, turned out to be a backstabbing spy. Then I found out my dad was living some secret life, and he winds up dumping the *Titanic* in my lap, and I can't do anything with it. Then maniac Lilith decides to make me her personal target. Now we have damn terrorists attacking New York and killing people who I've known most of my life. I guess I'm just at the end of my rope and I've had it with this kind of life. I'm just not cut from the same cloth as my dad and Ben are."

While Bria was trying to figure out something to say, Jack pushed his plate of food away and stood up. "I'm going for a drive. I'll see you later."

Jack started up *Fringe* and off he went. After a while, he found himself driving towards the 110 Garage. As he pulled onto the lot, he saw Paul outside working on a truck and Oliver in one of the bays under a car. By then, the garage was in pristine condition and had a secured lot around back for finished vehicles. They also hired a few employees so they could keep up with the service contract Jack gave them. As Jack pulled into a parking space, Paul recognized the sound of *Fringe*'s engine. "Hey, Jack, how the hell are you? It's been a while since you visited."

Jack stepped out of the car and shook Paul's hand. "How are you, Paul? Sorry I haven't been around, but I've had a lot to deal with lately."

Just then, Oliver came walking out. "Hey, Jack, good to see you. What'ya think about the upgrades?"

Jack looked around at all the improvements and smiled. "Looks good. I like the new security fence."

Before Jack could say anything else, Oliver interrupted. "Come on in the back and we'll show you around." Paul walked over and punched a code while Oliver and Jack waited for the fence to open. When it did, Jack stepped in and looked around. Oliver walked over to a car that had a protective cover laid over top of it and pulled it off. Jack's eyes grew wide as he stood staring for a moment.

"Oh my God. How in the world did you do this?" After Jack had the Ferrari towed back to the garage, he thought it was beyond repair, but Paul and Oliver had a different plan in mind.

As Oliver started the car, Paul walked over and shook Jack's hand. "Congratulations. We were able to put the dream machine back together again."

When the shock finally wore off, Jack walked over and climbed in. He revved the car a couple of times and ran his hands around the steering wheel. He suddenly had the strange feeling the car didn't belong to him anymore.

Although the car belonged to his father, it was clear to Jack it was time to let it go. He shut the car off and stepped out. He slid his fingers down the edge of the hood as he admired the workmanship. "I thought this car was gone. After that night with Lilith, there were pieces strung out all over that industrial park. I can't believe you guys were able to do this. I can't take this car with me."

Oliver's smile quickly turned upside down. "What are you talking about? We worked our asses off trying to get this thing back together for you."

Jack gave a small smile and handed Oliver the keys. "You're right. That's why I can't take it. This car belongs to someone who can take care of it. Obviously, you and Paul would be the perfect owners."

Oliver glanced over at the car then back to Jack. "But this was your father's car, Jack. We can't accept a gift like this."

Jack took one last look then walked away. While Paul took the time to cover the car, Oliver followed Jack around to the front of the building. "Jack, hold on a minute."

Jack stopped short of *Fringe* and turned around. "I'm not sure why my dad bought that car. I used to think it was because he used it to propose to my mom, but I'm thinking there was another reason. Maybe somehow he knew it would serve a future purpose, and now that purpose is over. I think my dad would be very happy knowing you and Paul will take good care of the car."

Although he still wished he could have finished his father's work, Jack left the garage with a good feeling, like a chapter of his life was finally closed. He drove to work feeling refreshed and ready to go. As usual, when he arrived, Ben scolded him for being late. There was a board meeting already in progress, and with the terrorist attacks still fresh on everyone's minds, there were many issues that had to be addressed. When Ben and Jack walked in, Robert was already reviewing the agenda for the meeting. "Glad you guys could make it. Why don't you grab some coffee and have a seat?"

Ben didn't like Robert's tone of voice, but from time to time, would tolerate it. After Robert finished speaking, Ben rose and stood at the head of the table. "Alright, there's no getting around the elephant in the room, so I'll just come right out and say it. With all that's gone on over the past month, there's no doubt our economy will eventually take a nosedive. It's not a matter of if, but a matter of when. Unfortunately, in today's world, war isn't profitable. Now let me just say this: Kotter Industries has always stood strong in the face of adversity, and I'm proud to say we've never had layoffs, but if it comes to that, and hopefully it won't, the company has a reserve of cash set aside to deal with whatever problems come our way."

While Ben kept talking, Jack suddenly realized what cash he was talking about. With a bit of anger, he took a deep breath and stood up. "Hold on, Ben. Why would you even think about telling anyone about that money without consulting me? That money was never intended to be used for this company or its problems."

With a look of disappointment mixed with some anger, Ben geared up for an attack. "First off, you don't address this meeting until I'm finished talking. Second, if you recall, that money is under my direction to be used as I see fit. Our government is planning to take this nation straight to hell in a handbasket. We need to prepare this company to handle the fallout if our economy falters."

As the other members of the board sat wondering what money was being argued over, Robert stood up and suggested Ben and Jack have a private argument elsewhere. Of course Ben declined and kept at it. "Listen, kid, you might have inherited this company, but you have no idea what it takes to maintain it and to keep moving forward, especially through tough times. Your father and I fought together through 50 years of wars, assignations, and government corruption to make this corporation what it is today, and I'll be damned if you think you're gonna just waltz in here and dictate to me what you think is best for this company, so either sit your ass down and shut up or get the hell out. Either way, you will have respect for the members of this board and the employees that count on us to support their families."

Ben was right. Although Jack did own the majority of the company, he knew he didn't have a leg to stand on. Like a dog with its tail between the legs, Jack gathered his bruised ego and walked out of the meeting. Robert watched as Jack walked slowly to the door and closed it gently behind him. "Come on, Ben, I'm not one of Jack's biggest fans, but you didn't have to slam him like that in front of everybody. What the hell is wrong with you?"

As everyone looked on, Ben sat down in his chair and contemplated what he was going to say next. "I'm sorry, everyone. Robert is right. Jack knows I love him like a son, but I guess sometimes I can be a real ass. Robert, please explain to the board about the money Jack Sr. left behind while I go talk with Jack. By the way, don't go through the whole story. Just let them know about the money."

Ben made his way to Jack's office just to find he wasn't there. He asked Bonnie if he had left for the day, but she wasn't aware that he had, so that left just one more place to look. He walked around the corner to Jack Sr.'s office and found Jack sitting at his father's desk. He seemed to be staring out the window into space. "Hey, kid, thought I would find you here. I gotta tell you, for someone who was never in the military, your dad sure had a strategic mind. Did he ever tell you why he spaced our offices so far apart?"

Jack didn't answer. He just stared out the window. Ben was trying to lighten the mood, but wasn't doing a good job.

"Well, he figured with four sides to the building, each one of us could take a side, and that way, we would always be able to keep an eye on what was going on."

With a smile on his face, Jack spun around in his seat and looked at Ben. "I don't think my dad was too concerned about what was going on outside of his office. If I'm not mistaken, you designed the layout of the floor plan."

Ben gave a half-smile then walked over and sat down. "You're right, kid. I just wanted to see if you were on your toes."

With a smile still on his face, Jack stood up and looked out the window. "All those days my dad would sit and stare out this window. What do you think he was thinking about?"

Ben stood up and walked around the desk, then stopped next to Jack. "I don't know, kid. Your dad had a lot on his mind. I guess it depends on what timeframe you're talking about. When he got the news about your mom, I think that was probably the worst for him. Many days he sat here staring out that window."

Jack thought for a second then came up with his own answer. "I think the death of my mom may have been a small part of something bigger. I think his entire life revolved around a master plan he set in motion as a young adult. Towards the end of his life, he sat and stared out this window, watching that plan slowly unravel and not able to do anything about it. Real big man. Wanted to do everything on his own, not even asking his best friend for any help until it was too late."

Ben looked at Jack for a few seconds and realized he was probably right. "Listen, kid, whatever reasons your dad had for doing the things he did are really none of our concern now. We have to deal with the present and whatever future problems we may have."

With a look of distraught, Jack stared out the window. "I don't want to wind up like my dad, sitting here when I'm old, staring out this same window wondering what could have been. I don't know what it is, Ben, but I just have this feeling there's something that we're missing."

Ben quietly turned away and looked down at the floor. Knowing Ben to never be short of words, Jack noticed the silence. "What's wrong, Ben? Right about now, you're usually throwing around some of your father-knows-best wisdom. So what gives?"

Ben didn't say anything. He walked over to a buffet-style cabinet, which had various picture frames lined up neatly across the top. In one of the frames was a picture of Jack Sr., Sergis, and Ben. As Ben lifted the picture up towards the light, Jack walked over and stood beside him. "I always liked that picture. You three looked so good together. I wish I could have met Sergis. I bet he was a lot like you."

Ben gently placed the picture back in its place. "This might sound funny, kid, but I could never hold a candle to my brother. I know sometimes you think I don't know how you feel, but you couldn't be more wrong."

Jack didn't feel like taking a trip down memory lane, but in order to find out what Ben was holding back, he needed to play along for the time being. "Come on, I find that hard to believe. Over the years I've watched you make deals that would probably break an ordinary businessman."

Ben smiled, but not because of pride. He smiled because he knew what Jack was up to. "Nice try, kid. Nowadays, flattery is way overrated. But just to let you know, my brother could talk the devil out of his soul, and in the end, the devil would be gracious about it. He would probably even thank him. That's how good Sergis was. With that said, let's get back to what you really want to know. The night we met Connie for dinner, I knew he had all the basic information, but I had the resources to dig a little deeper. I found out some information I don't think Connie knew."

Jack listened intently while Ben explained. "We told you about the New York company that has the salvage rights, but what Connie didn't know about was the continuous battle over trying to preserve the *Titanic.* Currently, there are four territories involved in creating laws specific to *Titanic*: the United States, Canada, France, and England. As of now, there's nothing concrete, but when they finally sign the laws into effect, that's when you might have a chance to make your father's dream a reality."

Jack listened, but wasn't quite on the same page as Ben. "Well, Connie did say something to me, but it seemed to be really shaky, so I didn't think anything of it. I'm a little rusty when it comes to maritime law. Whatever laws they come up with are being put into place to keep people like us from doing damage, and besides, I thought RMS Titanic, Inc. had exclusive rights."

Ben stared at Jack, shaking his head almost in disgust. "Come on, kid, have I not taught you anything over the years? Laws are made to be manipulated. That's why our court system is so screwed up. Besides, I don't particularly think any of these countries really care about a ship at the bottom of an ocean. They're just tired of hearing all the bickering over it so they have to play nice and act like they care. As for RMS Titanic, Incorporated, they're a salvage company. Usually, Kotter Industries doesn't partner up with anyone, but this is an extreme case. Remember, kid, mergers and deals are my specialty. When the time comes, you let me handle that end of the problem."

Jack suddenly had that excited feeling again. "Wait a minute. Why didn't you say anything before about this? Why were you just going to let the project fade away?"

Ben didn't have to think about it. He already knew the answer. "Well, kid, I told you I've been fighting my own battles on the inside. On one hand, your father trusted me with helping you complete what he started, and on the other hand, I had to think about Kotter Industries and the many people who rely on this company for their livelihood. I couldn't risk bringing this company to its knees by chasing a fantasy that may or may not work. But then there's the third hand, if I had one. Like I said before, many days your dad sat staring out that window. I can't imagine the loneliness he felt. You said you didn't want to wind up like him. Well, I wouldn't want you to wind up like him either."

Ben could be a hard ass, but at times, he could be just as kind, and Jack knew this. "Thanks, Ben. So does this mean you're with me on this again?"

Ben took a deep breath. "Well, kid, I'm with you, but I can't promise things will turn out in your favor. Don't forget, we have to get past the members of the board."

By the time Jack and Ben returned to the meeting, it was already over. Everyone had left for the day except Robert, Ethan, and the new guy, McKinnley. While Jack sat and had casual conversation, Ben pulled Robert out into the hallway. Jack could hear Robert becoming loud and knew Ben told him about the renewed interest in the project. After Robert stormed off, Jack stepped out into the hallway to talk with Ben.

"I'm guessing your little talk with Robert didn't go well."

Ben looked worried and was unable to hide it. "Well, kid, Robert is all about business. If he thinks for one moment that something is too risky, then he'll fight against it tooth and nail. I gotta tell you, kid, you think I'm hard, Robert is a beast when it comes to business decisions."

Now Jack had the worried look. "So, does this mean we're gonna wind up locking horns with Robert?"

With a smile from ear to ear, Ben wrapped his arm around Jack. "I hope so, kid. I think it'll be fun. What'ya say we put on our suits of armor and take a walk down to his office. We'll have ourselves an old-fashioned throw down." Jack was good with that as long as Ben was in his corner.

When they arrived at Robert's office, Ben opened the door and walked in. Right away, Jack's sarcasm kicked in as he whispered into Ben's ear, "I guess that whole knocking thing only applies to me, huh?"

Ben didn't reply. Instead, he walked over and greeted Robert. "Listen, Robert, we need to have a sit down so we can once and for all figure out a plan of action and decide whether or not we're going to honor Jack Sr. and his dying wish."

Surprisingly, Robert wasn't opposed to the idea. "Alright, Ben. You actually caught me at a good time. In the midst of everything that has gone on over the past couple of years, including the terrorist attacks, I've been sitting here thinking about the future of this company."

With some disappointment, Ben sat down. "Damn, Robert, I was really hoping for a knockdown, drag out fight."

Robert stood up and walked around and sat on the edge of his desk. He stared at Jack a little differently than usual. "I used to think you were just lucky, Jack, but I was really impressed with the computer deal you put together and how you presented it. You propelled Kotter Industries into a new age without taking any risks. Your ideas were solid and well thought out. To me, that's not luck. That was just plain old-fashioned good business sense. Your dad and I go back a long way, but you already know that. He never did anything to hurt this company and the compassion he had for his employees was second to none. So I find myself thinking, what if he was still here. I think no matter what his motives were with *Titanic*, he would never jeopardize this company or its employees. The more I sit here and think, the more I wonder why he didn't leave us some kind of blueprint on how to proceed."

As Robert and Ben sat staring at Jack, Jack stood quietly with his hands in his pockets. "What are you guys staring at? I've gone through everything my dad left behind in that storage shed. There weren't any kind of directions on how he planned on completing the project."

Ben shook his head and smiled. "Come on, kid, I know what Robert is leading to. Think about it. You're definitely your father's son. You think just like him, so therefore, you're the blueprint. Your father must have seen something early on in your life to know that if anything happened, you would have the ability to carry out his wishes."

Jack understood what Ben was saying, but wasn't sure he agreed. "I think my dad had things well-thought-out until *Titanic* was found to be in pieces. My only guess is that he figured after he was gone, the technology would finally become available to bring her up."

Robert walked back around his desk and sat down. "Alright, don't think this is a done deal, because it's not. There are still many obstacles to get over. There are also a lot of variables to consider."

With some renewed energy, Ben popped up out of his seat. "Alright, kid, if you're done playing pocket pool, we have a lot to do, but first thing is first. Just like everything else, we're going to have to take a vote. I'll have Hellen set up a meeting for tomorrow afternoon. In the meantime, be thinking about how we're going to sell the board on such a crazy idea."

Jack left work that day riding on cloud nine because the outcome didn't matter. He felt good knowing Ben and Robert had enough respect for him to finally try to complete his father's last wishes. He stopped by to see Connie, because Connie was planning on helping Warner with her research in Cyprus and they were leaving at the end of the week.

When Jack arrived at the house, there were mixed emotions. They were happy to see Jack before they left, but at the same time, they weren't sure if Jack would try to talk Connie out of going. After the hugs and kisses, Jack and Connie sat and talked while Warner continued to pack.

"Well, Connie, I'm happy for you. In a way, I kinda envy you. You have the career you always wanted and the girl you fell in love with. And now both of you are headed off into the sunset on this incredible trip."

Connie smiled with some reserve. "Come on, Jack. This isn't you. Something is going on that you're not telling me."

Like a little kid, Jack shook his head no. "I think I'm finally getting a grip on everything and it feels good."

As Warner hustled from room to room, Jack sensed the hint it was time to go. "Listen, Connie, I know you had your doubts about my project and I'm okay with that, but if in the future something does happen with it, would you consider helping me?"

Connie remembered back to the dinner with Ben and what Ben said. "Well, I know Ben was pretty sure the project was dead, but you're my best friend and I considered your father to be a second dad to me. So with that in mind, sure. I'll be glad to help you in any way."

Jack stood up and gave Connie a hug and shook his hand. "Be careful on your trip. Make sure you email me where you're going to be."

Just then, Warner emerged from the kitchen. "I know you weren't leaving without saying goodbye, Mr. Jack Kotter Jr."

As Warner wrapped her arms around Jack, he wished her the best. "I know we haven't exactly seen eye to eye lately, but you know I still love you, sweetie. You take care of Connie and make sure he stays out of trouble."

CHAPTER TWENTY-EIGHT

The next day, Jack was at work early. He even made it in before Ben. When Ben saw Jack's office door open, he didn't think anything of it. He thought maybe the cleaning crew left it open, until he walked in and saw Jack working hard at his desk.

"Who the hell are you and why are you sitting at Jack's desk?"

Jack looked up to see a bewildered Ben standing in front of him. "Ha, ha, Ben. Real funny guy you are. Grab some coffee and have a seat."

Ben turned to make some coffee then turned back around. "Wait a minute. Isn't it supposed to be me telling you to make coffee and have a seat? What the hell is going on around here?"

As Jack was printing out some paperwork, Ben poured himself a cup of coffee and added a touch of brandy. "I don't suppose you want a cup do you, kid?"

With a smile, Jack leaned back in his chair. "Hell, yeah, I do. I've been waiting all morning for you to get here so I could tell you to grab some coffee. And don't be stingy with the brandy."

After all the nonsense, it was time to get down to business. As Ben settled into his chair, Jack laid out some paperwork on the desk for him to look over. "I couldn't sleep a wink last night. It was so bad, I think I plucked Bria's last nerve, so I just came in here and started working on some plans this morning."

Ben grabbed some of the papers and relaxed back into his chair.

As he sipped his coffee, he read through some of the material and grunted every few seconds. Jack sat on the edge of his chair waiting for Ben to say something. Anything at all. Ben kept reading, but stood up and walked around, pacing the floor. By the time he was finished his coffee, he had read through several pages of ideas, pictures, and notes. The suspense was killing Jack, so with some anxiety, he stood up and waited.

"Come on, Ben, tell me what you think."

Ben stopped pacing and dropped his empty coffee cup in the trash can. "Unbelievable, kid. You actually came in early this morning and put this together to present to the board members?"

Jack felt like a little kid about to be scolded, but he stood strong and was ready to defend his ideas. Ben walked over to Jack and placed the papers on his desk. "These are solid ideas, kid. I would have never thought about coming at it from such a great angle. I'm impressed."

The relief Jack felt was like a huge weight off his shoulders. "Thanks, Ben. That means a lot coming from you."

Ben also felt good that he was able to commend Jack for his hard work. "Remember, kid, we have to make it past the board and then tackle the real problem: convincing all parties involved that it's a good idea to bring her up from her resting place."

After Ben left, Jack realized he hadn't been to sleep all night. He also knew he couldn't go home, because Bria would never leave him alone, so he did the next best thing. His father always had a comfortable sofa in his office just for those long, drawn out nights he would spend working. Jack quickly made his way down the hall before anyone else came to work. When he arrived at his father's office, he didn't waste any time slipping off his shoes and lying down. Only a few minutes went by and Jack was fast asleep.

Suddenly, with a twitching of the eyes and a brief moan, Jack was lost in a dream. He was floating in a lifeboat and Bria was floating next to him in a second lifeboat. Printed on the side of Jack's boat was the name RMS *Titanic* and the boat Bria was in bore the name *Marriage*. They were holding hands so they wouldn't separate and lose each other. It was dark and a thick fog started to roll in. For reasons unknown, their hands unlocked and they drifted apart. Jack yelled for Bria and tried desperately to sway his boat closer, but it was no use. Without saying a word, Bria drifted off into the dark fog until she was gone. Jack woke up and calmly sat up on the edge of the sofa. He wiped the sleep out of his eyes and took a few seconds to remember the dream. When he checked his watch, he realized the meeting was going to start soon.

Jack Sr. also had a personal restroom in his office, so Jack utilized it to freshen up before he made his presentation to the board. For once, everyone was on time and the meeting started when it was supposed to. Robert presented a few things concerning overseas business, then Ben stood up. He didn't really have anything to say. He just wanted to make sure nobody had any other business before Jack made his presentation.

"Alright, everyone, I know it's been a difficult time over the past few months, with all the extra meetings, the late nights, and the terrible takeout, so I apologize that tonight is going to be no different. So grab whatever drink or food you need and get comfortable. Jack has some business I think everyone is going to find very unbelievable, at best."

When Jack stood up, he was surprised to feel a sort of relief. All along he'd been carrying on his father's secret, trying to find ways to do the impossible project without anyone knowing, and that afternoon he was finally able to bring the huge secret out of the dark. He started his presentation with the story of his grandfather, Victor, and by the time he was finished, everything was out in the open. The mysterious box, the secret bank accounts, the *Titanic* project, and even the stories that were told by Winnifred Quick. The board members were astounded. Some of them had known Jack Sr. for a very long time and couldn't believe all that he was trying to accomplish. After Jack paused for a few minutes, he saw the looks on their faces and listened to all the whispers. Ben took the initiative to make Jack a stiff drink. After Jack downed it like it was juice, he came to the second half of his presentation.

"Alright, everyone. I know it's a lot to take in, but ever since Ben and I were able to figure out the puzzle, we've been going head to head. I would like to try to finish what my father started. It was something he obviously felt very compassionately about and I would like to be able to carry out his final wish. You now know my father already had the money set aside for the project. Unfortunately, there are several other obstacles to get over before anything happens. There are laws pending as we speak that are specific to *Titanic*. We don't know when they're going into effect. There is also the fact that the court system has ruled in favor of a certain New York company for sole salvage rights. Last but not least, with the recent attacks in New York, it's undetermined at this time how future events in the Middle East will affect our economy."

Ben called for a short recess, and Jack was more than glad to take a break. As the board members spoke among themselves, Jack sought Ben's opinion. "So, what do you think? Did I come off as sounding nuts?"

Ben smiled as he made himself a drink. "Well, I think you presented yourself very well, but the big test is going to come when you tell them what your plans are if you're successful at gaining their support."

Just then, Ethan came walking over. "I can't believe you didn't tell me anything about this, Jack. I thought our friendship extended further than this boardroom."

Without giving Jack a chance to respond, Ethan walked away. With a look of regret, Jack just stared at Ben. "Is it me or do I get crap thrown in my face every time I tell this story to somebody new?"

With a smile, Ben handed Jack another drink. "Don't worry about him, kid. You just stick to your A-game and you'll get through this."

As the meeting reconvened, there was still some whispering and grunting going on. With some interest, Kathy wound up asking the question that led Jack into the final part of his presentation. "I understand all the issues that are involved, including the moral issues, but let's say you're successful in your quest. What then? What are your plans for the ship?"

With some joy in his heart, Jack didn't waste any time tapping into the excitement he was feeling. "Well, I can't tell you what my father's plan was, but I know what I would do. My plan is to salvage every original piece we can then ship it back to New York, where I would have a team of shipbuilders try to put her back together the best they can. Obviously, some of the ship will have to be remanufactured. Eventually, over time, I would like to restore her back to her original beauty. If all goes well, maybe even sail her on her original route. After that, I'm not really sure. Maybe turn her into a floating museum. People will come from all around the world just to step onto the deck of the most famous ship of all time."

Once again, moans, groans, and whispers ran rampant through the room. Jack waited a few seconds then finished out the meeting. "Although proper procedure tells us to take a vote now, I'm not going to do that. The folders you have in front of you are yours to keep. They have all the information you need to make a decision. Take them home and go over them and we'll reconvene tomorrow and vote."

As the members of the board walked out, nobody said a word. Jack was expecting all kinds of questions, but there were none. Everyone quietly walked out leaving only Ben and Jack sitting at the table. Jack closed his briefcase with a smile and sat back in his chair. "Well, what do you think?"

Ben wasn't smiling. He didn't say anything. He stood up and walked over to the window. "I don't know, kid. Don't get me wrong. It was a great presentation, and I thought you really had them for a while, especially after you told the story Winnifred told us about Victor. I just wish you wouldn't have waited 'til tomorrow for a vote. That gives everyone too much time to think and reason everything out. I'll be honest with you, kid, I couldn't get a good read on anyone except Robert."

Jack walked over to the window and stood next to Ben. "What do you mean? Robert has already made his decision."

Ben thought for a few seconds as he glared out the window. "Listen, kid, there's a lot of 'what ifs' involved with this project. Let's say by some crazy chance we get the go-ahead to do what you want. If something happens, anything at all, it's going to fall back on to Kotter Industries. Make no bones about it, kid. By the time Robert is finished with you, you'll be standing on the corner with a cardboard sign that reads please shoot me."

CHAPTER TWENTY-NINE

LATER THAT NIGHT, JACK HAD DINNER PLANS WITH BRIA. LITTLE DID he know he was going to be in for another battle. After they ordered their food, Bria brought up the old taboo subject. "So, Jack Kotter, we keep coming to the same fork in the road. What about our future together? When am I going to see a ring?"

There was nothing Jack could do. He was trapped. "Come on, Bria. How many times do we have to have this argument? You know I'm working on some things and I just need some time."

Bria could feel her anger building because Jack always threw out the same old, tired excuse. "I know your dad was very important to you, and this project is something you really need to do, but come on, Kotter, you're the head of a corporation. You're always going to be busy with problems and projects. You can't keep using that as an excuse not to plan our future."

Jack didn't have a response. When the food finally came, they sat quietly and ate. Afterwards, Bria took a taxi home. When Jack arrived at his house, he was wide awake and anxious. He couldn't wait until the next day to see how the board would vote. He lay in bed looking up at the ceiling, thinking about the argument with Bria. She was right and he knew it, but he had more pressing issues to worry about.

The next day couldn't come fast enough. Jack rushed to work and prepared for the meeting. When Ben arrived, he wasn't very hopeful. "Well, kid, are you ready for the first obstacle?"

Jack tried to play it off and laugh. "I was ready when I walked out of here yesterday."

Slowly, the board members started to arrive. The atmosphere in the room was somewhat relaxed, which surprised Jack. He expected the tension to be thick, but instead, everyone seemed to be in good cheer. Ben started the meeting with a few unimportant memos then gave Jack the floor. Jack was ready and had a pretty good idea on how each person would vote, so he laid out his notes and jumped right in.

"Alright, everyone, there's no reason we need to dillydally around talking about it. You've all had time to go over the information in the packets I gave you, so let's put it to a vote. After you cast your vote, you can give an explanation or you can choose not to. I already have myself and Ben down as yeses. We'll start with Robert."

With his usual stuffy attitude, Robert cleared his throat and gave his answer. "I vote yes and that's all I'm going to say." After Jack marked his note pad, he moved on to Fitzgerald.

Always a lively soul, Fitzgerald was glad to speak up. "Your father was very good to me, Jack. He was an honest man and treated me like part of his family. I say yes." Jack marked more notes then called upon Anthony.

Anthony didn't say anything at first. He just stared at the table. He finally came up with the words he wanted to say. "I'm sorry, Jack. I have to vote no. Certainly nothing against your father, but with recent events in New York, we have to think about what effects if any it's going to have on this company."

Jack was surprised. He thought for sure Anthony would be with him, but he understood and accepted his reasoning. With some disappointment, Jack marked his notes.

"Alright, next is Jonathan."

With an arrogant smirk on his face, Jonathan spoke up. "Hell, yeah, Jack. I'm looking forward to seeing if you can pull this off." Jack knew that wasn't the real reason. It was greed for all the proceeds Jonathan was looking forward to.

"Alright, Stanley, what say you?"

Stanley wasn't much on drama. With him, it was always straight to the point. "I went through all the information you gave and it looks like a solid plan. I say yes." Stanley loved a good deal and that's what Jack counted on. Jack only needed one more vote in favor so he called on his friend Ethan.

After taking a sip of water and loosening his tie, Ethan gave his answer. "I gotta tell you, Jack. I'm not liking what I see. I think that money could be put to better use, instead of raising some old shipwreck off the bottom of the ocean just because it was the last wish of your dead father." Jack was stunned. He just stood staring with a blank look.

Ben jumped up, but before he could do anything, Anthony and Fitzgerald stepped in his way. Ben tried to force his way through at the same time, calling out obscenities. "You son of a bitch. Who the hell do you think you are?" When he realized Fitze and Anthony weren't going to let him through, Ben took a deep breath and backed off. "Someone get this punk out of here. Note his answer, Jack, and let's move on." As Ethan smiled and walked out, Jack was finally able to gather himself and noted the response given.

Ben noticed Jack was upset and thought it best the meeting take a break. During the break, Ben took Jack to his office and made some drinks. "Have a seat, kid. Don't worry about that ass. You're doing just fine."

Jack was still feeling very hurt, so he took a long swallow of his drink. "Here, Ben. Fill me up."

Ben took the glass and made another. "Come on, kid, you gotta snap out of it. Ethan is pissed off and he's taking his frustration out on this vote. Don't worry about him."

Jack took another drink, but this time, it was just a sip. "You don't understand, Ben. Ethan was one of the votes I needed to win the majority. I really don't think the others are going to see things my way."

Ben sat down and leaned back in his chair. "Well, kid, I don't know what else to tell you. I've been battling board members for many years. It's never a sure thing and there's no such thing as an easy battle. You were told by several people that there would be difficulties. Be ready to win, but also prepare yourself for defeat."

Jack perked himself up and downed the last of his drink. "Alright, let's go do this."

When they walked back to the board room, everyone but Ethan was already seated and waiting. Jack stood at the head of the table and continued on without skipping a beat. "Alright, this meeting is back in session, so let's move on. You're up next, William. Give us your vote."

William had the folder of information in his hand, acting like he was interested, but then he tossed it on the table like it was nothing. "My answer is no, Jack. It's not only bad business to keep secrets, but I just don't like the fact your father and now you want to use this company to work on some frivolous project."

All Jack could do was take it and smile. "Thank you for your honesty, William. Let's see what Richard says."

Richard didn't care too much about anything as long as his profit margin didn't decline. "It's going to be a no for me, Jack. Too many risks involved."

This didn't bother Jack. He expected shit from an ass. "Alright, Lewis. You're next."

For most of the meeting, Lewis had been slumped down in his seat, but he slowly pulled himself upright. "Sorry, Jack. I was up all night crunching the numbers you gave, and looking at the projection of profits, it just didn't add up. My answer is no." Jack had figured Lewis could go either way, but unfortunately, he had to note his answer in the negative column.

McKinnley Wilmington was the newest member of the board. Most of his time with Kotter Industries was spent managing some of the overseas facilities. This was another person Jack wasn't sure about. "Well, McKinnley, you can see that every vote is important. What say you?"

Although new to the boardroom, McKinnley wasn't new to business. "Well, Jack, I didn't know your father on a personal level, but the few times we did talk, he left a very good impression. I had genuine respect for your dad, but I have to say no. I just don't think it would be a very good idea at this time, given the circumstances of a questionable economy." Jack smiled and marked his note pad. He couldn't help but think to himself, *Poor guy. Probably doesn't know yet he's in a room full of wolves.*

Out of all the votes so far, his was probably the only honest one. Everyone else had ulterior motives. There was only one person left. Jack looked at his notes and saw the tally was even. Kathy was the only variable Jack was completely in the dark about. On one hand, she'd had a great friendship with his father and would do just about anything for him. On the other, she was a very shrewd businesswoman, which nobody, not even Ben, dared to mess with. Jack paused for a moment, thinking about how afraid he was around her when he was younger. After a cold shiver went up his spine, he gathered his nerves and moved forward. "This brings us to you, Kathy. You have the floor and the final vote."

Jack sat down in his seat and prepared himself for the worst. Kathy, who was actually looking through the material Jack supplied, placed the folder down on the table. When she stood up, she surprisingly walked over and stood next to Jack. With his nerves on edge, Jack slowly sunk into his chair.

Kathy stood with perfect ladylike posture as she prepared to give a little lesson in friendship and respect. "There's no doubt over the years we've all prospered from Kotter Industries. Jack Sr. was a kind and gentle man who was a friend to everyone, including the people in this room. He treated people like family and never had disgruntled feelings towards anybody. All this talk of raising *Titanic*, secret bank accounts, and stories of bravery come as quite a shock, and given all that has happened over the past few months, I know some of you might have reservations about starting such a massive project. There are moral issues involved, not to mention the fact that, like a fish out of water, we would be completely out of our element.

"Through the decades, we've pushed forward into new territories and taken advantage of new business opportunities. Most have worked in our favor and very few haven't. We're all in debt to Jack Sr., and I say we honor him by moving forward with this new business adventure and, hopefully, be able to give our friend the peace he so rightfully deserves. My vote is yes."

Kathy placed her hand on Jack's shoulder and gave a small

squeeze. When Jack glanced up, she shot him a big smile. Jack could feel the love and respect she had, not for him, but for his father.

When Kathy sat back down, Jack could have heard a pin drop. There were no whispers, grunts, or moans. All eyes were on Jack. Still feeling somewhat shocked, Jack stood up to address the board. "Thank you for your time, everyone. I know a lot of thought went into your decisions, and for those of you who voted yes, I appreciate your kindness and dedication. If no one else has any business to bring to the floor, I see no reason to keep us here any longer."

Before everyone could get up, Robert asked a question. "Just one thing, Jack. What if something does happen and we need that money for the company? Then what?"

Jack was caught off guard, but in any case, it was a valid question that had to be addressed. "I'm glad you asked, Robert. To be honest, I really haven't thought ahead that far. There are still many obstacles to get by, but if something were to happen, then this board would have to take another vote."

Robert agreed, so business was concluded and everyone left. Ben stayed behind as Jack gathered his paperwork and notes. "You did good, kid. I'm proud of you."

Jack just shook his head in frustration. "What the hell was Robert doing? He seems like a Dr. Jekyll and Mr. Hyde. One minute he's for you and the next minute he's not."

Ben picked up one of the folders that was left behind. He skimmed through it while he thought about what he was going to say. "Listen, kid, I told you before. If by chance this project takes off and something happens that reflects negatively on this company, then Robert is going to have a field day with you. Posing that question at the end of the meeting was just his way of warning you without actually warning you. It also gave him the chance to plant a seed for the board members to think about in the future."

Jack had been around and knew how things worked, but he never was able to get used to all the backstabbing and lies. "You know what, Ben? You really know how to throw a wrench into a good thing. With all your clout and connections, why can't you just make a phone call and make this project a reality?"

Ben knew Jack was only half-joking, but he decided to give a straight answer anyway. "Well, kid, I've had dealings all over the world, and I've made a lot of friends and even more enemies. I have contacts within contacts within contacts, and sometimes, none of that matters. Relax, kid, you just have to exercise some patience."

Jack left work feeling anxious. He thought back to when he was dealing with Lilith and how he felt like he was always looking over his shoulder, and now it felt the same to have Robert to deal with. Although Robert was supporting his idea, Jack knew he was just lurking in the shadows waiting for an opportunity to strike. He decided to try to call Ethan and maybe have dinner, but Ethan wouldn't answer his phone. Jack left several messages, but he was afraid they fell on deaf ears. He called Bria, but Bria was still upset over their last conversation, so he did the next best thing. He took a ride over to the mall to visit his friend Riley.

When he arrived, Riley had two patrons already occupying the seats, so Jack gave a polite wave and walked around the mall for a few minutes. It was actually perfect timing. He thought maybe he could find something nice for Bria as sort of an apology. While Riley huffed and buffed, Jack searched the jewelry stores. After browsing through and doing some window shopping, he realized unless it was a ring, Bria wouldn't be interested in jewelry.

On the way back to Riley's stand, he saw that a new store had opened up. They made carvings out of old beach wood, so Jack decided to take a look. After a few minutes, he noticed a small piece inside of a glass case. It was one solid piece carved into two hearts that intertwined. Jack thought it was interesting and asked the woman at the counter about it. The woman instantly became enthused and was eager to talk about the piece.

"How are you, sir? I'm so glad you're inquiring about this piece. It's my favorite. It represents two people who are in love and dedicate their lives to each other. Just like their love for one another, this piece is very delicate and needs to be handled with care." There was no hesitation at all. Jack made the purchase and asked the kind lady to wrap it up.

Afterwards, he walked back to Riley's stand, where Riley was waiting. "Hey, Jack. I figured you would be back soon. So, how are you?"

Jack hopped up into one of the chairs and stretched out his usual newspaper. "Well, old friend, I gotta tell you, my dad use to say life was full of ups and downs. He was absolutely correct. I always seem to be juggling several things at once. Every time I figure one out, another seems to collapse. And it just keeps going back and forth for me. If I could just line all my ducks up in a row just once, life would be pretty sweet."

Riley hopped up into the chair next to Jack and laughed. "I don't know why you think you have such a terrible life. You own the majority of one of the richest corporations in the world. That means you're sitting in the catbird seat, my friend. So, what's in the bag, if you don't mind me asking?"

Jack reached into the bag and pulled out the gift he bought Bria. "Since Ethan and Bobby Jo got engaged, Bria has really been pressing me about our relationship. She seems to think I'm turning out like my father. Married to my work instead of her."

Riley unwrapped the wooden hearts and admired them for few seconds, then handed them back to Jack. "It's nice you bought her a gift, but I have to agree with Bria. Money isn't an issue and neither is your commitment to each other, so why don't you marry her?"

Jack was a little surprised, but Riley was a good friend. "Wow. Are you serious? Has she been here talking to you? I can't believe you're asking me this. You of all people should know running a business takes up mega amounts of time. Especially a business like Kotter Industries. Besides, remember that project I told you about? Well, it's back on again. I can't really give you any details yet, because there are still some things pending."

Riley snatched the newspaper from Jack's hand then climbed down from his chair. With a displeasing look, he stood in front of him. "It seems like every time you have some sort of problem, you blame it on the fact that you have this huge corporation to run and you don't have time for anything else. There are many executives who lead busy lives but still have time for their wives and children, so please don't come in here anymore preaching to me about not being able to make a commitment."

Jack was stunned. He didn't know what to think. He climbed down from his chair and stood in front of Riley. "What's gotten into you, Riley? I can't ever remember a time when I've seen you angry at me."

Riley handed the newspaper back to Jack. "I'm not angry at all. I just think you need a swift kick in the ass. Stop making excuses all the time. You might find you can get more accomplished than you think."

Jack rolled up the newspaper and placed it under his arm. "Sorry, Riley, I didn't mean to burden you with my problems."

Riley spun Jack around and lightly kicked him in his tush. He then spun him back around and laughed. "There you go. That's your kick in the ass. You're my friend and I care about you. It just makes me angry that you have everything you could possibly ask for, including the woman of your dreams who would love nothing better than to spend the rest of her life with you, and yet you keep coming up with excuse after excuse why you can't make a commitment. Stop beating yourself down and just live the dream life that was meant for you."

Jack glanced down at the gift he'd bought. He thought for a few seconds and smiled. "You're right, Riley. I shouldn't let Kotter Industries dictate my life. I have the most wonderful woman in the world and a lifestyle that would make the rich and famous jealous. I wish you could walk in my shoes for a day and feel what I feel, but knowing you, you would probably come up with solutions to my problems."

Riley laughed as he once again grabbed Jack and twisted him around. He slightly booted Jack in the rear then twisted him back around. "Before you ask, I'll tell you why. You took on that crazy Lilith and you were damn lucky you didn't get hurt. Next time, let the police do their job. You're the owner of Kotter Industries, not the Caped Crusader."

Jack smiled as he shook Riley's hand. "Alright, Riley, I get it. I can't make you any promises, but I get what you're saying. Thanks for the talk and the kick in the ass."

Jack left the mall and made a beeline for Bria's house. He couldn't wait to tell her about the meeting. When he arrived, he had the gift behind his back, but when Bria opened the door, Jack saw she had been crying. Jack's feelings of joy quickly turned to worry. "Bria, what's wrong? Did something happen?"

Jack attempted to hold her, but she pushed him away. "Bobby Jo called a little while ago. She said she and Ethan had a conversation and she thought it best we didn't come to their wedding. When I asked her why, she started crying. She said it wasn't her idea then Ethan got on the phone. He said you still plan to go after that damn shipwreck."

By that point, Jack could feel his anger starting to grow. "What the hell does that have to do with their wedding?"

Bria grabbed a glass of wine from the table and took a drink. She then picked up an almost empty wine bottle and poured the rest in her glass. She took a breath then another drink to calm herself down. "Ethan said he wasn't comfortable having false friends share the most important day of his life. Damn it, Jack. What the hell did you do?"

With a heavy sigh, Jack sat down. "I didn't do anything. Remember back when we met with Connie and Ben to discuss my project? Well, as usual, Ben didn't lay all of his cards on the table. He recently told me several countries are contemplating laws specifically for *Titanic*. He said after everything is official, there might be a way to actually use the laws to our advantage, so we could go through with the project. We held a meeting earlier today and took a vote."

Bria downed the last of her wine then opened another bottle. "What is wrong with you people? How the hell can you vote on something that hasn't even happened yet?"

Jack stood up and took the bottle of wine. "Don't you think you've had enough?"

Still holding the gift in one hand, he took the bottle to the kitchen then came back. "Listen to me. Ethan is upset because he didn't know the whole story about my dad and everything Ben and I were doing after we opened that box. He doesn't understand all that was private until Ben and I put all the puzzle pieces together and figured it out. And even then, there was nothing definite, so there really wasn't anything to tell."

Bria walked to the kitchen and came back with the bottle of wine. "First off, you might be the owner of Kotter Industries, but in my household, I'll determine when I've had enough. Second, you're the only one who wants to do this project, Jack. Why can't you just let it go?"

Jack watched as Bria drank more wine. "I came over here tonight hoping you would understand and be happy for me."

Bria gawked as she slammed the glass down on the table. "Happy for you? I was supposed to be one of the bridesmaids, Jack, and now I'm not even invited to the wedding. You're losing everything that's important and you keep drifting further and further away from me." Bria tried to wipe the tears from her eyes. "How the hell am I supposed to be happy?"

Through all the arguing and crying, Jack remembered the dream he'd had of Bria drifting away in the lifeboat, but quickly realized he was the one drifting away. "I'm sorry, Bria, but if there's just a small chance I can fulfill my father's dying wish, then I'm going to try my best to do it." Jack walked over and handed the double heart to Bria. "I bought this for you earlier today. I thought maybe we could celebrate tonight, but I'm guessing that's out of the question."

Emotionally drained, Jack walked out and went home. He tried several times to call Ethan, leaving messages each time, but Ethan wouldn't return his calls. Jack was finally able to fall asleep, but there was no relief from his stress. Jack's emotional day haunted his sleep and turned his dream into another nightmare. As his eyes flickered and his sleep deepened, a dream started to form.

Jack was on a large pier filled with people looking out into New York Harbor at an anchored *Titanic.* All the people he cared about were on the top deck. They were all lined up waving with smiles on their faces. Suddenly, *Titanic* sank and his friends disappeared under the water. Everyone started to clap and cheer as a celebration broke out. As Jack watched in horror, his father and Victor approached him from behind. They were happy and shook his hand as to thank him for a job well done.

Jack woke up in a cold sweat and realized just how out of control his life had become. The rest of the night, he sat and weighed his friends against what he considered a family obligation. As the sunrise came and went, he was no closer to a solution. After a cold shower and several cups of coffee, he decided to take a ride over to see Ethan, hoping they could talk.

When he arrived, Bobby Jo answered the door. "I don't think it's a good idea for you to be here, Jack. Ethan is still pretty upset with you."

Before Jack could say anything, Ethan came to the door. "Why are you at my house, Jack? Anything you have to say can be said at the office."

Jack wasn't there to argue, but he wasn't going to back down from what he thought was right. "Come on, Ethan, you really think this is something to lose our friendship over?"

With that said, Ethan became even angrier. "No, you come on, Jack. You were my friend and I looked up to you. Obviously your father had some kind of plan, and he had every right to, but he's gone and whatever plan he had went with him. You, on the other hand, are here, and now you're trying to play God with people's livelihoods by trying to resurrect something that should be left alone. If you would have come to me and explained the situation like a friend would have done, then maybe I could have had a little more compassion for you. I could have been more prepared going into that meeting, and, just maybe, I would have voted your way. Instead, my ass was left flapping in the wind and I wound up looking like a damn fool."

By that time, Bobby Jo had faded back into the house. Jack definitely heard the anger in Ethan's voice, but he also could hear the hurt. "I'm sorry, Ethan. You're right. I consider you and me to be the best of friends, but I just didn't think it was important enough at the time to tell you. It was something of a personal nature, between my dad and me, and I needed to try to figure it out on my own."

Surprisingly, Ethan stood in the doorway listening, but he still wasn't feeling any better. "Listen, Jack, you didn't figure anything out on your own. I know Ben was involved, because there's no way he would have even let it get as far as a vote if he wasn't. I also know Connie was in town recently and he specializes in deep sea diving. That's not just a coincidence, so save your lies for someone that wants to listen to them. My house isn't Kotter Industries, so from now on, anything you need to say can be said at the office."

Jack was out of words and Ethan knew it. Without saying anything more, Ethan shut the door in Jack's face. Jack left feeling just as bad as he had the day before with Bria. He went to work thinking the day's activities would give him some kind of relief, but they didn't. He decided to leave work early and take a trip to the cemetery. The long drive felt good. *Fringe* had just been tuned up at the 110 Garage and she purred as Jack let loose on the highway. When he finally arrived at the grave site, there were fresh flowers on all the graves. Even the one reserved for Victor. This was puzzling. Jack was unaware of anyone besides himself who would take the time to visit the graves.

He sat for a while thinking about his father. Although there was still a chance the project would never get started, he knew if it did, he would have to try his best to make it work.

Jack left the graveyard feeling more determined than ever. He made his way back to town and decided to treat himself to a night out. He took a ride downtown to the Blue Water Grill. A great restaurant with cool jazz made for a nice night. Bria wasn't a fan of jazz, so it had been a while since Jack's last visit. With all that was going on, it was a perfect night to sit and listen to the house band play some soothing melodies. As the night progressed, Jack became more and more relaxed. Finally, it was last call, but that was okay. Jack knew the owner and sat around for another hour talking. When it came time to leave, it was early morning and Jack realized he'd drunk way too much, so he called Ben.

Ben was busy having his own little soiree with two dancers, so he sent Casey with the limo. When Casey arrived at the club, he had to help Jack into the backseat. The next day when he awoke, Jack could hardly remember anything. He finally made it to the office where Ben was waiting for him. With a smile on his face, he handed Jack a very large cup of coffee. "So, kid, pretty wild night?"

With his eyes bloodshot and barely open, Jack took a sip of coffee. "No, it wasn't like that. Bria and I are arguing again, and then on top of that, I tried to talk with Ethan, but he didn't want to listen. Now Ethan doesn't want either one of us at his wedding. Why the hell does life have to be so difficult? I thought rich people didn't have problems. What the hell am I going to do, Ben? I have to follow through with this, but at the same time, I'm losing everyone I care about."

Many times Ben found himself stepping into Jack Sr.'s shoes, and this situation was definitely a hard one to figure out. "Listen, kid, I know this has been a raw deal for you. I know you think I was just being practical when I told you to drop the whole idea of trying to complete your father's dream, but there was more. Something like this tears at the fabric of your life. You have to weigh the ins and outs when it comes to moral issues like this, and right now, I'm seeing nothing positive if you decide to go through with it. I will tell you this, I'm on the fence. I'll support whatever decision you make."

Jack didn't reply. He slowly turned and walked out. By the end of the day, he still felt horrible, and he was no closer to solving his problems.

When he arrived home, Bria was there waiting. Jack was surprised, but welcomed the opportunity to talk. "I thought you were still mad. What are you doing here?"

Bria wasn't in her usual playful mood, but she was calm enough to talk. "Well, after drinking myself to sleep, I woke up feeling guilty. I guess I finally realized the position your father put you in and how hard of a struggle you've been having lately. I don't blame you for not telling Ethan, and he should have been a good enough friend to understand. As for Bobby Jo, I know Ethan is pulling her strings, so I'm not blaming her for anything. I gotta tell you, Jack Kotter, I don't agree with disturbing that ship, but the only way I'll stand behind you is if you keep me informed. I'm getting tired of being out of the loop. I love you, Jack Kotter, and that should give me total access to you." With her soft touch, Bria walked over and grabbed Jack by his pants. "By the way, I loved the double heart you gave me." After a long passionate kiss, she led him upstairs to the bedroom.

The rest of the week was pretty standard. Business meetings, paperwork, delegating authority. When Friday came, Jack received an email from Connie. It was a letter informing him that he'd married Warner in a small Greek ceremony. There were a few pictures and an apology. Connie explained that it was a spur of the moment thing and that they were very happy together. Jack was happy for them, but decided for the time being to try to keep the news from Bria.

CHAPTER THIRTY

As the year progressed, Kotter Industries stayed strong, always vigilant of the idea the economy could eventually weaken. Every now and then, Jack tried to fix his relationship with Ethan, but Ethan considered the friendship to be over. He was content with keeping everything on a professional level. Eventually, Ethan and Bobby Jo's wedding took place and Bria was saddened by the fact she couldn't attend. Although she accepted the fact she played second fiddle to Kotter Industries, Bria still pressed Jack for a stronger commitment, but he always gave the same argument of company first.

During a mundane morning, Jack was sitting in his office contemplating his day and feeling quite bored. He decided to walk down to Ben's office and discuss the recent news of the space shuttle *Columbia*. It had disintegrated during reentry, killing all seven astronauts. Since Kotter Industries was still a strong force in the space industry, it was important to discuss the ramifications of any potential negative impact on the company. After having some friendly conversation along the way, Jack found himself at Ben's office door. Without thinking, he gave a hefty knock. He then opened the door and peeked in. Ben was on the phone and waved him in.

While Jack made himself a drink, Ben finished up his conversation on the phone. "Hey, kid, you're really getting good at that whole knocking thing. It's about damn time. While you're over there, go ahead and make me a nice stiff one. I've already had three, but what the hell. If drinking hasn't killed me by now, then it probably never will."

Jack laughed as he made the drinks. "After all the abusive things you've done to yourself over the years, I doubt anything will ever kill you." Jack handed Ben his drink and toasted him. "Here's to grabbing your dreams by the ass and holding on for dear life."

After one gulp, Ben's drink was gone. "Sit down, kid. We need to talk."

Jack took a deep breath as he sat down. He finished off his drink as he prepared himself for a serious discussion. "I can't believe it. What a disaster. Twenty-eight missions and now she's gone, along with her crew."

Ben shook his head in disbelief. "Yeah, kid, I remember when they started building her. Kotter Industries won most of the bids for supplying the building materials. But listen, that's not what I want to talk to you about."

Jack was already on the edge of his seat. Usually Ben went into depth about proceeding forward, especially after anything that connected Kotter Industries to a disaster. "So if not the space shuttle, then what?"

It was nothing new to Jack that Ben always looked serious, but there was something else. A look that Jack had rarely seen. "Well, kid, that little toast you did earlier was more appropriate than you think. Right before you came in, I was on a conference call with several high up officials. Who they are is unimportant at this time. What is important are those guidelines for *Titanic* we spoke about in the past. Looks like we might be able to work something out."

Jack heard the words, but he didn't have the breath to react right away. After a brief pause, he was finally able to speak. "Please tell me this isn't one of your distasteful pranks."

Ben stood up and walked over to the bar. He made two more drinks and handed one to Jack. "Here's to grabbing your dreams by the ass and holding on for dear life."

While Ben wolfed down his drink, Jack just sat in his chair feeling numb. "Are you serious, Ben? This is really going to happen?"

Before Jack could jump for joy, Ben quickly placed a hold on any celebration. "Listen, kid, the battle has just begun. Those officials I was telling you about only represent the five territories that made up the guidelines. Remember, you still have to give the executive board a chance to vote on it again. Then you have to deal with the company that has the salvage rights. Then there's always the fun-loving press that will condemn you to hell once they find out what you're trying to do. And last but not least, I would think any survivors or relatives of survivors would have something to say about it."

Jack didn't have an answer for any of what Ben was saying. "Damn you, Ben. Why do you do that? You give me this great news in order to get my hopes up and then you tell me about all the rings of fire I have to jump through. Sometimes I think you really get off on watching me suffer."

Ben smiled and let out a small laugh. "What are you talking about, sometimes? I get off all the time when I'm watching you faced with difficulties. Come on, kid, it's not the problem that makes or breaks us. It's how we react to the problem that makes us who we are. Now, it's decision time, kid. What are you going to do?"

With some vigor in his heart, Jack thought for a few seconds. "Well, I guess I'm gonna have to get my ducks lined up in a row. If I had to, I would guess it's safe to say you've already done the homework on the company that owns the salvage rights."

Ben didn't answer. He just gave a reaffirming smile. "Keep going, kid."

Jack continued on with his mental notes. "The media is going to have to be suppressed. I think our public relations department is equipped to handle that. At the same time, that will take care of any public scrutiny. As for the board, that's where the work begins. A lot of time has passed. Everybody might not feel the same as they did before."

Ben smiled with pride. "I gotta tell you, kid, sometimes when I watch you work, it's like watching your dad. I'm proud of you, kid. I'm guessing that you're going all the way with this."

Jack picked his drink up and downed it. "Hell, yeah, I can't stop now."

Jack left work with mixed feelings. He was happy about the project, but he still had to face Bria. After stopping by the Wiley

Roadster for a bite to eat, he made his way home, where Bria was waiting on the porch.

"Welcome home, Jack Kotter. I've been waiting for you." While still sitting, she grabbed Jack by his pants and started tugging, but Jack wasn't in the mood.

"Hold on, Bria. We need to talk."

Bria didn't stop though. She kept trying to pull Jack towards her. "What's wrong, Jack Kotter? Isn't this where you were seduced by that bitch Linda?"

With some anger, Jack pulled away. "What's wrong with you? I think sometimes you can really be warped in the brain."

Still angry, Jack walked inside the house with Bria following. "What's wrong, Jack Kotter, bad day at work?"

Jack suddenly turned and gave Bria a passionate kiss. "No, not at all. Actually, that's what I wanted to talk to you about. Would you like to sit down or stand while I tell you the news?"

Usually, Bria welcomed any kind of news from Jack because she enjoyed the communication, but this time, she could hear something in his voice. She grabbed Jack by the hand and sat down. "Well, I'm sure you're going to tell me no matter what I do, so what is it?"

Jack wasn't interested in beating around the bush, so he just came out with it. "Do you remember when I told you about the guidelines that were being created for *Titanic*? Well, apparently, it's a done deal. Ben says there might be a chance to proceed, which means I have to try to make it happen."

By that point, Bria was tired of trying to fight Jack on the subject, so she decided to switch gears and try to support him. "So, now what's the hold up?"

Jack was pleasantly surprised. He'd expected another blowup. "Well, we're going to have to review the guidelines to see if there are any loopholes we can exploit. Then there's the board. It has to be voted on."

Bria was smiling on the outside, but she was torn on inside. "I thought you won the vote already."

Still thinking about the other obstacles, Jack continued his thoughts. "We did, but too much time has passed and now other variables are involved."

Bria sat back in a relaxed position and stared into Jack's eyes. "Okay, I'm not going anyplace, so let's hear it. Maybe I can help you think of some solutions."

Jack was enjoying this side of Bria. Although he doubted she could help, he decided to take advantage of her newly found attitude. "Well, let's see. I'm not too worried about the guidelines. Ben is top-notch when it comes to maneuvering around the law. Although the members of the board voted in my favor once, that doesn't mean they'll do it again, but I'm not too concerned, especially with Ben on my side. The media can be handled, but once it gets out, it's the public opinion that could eventually be the biggest problem."

Bria sat rubbing Jack's inner thigh hoping to distract him, but when she saw it wasn't working, she sat up and blurted out her thoughts. "What about the guy who found the ship? I thought the law says whoever finds shipwrecks gets to do whatever they want with them."

Suddenly, the proverbial light bulb lit up in Jack's head. All kinds of thoughts ran through his mind as he contemplated some theories. "You might be on to something. I'm not sure what kind of role the original people who discovered the wreck play, if any, but it's definitely an idea worth exploring." With his newly found excitement, Jack decided to take Bria up on fulfilling her sexual needs.

The next day, Jack decided to take the day off and do some research of his own. After spending the day at the library researching maritime law, he had one last piece of the puzzle to take care of. Setting up a meeting with Dr. Robert Ballard. Jack rarely went to see Ben at his house, because he never knew what kind of exploits Ben was into, but he couldn't wait until the next work day. Luckily, when he arrived, Ben was sitting on his front porch sipping on wine.

"Hey, kid, something must be wrong, because you never come here just to visit."

With some excitement on his face, Jack stepped up onto the porch and sat down. "Listen, Ben, I've been doing my homework and I wanted to run some ideas by you."

Ben breathed a long sigh as he poured Jack some wine. "Listen, kid, I know your dad and I taught you to work hard, but sometimes you just have to take a break. If you keep going full speed, you're gonna crash and burn."

Jack was wound up tight so he took a drink of wine to calm his nerves. "Bria and I were talking last night and she came up with the idea of talking to Dr. Ballard. I think if we can get him on board with the plan, there won't be any type of opposition."

Ben downed his glass of wine and thought for a few seconds. "You're getting pretty good at this, kid. I think you're right. Not about being opposed, but about having Dr. Ballard's endorsement. I think his opinion would carry a lot of weight."

Ben stood up and walked into the house, then he emerged a few minutes later with some official-looking documents. "Listen, kid, take a look at this. It cost me a favor, but I had a friend of mine get ahold of the final draft of those guidelines. I think you're going to find them favorable."

With some enthusiasm, Jack skimmed through the paperwork. "This looks really good, Ben. I can't believe you were able to get your hands on this. I think we should meet in your office tomorrow so we can start putting together a plan."

Ben poured two more glasses of wine and handed one to Jack. "Sure, kid, but first, I want you to sit here and relax. Let's enjoy the breeze and talk about something other than work."

Jack couldn't help but see Ben was getting tired. Not just fatigued, but affected by life starting to take its toll.

The next day, Jack was in Ben's office bright and early. It wasn't long before drinking mixed together with the reviewing of laws. Although Ben had loads of knowledge when it came to interpreting laws, he had Lawrence Winder sit in to oversee the meeting. In order for Lawrence to understand the reason Ben was in possession of legal documents not yet made available to the public, Jack had to once again explain his father's secret life. Afterwards, Lawrence had several drinks to try to process the story.

"I don't know what to say, Jack. I like to think your dad and I were good friends. All the years we knew each other and he never once seemed to have any other interest besides Kotter Industries. What a fantastic story."

Ben ordered some food and everyone settled in for a long study session. Lawrence had some of his associates fax over various laws concerning the ocean, including the UN Convention on the law of the sea. Jack dusted off all the research he did for retrieving sunken vessels. At the end of an exhausting day, it was time to combine opinions, notes, and law, then role it all into one bundle.

Lawrence made some drinks then made a toast. "Here's to Jack Kotter Sr. A man with vision."

It was a nice toast, but after Jack took a drink, he asked Lawrence to elaborate. Lawrence thought for a minute before answering. "Well, Jack, I think your dad had the foresight to understand that if or when *Titanic* was ever found, there would be many questions, arguments, and controversies. With all his financial preparation, he must have somehow known he could get around all the red tape."

Jack looked bewildered, but worse, Ben also looked a little perplexed. "I'm an educated man, Lawrence, but I'm also tired and half-drunk, so can you give it to us in layman's terms?"

Lawrence stood up and stretched out all of his kinks. He picked up the outline of the laws concerning *Titanic*. "In layman's terms, I have good news and bad news. Which do you want first?"

With some disappointment, Jack just shrugged his shoulders. "Isn't that always how it is? Well, you might as well give us the bad news."

Lawrence pulled out his notepad and set forth the problems Jack was facing. "Alright, going over everything I could get my hands on, including these documents illegally in Ben's possession, there are a few problems you need to be aware of before you do anything. Funding the project. According to the guidelines, proof of adequate funding has to be provided. This means funding from beginning to end and then whatever follow-up needs to be completed. Second, you need a timeline. The timeline is based on when you start and a reasonable time of completion. The biggest problem you face, and the most important, are human remains. These laws are very specific about disturbing any human remains that are found."

Before Jack responded, he noticed Ben looked a little worried, so he thought carefully before he spoke. "Well, I know the funding isn't an issue and the timeline can probably be worked out, but why would human remains still be down there? I would think by now that wouldn't be an issue. What do you think, Ben?"

Ben sat up in his chair and pulled some papers from his desk drawer. "Well, kid, I've also done my homework. I can see why so many people are fascinated over this shipwreck. We all know that it split in two when it sank. The stern and the bow lay 2,000 feet apart from one another, facing in opposite directions. Here's a really interesting fact. As the stern sank to the bottom, there was air still trapped inside, so the deeper it sank, the more pressure built up. Ultimately, it imploded. From a salvage point of view, that's going to be your worst nightmare. The bow is another story. It flooded before it's decent to the bottom, so it's roughly still intact, which means it's a good possibility there could still be some kind of remains within the ship. Obviously, there's no way to be sure."

After Ben finished speaking, there was a quiet in the room. A sort of moment of silence out of respect. After reviewing all the negative aspects, Lawrence once again pulled out his notes so he could lighten the mood. "Alright, now that you've heard the bad, it's time for the good. The ship was declared to be irretrievable; therefore, it's become fair game for anyone. This is where all the lawsuits come into play. As you know, RMS Titanic, Incorporated won the salvage rights, but only to the debris field. The ship itself has to be left alone. Everything within these guidelines revolves around preservation for future generations. That's the kicker."

Lawrence could tell Jack was still waiting for the punch line. "You're looking a little confused, Jack. I'm guessing you're not getting the point."

Jack smiled because Lawrence was right. "I understand what you're saying, but I'm not seeing how this helps my cause."

Feeling his mouth to be dry, Lawrence paused. "For another shot of that bourbon, I'll tell you."

Jack was eager to hear the plan, so he poured the drink quickly and handed to Lawrence. Afterwards, Lawrence proceeded to educate Jack. "There have been some studies over the years about the deterioration of the ship. Scientist estimate it could be twenty to fifty years before *Titanic* is just an orange spot on the ocean floor. Because these documents are about preservation, it wouldn't take much of an argument to convince everyone involved that it would be of greater value to bring the ship to the surface rather than let her wither away to nothing until she is gone forever. This is where Ben comes in. I'm sure he has the connections and resources to do just that."

It had been a long day and everyone was tired. There wasn't anything much more to say, so Lawrence said his goodbyes and left. Jack was left feeling somewhat good, but as usual, Ben was the key to the success of the project. Everything was riding on his decision to help. It was Friday, so Jack decided he wasn't going to push the matter, so he suggested they take the weekend to think about what Lawrence had said. Ben was in total agreement, so the two had one last drink together and went home.

The next morning, Jack was up early making breakfast for Bria. Not that she wasn't grateful, but she had some reserve. "I take it your meeting went well yesterday?"

Jack was all smiles, but he knew there was still a chance Ben wouldn't go through with it. He plopped down some banana nut pancakes with sausage in front of Bria. The smell always mesmerized her.

"Hmm, my favorite. So, what's the occasion?"

With excitement in his voice, Jack told her about the meeting. Bria tried to be happy for him, but she knew once the project was started, Jack would engross himself in it. "So, I take it you're just waiting on Ben to give you the go ahead."

Jack took a drink of coffee and washed down some food. "Yeah, pretty much. There's still the board to contend with, but I'm trying to stay optimistic."

After breakfast, Bria went her own way while Jack prepared for a trip to the graveyard. There was still the question of the mysterious flowers.

A few hours later, Jack pulled into the graveyard and headed for the cemetery office. The caretaker knew nothing about the flowers and the office personnel had never noticed anyone out of the ordinary at the grave sites. The sites were towards the rear of the graveyard under some trees, so it wouldn't be too hard for someone to come and go and not be seen. As Jack drove slowly through the narrow paths, he could see off in the distance somebody standing at the graves. As he walked closer, he could see the person kneeling down placing flowers on one of the graves. When Jack approached, the person stood up and turned around. It was Ben. He was wearing a long somber face.

"What are you doing here, kid?"

After the initial shock, Jack was able to gather some words. "I should be asking you that question. It's you that's been placing flowers on the graves. I never knew you came up here." Ben turned back around as to finish a prayer while Jack watched in silence.

After Ben was finished, they walked back to Jack's car. Jack looked around wondering how Ben traveled to the graveyard. "I don't see your car. How did you get here?"

As he pulled out his handy-dandy flask, Ben leaned against *Fringe*. "Here, kid, have a swig. I hate driving all the way up here, so I have Casey drop me off. Some time ago, he met some chic down at the roadside bar, so he spends time down there while I sit and visit a while."

After taking a drink and making several faces, Jack handed the flask back to Ben. "So, why the big secret?"

Ben screwed the lid back on the flask and placed it back into his jacket. "No secret, kid. Am I supposed to place an ad in Time Square every time I pay my respects? Come on, kid, they were my family too. I loved your father and mother. After Sergis died, they were all I had. I've been coming up here for years. Sometimes to talk out decisions with your father. I've spent many days up here trying to figure out what to do. Ever since we opened that damn box, I've been spending more and more time here."

Jack took a load off and leaned against the car next to Ben. "I'm sorry, Ben. I've always admired your toughness and ability to make the difficult decisions. I didn't know you were still struggling with this."

Ben stood quiet momentarily then confided in Jack. "Listen, kid, I'm not the rock that you think I am. Your dad was a rock. Sergis was a rock. Even your mother had a built-in toughness about her. They're all gone and it's just me now. My thoughts keep referring back to what your dad and Sergis taught me. Company first. Always keep the employees' best interest at heart, and over the years, I've done just that. I just can't get over the fact that through all those years of hard work, your dad was off on some secret quest and didn't tell anyone. I know I said I would support whatever your decision was, but now that it's time, I find myself still struggling to decide whether or not to complete your father's last wish. I'm getting old, kid and I'm just not that strong anymore."

Ben could feel the water building up in his eyes. To say the least, it was difficult for him to let Jack know how he really felt. "I'm sorry, kid. I don't mean to lay all this on you. Everything was a lot easier when your dad was alive. I keep coming back here wondering if I'm doing the right thing, but my reasoning always has the same results."

This was definitely not the right time to push Ben into something, so Jack kept listening.

As Ben kept talking, the burden he was carrying seemed to go away. "I keep thinking about Old Salty and how Both he and your dad would take those trips. When we were on Salty's boat listening to him tell his story, I became envious. After you excused yourself, Salty and I talked some more. He asked me not to get in the way of you completing what your dad started, but I let my emotions get in the way and I blew you off. Then there was Winnifred Quick. I'm glad you didn't notice, but I almost fell off my seat when she told us that incredible story. I tried to play it off like it was no big deal, but I have to tell you, kid, my conscience was really hurting me that day. I've been coming up here thinking I could convince myself that I'm doing the right thing by not going through with it, but like I said, my reasoning just isn't working out."

After Ben was finished talking, Jack could tell there was some kind of peace about him. He didn't know how to react, but he dared to ask the question. "So, now what?"

Ben smiled then let out a refreshing laugh. "So now we go get that ship." Just then, Ben's phone rang. It was Casey wondering if it was going to be awhile before his services were needed. Perfect timing for Ben. "Hey, Casey, don't worry about me. Jack is here and I'll catch a ride back with him, as long as he doesn't crash me into a pole." After Ben hung up, he let out a small laugh. "Usually Casey will wait for me to call, but obviously, he has an agenda. About time. He's been trying to get his noodle wet ever since he met that girl."

It was a long ride back, but a good one. The stress Jack had been feeling for so long was gone, and Ben was so relaxed he talked about everything under the sun, except business.

CHAPTER THIRTY-ONE

When Monday morning arrived, Jack and Ben went back to their normal hustle and bustle of scheduled meetings and Kotter business. When the business decisions were done, it was time to really get to work. Ben made dozens of phone calls while Jack picked up where he had left off in regards to researching deep sea salvage. By the end of the day, Jack was exhausted and Ben was making arrangements to fly out that night. Before he left for the airport, he stopped by to see Jack. "Listen, kid, I've been on the phone all afternoon, but I still have to iron out a few details. I have to fly out tonight."

Jack knew whenever Ben made last minute plans to fly someplace, it was usually adventurous. He was up and out of his seat faster than he could say "kid at Christmas." "So, where are you going? Can I go?"

As he smiled and laughed, Ben felt a warm fatherly feeling. "Just like the old days, kid. Whenever your dad and I had to take care of business overseas, you were always volunteering yourself to go. Sorry, kid, not this time. I'm flying out tonight to smooth over some problems I'm having with the French."

As the bottom lip of Jack's mouth dropped, his eyes grew really big. "France? You're going to France? Come on, Ben, I've always wanted to go there. Come on, Robert can take care of anything that goes on here."

Ben put his arm around Jack as if to say okay, but then smiled as he gave the bad news. "No, you have to hold down the fort. Robert is going to meet me there in a couple of days. Sorry, kid." As Ben turned to walk out the door, he turned and gave Jack one last shot. "Tell you what I'll do for you, though, when I visit the red light district, I'll kiss one of those pretty little French girls for you."

Exhausted and hungry, Jack made a beeline for the Wiley Roadster. When he arrived, he saw Riley, the Mopar brothers, Paul, and Oliver all having a good time. So many polished cars and tricked out trucks graced the parking lot of the Wiley Roadster, but when Jack pulled onto the lot with *Fringe*, everyone sat up and took notice. It was such a beautiful car, not to mention that it was also a movie car driven by John Wayne. As usual, the Mopar brothers were chasing the women, and being the grease monkeys that they were. Paul and Oliver were walking the lot checking out everyone's rides like it was a car show. Of course they'd brought the Ferrari that took down Lilith, and they allowed everyone to take a turn sitting behind the wheel. With some nice shades on, cool and quiet Riley just kicked back and relaxed while he chomped down on a burger.

After ordering some food, Jack sat and talked with Riley. "Can I ask you a question?"

As he stared at Jack, Riley was enjoying his last bite. Afterwards, he took a drink to wash it down. "Jack, there's only three things I don't fool around with. My work, the love of a beautiful woman, and Wiley Roadster's burgers. So now that I'm finished, go ahead and ask away."

After his initial laugh, Jack asked his question. "If you had a chance to rewrite history, would you do it?"

Riley thought for a few seconds then scratched his head. "What'ya mean, any history or my personal history?"

Jack didn't answer right away. He thought about it then responded. "Well, let's say events that happened in the past that had a profound effected on society."

Riley sucked on his straw until the last bit of cola was gone and the air and ice that was left in his cup made a gargle sound. He then bent down and picked up an old rusty nail and placed it in his pocket. "Well, Jack, I guess I look at it this way. If I can prevent something from happening, like picking a nail up off the ground so somebody doesn't run it over, then I'm okay with that. If you're talking about going back in time to change something that's already happened, then I would say no. Whether good or bad, we learn valuable information from our history so we can do better in the future."

Jack pondered Riley's answer and understood his reasoning. "Fair enough."

Sometimes Jack would ask Riley for advice when he was working on something and Riley would tell him honest thoughts, but this time, the question had Riley intrigued. "So, what's up, Jack? You've been hinting at something for a long time. You wanna give me some kind of idea of what you're working on?"

Jack thought for a few seconds and smiled. "Well, I have to jump through a couple more hoops, but when I'm finished, I'll treat you to dinner and tell you the whole story."

The rest of the week was spent with Bria. Since Ben was gone, Jack decided to work on his relationship. Bria even helped scan the internet for salvage information. By the end of the week, Jack had most of the information he needed to start the project. The only thing left to do was to wait for Ben to get back to take it to the board.

When Ben and Robert finally did arrive back in town, Jack wasted no time in sending Casey to the airport to pick them up. Of course Jack went along for the ride. When Ben and Robert climbed into the limo, Ben noticed Jack could hardly contain his excitement. "Alright, kid, go ahead. I know you're dying to pick our brains, so ask away."

As the limo pulled off, Jack made some drinks. "I don't want to pick your brains, I just want to know the lowdown on why both of you had to go to France." Ben was suffering from jet lag, so he laid his head back and let Robert do the talking.

"Back in 1980, France was having some difficult times with unemployment. Their unemployment rate was at an all-time high. The president's economic policy wasn't very popular. As usual, your dad saw opportunity amongst crisis. We had had conversations in the past about trying to expand into the European market, but we just couldn't get a foothold. We had some small potatoes stuff going on over there, but nothing of significance. Anyway, your dad didn't waste any time going over there and smooth-talking some government officials into letting Kotter Industries set up shop. I considered myself lucky enough to be invited along to help negotiate a deal. Besides, if I remember correctly, Ben had the flu and couldn't go."

As Jack sat and listened to Robert, he tried to fit the pieces together in his head. "So now we need something from their lawmakers concerning *Titanic*, and we have something that they want."

Cool as a cucumber, Robert finished off his drink, sat back, and crossed his legs. "Well, Jack, you're kind of right. Since we set up shop over there, other companies have been formed, and it's been a political nightmare ever since. Ben and I have pretty much been worn out from the constant harassment over the years, so we figured this would be the perfect opportunity to try to resolve some differences. We were finally able to come to an agreement."

Jack didn't like the sound of it, but decided to ask anyway. "So, what was the final outcome?"

Like a long awaited sigh, Robert took a deep breath. "Well, we're going to continue to operate the property over the next five years, at which time our three main competitors are going to bid for the buyout. It worked in our favor. Back in 1980, we put a lot of people back to work, and over the years, we were able to make significant financial gains. Five years from now, somebody else can take over the headache. In return, we have their blessings concerning the project."

This was definitely a win-win for Jack and Kotter Industries. Now the only thing left was a final vote. Ben was fast asleep and Jack could tell Robert was tired, so he kept his mouth shut the rest of the way home.

When Monday came around, Ben called Jack to his office. Robert was there, so like a school kid, Jack quietly took a seat. Jack already had an idea what the meeting would be about, so he had all of his research ready to distribute. When Jack asked about the next vote, Ben and Robert didn't say anything. Jack could tell something was going on, but he was almost afraid to ask. Almost. "So, what gives? Is there something you're not telling me?"

Robert sat looking through Jack's research as Ben gathered up his thoughts. "Listen, kid, don't worry about the vote. That's been handled already."

Jack could feel his anger quickly rising. "Come on, Ben, this is my company, so if something unethical is going on, I want to know about it."

Robert paused momentarily from reading through some notes and glared over at Ben. Ben smiled and laughed. "Listen, kid, I know how you think, but you have to come to terms. Yes, your father kept controlling interests, but he did make the decision to go public with a percentage of stock, which means your ass is still susceptible to whatever the stockholders vote for. Now if you think the backdoor deals Robert and I make are unethical and immoral, then maybe you need to get the hell out of this game."

It was one thing to take a tongue lashing from Ben, but receiving it in the presence of someone else made it that much more humiliating. "Come on, Ben, you know what I meant. You didn't have to put me down like that in front of Robert."

Robert took that as his cue to leave so he stood up and headed for the door. "Hey, Jack. What I've read so far is impressive, so I wanna go to my office and continue reading while you and Ben hash out your lover's quarrel."

When Robert was gone, Ben continued his speech. "Listen, kid, projects of this magnitude don't get done unless deals are made or palms get greased, so if you're in it for the long hall, you're gonna have to set your ethics aside and play ball. This is business and you know as well as I do business can be brutal."

Like a scorned little boy, Jack slumped down in his chair. "Well, are you at least going to tell me what kind of backdoor deals you and Robert made?"

Like a tired old bull elephant, Ben let out a low monotone groan then moved slowly to the bar. "Listen, kid, I'm getting old. It's been made no secret that the board members would love to see me retire. They want Robert to take the helm. It seems your father's and my way of thinking is obsolete. They think it would be more prosperous if the company cut employee benefits and considered layoffs during difficult times. Well, I guess time finally caught up to me."

Jack definitely didn't like the sound of what Ben was saying. Suddenly, he came alive with worry. "So, what was the deal? You're stepping down if they vote this project in?"

After making some drinks, Ben walked over and handed Jack one.

"No, kid, at least not yet. Robert found out that most of the members were going to vote it down, because quite frankly, they never thought it would even get this far. So I put my personal reputation on the line and I made the deal that if anything would go wrong, anything at all, I would step aside as chairman and retire."

This didn't go over well with Jack, but in the same regard, Jack wasn't anticipating any real difficulties. "I don't like it, Ben. I don't foresee any problems, but I remember what you and my dad taught me about having a positive attitude, but be ready for the worst. I wish you would have told me this before you did it. This puts me in a really bad position. You know how important this is to me, but I don't want you being sacrificed in the process. This really sucks."

Although Ben shrugged it off like it was no big deal, Jack knew deep down he loved being in the position he was. He loved every minute of every battle fought. Where most people can't stand to get out of bed, let alone go to work, Ben leaped at the opportunity to be at work every day. If he could, he would work seven days a week. His whole life revolved around Kotter Industries.

The next day, the board met in the early afternoon. Jack was irritated by the fact he had to sit in a room with a bunch of backstabbing hypocrites. As the meeting went on, several problems concerning the business had to be addressed, but nobody was talking about Jack or his project. At the end of the meeting, everyone placed their mark on a paper ballet and walked out. As Ethan made his way to the door, he turned to face Jack who was staring off into space. "What's the matter, Kotter, don't like all this secret backdoor nonsense?"

Laughing as he walked out the door, Ethan made his exit leaving Jack and Ben alone. "Well, kid, it's done. Looks like your father's dream is going to become a reality."

Jack stood up and walked over to the window. He looked out at some of the board members that were walking out the front door. "Pretty anticlimactic end to this meeting. Just out of curiosity, which board members were actually for the project?"

Ben walked over and stood beside him. "Does it really matter, kid? I think you already know in your heart who was really on your side. Besides, who the hell cares? You have to look at the big picture."

With his hands in his pockets and his head down, Jack breathed a long sigh and then laughed. "The big picture. The big picture has been nothing but a rollercoaster ride from the very beginning, and you kept trying to warn me, but I just wouldn't listen. The big picture. Sometimes I just can't believe my dad left this behind for us to endure."

With little hesitation, Ben made two last drinks. After handing one to Jack, he made a toast. "Here's to our success and the peace your father sought all his life."

Throughout the week, Jack and Ben worked on the beginning stages of the project, following protocol by creating an outline for cost and a timeline for completion. There were companies with special skills that bid on certain aspects of the project, and of course, Ben took care of the dirty politics. The two men who originally discovered the ship back in 1985 were also on Jack's agenda. Mr. Jean-Louis Michel and Dr. Robert Ballard. Jack knew it would be a while before the media found out, so he needed to utilize the time he had to try to gain as much support as possible. Unfortunately, Mr. Michel couldn't be located, but Dr. Ballard happened to be between projects. He was spending much of his time at the University of Rhode Island working on creating the Institute for Archaeological Oceanography. Jack had Bonnie make the appointment.

The next day, Jack chartered a private jet and flew out to Theodore Francis Green State Airport where he had a rental car waiting. During the trip, he tried to study information that would help his cause, but the excitement of meeting Dr. Ballard flooded his thoughts. When he arrived, his nerves kicked in. During the ride to the campus, he thought about how he would open the conversation, and then he thought about what his dad would do. Jack Sr. was very direct. He didn't believe in dancing around any subject, especially when it came to business.

Jack finally arrived at the Narragansett Bay Campus and had no problem being directed to where he had to go. When he entered the building, the first thing he noticed was the quiet. There weren't any students around, nor were there any professors or personnel walking the hallways. Jack noticed an information desk off to the side with an older secretarial-type woman. When he approached, Jack tried to think of a nice greeting, but his nerves wouldn't let him so he just smiled. "Hello, my name is Jack Kotter. I have an appointment with Dr. Ballard."

With an unimpressed look on her face, the woman looked over at a list of campus phone numbers and dialed an extension. After she hung up, she gave Jack another unimpressed look. "Dr. Ballard will be with you shortly. There's a waiting area over there." As the woman pointed, Jack gave a half-smile and thanked her.

Before he could get comfortable, he heard footsteps echoing towards him. As they grew closer, Jack stood up and adjusted his tie. As the footsteps rounded the corner and came to a stop, Jack had no problem recognizing who it was. Still nervous, he eagerly stretched out his hand and smiled. "Dr. Ballard, thank you for seeing me today. I appreciate you taking time out of your busy schedule."

Dr. Ballard shook Jack's hand and greeted him with some delight in his voice, "Not a problem, Mr. Kotter. I know who you are and I'm quite curious about why you wanted to meet with me."

After their initial greetings, Dr. Ballard motioned Jack back towards the way he came from. As the two men walked back down the hall, the clip-clop of their shoes was the only sound that could be heard. When they arrived, Dr. Ballard invited Jack into his office. As he walked through the door, Jack slowed to a pause. He admired all the photos of lost ships and shipwrecks on the wall. With a little pride and a big smile, Dr. Ballard walked past Jack and took a seat at his desk. Still standing just within the door, Jack took notice of a photograph hanging off to the right. It was the research vessel *Knorr*, the ship used to locate the *Titanic*. As Jack turned to express his interest, he noticed, off to the left, a four-foot scale model of *Titanic* encased in glass. It was very impressive. Jack stared at it for a moment, as he was taken by its beauty. There were other models of ships in the room, but nothing compared to *Titanic*.

As Dr. Ballard leaned back in his chair, he watched Jack as he admired the model. "She's beautiful. I couldn't believe it when we first discovered her. She was so majestic, even after being broken in her final resting place."

Feeling somewhat intimidated, Jack walked over to the desk. Dr. Ballard leaned forward and motioned for Jack to sit. "Please have a seat. When I was told you wanted to meet with me, I gotta admit, I was really intrigued."

Jack cleared his throat and gathered his thoughts. "Well, Dr.

Ballard, I know your time is valuable and I wouldn't be here if it wasn't important. I hate to beat a dead dog, but I wanted to talk to you about *Titanic*."

With very little surprise, Dr. Ballard tried to push out a smile. "Well, Mr. Kotter, she's not a dead dog, and I'm hoping you didn't come here wanting to take a trip down to see her, because we don't do that. Yes, it's true I was one of the men who discovered her, but since then, there have been many lawsuits, none of which concern me."

Jack knew it wouldn't be easy, but he had to continue. "No, Dr. Ballard. I don't want to visit *Titanic*. I came here to discuss a project in hopes of gaining your support."

Dr. Ballard eased his tensions just enough to want to hear more. "Mr. Kotter, I told you I was intrigued, because I've read about you in magazines. One of the youngest multi-millionaires, with a company known worldwide. When I found out you wanted to meet with me, I couldn't imagine why. Corporations like yours usually finance cutting-edge projects that, for the most part, produce some kind of return on your investment. The only thing left to do with *Titanic* is to let her rest in peace."

Jack wasn't prepared to go into detail, but if that's what it took, then so be it. Feeling somewhat melodramatic, Jack stood up and walked over to the lifelike model. "Dr. Ballard, 2,223 people sailed on *Titanic*'s maiden voyage; 1,517 died during the sinking. We've heard just about every story possible from the survivors, but how many stories did we hear from the people who perished?"

Dr. Ballard stood up and walked over to Jack. "Well, Mr. Kotter, at the risk of sounding obvious, I would say none."

As his eyes scanned the decks of the model, Jack smiled. "You're right, none. But if you would allow me the time, I have an incredible story of one of the passengers that didn't make it."

Once again, Dr. Ballard was intrigued. "Alright, Mr. Kotter, tell me your story."

Jack started off by telling Dr. Ballard about the box. He continued on with Victor being on the maiden voyage and the story Winnifred had told about Victor's heroics. He even pointed out on the model where Winnifred's story unfolded. He finished with explaining his father's lifelong quest to find *Titanic*.

By the time Jack was finished, Dr. Ballard was feeling a little more sympathetic. "You're right, Mr. Kotter. That was an incredible story. Sounds like your father and I had a lot in common. I started looking for her back in 1973. It wasn't until the Navy needed an underwater study done that I received the proper funding. So you're here because you want to create some kind of memorial for your family?"

Jack didn't answer right away. With an intense desire, he stared at the model. "No, Dr. Ballard. My father's dream was not only to find *Titanic*, but to bring her to the surface and bring my grandfather home."

Dr. Ballard heard the words, but was astounded at what Jack said. "If that's a joke, Mr. Kotter, then it's a bad one. I can't say I understand your father's pain, but he had to have known the ship is considered a massive grave site. That was the main reason why, initially, no salvage was attempted. Besides, there're laws in place to protect her now."

Jack could feel his frustration starting to build, not only with the project, but with Dr. Ballard. "Do you really think I would come here and tell you something like this without having a plan?"

Dr. Ballard walked back to his desk and sat down. He pulled a folder from his desk drawer and laid it out for Jack to see. "These are all recent articles that concern the *Titanic*. Since her discovery, she's become a three-ring circus. More and more trips are causing damage to the integrity of the ship." Dr. Ballard stood back up and walked over to Jack. "Mr. Kotter, I have no doubt your company has the resources to make this happen, but I'm pleading with you not to do it. Leave her alone and let her rest quietly."

With his hands in his pockets, Jack stood glaring at the model. "Everything aside, you yourself said she's rapidly deteriorating. Fifty years from now, she'll be an orange spot on the ocean floor. Don't you think it would be better to try to preserve her for future generations?"

Dr. Ballard admired Jack's resolve and determination, but his curiosity started to set in. "Mr. Kotter, it sounds like you have the political connections and resources, but why are you here politicking for my support when you obviously don't need it?"

Jack paused and looked around the room, because he realized he was doing what his father taught him not to do. Beating around the bush. "The bottom line, Dr. Ballard, is public perception. Once the media gets ahold of this, it might not go over too well with the public. Kotter Industries doesn't want to be looked upon as grave robbers. That isn't our purpose. I thought it wouldn't be such a bad idea to try to gain your support. This way, public perception might be more positive."

Dr. Ballard shook his head in disbelief. "Mr. Kotter, if you came here looking for my okay, then you've made a trip for nothing. My reasoning won't ever change. It's a grave site that shouldn't be touched."

Jack took one last look at the model then turned away. "I was hoping for a more positive outcome, but it seems my words have fallen on deaf ears. Dr. Ballard, after reading so much about your accomplishments, it was really nice to finally meet you. Thank you for your time."

Jack left the campus and headed back to the airport. He wasn't disappointed; he was rather relieved. He was opposed to Dr. Ballard finding out secondhand about the project. When he finally arrived back home, he contacted Connie. Warner and Connie happened to be flying back to New York within the week, so Jack set up some dinner arrangements.

During the next few days, Jack spent most of his time working out details and, of course, neglecting Bria. When Connie and Warner arrived in town, Jack and Bria met them at Benjamin's. Luckily for Jack, Sarah wasn't working. After all the formalities and ordering food, Jack went straight to work. "Connie, you're not going to believe what's happened since you left last year."

As he held Warner's hand, Connie smiled. "Same old Jack. By the way, our trip was good and Greece was a great experience."

While waiting for their food, Warner and Bria stood up and walked over to the bar. Although Jack was anxious to tell all, he settled down and apologized. "I'm sorry, Connie. I appreciate the letters and pictures you sent me from Greece. It looked like you were having a great time."

Connie took a second and quickly ran through his memories. "Yeah, it was. Don't get me wrong, though. There was a lot of work involved, but the energy Warner had for the project was enough to keep us both going. Unfortunately, our funding ran out. The Greek government didn't give any explanation as to why. It was a real gut shot, so that's why we're back in the States. So, enough about my misfortune. Tell me what you're so amped up about."

Jack was about to burst, but he kept his composure and settled back into his chair. "Well, before you left we had that meeting with Ben."

As he took a drink of water, Connie laughed for a few seconds. "I remember that. Thanks for reminding me, but go on."

Jack smiled as he kept talking. "Anyway, that info you and Ben told me about worked out. Without going into all the details, several countries got together and created specific laws concerning *Titanic*. After making some phone calls, the company law firm found some loopholes. That's all Ben needed to hear. He did some politicking and we're now in the planning stage."

The look on Connie's face didn't paint a pretty picture. "What do you mean by 'planning stage'?"

Jack's smile stretched from ear to ear. "The project is a go, Connie. Can you believe it?"

Connie didn't share Jack's enthusiasm, nor was he smiling. "Jack, we've been friends ever since we were kids. You're like a brother to me. Please don't take this the wrong way. Don't go through with this project. I'm begging you. I didn't know the specifics about the laws, but I knew the powers to be were working on some litigation concerning *Titanic*. Jack, I know I said I would help, but that ship met its fate 91 years ago. Let her rest."

Jack remembered the gut-wrenching feeling he had when Ben told him the project was dead, and now it had returned. "How can you do this to me, Connie? After all these years as friends, you're going back on your word like I was nothing."

Connie tried to throw a positive spin on it, but was having no luck. "I'm sorry, Jack. I knew how important this was to you and I respected and loved your dad, but my belief was and still is to just leave the ship alone. It's considered by most people to be a grave site, and I share that belief. I really didn't think Ben would have the connections to make this happen, plus I figured once those laws were in place, there would be no way around them, then there would be no more talk about disturbing the ship. I'm really sorry, Jack. My intentions weren't to hurt you."

Jack listened to Connie apologize several times, but he was still numb. As the waiter placed their food on the table, Jack stood up and walked over to the bar. Warner could feel the tension, so she walked over and sat down next to Connie. After drinking a shot of Jäger Bomb, Jack took Bria by the hand. He led her out the door and went home. Although Bria had an idea of what the conversation was about, she didn't know exactly what Connie said to upset Jack. The mood was quiet all the way home.

CHAPTER THIRTY-TWO

THE NEXT DAY, JACK WAS BACK IN HIS OFFICE HARD AT WORK. STILL angry from the night before, he was more determined than ever to complete the project. While he was researching underwater archaeologists, Ben walked in. "Hey, kid, I heard about what happened last night."

Before Ben could take two steps in the door, Jack lashed out in angry sarcasm. "I'm sorry, I don't remember hearing you knock, and what the hell do you think you know about last night?"

Ben paused then quietly closed the door. He walked over and made himself a drink, then sat down. "Well, kid, you're right. I didn't knock, but then again, there will never come a time when I knock on your office door, so get used to it. As for last night, Bria called me. She was worried about you and wanted me to talk to you. Most importantly, I didn't bother making you a drink because you yelled at me. So if you don't feel like talking, then I'm going back to my office."

Jack took a deep breath and leaned back in his chair then spoke in a calm voice. "I told Connie about the project and he backpedaled on me. Just before he left for Greece, he told me if I got the project off the ground, he would help me. When I told him about it last night, he was like a deer in headlights. He figured once the laws were in effect, there would be no way around them. I guess he figured the project would just go away and that was the real reason he said he would help. He's my best friend and he backstabbed me."

Ben walked over to the bar and made another drink, then he handed it to Jack. "Listen, kid, I'm not a big fan of Connie, but in his defense, I don't think he did anything wrong. He's devoted his life to conducting research beneath the oceans. He probably feels very strongly about disturbing something that's been down there for so many years. You can't condemn the guy for his beliefs."

After Jack thought about it, he knew Ben was right. "I guess it's just starting to bother me that I'm the only one interested in seeing this through."

Ben downed his drink and laughed. "Well, kid, it does seem like you're alone in your thinking. By the way, how did your meeting go with Ballard?"

The look on Jack's face told the story. "Well, he was opposed to the idea. Just like Connie, he looks at the wreck as being a mass grave site."

Ben looked down at his empty glass then gathered his thoughts. "Listen, kid, despite what I believe, I'm behind you all the way. As for Connie, why don't you give him a call and listen to what he has to say. Just don't be so judgmental."

After Ben left, Jack called Connie and offered to treat him to lunch at the Wiley Roadster. When Jack arrived, Connie was already there waiting. Jack didn't know how to start, so he started by apologizing. "Connie, I should have been more receptive to your beliefs and I wasn't. I know you have strong convictions when it comes to the world's oceans, but I was hoping, just this once, you would maybe stand with me."

Connie could feel his stomach growling, so he decided to lighten the mood. He looked into Jack's eyes and gave him a really serious look. "Well, Jack, I gotta tell you. When you invite somebody to lunch, it usually means there's food involved sometime during the get-together."

Jack cracked a smile then started to laugh. "You're an asshole. You get me every time."

After lunch, Jack discussed several plans for retrieving the ship, but Connie was still hesitant to respond. "Jack, we'll always be best friends, but I just don't think I can help you."

This time, Jack wasn't as sensitive. "Alright, Connie, I understand, but it would be great if you could just be a sounding board for me. Let me know if I'm on the right track."

Connie reluctantly agreed, and so Jack started spurting out ideas. "I know the ship is in two pieces, so I thought about just hooking both pieces like a fish and pulling them up, but I'm not sure if that's the best way. Then I remembered one time my dad came back from one of his long trips. He wanted to spend some time with me so we went to the movies. We saw that movie called *Raising the Titanic*. Remember that? It was pretty good. Anyway, they used some kind of balloon system. They somehow stuck these balloons inside the ship then pumped them full of air. The ship floated to the top and burst out of the water. What'ya think?"

Connie was waiting for the punch line, but Jack didn't flinch. "I can't believe you just told me that with a straight face. You're either jerking my chain or you're dumber than a box of rocks. I'm gonna guess that you're jerking my chain."

Finally Jack burst out laughing. "Gotcha. The look on your face was a Kodak moment. To be honest, we're still lining up engineers and we still need underwater archaeologists. This is going to be one massive project."

Jack could see the gleam in Connie's eyes as his interest started to peak. "Come on, Connie, you know you can't walk away from this. You would never forgive yourself knowing you had a chance to be associated with *Titanic*. Truth be said, I need you to be one of the project managers. I just don't trust anyone else."

Jack was right. Connie was most definitely interested, but he had his convictions to deal with. "Let me think about it, Jack. Either way, I'll call you tomorrow."

Jack smiled as he shook Connie's hand. "Sounds good. Now I have to go home tonight and deal with Bria. She saw the ring on Warner's finger last night. It's just a matter of time before she hounds me about it."

With a heavy conversation waiting, Jack went home; Connie knew Warner would also give him grief, but he went home with the added stress of having convictions in his heart. When Connie arrived home,

Warner could see he was struggling with something. "He wants you to be part of that fiasco, doesn't he?"

With a perplexed look, Connie rubbed the stress from his eyes and sat down. "I'm guessing Bria told you what was going on last night."

Warner sat down beside Connie and gave him a hug. "Bria told me a lot last night. Not just about this project, but also how it's consuming their relationship. This project is no good for anyone, but Jack just can't see that. He's blinded by his honor to do well by his father. It's just not right, Connie."

Connie stared into Warner's eyes and knew she was right. "He's my best friend and his dad treated me like a son. Besides, Jack knows me all too well. He said it would be impossible to walk away because I would hate myself for it. I didn't say anything, but he was right. For a guy like me, it's a chance of a lifetime to be part of such a historical ship."

Warner shook her head in frustration as she continued to disagree. "This isn't right, Connie. It goes against everything you believe in. I just don't like it. It doesn't feel right. I can't get over the feeling that something bad is going to happen."

Connie smiled as he leaned over and gave Warner a kiss. "He wants me to be one of the project managers."

With a disgusted hiss, Warner stood up. "I think you're using every excuse you can find to talk yourself into this. What about me? What about our work in Greece?"

Connie stood up and started to pace the floor. As he stood in the middle of the room, he brushed the hair back from his face. "I don't think funding is going to come through anytime soon. The Greek government seems to be having problems of their own. I'm sorry, sweetie. Maybe if I help Jack, I can talk him into funding our project. This way, everyone gets what they want."

Warner thought about it, but was still apprehensive. "I don't know. I still don't like it, but we need to finish our work so we can get funded for future projects."

After a few more minutes, Warner walked over and gave Connie a hug. "I'll go along with whatever you decide."

The next day, Connie was up early and on the phone. Jack was already in the office when the call came. With her usual unexciting voice, Bonnie transferred the call. Realizing how early it was for

Connie to be calling, Jack was nervous and excited at the same time. When he picked up the phone, he didn't waste any time inquiring about Connie's decision. "Well, Connie, no doubt you talked things out with Warner and I know she's dead set against it."

Connie wanted to make Jack sweat a little, so he gave a long pause. Afterwards, he spoke in a low-key voice as to seem disappointed. "Well, Jack, we did talk it over, and it wasn't an easy decision. There were a lot of things to take into account."

Jack wasn't in a mood to hear a bunch of reasoning just to be shot down at the end. With some frustration, he interrupted Connie. "Come on, Connie, just say what you called to say and don't worry about it. I'm okay with you holding to your morals."

As Jack braced for the worst, Connie gave another long pause. "Well, Jack, you don't leave me a choice. I guess there's only one thing to say. Let's make some history and raise the *Titanic*."

Jack heard the words, but it took a second or two for them to register. "Are you kidding me? You dirty dog. All this time you had me believing you were going to turn me down. Thank you, Connie. It really means a lot that you're heading this huge project for me." After laughing at each other for a few minutes, Jack and Connie discussed the terms for the unfinished project in Greece.

The rest of the day, Jack walked around like he was on cloud nine. When the afternoon came, Ben arranged a meeting in his office. When Jack arrived, he saw a familiar face. Ben stood up and introduced the familiar man to Jack. "Hey, kid, glad you could make it on time. You remember the taxi driver from San Francisco? This is Samuel Yedidya."

Samuel stood up and shook Jack's hand. "How do you do Mr. Kotter?"

Jack quickly remembered the embarrassment Ben caused during their conversation and was quick to make a joke. After shaking hands, Jack invited Samuel to have a seat. "I hope Ben hasn't given you any more grief about your English. By the way, my friends just call me Jack."

Samuel gave a polite laugh at the joke and sat down. "Well, since we're going by first names, you can call me Sam."

One of the first things Ben suggested was drinks, but unfortunately for Ben, Sam declined the offer. Out of respect, Ben didn't pursue the idea. Instead, he proceeded with the meeting. "Okay, kid, this is what I got so far. I remembered Sam, because after you left me hanging, we spoke for a couple of minutes and Sam told me he had degrees in oceanography. I think he would be a great attribute to the team. I've already explained what the job is and he's really excited about it. Now, I know you've been researching salvage companies, so I've been recruiting some of the best seamen, rig workers, and divers in the industry. I've already compiled a list of workers who are interested. Now we're going to have to find some top-notch management, because to be quite honest, I don't plan on spending months at a time out in the Atlantic unless I'm on a cruise ship. Besides, there are never any women on these jobs."

Before Ben could continue, Jack cut him off. "I already have at least one of the project managers lined up."

Ben's curiosity was peaked. "Sorry, kid, I thought I was hiring all the personnel. Who did you get?"

Knowing it would cause him some grief, Jack came right out and told him. "I presented the opportunity to Connie and he agreed to the task." Ben didn't say anything and Jack could tell he was processing the information. "Come on, Ben, you know he's one of the best out there. You need to set aside your differences for the greater good."

Sam could feel the tension and just sat quietly while Ben geared up for his response.

"Okay, kid, you're right. I don't like Connie, but he's very good at what he does. Good job, kid. We could really use the talent."

Jack was shocked. He expected a blow up but instead, he received reason. It felt really nice to be appreciated.

After Ben was finished and Jack had nothing else to present, Sam stood up and let them know about his contributions to the project. "Well, Ben has given me all the timelines, so I'm going to start mapping out the oceans currents, and I'm also going to have to be the one that maps out the projection of any icebergs that make their way down Iceberg Alley into the Atlantic. I also need to study the mapping of the ocean floor around the wreck. I know there are some marine organisms that are currently eating away at the wreck. We're going to have to take that into consideration when doing the heavy lifting."

CHAPTER THIRTY-THREE

WITH EVERYTHING, INCLUDING TIME, ON THEIR SIDE, THE PROJECT went forward. Over the next year, plans were drawn up, equipment was acquired, people were hired, and Robert waited in the shadows for something to go wrong. Bria constantly hounded Jack about wedding plans, and while Ben kept Kotter Industries running smooth, Jack oversaw the entire project, keeping everything tightknit so the media wouldn't get ahold of it.

After all the preparations and coordination, there were several plans on the table. The first idea was to completely dismantle the ship by using manned submersibles armed with underwater torches, but the cost would be extreme and the risk to human life would be even worse. The second idea was somewhat similar. Using the same submersibles, they would cut large chunks of the ship away and then use heavy cranes on barges to bring the pieces of ship to the surface. This, too, would take a lot more time and expense than what Jack was willing to do. Although the ship was already in two pieces, Jack wanted desperately to keep both pieces intact.

With more questions than answers, Jack knew his back was against the wall. Ben never told Jack exactly how much money his father set aside, and he knew Ben had already written some hefty checks to cover the current expenses. It seemed the project was at a standstill. With constantly being at odds with Bria and having

Robert lurking over his shoulder, and with the fact that nobody had a doable plan Jack agreed with, the dream project was quickly turning into a nightmare.

Just when Jack thought things couldn't get any worse, a devastating disaster happened. In December of 2004, an underwater earthquake measuring 9.1 set off a tsunami in the Indian Ocean, affecting fourteen countries, including Indonesia, India, and Thailand and killing 230,000 people. Being a leader in various types of industries around the world, Kotter Industries had interests in several of the countries affected. An emergency meeting was called and Jack knew Robert would use the situation to try to manipulate the board.

After several weeks of evaluation and meetings, it was determined that none of Kotter Industries' properties were affected. Unfortunately, several employees were lost in the disaster, and out of respect for their families, Ben took the time to visit them in person. After traveling for several months, he was back in the States and ready to move forward with the *Titanic* project.

While Jack bickered with the salvage company, Ben sought out a different approach. He called Jack to his office in order to discuss his thoughts. When Jack walked in, Ben could see the wear in his face from the stress taking its toll. "Sit down, kid. Take a load off. I think I might have something we can work with, but I have to fly to Maine."

By that point, Jack was feeling pretty numb about any ideas that were presented, but he was always willing to listen to anything Ben had to say. Never short of humor, Jack sat down and smiled. "So besides the Sasquatch, what else is up in Maine?"

Ben stood up and walked around to Jack and sat on the corner of the desk. "It's not a what, it's a who. Back in 1968, the Russians lost one of their submarines. It went down about 1,500 miles northwest of Hawaii. After several attempts from the Soviets to try to locate the sub, they gave it up for lost. Because it was during the Cold War, the United States was interested in its potential value for information. Long story short, they were finally able to locate her three miles down, but the challenge was exactly that. At that time, no salvage had ever been attempted that deep before. The technology just didn't exist back then."

Jack loved history, especially when he was growing up and Ben would tell stories about his life. "So, what happened? Were they able to retrieve the sub?"

Reminiscent of those storytelling times, Ben smiled as he walked over and made some drinks. "Yeah, kid. In order to keep the project from prying eyes, the CIA contracted the Howard Hughes Corporation to build a ship just for the salvage of the sub. As you know, your grandfather on your mother's side was a shipbuilder. The company he worked for found out about it and tried to bid on the contract. Unfortunately, Howard was as tough as they come. He already had the situation on lockdown. I really miss that guy, but anyway, his company built a ship called the *Hughes Glomar Explorer.* Now, this is where it gets interesting. Along with the ship, the engineers built an underwater work platform that could support anything ranging from a workstation to various other types of equipment. The ship was also equipped with some kind of claw system that could snatch the sub up and bring it to the surface."

By this point, Jack's eyes were as wide as silver dollars and his interest in the story had just skyrocketed. "I'm liking where you're going with this, but you still haven't told me why you have to fly to Maine. Is that where the ship is now?"

Ben handed Jack a drink and sat down. "No, kid. Actually, the ship is still around, but she was converted into an offshore deep sea drilling ship. She no longer has the functions she was originally built for."

As he forced his drink down, Jack's excitement took a nosedive. "Except for watching my emotions go up and down like a rollercoaster, what's the purpose of you telling me this story?"

Still reminiscing, Ben paused as he smiled at Jack. "I really miss those days, kid. Telling you different stories about world events and history. Anyway, I'm not worried about your rollercoaster feelings. One of the primary engineers that worked on the project has since retired and lives up in Lubec, Maine. He's agreed to meet with me and discuss our project. I'm hoping he has no sentiment about what we're doing. Maybe I can talk him into helping us."

With some reluctant feelings, Jack still had questions. "This guy has to be pretty old. I'm thinking he probably doesn't have anything to offer in these current times. On top of that, I wasn't exactly thinking about constructing any special equipment."

Jack could see Ben's face turning red so he decided to slow his roll. Huffing and puffing, Ben stood up and started pacing. "Well, kid, the guy is probably about my age and I'm okay with that. Once more, if you have some fantastic idea rolling around in that head of yours, I would love to hear it."

Knowing he'd overstepped himself, Jack stood up and walked over to Ben. With a kind smile, he put his arm around him. "I too miss the history lessons you use to give, and no, I don't have any ideas rolling around in my head. For all that you're doing, you've been a true friend to me. Thank you."

With a sarcastic look on his face, Ben just stared at Jack for a moment. "You're so full of crap. I don't need you to patronize me, so get off me and get the hell out of here. I need to get to the airport."

Jack let out a small chuckle and smiled. "Alright, Big Ben, call me after your meeting and let me know something good."

CHAPTER THIRTY-FOUR

After packing a few things for the trip, Ben had Casey drive him to the airport. After the plane landed, Ben didn't waste any time meeting with Mr. Lincoln Henry Smith. Mr. Smith agreed to meet with Ben at Cohill's Inn, a quaint restaurant located on the tip of Maine. When Ben arrived, it was late and the dinner crowd had already left. He noticed a white-haired gentleman sitting at a table overlooking the water. The wrinkles in his face showed his age. With his arthritic hands, he struggled to take a sip of his coffee. When Ben approached, he stood in front of the gentleman.

"Hello, are you Mr. Smith?"

The gentleman placed his cup on the table and stood up. He shook Ben's hand and asked him to sit down. "So you're Benjamin Marcus."

Ben smiled as he asked the waitress for coffee. "Yes, sir. Do I know you?"

The gentleman smiled back. "No, sir, but anyone who hasn't been living in a hole has heard of you. I've been sitting here wondering why a man such as yourself would travel way the hell out into the middle of nowhere to meet with me."

As Ben glanced out over the water, he tried to keep his pride from showing. "Well, sir, you worked on the *Glomar Explorer* so you have a unique perspective for deep sea salvage."

The gentleman smiled as his thoughts took him back to younger days. "Well now, that was some real Cold War spy stuff going on back then. By the way, calling me sir is like putting an outhouse in a five star hotel. It just doesn't fit. People just call me Henry. Anyway, the *Glomar Explorer* was a very unique project. Nothing like that had ever been designed and we didn't even know if it would work, but it did."

As the waitress refilled both coffees, she brushed her leg up against Ben. "If you need anything else darlin', you just holler."

Ben took a sip of his coffee and smiled. "Nice friendly town you have here. What'ya say we stop with the mental chess game and get down to business. A man like you never really retires. I have a feeling you still keep tabs on what's going on, especially anything unique that pops up."

Henry broke open some cream and sugars and piled them into his coffee. "Well, Mr. Marcus, I wasn't lying when I told you I was wondering why you trekked all the way out here to see me. On the flip side of that coin, I know Kotter Industries has been contracting seamen, rig workers, and laborers, along with accumulating tons of equipment for over a year now. You're gearing up for something big, so I'm guessing you're stuck in a rut and need some ideas."

Ben liked Henry from the start. There was something about him that sparked his interest. Maybe it was the fact he wasn't easily intimidated. Or maybe he was just looking into a mirror. In any case, it had been a long time since Ben was this impressed with somebody. "Well, Henry, call me Ben. What'ya say, friend, I buy you something a little stronger than this coffee?"

Henry glanced over at the bar and barked out an order. "Hey, Kelly, get us a couple of Jägermeisters and a pitcher of beer."

Ben's face lit up like a Christmas tree. "Now you're talking my language, and I get the double bonus of seeing that pretty little waitress again. I think she likes me."

Henry stared at Ben the way only a father would stare at his daughter's first date. "That pretty little waitress is my daughter and I would remind you to mind your manners. I have a shotgun in my truck and I'm not opposed to using it."

As Ben tried to think of his next words, Kelly walked over with the drinks. "Here you go, fellas." After Kelly set the drinks down, she slid her hand across Ben's shoulder. "Don't worry, sweetie, the first one is on me."

Before Ben could get two words out, Henry's Jägermeister was gone and he was chasing it with a mug of beer. "Gotta be quick up in these parts, old man."

Ben quickly swallowed his shot and grabbed his beer. "That's what I'm talking about. You better be careful, Henry, I might start liking you."

After several more shots of the Meister with beer chasers, Ben and Henry finally had their minds ready to talk business. After drinking the last of the beer, Henry slammed down his glass. "Now, tell me why you came all the way out here to see a crumpled up old man."

Ben paused for a moment then quietly placed his mug down on the table. "Well, Henry, we have something that we want to bring up from the Atlantic Ocean. Now, we've come up with several ideas, but the bottom line is we want to try to keep it in one piece."

Suddenly, Henry had a gleam in his eye. "Well now, there are a lot of things at the bottom of the Atlantic. If you were looking for treasure, you wouldn't need me, so that means it's gotta be a ship of sort. How deep would this mystery ship be?"

Ben could tell Henry really liked the mind games, and that was alright because Ben was having a blast. "Well, she's about two and a half miles down."

Henry looked around and noticed all the customers were gone. Kelly was locking the doors and cleaning up for the night. "Well now, let's see. There are many, many wrecks at the bottom of the Atlantic, but in my opinion, there's only one worth going after. And she just happens to be about two and a half miles down." With that same gleam, Henry leaned across the table. "You wouldn't happen to be going after the *Titanic*?"

Ben smiled as he drank down the rest of his beer. "Not bad, Henry. As a matter of fact, we are."

With his arms stretched behind his head, Henry sat back in his seat. "Oh, Benjamin, my friend, I've been waiting such a long time for somebody to have the balls to do it, and like a gift from God, here you are."

As Kelly finished with her cleaning, Ben and Henry sat laughing and talking about the old days. In between their laughing, they talked about the *Titanic*. Henry had some sound ideas and that made Ben very happy. After everything was said, Ben made arrangements for Henry to come stay in New York in order to breathe new life into the project.

The next day, Ben flew back to New York and met with Jack and Connie. There was a lot to go over, so they met in Ben's office and had lunch delivered. When Connie arrived, Ben was in his office, but Jack was still en route. Knowing he didn't get along with Ben, Connie felt awkward. Ben could feel the tension, so as a nice gesture, he made Connie a drink and, of course, himself one also. "Please have a seat, Connie. For once, it's a good thing that Jack is late. I wanted to clear the air between us so we can start fresh before this project gets into full-swing. I know we've never seen eye to eye and that's mainly my fault."

The leather made rip noises as Ben leaned back in his chair. "So many times Jack got into trouble as a boy, and he would call me for help. It's just that he never wanted his father to be disappointed in him, so I would always keep everything hush-hush. With his father being my best friend, that never really sat well with me. In my mind, I used to blame you, because, I guess, I always looked at Jack as being a little angel. It wasn't until he got older that I realized he was just as much of a troublemaker as you were. All these years, I've been carrying around that anger when there was nothing to be angry about. I'm sorry for that, Connie. I don't know if you can forgive and forget, but I'm hoping we can start over and at least be civil towards each other."

After letting the ice cubes melt a bit, Connie took a sip of his drink. "Wow! You really know how to spike a drink. I appreciate your apology, Ben, but I've never held any ill will towards you. I always knew when Jack and I were kids you held me responsible for all the trouble, and I was okay with that. Somewhere deep inside, I guess I was jealous, because no matter how much trouble Jack got into, you were always there as his guardian angel."

As hard as Ben was, there were certain times he could be very pleasant. "Thanks, Connie."

With a toast, Ben raised his glass. "Here's to future relations."

Just then, Jack walked in. "Sorry I'm late, guys. What are we toasting?"

Ben smiled and shook his head. "Nothing, kid. Connie and I were just talking about younger days. Grab a drink and have a seat. Our lunch should be here any minute. After we eat, we'll get started."

Over the next couple of hours, Ben told Jack and Connie about his trip to Maine and about Henry. He also reviewed the plans Henry had in mind. Although, it wasn't exactly what Jack had planned, he was alright with it.

The next day, Henry flew in from Maine and set up a dinner meeting for later on in the evening. Jack could hardly keep still. He was excited, worried, and anxious all at the same time. He was so wound up, Bria decided to take him out to see his friends. They met at the Wiley Roadster. The Mopar brothers were there as usual, along with Paul and Oliver with the Ferrari. Like two kids in a candy store, Jack and Bria walked around admiring all the new cars of the up and coming cool kids. After a day of fun, Jack checked his watch as the sun started to set. Bria smiled because she was thankful for the day. She kissed him goodbye and sent him on his way.

Jack made his way to the Ace Hotel, where Henry was staying. Henry was interested in trying the John Dory Oyster Bar and restaurant. When he arrived, he saw Ben walking in. By the time Jack parked his car and walked in, Ben and Henry already had drinks on the table. "Damn, Ben, anyone ever tell you, you drink too much?"

Ben glanced over at Henry as Henry was halfway done with his. "I gotta tell you, kid, sometimes I don't think I drink enough."

Before Jack could sit down, Henry stood up and introduced himself. "Hello, Jack, my name is Lincoln Smith, but most people just call me Henry. Now sit your ass down and have a drink."

Jack smiled as he sat down. He realized it was going to be a long dinner dealing with two people with the same personality.

Connie arrived a short while later, and after some small talk and a few more drinks, Jack asked Henry about the ideas he had for *Titanic*.

As an engineer whose mind never stopped working, Henry was all too happy to go over his plans. "Well, from what Ben tells me, you already have most of your people in place. I see you're staying away from the big names. That'll probably ruffle some feathers, but I like your style, Jack. On the other hand, your way under equipped. My plan is somewhat simple for the bow. Picture the concept of a claw machine. I think after digging out 93-years' worth of soot, she'll come up just fine. As for the stern, we don't have a choice. It's gotta come up in pieces. If we're lucky, we can pick apart everything that collapsed on itself, then maybe, just maybe, we can bring what's left of the hull up in one piece. After that, everything else around the wreck is gravy."

That was a little too fast for Jack. He was more interested in details. "Alright, I'm okay with the stern, but let's go over the plan for the bow. You do know the bow buckled when it hit the bottom?"

Henry looked at Jack for a moment and smiled. "Don't worry, Jack, I've been doing my homework on *Titanic* ever since they found her. The idea I have is similar to the *Glomar Explorer*. We're going to use a grappling system, built by Kotter Industries, of course, to do exactly what we did back then. Just like a claw machine, we're going to strategically place two hooks on each side of the bow then pull her up. Obviously, she'll moan and groan, but I think, in the end, she'll surprise everyone and hold her composure."

Connie liked what he was hearing, but was also a little leery about the details.

Henry's words ran through Jack's mind like a rollercoaster. He understood the concept, but was worried about the outcome. "I don't know, Henry. You think she'll rip apart after being down there for so long?"

Henry glanced down at his empty glass. He paused to try to get the attention of the waitress. Henry's silence worried Jack, but he waited patiently for an answer. As his eyes rolled around, Henry finally took a deep breath. "Well now, Jack, that's the million-dollar question. I know over the years she's been weakened by bacteria, but those boys in Belfast really knew what they were doing when it came to shipbuilding. I think she'll do just fine. If there is a problem, I think it would be minimal." Henry could see the worry in Jack's face. "Don't worry, Jack, we're not just gonna yank her out of that watery grave. It'll have to be done in stages, and after each stage, we'll assess how to proceed with the next."

Jack glanced over at Ben and Connie to try to get some input, but it was obvious Ben was out of his comfort zone, and Connie was still trying to process the information. Connie fiddled with his empty glass as he tried to picture the scene in his head. "Well, Henry, the

Atlantic Ocean isn't a very friendly environment and can downright be unforgiving."

Before Henry could respond, the waitress stepped to the table and gave everyone a refill. Jack sat contemplating in his head the various outcomes of Henry's ideas while Henry, Ben, and Connie talked about the minor details. Jack realized he was running out of options, so he agreed to follow Henry's plan.

Before the project could get underway, an expedition was conducted east of the wreck in August 2005. The idea was to find missing pieces of *Titanic*'s hull. The results would explain a new theory that claimed *Titanic* not only side swipe the iceberg, but that she also bottomed out on part of the berg beneath the water. This would also explain eye witness accounts of water coming up through the floor in Boiler Room Four. After several dives, the missing pieces were found far east of the wreck site, in an area that had previously been overlooked. This gave experts a more accurate picture of how *Titanic* spent its last moments. This also gave Jack a better picture of his final plan.

With all the recent attention and the ongoing fascination with *Titanic*, it was obvious Kotter Industries wasn't going to be able to keep the project secret for much longer. The window of opportunity was rapidly closing and the project needed to proceed. During that same month, all the equipment needed was placed at the site. The grappling hooks were still being constructed, so the first phase of the plan was to gather up all the scattered debris around the ship, including the newly discovered pieces of hull. The second phase would involve the stern. Since it imploded on itself, the idea would be to recover anything not still attached. This would make it easier to concentrate on separating the top layer pieces from the body. In the end, they would have to determine whether or not to try to lift the remaining hull, rudder, and propellers together. The third phase was a bit more direct. No deconstruction involved. Dig out the soot, attach the grappling system, and hoist her up, but they knew looking at it on paper was one thing. Actually doing it was totally different.

It wasn't long before passing ships off in the distance became curious. Eventually, word made it to the press that something big was happening out in the Atlantic. Although, curiosity from workers on commercial ships came and went, it was the passengers and crew from the cruise lines passing by that made inquiries. Of course, in the end, curiosity always wins. After receiving so many reports, various news stations had no choice but to investigate. After realizing all the activity was taking place in the vicinity of *Titanic*, speculations and rumors spread of yet another documentary. After a while, the hype died down and interested parties awaited the next History Channel special.

This played well with Kotter Industries. The less attention, the better. Jack was ecstatic because the project was underway and going well. After being out in the Atlantic for a few months and conducting several investigative dives, Jack made a trip back to New York to spend time with Bria. While at dinner, the waiter delivered a bottle of champagne to the table. After a few refills, Bria noticed something shiny at the bottom of the bottle. When she lowered her head down to the table to take a closer look, she became puzzled. It looked like a diamond ring. When she raised herself upright, she saw the smile on Jack's face. As with a traditional proposal, Jack knelt down on one knee.

"Bria, you've stood by me through good and bad. You love me for who I am and not what I can give. You've been my rock through some of the toughest times of my life. You've seen the ugly in me and have still loved me just the same. You're an incredible person, magnificent lover, and the woman I would love to spend the rest of my life with. Bria, I kneel before you today as a king would kneel before his queen. I love you, Bria. Would you have me as your husband?"

Bria was speechless. So many arguments over the years. Just as she was about to respond, she caught a glimpse at everyone staring. At some point during Jack's words, everyone in the restaurant stopped what they were doing and gazed at the young couple and their love. A lone tear ran down Bria's cheek as she turned back to Jack who was waiting with anticipation. "Yes, Jack Kotter, I would gladly be your wife."

As Jack and Bria shared a hug and kiss, the other customers broke out in applause and cheers. Jack and Bria couldn't finish off the bottle of champagne quick enough. Drink after drink, they guzzled down what was left until the bottle was empty. Finally, Bria was able to get the ring out and place it on her finger. A little sticky, but that was alright by her.

The end of the night finally arrived as Jack and Bria lay in bed discussing plans for the big day. Unfortunately, that day would have to wait. Jack wanted to finish the *Titanic* project before committing himself to Bria for a lifetime. Feeling that she finally corralled Jack, Bria was happy just to finally have a ring on her finger. She didn't have any arguments for him.

The next day, Jack made the trip back out into the Atlantic, while Ben took care of the day to day business. Periodically, Sam would hold meetings concerning arising storms or rogue icebergs drifting down from Iceberg Alley. On occasions, the workers would take breaks to view such an iceberg off in the distance. Usually with a pair of binoculars. Ironically, because of the *Titanic* disaster, a new type of agency was created. The International Ice Patrol. Since 1914, the Coast Guard had had the duty of being the watchful eyes for ships passing through iceberg territory. As an added bonus, Sam had the idea of having several tugboats on standby to give a gentle bump to an iceberg if necessary to avoid any complications with the equipment.

Unfortunately, tropical storms and hurricanes could sometimes reap havoc, especially when there were interests in various areas. On 29 August 2005 hurricane Katrina struck the Gulf Coast, destroying life and property stretching from Florida to Texas. Several Kotter Industries employees were killed, and many more lost everything they owned. Because of the disaster, the *Titanic* project was temporarily stopped so Jack and Ben could visit the families affected. During that time, Kotter Industries wrote checks to many of the families to compensate until the insurance companies paid for damages.

After several weeks, and some time spent with Bria, Jack was back out in the Atlantic with a full head of steam. Many times, Warner and Bria would also make the trek out to the project site, but they would always long for the nightlife of New York, so they would rarely stay. On a quiet night with calm water, Jack looked out over the ocean. Enjoying the cool breeze, he watched the sun go down.

Puffing on a fat stogie, Henry emerged onto the deck. "Beautiful night isn't, Jack?"

After making several attempts to whisk away the smoke, Jack laughed. "Next time Ben makes the trip out, I'll have him bring you some Cubans."

Henry took one last puff and tossed the worn down cigar overboard. "You have a connection for Cubans?"

Jack smiled as he tried to avoid the last of the smoke. "No, Ben has the connection. He's got connections on top of connections. Whatever you want, he can get it."

Henry leaned against the rail and peered out over the calm water. "I remember back in the day when I worked for Howard Hughes. He was the same way. That man was so eccentric he had no problem lighting up a cigar using a Ben Franklin like it was nothing."

Jack paused as he thought back to when Ben used his second Lamborghini to help stop Lilith. "Well, I don't know about the money aspect of it, but I guess when men such as Ben or Howard achieve such a lavish lifestyle, one can easily get carried away. One thing about Ben, though, he'll help just about anybody. All my years of knowing him, I've witnessed some extraordinary generosity."

Henry seemed delighted with the respect Jack had for Ben. "It's nice to see someone as young as you have such admiration for a mentor such as Ben. I think you'll go a long way in this world, Jack."

As he took a deep breath enjoying the clean air, Jack graciously accepted the compliment. "So, Henry, how are you doing with all this?"

It didn't take Henry long to give Jack his answer. "Well now, Jack, I have to tell you. It feels good to be active again. I wasn't ready to retire, but my daughter forced me to. I'm not getting any younger and my bones are starting to fail, so she talked me into coming to live with her. I still wonder if I made the right decision. But enough about me. What about you? This isn't exactly a pet project and you're sure not out here just for the hell of it. So, what's your story, Jack?"

A chill started to set in, but Jack enjoyed the brisk air and it didn't seem to bother old Henry. "Well, it's one hell of a long, far-fetched story, but I'll give you the short version. My grandfather was on *Titanic*. According to one of the survivors, he apparently gave his life for a young woman and her children. My father spent his entire life searching for *Titanic* just so he could bring my grandfather home to rest. When he died, he left the task to me."

Jack expected some kind of surprised response, but Henry didn't say anything. He just stared out over the water. After glancing up at the sky a few times, Henry finally spoke. "You're gonna have to tell me the long version of that story one day, but for now, I'll say a prayer for your family and for the success of this project."

After some time admiring the ocean and enjoying the cool weather, Jack began to question the integrity of *Titanic*'s hull. "Tell me what you really think, Henry. You really think the two front pieces of the bow are going to come up without a fight?"

Henry could hear the uncertainty in Jack's voice, but it wasn't about the ships condition. "Over 1,100 souls went down with that ship. What is it you really want to know? Was your grandfather one of them? Or maybe you're thinking there's a chance some of the remains of those unfortunate souls may still be sealed inside? What about it, Jack? Getting nervous?"

Jack knew Henry saw right through him. "Well, when we bring her up, I'm going to have several clergies on hand to oversee anything we find. I'm also going to have a couple of film crews here when we start bringing up the stern. I don't want any questions raised about our intent."

The next morning was a big day for the project. After gathering all the data from previous dives, a course of action was plotted out. The first target was going to be the dome of the aft staircase. Not to be mistaken for the Grand Staircase, this was the staircase originally located between the third and fourth stack, which led down to a beautiful restaurant. After the sinking, it broke off, landing 1,000 feet east of the stern. After a few hours of preparation and rigging, it was time to pull it up. Jack couldn't wait. Although Ben couldn't make the trip out to see it, everyone else waited impatiently, leaning over the rail and looking on.

As it broke the plain of the water, everyone cheered and clapped. It was carefully lowered onto a waiting barge that was chained to several other barges. The size of several football fields, this floating platform was going to house all of the miscellaneous pieces outside of the wreck. That way, archeologists could work on and prepare the pieces for transport.

Over the course of the following eighteen months, with several crews working, time dragged on, but the results were great. Everything around the wreck was recovered, including any small items that were lying about, and plans were being made to start on the stern. Kotter Industries was successful in building the new grappling system and was ready to test it out. Jack made plans for Ben to come out to the site so they could meet and discuss how to proceed. As usual, when he arrived, he was grumpy and belligerent. After giving his sea legs a chance to adjust, he turned to his friend Henry. "You old dog, I know you have a bottle stashed someplace. What'ya say we go have a drink and smoke a couple of these Cubans I brought?"

Henry didn't even blink an eye. "Hell, yeah, let's go."

Knowing Ben and Henry were going to be awhile, Jack decided to sit down with Sam and Connie to discuss some of the smaller details. Afterwards, they met Ben and Henry for dinner. Even though the vessel they were on was 300-foot long, it didn't stop the Atlantic winds from rocking it at times. Ben wasn't exactly an admirer of ships, especially when it felt unstable. "How the hell is somebody supposed to eat with all this damn rocking back and forth going on? Come on, kid, let's get this meeting over with so I can get the hell out of here."

Jack and Connie laughed at the fact that Ben's face was turning a darker shade of green with every bite. "Alright, Ben, next time we'll have the meeting on your turf, but for now, we need to discuss the stern, and also I want to bring in the film crews."

After taking a few deep breaths so the color would come back to his face, Ben expressed his opinion. "Well, kid, if you do that, it's going to open up a can of worms. Once the press finally figures us out, all hell is going to break loose."

Henry also joined in with some negative views. "Also, Jack, we have to dig her out first and hope that everything is still connected to her bottom. From there, we have to decide whether or not to keep her rudder and propellers attached."

Connie had no shortage of worries. He was more concerned with the 94 years of soot inside and outside the massive ship. "Well, Jack, I have a couple of dredging ships on standby, but we're going to have to figure out a way of not only sucking it up, but displacing the soot so it doesn't resettle around the wreck. Usually, it's not a problem, but we're not bringing the soot to the surface. We're just moving it from one spot to another. It's almost certain we're gonna have to somehow modify the equipment."

As Sam sat and listened, his thoughts raced with ideas. "Listen, I'm no expert, but why don't we go by way of caution. This is too important to make any mistakes. With all the footage we have, it's pretty plain to see the stern is in piss-poor condition. When she hit the ocean floor, she hit hard. Both port and starboard sides of the stern collapsed, so why not stick with the original plan? We know at least the top three or four decks collapsed on each other, so let's peel them off one by one and bring them up in pieces. Afterwards, we can dig her out a bit to see if her port and starboard sides are still attached to the keel. If they are, I have an idea on how we can proceed and save some time and money."

Ben definitely liked the idea of saving money. "Alright, Sam, you have our complete attention. Let's hear what you have."

Sam smiled and continued on. "Okay. Hopefully she's still holding together. If she is, then let's dismantle her rudder and her propellers and bring them up one by one. Now, all that is left are the lower decks, which are still intact, and the port and starboard sides, which are lying flat on the sea floor. So, picture, if you can, a soft-shell taco. We should be able to just lift her two sides back into a vertical position, which would then lift what's left of the stern."

Jack and Connie had had plenty of tacos in their youth, so they could easily picture what Sam was saying. Ben, on the hand, was lost. "What the hell is a taco, and how the hell is that saving us money?"

After Henry finished laughing, he stood up to respond to Sam's ideas. "I don't eat Mexican food either, so like Ben, I've never had a taco, but I understand the concept. That's an excellent idea, Sam. I like it a whole lot better than mine, but we can't do it with just one grappling system. We're going to need at least two."

This was good news. At least Kotter Industries already had everything in place to build several more systems if needed, and it wouldn't take as long. Jack glanced over at Ben, who was still trying to figure out what a taco was. "Well, Ben, what'ya think? Maybe a month or so?"

Ben stood up and shook off his motion sickness, which was slowly starting to return. "Well, kid, the plans are already drawn up and we have all the materials, so sure, probably a month, give or take a day. Listen, I gotta get the hell out of here before I pass out. All this rocking back and forth isn't good for a man my age."

Before Ben could say anything else, Sam interrupted with some bad news. "Sorry, Ben, you can't leave tonight. There's a storm coming through. It's nothing major, but it's enough to make it hazardous for a small craft to travel back to New York."

Ben scratched his head and looked at Henry. "Did he just call my forty-foot yacht a small craft?"

Henry shook his head and laughed. "I think he did. Don't worry, Benjamin. We'll have ourselves a good time tonight. We'll drink 'til sun-up, then we'll sneak over to one of the barges and do some fishing. What'ya say old man?"

Ben didn't like the idea of staying overnight, but hanging out with Henry would make it bearable. "Alright, but I'm not sleeping on this tub. Henry and I will stay on the yacht for tonight. Besides, I just had the bar restocked."

As the team prepared to make history and bring up the stern of *Titanic,* Robert was still back in New York lurking and waiting for an opportunity to sink his teeth into Jack and Kotter Industries. Ben was the best when it came to business, but Robert was equally as ruthless and savvy. Robert's success came by way of economics. Robert was a huge reason why Kotter Industries managed to stay at the top of the food chain for so many years. Kotter Industries relied on him to guide the company through tough economic times.

As intelligent as he was, in 2007 Robert saw the various economic trends within the real estate market and knew it would have a ripple effect. During board meetings, America's economy was always a hot subject. Even though he was the go-to guy, Robert wasn't playing by the rules. Along with false information, Robert always reassured the board members the U.S. economy could survive any short-comings. In reality, the economy was headed downhill fast and he knew it.

CHAPTER THIRTY-FIVE

As winter gave way to spring, it was time to tackle the task of separating the three propellers and the rudder from the stern. As always, Connie was on point, dredging out the ocean floor just enough to get a submersible in to cut away the four mammoth pieces. By the beginning of the summer, the team had raised the 78-foot-high, 100-ton rudder, along with two of the propellers. A second team managed to collect all the material from the collapsed decks. Following suit, Kotter Industries was successful in manufacturing the other grappler needed to lift the ship. Without getting too excited, Jack could finally see the light at the end of the tunnel. One more propeller and then the stern itself.

After succeeding in bringing up the third propeller, the project had to be temporarily stopped due to a severe storm that was expected to last several days. The first day was mild, but by the second day, the seas started to swell as the wind pushed and pulled on the equipment, including the barges that stored the miscellaneous pieces of *Titanic*. It was a full-on, all night battle with all hands making sure none of the equipment broke loose. By the morning of the third day, the ocean swells had shrunk down to a manageable size, but the winds stayed strong.

Finally, after three days of pounding seas, some of the rigging broke loose. Connie and several other workers were on a barge where one of the 1,200 ton massive cranes had broken loose. A few of the men managed to manipulate some chains in order to help stabilize the equipment, but Connie wasn't so lucky. One of the hooks that broke loose struck Connie in the back of his head pushing him forward and overboard. Jack saw Connie hit the water, but was on another barge assisting other workers. Although the water was cold, it was the barges being pushed and pulled from the strong winds that posed most of the danger.

In desperation, Jack radioed the main ship to have a small craft launched, but Connie had no time. He was unconscious and floating between two of the barges. With the rain coming down heavy and the wind changing direction every few seconds, the two barges started to close the gap. Jack could only watch in horror as his best friend was crushed. With the storm still raging, Connie's body disappeared under the water. The next day, the storm had passed and a search was underway. It wasn't long before Connie's lifeless body was found. With a ghostly stare and mangled limbs, Connie was found floating ten miles from the sight.

It was up to Jack to notify the authorities and, more importantly, Warner. After Connie's body was recovered, the Coast Guard was called. Jack also notified Ben, who responded by coming out to the sight immediately. When he arrived, he was emotionally upset at the death of Connie, but he was also angered over the fact that if the project never happened, Connie would still be alive.

When the Coast Guard arrived, Jack explained the incident. The explanation was also corroborated by the other workers. As with everything else, Ben had connections in the Coast Guard. He knew half the crew and the ship's commander. There was no dispute over the accident, so it was just a formality of filing the proper paperwork and notifying the next of kin. After Ben spoke with the captain and explained the relationships, it was agreed that Jack would personally notify Warner.

Although it was officially considered an industrial accident at sea, it still fell under the responsibility of Kotter Industries. This was the first incident in the history of the company. Jack and Ben both knew it wasn't going to go over too well with the board members, especially Robert. Once again, the project had to be temporarily suspended, and that meant paying workers to sit around and do nothing. This was also a problem that would have to be addressed.

On the way back to the mainland, all Jack could think about was the daunting task of facing Warner and the long week of board meetings. When Ben's yacht finally docked, it was late. Jack could tell Ben was still very upset at the situation, but he still offered to tag along for moral support. As they stood on the dock, a cool breeze blew in off the water. "Listen, kid, I'm not going to lecture you or hound you about what happened, but if you need me to go with you to Warner's house, I will."

With everything happening so fast, Jack hadn't mourned the death of his friend until then. A single tear ran down his cheek as his thoughts replayed the horror of Connie being crushed. "I don't know what I'm going to say or how to say it, but whatever I do, it's going to have to be me on my own. I pushed Connie into this and now I have to bear the burden alone."

As they made their way to the parking lot, Casey was there waiting with the limo. "I know you're pissed, Ben, and you have every right to be."

Before Jack could say anything else, Ben's anger erupted. "You think I'm pissed? After all these years, I thought you knew me better, kid. I was pissed this morning when I found out about Connie! I'm way above that now!"

Casey had seen Ben's anger many times, but he had never seen Ben that crazy. After taking a few deep breaths, Ben continued his rage. "Can you even fathom what is going to happen? Not only is the media going to have a field day, but Robert is going to carve you up like a God damn Thanksgiving turkey, and there's not a damn thing I can do to protect you!"

Angry and disgusted, Ben didn't want to hear any more of what Jack had to say. He turned and stepped into the limo, leaving Jack to his fate. Jack stood on the empty parking lot watching the limo drive away as it disappeared into the night. Afterwards, he gathered his remaining strength and drove over to see Warner.

When he arrived, it was after midnight. When Warner answered the door, she was wiping the sleep from her eyes. At first, she thought maybe Connie forgot his key, but when she saw it was Jack, she was somewhat surprised. "Come in, Jack. What are you doing here? The last I heard, Connie said you guys were about to bring up half the ship."

Jack's heart was beating way too fast and he knew he had to somehow calm himself down. As he sat down, he tried to take a couple of breaths, but it just wasn't enough. "I'm sorry for coming here so late, Warner, but I needed to talk to you."

By then, Warner had yawned several times and was wide awake. "So, what's going on? Is Connie in some kind of trouble? Don't you dare cover for him like you used to. You might as well tell me."

Jack knew there was no easy way to say it, so he just blurted it out. "Several days ago, a violent storm swept through the north Atlantic. Last night, it got really bad when some of the equipment broke loose. We were able to re-secure it, but not before the accident."

Jack could see the worry starting to appear on Warner's face. "Why are you here without Connie? Was he hurt? Is he in the hospital?" Before Jack could answer, Warner started crying as she stood up in a panic. As the tears rolled down her face, her voice became louder. "Where's Connie at, Jack?" When Jack stood up to hold her, Warner became even more enraged. "Where's Connie? Why isn't he here?"

As his shoulder blades started to droop, Jack's arm went limp. "I'm sorry, sweetheart, Connie isn't coming home."

Suddenly, Warner gasped for air as she started to hyperventilate. "No, Jack. You're wrong. Connie is coming home. He's just trying to play a joke on me. Tell me he's playing a joke, Jack."

With tears still pouring out and breathing heavy, Warner stepped closer to Jack. "Tell me, Jack. Tell me you're joking."

With his body feeling like Jell-O, Jack was out of words. "I'm sorry, Warner."

With speed and accuracy, Warner slapped Jack across the face. "No, Jack. Connie's outside my door laughing isn't he? Tell me, Jack."

Jack slowly rubbed his fingers across his cheek to try to take away some of the sting, but it was premature. Once again, Warner slapped him. This one was more intense than the first. "You promised me, Jack. You stood in this very room and made a promise to take care of my Connie." Warner was crying uncontrollably. "God damn you, Jack Kotter. God damn you for what you are."

Once more, Jack attempted to hold Warner, but instead was met with more rage. Warner slapped him several more times. "Get out! Get the hell out my house, you bastard. Get out!"

Finally, with her weakened legs, Warner collapsed into Jack's arms crying. "Why, Jack? Why did you have to go after that ship? Why? You took Connie away. Why, Jack? Why?"

Jack gently kissed Warner on the forehead then turned to leave. Warner wiped her face on her sleeve then picked up a vase full of flowers that Connie sent her. As Jack opened the door to leave, Warner threw the vase. Just barely missing Jack, it broke against the wall. "You son of a bitch."

With Warner's words still fresh in his head, Jack gently closed the door and went home. With a broken heart and a broken soul, Jack was numb all over. Like a zombie with no feeling, he dragged himself up on the porch and flopped down in the chair. It wasn't long before he fell asleep. A few hours later, he awoke as the sun was starting to rise. Suddenly, the front door opened and Bria walked out. She was going for her morning jog and was surprised to see that Jack had slept outside.

"What are you doing here? You usually call me first before you come home."

As Jack stood up to stretch, she could see the wear and tears on his face. Jack was groggy and didn't speak right away, but as he rubbed his face and wiped away the leftover tears, he leaned over and gave Bria a kiss on the cheek, then slowly walked into the house.

With some worry, Bria followed behind. "What's wrong, Jack? You don't look so good. Did something happen with the project?"

Jack heard all the questions, but was too worn out to try to keep up. It took all of his remaining strength to turn and look Bria in the face. "Connie is dead."

Bria stood quietly as she tried to process what Jack had just said. Her lower lip dropped as her mind accepted the words. "What do you mean Connie's dead? Please tell me this is just a cruel joke."

Jack could barely look Bria in the eyes. When he turned to walk into the kitchen, Bria grabbed him from behind. Her voice became elevated. "Tell me what happened, Jack, and it better not have anything to do with that damn ship."

After telling Bria about the storm and the accident, Bria became even angrier. She quickly changed her clothes and rushed out of the house. Jack figured she was going to see Warner and didn't see any reason to try to stop her. Afterwards, he took a long shower and passed out on his bed.

CHAPTER THIRTY-SIX

As Jack lay sleeping, New York was just waking up. Businesses were unlocking their doors, people were coming and going, and the media was all over Kotter Industries. As the reporters were being kept at bay, the secretaries' phones rang off their hooks. Kotter Industries' public relations department was overwhelmed. They had no choice but to make an official statement. After everything was said and done, the media released the story during the afternoon news. "*Titanic* Takes Another Life."

When Jack awoke in the late afternoon, it wasn't long before he found out Ben was right. It was a media frenzy and Kotter Industries was caught in the middle. When Jack arrived at work, he was quickly surrounded by reporters rudely shoving their cameras in his face. After pushing his way through, he was finally able to get into the building. For the moment, he was safe from the battle, but he was headed upstairs where the war was waiting for him. As he entered the boardroom, all eyes were on him. The tension was thick as Jack could feel the looks piercing through him. He knew he had a lot to answer for, but at the same time, he was still morning Connie's death. Still feeling everyone's eyes, he quickly made a cup of coffee and sat down. He expected condolences, but instead was looked upon as reckless and immature. As Ben and Robert stood off to the side talking, Jack sat and listened to the whispers and ridicule.

When Ben and Robert finished, Ben addressed the meeting. "Alright, everyone, grab whatever refreshments you need and have a seat. It's going to be a long meeting and a long day."

After the events of the past couple of days, Jack noticed Ben was unusually calm, or maybe he was just worn out. Either way, Jack still knew he was very upset and disappointed. After Robert's presentation of lies and deceit regarding the economy, it was Jack's turn to face the board.

With some hesitation, he stood up and addressed everyone. He didn't know quite what to say, but as usual, he always recalled how his father spoke during tough times. *Speak as though you're the biggest man in the room, but whatever the situation, treat it with your utmost respect.*

"Well, everyone, I know how important a company's reputation can be. We do one good deed after another and get praised, but as soon as something negative happens, that's the one thing everyone seems to remember. I know the death of my friend has placed a considerable amount of pressure on this company, not because of the accident, but because of what we're trying to accomplish. By now, every television station and newspaper is preparing to tell the world what we're doing. There's no doubt in my mind the public is going to be outraged. My guess is that Kotter Industries will be looked upon as grave robbers."

Jack paused as he glanced around the table in order to get a feel for how the board members were reacting to his words. As he reached down for his cup of coffee, he could feel a slight tremor in his hand. Assessing everyone's facial expressions, he took a small sip and continued on. "Sometimes I stand before you and tell you stories about my dad and how he would handle certain situations, but I realize I need to stop doing that. My father is gone and I'm here. As I stand here before you today, I will give you my word and make each and every one of you this promise. Kotter Industries has faced adversity many times in the past, and this time is no different. We will make it through the darkness and come out shining on the other side. Although the media has already advertised that *Titanic* took another life, that phrase can't be further from the truth. Kotter Industries took every precaution and followed every safety regulation known, and I will not be intimidated by the media or public perception.

When the time comes, I will let everyone know about the funeral arrangements. Afterwards, the project with proceed as planned."

Jack didn't bother to stick around to hear any of the grumbling, and he certainly wasn't in any mood for anything Robert or Ben had to say, so he went back to his office. Afterwards, the meeting took a break.

Ben went back to his office with Robert hot on his heels. Mentally, Ben was preparing himself for a difficult battle, and Robert didn't waste any time throwing down the gauntlet. "Listen, Ben, I went along with this crazy idea knowing eventually it would fall apart, and if you remember correctly, I told you I would take Jack down if anything reflected negatively on this company. You also gave your word you would step down as chairman."

For a pleasant change, Ben made two cups of coffee and handed one to Robert. "You and I have been friends a long time, Robert. We seem to be a couple of old war dogs and we're not getting any younger. We haven't always seen eye to eye, but that's what I liked about our relationship. Through the years, I've enjoyed the little skirmishes and the constant battles in and out of the boardroom." Ben paused as he sipped his coffee. "You don't have to tell me this project stinks to high hell. I already know that. But you and I agreed to back the kid, not only because of persistence or because we felt obligated to the old man, but deep down, we both wanted to see this project succeed. I think eventually, the public will come around. They always do. No matter what the circumstance, the media builds it up, and over time, the public forgets. Eventually, they'll find something else to chew on. Now, let me save you from wasting your words. We've already gone beyond the point of no return, so instead of trying to work against us, why don't you place all your energy into helping contain the situation so we can move on?"

During Ben's speech, Robert sat listening and sipping his coffee, knowing eventually he was going to hold Ben and Jack responsible for the failure. "Alright, Ben. You'll get no argument from me, but we still have to deal with the death of Connie."

Even with the rocky relationship Ben had with Connie, he was still saddened by his death. "Well, it's already been determined as an accident, so there's not going to be any further investigation. Connie's father died about 12 years ago and his mom passed away shortly afterwards. Besides his wife, he has no other family that we know of. Warner has already made up her mind to have him cremated. She plans to throw his ashes into the Mediterranean Sea. I don't think any of us, including Jack, are invited."

When the meeting resumed, Jack wasn't there. He'd decided to go home for the day to try to smooth things over with Bria, but Bria wasn't home. Instead of sitting around thinking about his troubles, he decided to go see Riley. When he arrived, Riley was up in his chair reading about the Kotter Industries scandal. With all that was going on, Jack tried to remain upbeat. With a smile on his face, he hopped up into the other chair and greeted his friend. "Hey, Riley, how's business?"

Riley folded his newspaper and placed it in his lap. After a few seconds, Jack could tell Riley was disgusted. "Oh, I see you've heard the news."

Just when Jack was about to try to explain, Riley cut him off. "So this was your big project you were talking about? I thought I knew you better, Jack, but I guess not. I just can't believe Kotter Industries would stoop so low as to invest stockholders money into grave robbing."

Suddenly, Jack felt like he was being ambushed. As he waited patiently for an opening, Riley wouldn't let up.

"As your friend, why would you not tell me before doing something like that? Or maybe all these years, you've just been jerking me around so I would keep pouring money into Kotter stock. I guess it really doesn't matter. This time tomorrow, I'm dumping everything I have that's connected to your company."

Before Jack could respond, Riley threw the newspaper down and walked away more disgusted than he was before. Jack felt he was rapidly losing friends, and with them any support he may have had, so he paid a visit to the Wiley Roadster. As he pulled onto the lot, everyone stopped and stared, but this time it wasn't the glad-to-see-you stare he used to, but a more ominous stare. As he slowly cruised through the lot, everyone looked on in dissatisfaction. Although Jack knew most everyone that hung out, he didn't see anyone he called a friend, so he just kept going.

After driving around for a couple of hours trying to clear his thoughts, he decided to go home. When he arrived, it didn't take long to realize there was something different. As he stood in the doorway, he glanced around the room. None of Bria's clothing was lying about. When he walked into the kitchen, there were no dishes in the sink. Bria always left her dishes for him to clean up. Jack walked back out to the living room and, once more, looked around. All the small knickknack items Bria usually kept around were gone.

As Jack climbed the steps to go to the bedroom, his heart started to weigh heavy. When he walked in, he walked quickly to the closet. With his eyes moving from side to side, he stood for a few seconds in total awe. All of Bria's clothing was gone. There were a few times in the past Bria had been mad and left, but she'd always left her belongings behind. This time was definitely much different. Everything was gone. He turned to the bed and saw the ring he gave her laying on the pillow. Beside it was a letter.

We met and our love for each other happened in an instant. The man I wanted to spend my life with was warm and kind. The man I loved from day one had compassion in his heart and his soul was pure. The man whose thoughtfulness had no match and who would gladly humble himself during the worst of times is no longer part of me. The man I knew no longer exists. I realize now that man went away long ago, and I have to accept the reality I will never see him again. He gave up his life and friends for a cold, emotionless company.

Let someone go and if they return then you're meant to be together, but I realize I've let you go many times in my heart and you've never returned. The man reading this letter is not the man I met, so if someday this letter finds its way back to him, I wanted him to know I loved him with all my heart.

When Jack finished reading, he noticed some dried tear drops at the bottom of the paper. He could feel his heart breaking and could think of no relief. His legs felt weak as he sat down at the edge of his bed. As he reviewed the words on the paper, he remembered the dream he had about him and Bria in different boats drifting apart. It all became clear like a great revelation. Everyone he cared about had tried to keep him from a path of destruction, but he was blind. Suddenly, he remembered his father and a Bible verse he had taught him at a young age. *What good is it to inherit the world if you lose your soul? Mark 8:36.*

Trying to keep up with a fast-paced world could destroy everyone and everything he cared about. Jack was feeling the effects of exactly that.

The next day, he met Ben at the diner for breakfast. Ben could tell there was something wrong, but thought maybe it was stress. "Don't worry, kid, Kotter Industries has seen its fair share of dark days. We'll get through it."

Jack sat staring at Ben for a few seconds. "I'm sorry, Ben."

As Jack took a sip of coffee, Ben's mind ran rampant trying to figure out what the apology was for. "Alright, kid. I told you, we'll get through it."

Emotionally drained, Jack placed his coffee down on the table. "No, Ben, you're not hearing me. I'm sorry for everything. You were right about the box. I should have just buried that damn thing in a deep hole and forgotten about it. At times, I was selfish and I was blinded by greed. I used you and the company resources to get what I wanted when I should have been more careful to make more intelligent decisions. I became a cold, hard machine to Bria, and I did nothing but push my friends away. I kept trying to use my dad as an excuse, when all along, I was trying to play king of the world. I've been trying to figure out where I went off track and I just can't remember. I guess it really doesn't matter now. Connie's dead and that was enough for Bria. She's gone. Most of my friends have disowned me. Robert is just itching to force me out and I'm still not sure why you're still here talking to me."

Ben appreciated the fact Jack had come to terms with himself, but in usual Ben fashion, he had no time for sympathy. "If you're done feeling sorry for yourself, maybe we can sit here and work on a solution to your problems. There's no doubt in my mind you have to see this project through. The ramifications would be astronomical to the company, not to mention all the lawsuits, if you chose to stop now. As for Robert, I have him under control for now, but I don't know how much longer he's going to stay that way. The media, they'll eventually give up when something else newsworthy comes along. The public will forgive and forget, but your friends are a different story. You're gonna have to find a way to make peace with them."

After breakfast, Jack made arrangements to get the project back on track. While Ben kept Robert and the media at bay, Jack set up a meeting with Henry and Sam to discuss the retrieval of the stern. While he waited for the arrival of Sam and Henry, Jack sat on the edge of one of the barges. He sat reminiscing about all the childhood adventures he and Connie had managed to get into and laughed. He then said a small prayer and realized Ben was right. Jack had nobody to blame but himself, so he shouldn't waste time feeling sorry for himself. Although the idea remained the same, the project took on new meaning. It was no longer about completing a family obligation, it became more about getting on with life.

When Henry and Sam finally arrived, Jack was eager to get started. It took a few weeks of prep work and excavation before Henry's designed claw system could get its first crack at *Titanic*. During those weeks, there were several dives to the sight to determine whether or not the collapsed sides of the stern were still connected to *Titanic*'s bottom.

After the initial work and hundreds of photos, it was determined she was still intact. But even with this revelation, Jack was still skeptical about moving her, and with good reason. After everything was said and done, Jack had one final meeting. He looked Henry in the eyes and asked him about the integrity of the ship. As optimistic as Henry could be at times, even he couldn't give Jack the answer he wanted to hear.

"Well, Jack, we've come too far to turn back now. If you're asking me to give you a yes or no answer, I can't do that. If you're asking me for my professional opinion, I can tell you those Irish really knew how to build ships back then. They built them to last and I have no doubts about their workmanship. Is there a good chance she'll break apart? Sure. She's been down there for 95 years. Anything could happen at this stage in the game."

With some worry, Jack looked at Sam for a moment. "What do you think, Sam?"

Sam took a deep breath. "Well, I've made many dives on old wrecks and it always seemed to amaze me that, over the years, most of the ships I dived on had remained intact."

Jack knew he had a huge decision to make. After the meeting, he tried to think about all possible scenarios, but he kept coming up with the same outcomes. Anything but success would devastate Kotter Industries. The number of lawsuits combined with several countries being enraged would simply wipe the Kotter name from history. While he was in his cabin resting, Jack received a message that he was needed in the boardroom for a meeting the next day. Jack was so preoccupied, he didn't think to call ahead to find out why he was needed.

The next day, he arrived at work to find everyone in a dismal mood. When he stepped off the elevator, there weren't any pleasant hellos or conversations. There were no smiles or laughter. Mostly, people were trying not to make eye contact. When Jack made it to his office, Bonnie informed him Robert was waiting in the main conference room. When he walked in, Robert was already seated at the table, sipping his coffee. "Please have a seat, Jack. I appreciate you taking time out of your busy schedule to meet with me."

Jack's eyes quickly scanned the room for other people, but saw nobody. With a smug look and arrogant grin, Robert laid some paperwork out on the table. "If you want, help yourself to some coffee. I just made it so it's fresh."

Although Jack knew Robert always had an arrogance about him, there was something different this time. He didn't bother with the coffee and cautiously sat down. "Alright, Robert. You obviously have some kind of agenda, so let's hear it."

With his grin turning into a smirk, Robert stood up. "Just like your father, a chip off the old block, or maybe not. Your father was a great man despite his eccentric way of life. He was my friend and I had a tremendous amount of respect for him." With his arms folded, Robert walked slowly around the table. "But for you, I have no respect. I don't like you, nor do I think you have what it takes to be half the man your father was. You're a minnow trying to disguise yourself as a shark. You constantly use Benjamin as a shield to hide behind, and I don't like that."

When Robert finished circling the table, he sat back down. By that point, Jack was attempting to stay calm. "So, you called me back to New York to insult and belittle me?"

Robert glanced down at the paperwork on the table and slid some of the papers over to Jack. "I couldn't care less about why you think you're here, so let me get straight to the point. I'm tired of hearing about your so-called family honor. I think it's bullshit. I told Ben your little project would cost both of you, and now I'm here to collect."

Jack briefly read through some of the papers and didn't like what he saw. It seemed to be reminiscent of the situation with Nicholas. "This says I'm giving my stock up for public sale and resigning. If this is your way of playing a joke, I'm not laughing."

Robert's smirk quickly changed to anger as he slammed his briefcase shut. "This is far from being a joke, Junior. You're out of money. This company has been supporting your project for the last few months."

Jack was a little surprised, but only because Ben didn't say anything. Jack smiled as a he stood up to get a cup of coffee. "I can't believe you would even try something like this, Robert. You think I would just quiver in my boots, tuck my tail, and run? That's funny. So the money set aside for the project ran out, okay. I already have the executive board backing this project. They're not going to support the idea of just stopping halfway through. At least not just on your say-so."

Robert smiled as he leaned back in his chair. "So quickly you forget part of what I do, Junior. I'm an economist, and I'm guessing you haven't been keeping up with the news lately. I guess that's one of the prices you pay for being out of touch with the world while you're at sea. The U.S. economic situation is starting to look grim. The dominoes are starting to fall. The bursting of the housing bubble has the banks scrambling to avoid a crisis. The world markets have already started to weaken, and with no end in sight with the Middle East, by this time next year, we'll be facing a recession that might rival the Great Depression. When it happens, it will take years to fully recover. You are right about the board, though. They are backing your little project for now, but when push comes to shove, those greedy vultures care more about their bank accounts than loyalty."

Suddenly, Jack was feeling like the minnow that Robert had called him earlier. "What the hell is wrong with you? You've been feeding the board members the idea that our economy was strong and could withstand anything. You want to bring this company to its knees just to get rid of me? Ben will eat you up and spit you out when he finds out."

Robert paused for a moment and geared up for a final attack.

"Well, Junior, you're right. I may have fabricated certain information, but that won't matter once the board realizes I'm the only one that can fix the problem. I've just been lying and waiting like a lion watching its prey, but that doesn't matter now. Ben made a deal with me and will be stepping down as chairman of the board. As for you and this silly little project, I couldn't care less. What I do care about is this company. Yeah, we might have to shut down some factories and lay off some employees, but this company will survive as it always has."

So far, Robert had the upper hand during the game of mind chess, but Jack still had a few moves left. "I gotta tell you, Robert, I've always known your potential for taking over. I just didn't think you would go to these lengths to do it. What makes you think I'm going anywhere? I still have majority control, and all I need to do is exercise patience. I can bring this project to a halt and pick it back up later when the bad times pass. As for Ben and whatever deal he made, it's irrelevant. The board won't go for him stepping down."

Robert sat staring at Jack like a cat stares at a mouse when it's toying with it. "I really didn't think you would put up this much of a fight, Jack, so let me just give you something to think about. First off, the public is already outraged over your grave robbing escapades. Second, if you let this project sit without finishing it, the amount of lawsuits combined with the fact we will lose every government contract we have will start the downfall of Kotter Industries. Now, add the fact that private business sectors here and around the world will cease to do business with us because of your incompetence. In the end, the Kotter name will be spoken in such company as Bethlehem Steel and Enron."

Robert opened his briefcase and surprisingly pulled out a Bible. He turned to 1 Kings 3:25 and handed it to Jack to read. The verse dealt with two mothers fighting over one child. King Solomon made the decision to chop the child in half, knowing the true mother would surrender the child rather than see it killed. Jack knew the story well. He realized the added financial burden of the *Titanic* project could possibly bankrupt Kotter Industries and send the company into a downward spiral. Feeling like the heartbroken mother in the story, it was a difficult decision to give up the company, but the right one. With a heavy heart, Jack stood up and walked over to the window. He took a few minutes to stare out over the parking lot. "You're a real bastard. You came up with this backstabbing plan and played it out perfectly, and then you throw Bible verses at me to justify yourself. There are more terrible words for people like you, but I'll save my dignity and won't use them."

Robert placed the Bible back into his briefcase, along with his copies of the paperwork. "Give up the company your dad built or watch it die. I'll give you some time to sign the papers. I'll be in my office when you're finished."

After Robert left, Jack stood at the window and gazed out at the traffic in the distance. He thought about calling Ben, but then Robert's words kept playing over and over in his mind. He was right. Jack thought about all the times he had used Ben to hide behind. This time had to be different. He had to accept responsibility for his actions and finally stand on his own. He felt he had no real choice but to see the project through. Selling off his majority of the company would guarantee the completion of the project.

The next day, Jack made plans to be transported back out to the sight. He had Sam and Henry meet him on the deck. When Jack arrived, he was surprised to see Ben waiting. Several film crews were also waiting and everything was in place, ready to go. Henry was just waiting on Jack to give the go ahead. "Listen, Henry, I know this is the moment we've all been waiting for, but I need to talk with Ben for a few minutes."

Henry glanced over at his friend Ben and gave a small respectful nod as to say go easy on him. After Sam and Henry walked away, Jack turned to Ben. "So, when did you find out?"

Ben was saddened by the fact this conversation was even taking place. "I've been in Ireland all week and I just got back last night. Bonnie called me in tears. Apparently, Robert wasted no time in moving her to another office. He went as far as to put out an email about your departure. I love that man, but sometimes he can be a real jackass. Anyway, kid, why did you do it? You should have never faced off against Robert on your own. I should have been there with you."

Jack smiled because so many times Ben had protected him. "No, Ben, not this time. I have to stand on my own two feet some time. Besides, by the time I realized what was going on, it was too late. Robert had this whole thing planned perfectly, which brings me to you. You're not seriously thinking about going through with that non-binding deal you made?"

Ben paused as he enjoyed the cool breeze blowing off the ocean. "Well, kid, you're right. Robert definitely played us pretty well. In our last conversation, he assured me he was still okay with the project. I should have known better. And to answer your question, yes. No court would ever uphold such a deal, but that's not how men like Robert and I operate. It was a gentleman's agreement, bound with a handshake, and that's more important to me than any paper contract. The deal was if anything went wrong that reflected negatively on the company then I would step aside as chairman and retire. Stepping down didn't really matter to me anyway. I never wanted that position. Besides, it always interfered with my afternoon delight with my lady friends. Retiring is something completely different. There are many ways of retiring, and this old pony has one last trick. I might have agreed to retirement, but I never gave a timeframe."

It had been awhile, but Jack let out a laugh. "Well, aren't we a couple of misfits with no place to go?"

Though Ben and Jack enjoyed a few seconds of laughter, it wasn't long before the conversation turned serious again. "Listen, kid, I'm still a board member for now, but I'm tired. With everything that went down, I'm looking forward to just walking away. Maybe I can be one of those people I told you about. Sleep until the afternoon and party all night. What'ya think, kid?"

Jack smiled as he placed his arm around Ben. "I think you would make a great party animal. What'ya say you stick around long enough to see history get made?"

Ben's facial expression suddenly became serious, then a small smile crept out. "Don't worry, kid. I wouldn't miss your father's final dream for the world. Besides, last time I came out here, Henry beat me in a poker game. I gotta get my money back."

With that said, Jack lifted his radio up to his lips and gave the word. "Hey, Henry, I think we're ready to do this."

Henry was just inside the door and quickly poked his head out. "'Bout damn time you two mush-heads finished crying to one another. Now let's get this dog and pony show on the road."

Henry grabbed the radio and asked for confirmation, and it was quickly relayed back that all systems were online and ready to go. There were four grappling systems in place. After 95 years of being completely still, the stern started to grumble and moan.

The murky soot started to kick up and create a fog-like haze as the underwater film crew carefully filmed every aspect of movement. Suddenly, the massive stern slowly rose out of its grave. Before it could make its ascent, the ship's bottom had to be checked. Sam checked the keel and had nothing but good news. Although the port and starboard sides had to be twisted back into place, they were holding steady with the help of the grappling system. It would take several hours before the stern reached the surface of the ocean.

While the cranes were slowly doing their jobs, the team took the opportunity to sit and plan out the next phase. They set up a table on the deck so they could watch with pride as the grappling system was hard at work. As the designer, Henry was in his finest moment. Sam had his radio glued to his ear monitoring everything going on with the project. Ben sat staring at Jack as Jack stared off into space.

"I see you're really deep in thought, kid. You mind sharing with the rest of us?"

As his daydreaming gave way to Ben's scratchy voice, Jack let out a wondering smile. "Well, I was just sitting here wondering about what my life would be like if the *Titanic* disaster never happened."

Henry laughed as he pushed his chair back onto two legs. "Well now, that's a millennium-old question that everyone seems to ask. What if wars never happened? What if disasters never happened? What if life was just a bowl of cherries? What if? What if? What if?"

Before Henry could finish, Ben cut in with a laugh. "It would be one hell of a crowded planet."

The laughter didn't last long because something came over the radio. Crane number four was starting to blow out smoke. All systems came to a stop while repairs had to be made. In the meantime, Jack and Ben discussed plans for the bow while Henry supervised the repairs. Afterwards, Ben decided to go back to New York for a day or two to wrap up a few loose ends.

CHAPTER THIRTY-SEVEN

A FEW DAYS LATER, REPAIRS WERE DONE AND BEN WAS ON HIS WAY OUT to the site. By the time he arrived, the stern was only 100 feet from the surface. As everyone watched with anticipation, the stern finally broke through the waves. With all the cheers and the applause, it sounded like the conclusion of a heavy weight bout that went the distance. Unfortunately, there was still plenty more work to be done. It would take months to assess all the damage and determine the best course of action. Although Ben was right, the media slowly lost interest due to bigger stories, that didn't keep the occasional tabloid papers from sending out small crafts to try to get pictures. They would never stay long because of the rough Atlantic having its way tossing them around like toys. Every now and then, a small boat or two would circle around, usually within binocular range, but that didn't bother Jack. Shortly after his departure from Kotter Industries, Robert made sure the company was disassociated with the project and any lawsuits. Jack knew he was alone and facing an uphill battle with public perception.

Summer came to an end and fall was setting in. While Ben was still working on his final plans for retirement, Jack decided to break for the winter and resume the project in the spring. That meant Jack had absolutely nothing to do. He decided to take a trip out to California to visit the old homestead.

In the meantime, Ben purposely utilized the company bank account to take a trip back to Belfast, Ireland. Years ago, he and Jack Sr. had agreed they would never travel using company money, but given the circumstances, Ben wanted to piss Robert off as much as possible. While he was away, Henry and Sam stayed behind to manage the site. To prepare for the stern, Jack had a floating dock built to keep the massive wreckage of steel afloat.

Although history was made in America with the first African American president being voted into office, it was politics as usual in the nation's capital. Along with smiles, speeches, and the blowing of kisses came promises of prosperity and better days. What happened instead was obsolete wars, natural disasters, and good old-fashioned red tape, along with a dysfunctional government.

For Kotter Industries, it was inevitable, with the economy in a downward spiral, that Robert would make good on his threats. With Jack gone, Ben stood alone in the boardroom and had little power left. Like most other large corporations, Kotter Industries was bleeding money. Some of the overseas operations had to be shutdown. The decision to make large numbers of layoffs, not only overseas but across the United States, was made. Naturally, with the economy in a nosedive, the stock markets wavered, and Kotter stock, along with many others, decreased in value.

Although Jack wasn't part of his father's company anymore, he still kept his eyes and ears open concerning the company's activities. From time to time, Ben would keep him updated. As winter gave way to spring, Jack geared up to finally bring his father's lifelong dream to an end. He left the comforts of sunny California and made his way out into the still frigid Atlantic. He met with Sam and Henry to discuss the final preparations of the project. One last piece of the puzzle lay just two miles beneath them. The infamous bow. This was the crown jewel of the wreck. This was also the piece that was, for the most part, intact.

As Jack and Sam stood watching the calm, cold water, they could still feel a bit of winter in the breeze. "Well, Sam, what'ya think?"

As he took a deep breath, Sam smiled. "I think I'm grateful for just being here and for you and Ben letting me be part of history."

Now it was Jack's turn to take in the brisk air. "I appreciate your sentiment, Sam. Now what'ya think about the bow?"

After a brief laugh, Sam started to look worried. "Well, Jack, I don't know. Ever since they found her, I've always wondered what kind of damage is underneath. When people watch the specials and the movies, they don't realize when the bow hit, she dug herself a sixty-foot hole. We won't know anything about the damage until we dig her out. All the film we've been shooting is nothing compared to what we'll see if or when we raise the bow section."

Just then, Henry came walking out on deck. "If or when? Come on, Sam, you gotta have some positive thoughts. Anyway, I think we're all going to be very surprised. If you look at the pictures and the video footage, it's obvious she buckled when she hit, but I think we'll be just fine. I keep telling everyone those Irish knew what they were doing."

A few days later, Ben arrived just in time for the final prep work. The dredging ships were finished and the workers were attaching the grappling systems. It was June, and the cool breezes had warmed, and the workers were noticing more and more commercial and cruise ships off in the distance.

Finally, it was time. Jack gave the order and the massive system started to turn. As they slowly lost their slack, the massive chains started to pull and lift. Once again, Sam was below watching to make sure nothing went wrong. When the bow started to move, it crumpled together back to its original shape. Like a ghost in the darkness, it slowly disappeared as the soot started to churn and create a fog-like haze. Sam's voice came on the radio and informed Henry he could no longer see what was happening. He advised they halt the operation until the soot could resettle, but Henry advised against it. In Henry's mind, it was now or never and all systems were go.

With some aggravation, Sam decided it would be better to have the submersible rise above the massive soot cloud in order to get a better view. As he stared downward out of the small porthole, his heart started to pound with anticipation. Compared to the *Titanic*, being in such a small craft left Sam feeling quite intimidated. Out of the soot and darkness came the massive bow of *Titanic*. Like something out of a sci-fi movie, the massive bow rose slowly, becoming more and more prominent as the soot sank to the bottom. Sam gave a wide berth as *Titanic* slowly rose above him. On the other side was a film crew filming the entire process. After the initial awe, Sam finally took notice of the damage the iceberg did when she first hit. Once again, he picked up the radio and informed everyone she was free from her watery grave.

Jack gave the order to stop so they could assess the damage, if any, to the bottom. After several hours of photographing the bow's keel, Sam ascended to the surface. His first thought was to scold Henry, but he took into consideration Henry's age and took a few breaths. "I think we're okay, Henry. You got lucky."

Sam could see the gleam in Henry's eyes. Luck was far from what Henry was feeling. "Come on, Sam, give an old man some credit, will'ya? I've been studying this wreck for years. I know how she went down and how she landed. Luck had nothing to do with what we did today, so let's get these photos processed so we can get on with it."

The film crew worked through the night and by mid-morning was done processing everything. While Ben, Henry, and Jack reviewed the footage, Sam prepared for the final dive. Henry paced the floor looking at still photos while Ben and Jack reviewed the film footage. "Well, Jack, I think she's been pretty well-preserved. Except for the initial buckling and the rips that it caused, I think we're in good shape."

Just like old times, Jack glanced over at Ben in order to get some idea from his expression, but Ben gave his usual attitude. "Don't look at me, kid, it's your show now. For all I care, you can dump this heap of scrap metal back down to the bottom of the ocean."

Jack gave a small sarcastic smile. "Thanks, Ben. I knew I could count on you. Alright, Henry, let's do it."

Henry didn't waste any time. Within seconds, he was on the radio barking out orders. Thirty minutes later, Sam was in the water ready to go. It would take a couple of hours for Sam to get the submersible in position, so it was just a short wait. As the afternoon approached, Sam gave the go-ahead. He was in place and everything looked good. With excitement in his voice, Henry gave the order to start *Titanic*'s final ascent. It would be another couple of hours before *Titanic*'s bow would see daylight.

As the grappling system did its job, the trio took advantage of the time and took a closer look at the stern. Two teams of underwater archeologists worked diligently to try to piece together *Titanic*'s last moments. There was also clergy on standby. A variety of easy maneuvering cranes were available, along with temporary scaffolding built in order to navigate what was left of the Goliath. The dripping of water and the moving of shadows made it an eerie visit. The ocean was calm, but it didn't stop the hull from bellowing out a moan every now and then. After just ten minutes in, Ben decided he had had enough. Too many uneasy sounds and unexplained shadows moving about. But Henry was like a little kid in a candy store. Although the amount of damage and decay made it hard, there were still many things still intact. Showcases with dishes in perfect condition. Stain glass windows and much more.

For Jack, it wasn't about the ship. It was about his family. He tried to imagine Victor having a drink in the lounge, laughing with other businessmen. He tried to picture his father as a child walking along the deck and looking out over the ocean. He remembered the diary page his father had written about the tragedy and how he never saw Victor again. Suddenly, he was overcome with emotions. Three generations and it was finally time to make the dream a reality.

Jack decided he, too, had had enough, so he left Henry to wallow in his curiosity. Jack went back to the operations boat and saw Ben leaning over the side. "I don't know why the hell I can't stay on my yacht. The seasickness is really getting on my nerves."

Jack smiled as he patted Ben on the back. "Because, Ben. Whether or not you want it, you're a huge part of this project, so I need your wisdom and input. Besides, it will all be over soon."

Just then, Sam came over the radio. *Titanic*'s bow was approximately 100 feet from the surface. The film crews were in place and ready to shoot. Henry was just getting back and was smiling from ear to ear. He laughed at Ben's face, which was still partially green from being sick. "Come on, Benjamin, it's almost over."

Ben finally caught his composure and straightened up. "If either one of you tells me it's almost over one more time, I'm gonna wrap a lifejacket around you and drag you from behind my yacht all the way back to New York. Now, let's get the show on the road so I can get the hell out of here."

Sam gave the okay and Jack gave the order. Once more, the

massive chains started to pull. The workers stood by and watched the water part like the Red Sea. As air bubbles trapped inside pushed their way to the surface, the bow finally emerged. Like a great goliathan waking up from a long slumber, she rose above the waves with a sense of new life. The applause was loud and the pride the workers displayed was even louder. They carefully maneuvered her over to the floating pier that awaited her arrival. She was in pieces, but after 97 years, *Titanic* was again on top of the Atlantic Ocean. After securing the final piece of the puzzle, the workers and crew broke out in celebration. Of course Henry and Ben supplied the liquor, and the party went on through the night.

The next morning, Jack woke up at sunrise and decided to survey what he had accomplished. As he stood looking out at the massive sight, he heard a groggy voice come from behind. "There she is, kid. All that remains. Now what?"

When Jack turned around, Ben was there looking like Mr. Professional GQ man. "I don't know how you do it, Ben. Party all night and still look great in the morning."

Luckily, the ocean was calm and Ben felt good. He walked over and leaned on the rail. "Listen, kid, I always look great no matter what, and don't you forget it. Now, back to my original question. Now what are your plans for this heap of scrap?"

Jack thought about it and just shook his head. "Well, I don't know. We know my dad wanted to somehow put this thing back together, but he didn't exactly draw up any blueprints for us."

Although Ben was technically one of the project managers, he would sometimes have to remind Jack exactly where he stood. "Listen, kid, I know we started this together, but I can no longer make any decisions. Robert cut all ties between this project and Kotter Industries, and whether I like it or not, I'm still a board member until my final resignation. Think about what you want to do. If you need me, I'll be in New York."

A few days later, the celebrating came to an end when Jack received a newspaper with *Titanic* plastered on the front page. Somehow the word had leaked out that *Titanic* had been fully excavated and was no longer at the bottom of the Atlantic Ocean. Once again, Jack was center stage with disaster. The public was outraged and the mainstream media showed no mercy. Melvina Dean was the last survivor of the tragic *Titanic* story and had passed away a couple of months earlier, so various news stations interviewed so-call shipbuilding experts and deep sea salvage experts to try to get an idea of the consequences of bringing *Titanic* to the surface. They also tried to get comments from Dr. Robert Ballard, but he declined to be interviewed.

All the negative attention brought on a whole new set of problems for Jack. The public outcries created demonstrations and protests at City Hall. This forced the mayor of New York to make an official statement. After everything was said and done, New York wanted nothing to do with grave robbing and would not welcome Jack or any pieces of his project into New York Harbor. With the detachment of Kotter Industries and an entire city telling him to stay away, Jack was out of ideas. The project had used up all of what his father had saved and was draining Jack's personal accounts. He was in no mood to hear any of Ben's speeches, but Jack felt he had no choice.

A few days later, Ben arrived back on site and Henry was there waiting with a bottle and a deck of cards. "Benjamin, my friend, we seem to have run into some problems."

Ben was already disgusted with the situation and it clearly showed. "I appreciate the welcome, Henry, but where the hell is Jack so we can get this damn meeting started?"

Jack and Sam were already sitting down discussing various options when Henry and Ben walked in. As Henry sat down, Ben wasted no time in going off. "Damn you, Jack. Damn you for not listening to me when I told you not to open that godforsaken box. You had control of one of the largest corporations in the world and all you had to do was live your life. Now look at you. Out here in the middle of nowhere with a broken down ship that nobody wants. Tell me something, where did your father and I go wrong? We handed you everything you could ever want on a silver platter and you threw it all away."

Jack paused for a moment then smiled. "Good to see you too, Ben. Now cool your jets and have a seat so we can get down to business."

With some surprise, Ben stood looking at Jack then sat down. "Listen, kid, for someone with no options, I suggest you don't bite the hand that feeds you. Now, you know I can't make any official decisions about this project, so let me just say this. Either let this monstrosity sink back down where it belongs or throw it up on some barges and let's get the hell out of here. Either way, I don't give a damn."

Jack knew Ben was just blowing off steam and that was normal. He also knew Ben was probably right all along. Why give a once in a lifetime life away to do something nobody agrees with? Jack knew his heart was in the right place, but that didn't mean he was doing the right thing. As the tension in the room started to grow thick, the silence set in. Jack stood up and leaned against the door jam. As he stared out into the ocean, he was reminded of something Lilith had said. She wanted to right all the wrongs, but did raising the *Titanic* right the wrongs or make things worse?

As Jack continued to think about his woes, Henry and Ben made quick work of Henry's booze. While they laughed and drank, Sam stood up and walked over to Jack. "What do you think about taking her back to Belfast, Ireland? I think they would probably welcome the chance to get their hands on *Titanic*. I'm sure with Ben's connections, he could make it happen."

As Jack tried to rub the stress from his eyes, he looked at Sam then glanced over at Ben and Henry. "I think you might be on to something, Sam."

With some renewed energy, Jack walked back to the table and sat down. "Sam has the idea of taking *Titanic* back to Belfast. What do you think, Ben?"

Ben was still enjoying his time with Henry, but he heard what Jack said. He scratched his head then shook his head no. "Sudden storms, rogue waves. Anything could happen between here and Belfast. It's not a bad idea, but I wouldn't recommend it. I gotta tell you, though, you're on the right track."

Just then, Jack realized Ben was about to unveil one of his master plans. "Come on, Ben, you gotta be kidding. You come here ragging me about how I screwed up, and all along, you have some kind of solution in mind."

Ben glanced over at Henry and they both burst out laughing. "Well, kid, Henry and I came up with an idea when I first went to go meet with him up in Maine. Listen, kid, this project was doomed from the beginning. I can't really tell you what your father's thinking was, but if I had to guess, I don't think there was any wrong choice.

Either you completed his final wishes or you just simply lived out your own life with Kotter Industries. I think your father would have been proud of you either way."

As Sam and Jack listened, Ben laid out the final plan. "We know your father's ultimate plan was to somehow get this ship back to New York and possibly put her back together. With all the hype about it now, you can probably kiss that idea goodbye. You can't take the chance of transporting it back to Ireland because there are too many unknown variables involved. So, what's the next best thing?"

Jack looked at Sam while Sam just shrugged his shoulders. Ben stared at Jack for a moment then smiled. "Come on, kid, just because I got knocked off my perch doesn't mean I'm still not well connected. While you boys have been out here playing Popeye the Sailorman, I've been dealing with Harland and Wolff."

As the bewildered look became apparent on Jack's face, his mind started to wander. "Are you talking about the Harland and Wolff Shipyard that built *Titanic*?"

Ben paused to finish off the drink in his glass. "Well, they're actually called Harland and Wolff Heavy Industries now. We've had some good dealings with them in the past, so we've managed to stay out of each other's way. Although most of their resources are placed on offshore projects, they still find time to build ships, and more importantly, they do ship repairs. When Henry and I first told them about this project, they were ecstatic." While Ben decided to finish off the bottle, he gave Henry a nod to finish the story.

"Think about it, Jack. Back then, shipbuilding was a family affair in Ireland. There was a lot of pride that went into every project. Grandfathers, fathers, and sons all working hand in hand to finish a ship. When *Titanic* was lost, a lot of pride was lost with her. There are third and fourth generation shipbuilders still working at Harland and Wolff, and they would like nothing better than to remove a blemish from their family history."

Jack was still trying to grasp the idea that was being presented. "Wait a minute, fellas. Let me get my head around this. You want to bring workers from Ireland way out here to put *Titanic* back together. You do realize we're in the middle of the Atlantic Ocean? And I can only fathom how I'm going to pay for all this."

Henry glanced over at Ben and shook his head. "You're right, Ben, no imagination."

While Henry went to fetch another bottle, Ben continued with some answers. "Listen, kid, Robert might have control of the board members, but I still make the decisions when it comes to wheeling and dealing overseas. The workers will be here next week. I also have a few stories I'm going to have leaked to the press. Watch and learn, kid. All this bad press you're getting will soon turn around."

The following week, reporters from around the world were competing for interviews with the workers from Harland and Wolff. They also tracked down surviving relatives of the victims who'd lost their lives aboard the doomed ship. When the media finally printed their stories, it was learned that the majority of workers picked for this occasion were in some way related to the original 3,000 workers who built *Titanic*. Grandsons, distant uncles, second and third cousins. All wanting a chance to repair history. It was also learned that the relatives didn't seem to mind seeing *Titanic* finish her maiden voyage. Come to find out, most felt as Jack Sr. did. It would correct a fatal mistake in history, and at the same time, give true closure to those who needed it most.

When the stories finally reached New York papers, the public was astounded. One of the headlines read "Who says you don't get a second chance to make a first impression?" Another simply read "Harland and Wolff back in the saddle." There were no more protests or ridicule. Public perception changed almost instantly. Just when Jack thought he was down and out, Ben came through with another one of his miracles. When the Irish workers finally arrived, they were greeted with applause.

Mr. Finnigan O'Leary was the master shipbuilder who was among some of the first volunteers recruited by Ben. His grandfather was just a young lad when he worked on building *Titanic*. In his later years, he would tell young Finnegan stories and show him pictures of the grandeur *Titanic* was made of. When Ben presented the opportunity, there was no hesitation. Finnegan had no interest in celebration or being patted on the back. He was a serious man who had one goal in mind: Set the record straight. He quickly held a meeting to set a plan of action in motion. While Sam helped with the excavation of the bow and stern, Ben, Henry, Jack, and Finnegan discussed materials, specifications of the ship, and the various types of equipment that would be needed. One of the biggest concerns were the gantries needed for the ship and the project. Gantries were a type of frame used to support the ship while it was being built. They were also equipped with cranes to move heavy materials into place. They would have to be attached to a floating platform, which would be tricky, but not impossible.

It would take another couple of months to prepare, but eventually summer gave way to fall. The cool air set in and everything was in place. Ben had to set up a special account due to large amounts of funds being donated to the project. When it came to donated materials, Ben threatened Robert to use one of Kotter Industries biggest competitors, China Steel Corporation. With very little choice, Robert finally came around to Ben's way of thinking and made the commitment of donating all the new steel needed to complete the project. With so many connections, Ben had half a dozen companies involved with fabricating most of the materials that would be used.

After the excavation of the stern and bow, it was finally learned there were no human remains left. However, there were some articles of clothing found along with a small portion of jewelry scattered about. Even some old coins managed to stay preserved. There was no question of what to do. A small ceremony was held with all of the items placed in a sealed container and attached to an anchor. It was then dedicated and dropped into the ocean.

After the dedication, Jack became a bit emotional, so he quietly slipped away from the crowd. As the sun started to set, he looked out over the ocean and watched a ship way off in the distance as it appeared to glide across the water. He couldn't help but think about his father and what he would be feeling if he was still alive. Just as he was enjoying a few moments of peace, Ben snuck up from behind and cracked the silence with his voice.

"Hey, kid, your father would have been proud of you."

Jack turned to see Ben actually smiling. "Thanks, Ben, for the kind words. I also haven't had the chance to thank you for all that you've done. You were absolutely right and I should have never doubted you. Public perception, the funds, everything. I can't believe you pulled this off, but somehow, I knew you cared."

As the sun continued to fade, Ben handed Jack a beer. "It's been a long ride, kid. Here's to success."

Just then, Finnegan came walking over. "Well, Mr. Kotter, I think we should be ready by next week."

Jack smiled as he reached out and shook Finnegan's hand. "So you really think you can put Humpty Dumpty back together?"

With a frown on his face, Finnegan made a feeble attempt to try to smile. "No, Mr. Kotter. We're going to rebuild *Titanic* and maybe restore some pride. Ignorance combined with an iceberg may have sunk her, but I'm gonna make damn sure she reclaims her dignity and glory." With even more determination, Finnegan walked away.

Ben just laughed and shook his head. "Don't worry, kid. Hopefully, he didn't take that as an insult."

Jack thought for a second then took a drink. "Connie would have loved this. He probably would have been going in a hundred different directions right about now, but he would have been loving every second of it. I guess I just miss my friend and I wish he was here."

Ben knew it was a sensitive subject, so he took a long breath and thought about what to say. "Listen, kid. Once this is all over, you're going to be missing a lot of people. Life will go on, and when it does, you'll face new challenges. I'm sorry he's not here, but you are. You're right. He would have been thrilled at the possibility of sailing *Titanic* into New York harbor, so let's keep his memory alive by finishing this thing and moving forward with our lives."

The following week, the first shipment of material arrived and the men started the work. They wasted no time cutting, welding, and hammering away at what was left of *Titanic*. Obviously, over the years, many of the notable pieces of *Titanic* deteriorated and disappeared, such as the crow's nest, all four funnels, the docking bridge, and even the wheelhouse had disintegrated. On the flipside of the coin, much of the material and artifacts that were salvaged years before were slowly being donated back to the project. Even a 15-ton piece of *Titanic*'s hull salvaged in 1998 was transported back to the sight to be reused and welded back into place. In 1993, one of the four famed whistles made of bronze weighing in at 750 pounds was salvaged and painstakingly restored. It too was being stored and waiting to be returned to its rightful place on *Titanic.*

The excitement of the project, combined with the rambunctious energy of the workers, continued into 2010. As usual, the media found new dilemmas to pursue and drama to report. They eventually stopped trying to get sneak peeks at any progress and gave up on chasing Jack for interviews. However, Jack was able to mend his reputation and was once more admired by most of his friends.

Good and bad fortune came and went throughout 2010. Another famous ship from the Cunard Line, the RMS *Queen Mary 2,* continued its voyage circumnavigating the world. Hundreds of thousands of people were stranded after airports all around Europe were shut down due to a volcanic eruption that thrust clouds of ash into the sky and blanketed Europe. Thirty-three Chilean miners who were trapped for 69 days in a Chilean mine were finally rescued. And Greece's' economy continued to falter as protesters clashed with local authorities and government forces.

As world news continued to unfold, *Titanic* sat silently in pieces as the workers diligently worked day and night to do the impossible. Through all the rigorous work, Finnegan remained solid as a rock and confident he could repair history. Due to passing storms and various types of equipment failure, time restraints started to be a factor, so eventually, more workers were brought over from Ireland.

Although much of the restoration was going well, some of the original artifacts were just too far gone. By 2011, Ben managed to have every type of material needed being donated to the project, including steel, fabric, glassware, fine China, wood, and even reproductions of original furniture. Piece by piece, *Titanic* started to look like a ship again. Even with several project managers, Jack remained a constant presence during it all. Just like any other company, he held regular meetings to review progress reports. Time was ticking away and Jack knew it.

By winter's end, the hull was complete and most of the decks that had been destroyed were nearing completion. There were two large sections in the rear of the ship left open for the engines. Although he never looked concerned, Finnegan's biggest worry was the engines. Could he get *Titanic*'s boilers and engines to work again? After being at the bottom of the Atlantic for 99 years, it was going to be a challenge, but not impossible. At 30 feet tall and weighing 1,000 tons, the two triple expansion steam engines, along with a smaller turbine engine and 29 boilers, were loaded into a cargo hold of a tanker and shipped off to Belfast, Ireland. Jack, along with Finnegan, Ben, and Henry took a flight out to meet with the company that would help restore the mammoth machinery.

In 1912 the engines ran off steam that was supplied by coal. In order to keep the engines running, firemen, which was what the workers were called, kept the boilers filled with coal day and night. Due to the craftsmanship and the heavy duty steel, Finnegan knew the machinery could be restored, but he had the unique idea of combining modern day technology with the old-school quality. For obvious reasons, he wanted the engines to be modified so they would no longer require coal as their source of power.

It was a long two weeks with meetings that ran forever, or so it seemed to Jack, but in the end, several plans were on the drawing board. Finnegan was pleased with the designs that were being presented, and Ben was even more pleased that it would cost next to nothing. Once again, he worked his magic and made some deals that would benefit both the company doing the work and Kotter Industries. Although Kotter Industries separated itself from the project, the company still prospered from it in many ways. With the project well in hand, Ben and Henry flew back to New York while Finnegan stayed behind to help get the massive restoration started.

Jack decided to look up his family's past and visit Southampton, England, where his father first boarded *Titanic.* Some of the companies that Victor was associated with were still operating, so Jack toured some of their facilities. He was well received, not only because of the *Titanic* story, but because of his name. Being a world leader in industry, the Kotter name was well respected and liked.

During the summer, there was nothing much to do. With Finnegan's leadership and Henry's tenacious attitude, the project was in good hands. Ben was still prolonging his retirement and terrorizing Kotter Industries with his wheeling and dealing, while Sam stayed on as Henry's right-hand man to see the project through. So Jack decided to take some time off.

His first stop was the Wiley Roadster. When he arrived, he saw the Mopar brothers conducting their usual shenanigans. Annoying the women and copping free food. Jack was driving *Fringe,* so of course, everyone saw him drive onto the lot. As he stepped out of his car, Jimmy came running over with something that looked like a cheeseburger and ketchup running down his face. Walley wasn't too far behind, yelling across the lot. "Jack, where the hell have you been? So much going on, but we never see you."

Jack smiled as he made a beeline for the food stand. He met Walley halfway and gave him a hug. "Hey, Walley, how the hell are you?"

Walley was glad to see his friend and walked with him to the food stand. "We heard about your friend Connie. We didn't know him too well, but I'm really sorry, Jack."

Jack gave a gracious smile as he approached the order window. "I guess you guys haven't had too much excitement since Lilith got caught."

Walley leaned against the wall as he let out a laugh. "No. Not too much. The police department was supposed to give us some kind of reward, but it's been so long, I'm not holding my breath. Jimmy still likes to run around telling the stories, but I seem to have grown tired of hearing the same story told 50 different ways."

As the counter person handed Jack his food, he noticed something different. "I know I haven't been around, but there's something different about you."

Walley looked off across the parking lot and saw Jimmy sneaking up behind and slapping girls on their bottoms. "I don't know. Guess I'm getting tired of this lifestyle. Tired of being on this lot all day, every day, doing nothing and having nothing."

Jack listened to Walley as he swallowed down the first bite of his sandwich. "I gotta tell you, Walley, I've known you and Jimmy all these years, and never once did you guys ever ask me for jobs, or for anything else, for that matter. I guess I just always thought you guys were happy hanging out and having fun. Sounds like you're ready for something better."

Walley watched as Jimmy faked like he was falling down then snuck a peek up a girl's miniskirt. "Well, I know I am, but I'm not too sure about Jimmy."

Jack stared over at the old truck Walley had. "Well, let me know if I can help. I still have friends in high places who could use some energetic guys."

When Jack left, he cruised the boulevard for a while, then found himself pulling onto the mall parking lot. He thought about his last encounter with Riley, but was determined to talk to him. When he walked in, Jack was astonished to see Riley's stand was no longer there. He asked one of the other merchants about it, and he informed Jack that Riley called it quits about a year earlier. He said Riley just came in one day and packed everything up and left. Jack was stunned. Riley was a friend of integrity whom he admired very much.

After leaving the mall, Jack thought a few times about trying to contact Bria, but he decided just to leave things alone. Later that night, he made his way to Benjamin's Steakhouse, and to his surprise, saw that Sarah was still working as a hostess. "Well, well. Jack Kotter. It's been a very long time. How are you?"

Jack smiled then leaned over and gave Sarah a hello hug. "I'm doing well. I wasn't expecting to see you still working here. Figured you would have moved on to bigger and better things by now."

As Sarah walked Jack to his table, their conversation continued. "So, your buddy Ben has been in and out a few times, and I always give him the message to tell you I said hello, but I'm guessing it never gets delivered."

As Jack sat down, Sarah sat down across from him. "I heard about your break up with Bria, and I see you have no one on your arm tonight."

Jack was a little surprised, but he shrugged his shoulders and played it off. "Yeah, we disagreed on some important issues, and we just couldn't work them out."

Before Jack could say anything else, Sarah leaned across the table and whispered into his ear. "I get off at eleven and I would love to get you off shortly after."

As Sarah swiped her cheek against Jack's, he could smell her enticing perfume. When she stood up and walked away, his eyes were fixed on her tight skirt and tush. With a come-hither smile, Sarah gave a short glance back at Jack. "Your waitress will be right with you."

When Jack finished his dinner, he walked over to the bar area and had a few drinks. Before he knew it, it was eleven o'clock. Like the spider to Little Miss Muffet, Sarah sat down beside him. After a few more drinks, they left and went back to her house. The next morning when Jack awoke, he felt good. He had known Sarah for many years and felt no guilt in having frivolous sex with her. After she made him breakfast, he gave her a gentle kiss on the cheek and left.

After stopping by the 110 Garage for a visit, he decided to cut his time short and head back to the site. When he arrived, Ben was there having a meeting with Finnegan and Henry. "Hey, Ben, I wasn't expecting to see you here."

Although Jack had been away from the business world for a while, he could still recall the various types of expressions Ben would display during stressful times, and the look on his face wasn't good. "Hey, kid, I could say the same for you. What happened to taking the summer off and spending some time back home?"

Jack was still trying to figure out Ben's initial expression. "Well, I saw some friends and had a good time, so I decided to come back here to see if I was needed, but instead, I find you here having a meeting with an all too familiar worried look on your face. So, what gives? What's going on?"

With a half-smile on his face, Henry stood up to greet Jack and to welcome him back. "Good to see you, Jack. Have a seat and Finnegan will fill you in." With some reservations, Jack sat down and prepared himself for bad news.

Finnegan was busy looking over some paperwork, but quickly placed it aside to greet Jack. "Well, Jack, it's just as well you cut your time short. We seem to have run into a bit of a dilemma. Our friends back in Ireland are having some issues with several of the plans for the engines. They can't seem to incorporate the new technology using the old materials. Henry is going to fly back tomorrow morning to see if maybe he can help with a design. I hate to say this, Jack, but if we can't get these engines to work, we're gonna have one hell of a big paperweight floating in the middle of the Atlantic Ocean."

Jack didn't say anything. He wasn't worried, but at the same time, he became annoyed. So many obstacles. So many delays. He had the perfect plan and it seemed like everything worked against him. With his head down and his hands fiddling around in his pocket, he walked out to the deck. There was a cool breeze blowing and the usual fishy smell wasn't in the air.

Eventually, Ben walked out to try to talk, but even he had little to offer. "Listen, kid, worst-case scenario, we shove a couple of updated engines in this tub and be done with it."

Jack just shook his head, but the smile he tried to push out just wasn't happening. "Come on, Ben, you know we can't do that. For this project to be a success, everything has to be as original as possible, or else this whole thing would be for nothing."

Ben paused for a moment then breathed a heavy sigh. "Come on, kid, I wanna show you something"

As they walked to the other side of the research vessel, *Titanic* slowly emerged into their line of sight. Floating like a majestic swan, she was beautiful. Except for the external painting, some interior work and, obviously, her engines, she was about eighty percent finished. Her four funnels were expected to arrive from Belfast any day. "What'ya say we have Sam take us for a little tour?"

Since work began on the restoration, the workers had been somewhat apprehensive about allowing people to board her, for safety reasons. On the flip side of that coin, Finnegan refused to allow any outsiders besides Henry and Sam simply because of his way of thinking. *Titanic* was beyond historical; Finnegan now considered her sacred. She was not to be boarded until once again complete.

"I don't know, Ben. Finnegan is really determined to keep *Titanic* to himself. He doesn't like outsiders on his ship."

Ben gawked as he shook his head. "First off, it's not his ship. Second, it's your project, and third, I don't give a rat's ass about Finnegan's rules."

Jack laughed as he picked up the radio and called Sam. It took a while, but Sam finally arrived to pick them up. Ben wasn't use to waiting. "What the hell did you do, Sam, go by way of the Pacific Ocean? We only called you forty minutes ago."

By that point, Sam was used to dealing with Ben's sense of warped humor and just laughed it off. "I don't know about this, Jack. Finnegan is ..."

Before Sam could say anymore, Jack finished for him. "Yeah, yeah, I know. Finnegan doesn't want anyone on *Titanic*."

Jack kept his eyes on *Titanic* as Sam navigated his way through the waves. Bigger and bigger it became until, finally, they were alongside it. Both frightening and intimidating, *Titanic* was way more than he expected. He tried to imagine what people thought while boarding her for the first time. The thought process was overwhelming. From the barge it was attached to, the trio climbed the ramp and entered the original doorway. What an amazing feeling Jack felt. Even Ben was silent while he looked around and took in all that *Titanic* had to offer.

There were still some open areas where workers were welding and hammering, and some of the walls were missing, but all in all, she was incredible. It took a few hours, but the tour was well worth it. Jack couldn't believe the restoration efforts. Most of the stained glass was original. So beautiful. Some original pieces of furniture and original stacks of China were also restored. The wheelhouse had been rebuilt and it was perfect. The crow's nest, docking bridge, and even the aft and fore Grand Staircases were finished. Such incredible sites. From stern to bow, *Titanic* was magnificent.

Jack wanted to take a look at A Deck where lifeboat number 11 would have been. This was where Victor was last seen by Winnifred. As they made their way up to A Deck, they walked around to the area in question. Once there, they saw Finnegan waiting. "Well, well, Mr. Kotter, I was wondering how long it would take you to come aboard."

Jack stopped and stared for a moment because he wasn't sure what Finnegan was talking about. Finnegan walked over and shook Jack's hand. "Ben told me about your family history, Mr. Kotter. Considering your loss, I think you have every right to be on this ship."

As he gave a humble smile, a feeling of relief came over Jack. "Thank you, Finnegan. Your kind words mean a lot."

CHAPTER THIRTY-EIGHT

In March of 2011, an earthquake off the Pacific Coast of Tohoku, Japan struck causing a massive tsunami. In the end, over 16,000 people were killed or declared missing. With post-WWII interests still going strong in Japan, Kotter Industries became heavily involved in the rebuilding stages. Because Jack was no longer part of Kotter Industries, the project was able to continue on.

By April, Henry had flown back to New York with great news. There was finally a working plan for *Titanic*'s engines. About that same time, Ben concluded his tour of Japan's devastation and was also back in New York. After a night of whiskey and women, they wasted no time getting back out to the site where Finnegan and Jack were waiting. Henry was all too happy to tell of the progress he'd had in Belfast.

"Well, Jack, we're back in business, and I think you're going to be very pleased with the results. We combined some eco-friendly technology with some modern mechanics and kept the original look of the engines. They're even going to restore most of the original heavy duty moving parts and reuse them. As for the boilers, they're finished and they look great. Once they're back in place, they should make great show pieces."

This was great news, but Jack wondered if Finnegan could get back in sequence with the original timeline. Unfortunately for Jack, not only was it important that nothing happen to *Titanic*, but it was equally important to finish the project on time.

In April, Ben and Jack took a break to attend the royal wedding. Another fairytale wedding that had worldwide coverage. Like with most other mainstream countries, Kotter Industries was intertwined with England's industrial and manufacturing facilities. Before passing away, Jack Sr. had been a longtime friend of the royal family. On May 2, during their flight back to New York, the crew gave a stunning announcement. A United States Seal team conducted a raid on a compound in Abbottabad, Pakistan. During a gun battle, the once feared leader of Al-Qaeda was killed. As England celebrated the royal wedding, the world celebrated the death of Osama Bin Laden.

After the initial cheering by the passengers, Jack expected some good conversation with Ben, but he was not in a talking mood. With a frown on his face, he just simply said, "Not everything is what it seems to be, kid," then closed his eyes and went to sleep.

During the next couple of months, work continued and the progress was incredible. Such pride and extraordinary beauty in the craftsmanship. Sometimes, Jack would just sit and admire the workers as they seemed to work in harmony, never hearing any complaints about the labor.

Work did temporarily stop on July 21 as everyone watched the space shuttle *Atlantis* make its final descent and land at the Kennedy Space Center. Although this concluded the space shuttle program for NASA, Kotter Industries would still play a huge part in the development of future spacecraft. Not that Jack really cared.

While Jack sat watching from the research vessel, Finnegan came up and sat beside him. "Looking at her now, it's hard to believe she was in pieces at the bottom of the Atlantic for so many years. What do you think of her now, Mr. Kotter?"

Jack smiled as he peered out over the water. "Well, Finnegan, I'll tell you what I think. My father's name was Mr. Kotter, so I think you should just call me Jack. With regards to *Titanic*, I don't have any words that can describe how I feel."

Finnegan watched as the men painted the outside of the hull. "I know what you mean, Jack. My grandfather worked day and night on that ship. He used to tell me about the excitement everyone felt as the ship neared completion. Back then, I could only imagine those feelings, but now as I sit and watch her floating like a beautiful swan, I now know what he was talking about."

As the cool breeze continued to blow, the waves seem to go on forever. Jack could tell Finnegan had some curiosity, but seemed to be holding back. "Come on, Finnegan, spit it out. I can tell you're dying to ask me something."

Finnegan paused for a moment. "Sorry, Jack, I'm not usually short of words. I know about the family history, but I guess I'm wondering if there's more to this than just a final wish."

Now it was Jack who was short of words. After some deep thought, he was finally able to put everything into perspective. "Well, this whole idea started with me making a decision to open a mysterious box my dad left for me. Wow, talk about a snowball that rolled into an out of control avalanche." For the next hour, Jack told Finnegan about everything from finding the shed to the stories told by Old Salty and Winnifred to losing the company his father built. After everything was said and done, *Titanic* was more than just a ship from another time. For Jack, it had become a test of manhood. A battle that he needed to win. It was the end of the life he knew and the beginning of a life still to come. He needed to see this through not only for his father and Victor, but for Connie and every other soul that was cut short.

By September, people across America had had just about enough economic hardships. The economy showed little to no sign of improving. The government kept bailing out big business and banks, and in general, people were bothered by the role Wall Street played in the collapse of the economy. Protests soon followed, and the Occupy Wall Street movement was started. Since he was no longer part of the business world, Jack could only sit and watch as Americans became more and more frustrated. Although Ben was no longer chairman of the board and was on his way out to pasture, he remained vigilant in his old school ways and kept Robert from closing down factories and laying off more workers. With all the fighting, both at home and overseas, there were enough news-worthy stories to go around. Jack and his restoration project faded away into the old dusty storage rooms of media empires.

By December the restoration of the engines was complete and were being prepared to be transported back to *Titanic* to be installed. That time of year was always big for Jack. His family and friends were very important, but it seemed that that life was long gone. Of course he still had Ben and a couple of his old friends were still around. He also considered some of his new-found friends, such as Henry, Sam, and the brothers from 110 Garage. He even found a connection with Finnegan when it came to *Titanic*. Everything considered, Jack was going to make every effort to have a nice Christmas. After consideration of the hard work everyone was doing, Jack sent the workers home for the holidays in order to spend time with their families.

On Christmas Day, Jack sat on his front porch reminiscing. He enjoyed the cool, brisk air as he thought about Christmas days from long ago. Then he closed his eyes and laid his head back. Just as he was about to drift away, that all too familiar groggy voice broke his tranquility. "Merry Christmas, kid. What the hell are you doing out here in the cold?"

Jack's eyes opened abruptly as he focused in on Ben standing over the top of him. "Damn you, Ben. It's Christmas Day and here we are cussing at each other. You're the only person I know who can mention Christmas and hell in the same breath. I can see you getting struck by lightning and me being collateral damage."

Ben handed Jack an envelope then sat down beside him. "Why so moody, kid? It's Christmas."

As he sat up, Jack tried to rub the stress from his eyes. "Sorry, Ben. I just have a lot on my mind."

Ben could see the sadness in Jack's face and had a good idea what it was about. "Listen, kid, people come and go and some pass away. That's just life. I've lost people in my life who I cared about deeply, but we remain steadfast, and eventually, we become a stronger person."

Jack didn't say anything. He fumbled around with the envelope and stared off across his property. "I miss the times we used to have around Christmas. You and dad always cracking jokes. Mom getting irritated at the both of you. Then there was Connie running around playing jokes on anyone who would fall for them. I was looking forward to maybe having a family with Bria and having those same kind of times. I guess I really screwed that up. Wanna hear something funny? I find myself getting upset because I don't think about her as much as I think I should. Crazy, isn't it?"

Ben sat silent for a moment then stood up. He walked to the edge of the porch and leaned against the post. "Around the holidays, before you were born, we would have some crazy parties at the office. You talk about fun. Back then, we had some pretty freaky secretaries working for the company. By the end of the night, we were wasted and half-naked. I really miss those days, but we can't freeze time forever. Times change, kid. That brings me to our business."

Jack was listening, and at the same time, thinking about his own memories. Then he realized what Ben said. "Business? What are you talking about? It's Christmas Day."

Ben walked over and snatched the envelope from Jack's hands. "Sit up and pay attention. Here, open this before I change my mind."

Jack gently took the envelope back and opened it up. As he reviewed the contents, he saw it was some legal documents. "What is this, Ben? It looks like some kind of transfer of property."

Ben took a deep breath and explained. "Listen, kid, your dad left me the job of watching over you and I failed miserably." Before Jack could interrupt, Ben continued. "I let Robert trap you into giving up your holdings, and for that, I'm really sorry, kid. Despite what we found out about your father, I think Kotter Industries was very important to him. I think it was equally as important that you remain a vital role in its future. Remember what I told you, kid. There are many ways a person like me can retire."

With the papers still in his hand, Jack stood up. "Come on, Ben, this company was your life's work as well as my fathers. You can't just give it away."

With pride in his eyes, Ben smiled as he tried to hold back the tears building up. "Listen, kid, I've worked hard, played hard, and lived hard. At times, I've even had women ride me hard. It's time for me to kick back, relax, and live my rock star life. I promised your dad I would take care of you, and that's not a promise I'm willing to break. Besides, Robert is going to flip his wig once he finds out you now own controlling interest again."

Jack was speechless. He stood staring at Ben, trying to come up with words. Just then, Ben reached out for a handshake. "What'ya say, kid? Give an old friend one last chance to make things right?"

By then, Jack was fighting back his own tears. He shook Ben's hand then quickly moved in for a hug. Afterwards, Ben told Jack the transfer of stock wouldn't take place until mid-summer of the following year. That was actually good news for Jack, because it would give him time to bring closure to his father's last wish.

When the new year started, so did Jack's countdown. The boilers and engines were in transit back to *Titanic*. Various areas of work on *Titanic* were being completed on a daily basis, and even Finnegan was showing signs of excitement. As the media concentrated on the 2012 presidential race, Jack and his team quietly and diligently worked on the completion of *Titanic*. By the end of January, the boilers were back where they belonged and were looking great. Henry was absolutely correct. They made great show pieces. By the end of February, the engines were installed and ready for testing. By then, *Titanic* was back in the news. As the media reported the up and coming 100-year anniversary, the various cable networks were replaying any and all documentaries. Once again, reporters were jockeying for exclusive interviews. When Jack gave a press conference, there were many questions asked. At the end of the day, only one thing mattered. Jack was going to make good on his promise and bring *Titanic* home.

The next day was a media frenzy. Headlines read, "From Zero to Hero," referring to Jack. "Best of the best. Crew needed to bring *Titanic* into port." And one headline simply read, "History Rewritten." The clock was ticking down for *Titanic* to complete her maiden voyage. After the engines were tested several times and found to be in sound condition, there was only one thing left to do. In March, the last pieces of the jigsaw puzzle were installed. The four iconic smoke stacks. By the end of the first week of March, *Titanic* was complete. She was an incredible sight to behold. Everything was perfect, from the fixtures to the carpet and right down to the linens. It was like she had never sunk. There was so much pride in her completion that the workers wouldn't even allow her to collect dust. It was hard to do, but they kept her polished around the clock.

With the restoration complete, there were some decisions to be made. Jack called for a meeting and had everyone meet on *Titanic*.

The first class reception room located at the base of the famous Grand Staircase was to hold *Titanic*'s first order of business. One by one, they found their way. As Jack sat waiting, Finnegan and Sam walked in. Afterwards, Henry and Ben walked in with bottles of whiskey and champagne and, of course, glasses for all. Ben looked around as he took a seat. "Congratulations, kid. You did it. Now what the hell are you going to do?"

Without hesitation, Henry popped the cork and poured everyone a glass. "A toast. To those who lost their lives, to those who gave their lives for others, and to those who had courage enough to survive."

After a couple of drinks and some casual talking, Jack started the meeting. "Alright, let's get down to why I called everyone here. We all know the plan was to restore *Titanic* and sail her into New York, but we never discussed a timeframe. Well, when Finnegan first arrived, we discussed the idea of an anniversary date. I'll give Finnegan the floor so he can explain."

Finnegan grabbed the whiskey bottle and opened it up. After pouring everyone a shot, he gulped his down. "So smooth. You Americans really know your whiskey. I won't waste anyone's time, so I'll get right to it. *Titanic* struck an iceberg on April 14. She sank on April 15. Now, Jack and I have tossed around various ideas on which date to use, but in thinking about it, Jack came up with another idea. What most people don't know is that *Titanic* had two captains. Captain Herbert Haddock was the original captain on *Titanic* and had made plans to be in New York on April 16. After relinquishing command, Captain Smith altered the plan and wanted to get to New York on April 17 at 5:00 a.m. So, the dilemma now is which date would be the right course of action. We've already succeeded in doing the impossible. We've raised the *Titanic* from her watery grave and restored her back to her original splendor. I say we maintain our way of thinking in keeping everything as original as possible. Let's complete her maiden voyage as planned. I say we arrive in New York on April 17th at 5:00 a.m."

There was silence in the room as everyone looked around to get a feel for what everyone else was thinking. Ben stood up and poured some more drinks. "Listen, kid, like I said before, I'm out of the loop, but from knowing your dad for so many years I can say with a definitive answer, he would agree with Finnegan. But, whatever you decide, count me in. Now, if you'll excuse me, I'm gonna take another walk around this old girl to see if I can spot some other kind of spirits." Henry also agreed with the date and decided to go with Ben. They grabbed what was left of the whiskey and off they went.

Jack noticed Sam was staring off into space. He had a worried look about him. "Sam, you're part of this team and I value your opinion very much, so if there's an issue, you need to let us know."

Still wearing a worried look, Sam looked around. "I don't know, Jack. I've dived on many wrecks. Each one with its own personality. I know we were all excited about the completion of this project, but there's still that deep dark feeling you get when your thought process starts to wonder if you did the right thing. I'm just not too sure we want to be on this ship during the 100-year anniversary of its sinking. Especially at the exact location it took its last breath before sinking beneath the waves. I say we leave now and don't tempt fate."

Although Finnegan would rather have been drinking whiskey, there was none left, so he grabbed the champagne and poured some drinks. He then raised his glass for another toast. "Here's to Sam. The only one among us men who had the guts to say what we were all thinking. There have been whispers among the workers as the ill-fated date approaches. As much pride as they have, come April 15, they don't want to be on *Titanic*. To be honest, I lay in my bunk at night with cold sweats thinking about it. If we've undone God's will, let us pray for His mercy. My grandfather used to tell me wisdom begins with the fear of the Lord, and fear the Lord we shall. It's your decision, Jack."

While Jack and Sam pondered the possibilities, Finnegan gently placed his empty glass on the table and walked away. Whatever worry Sam had before, it had grown worse while listening to Finnegan's little speech. "I just don't know, Jack. It's always been my opinion the ocean takes what it wants and very seldom gives it back." Sam stood up and walked around the table to Jack. "You're my friend, Jack, and I greatly appreciate this chance of a lifetime, so I will go along with whatever you decide."

After Sam left, Jack sat quietly with his thoughts. Although, he had already made his mind up about the date, it didn't stop him from having thoughts of disaster. Eventually, he walked up to A Deck, where he stood thinking about Victor. Jack tried to reenact in his mind what Winnifred had told him. It was horrifying just to think about, but he kept forcing the faded images into his head. He needed to feel the intensity of the moment. He wanted to know the same feeling of despair the passengers felt.

The following day, Jack informed everyone *Titanic* would sail as originally scheduled. The job of picking the cream of the crop personnel to sail *Titanic* home fell on Finnegan. Jack new Finnegan would take no chances when it came to sorting through and picking out the best sailors available. Although the stench of superstitious beliefs clouded the judgment of most applicants, Finnegan did a great job weeding through all who applied.

Anxieties flew high as March faded away and April brought its promise of fresh flowers and showers. Last minute preparations, along with a slew of inquiries, took their toll on Jack. Everyone wanted to book passage for the completion of *Titanic*'s maiden voyage. Offers poured in from around the world. Some people offered up to a million dollars for one ticket, but there were no tickets being sold for the ride. Finnegan and Jack stood strong against any and all offers. All the blood, sweat, and tears that went into bringing *Titanic* back to life was only for those who participated and contributed to its success. However, after discussing it with Finnegan, there were two exclusive invitations sent out. Dr. Robert Ballard and Jean Louis Michel, the two researchers who discovered the *Titanic* in 1985. It was no surprise to Jack when neither one replied.

Although *Titanic* was complete, there was still plenty to do. When it came time to handle the politics of New York, Ben was the undisputed champ. His connections, along with a silver tongue and business savvy, had the local politicians begging for *Titanic* to come into port. As New York City prepared for the event, Finnegan finished out hiring the crew complete with chefs. Although he hired several capable personnel to handle the ship, Finnegan decided nobody would have the title of captain. Instead, hanging on the wall of the wheelhouse was a picture of Captain Edward John Smith.

The stage was set, and on 13 April 2012, Jack made arrangements for dinner to be served in the grand dining room. This was to make sure nobody had second thoughts. Although some of the workers took their superstitions back to Ireland, for better or for worse, most stayed behind. It was a great dinner, followed up by drinks and conversation. Everyone had a good time, but nobody wanted to talk about the elephant in the room. The clock was ticking. They were less than 24 hours away from *Titanic* sailing off into history. As the night wound to an end, the dining area slowly started to empty out.

The next day was spent preparing the last of the equipment to be shipped out. The platforms and barges were already gone and the last of the cranes were being secured for transport. By dinnertime, *Titanic* was on her own. As Jack stood on the poop deck, he looked out over a calm sea. There was no wind and the water was flat with no swells. The stars were out in force and the moon barely gave off light. He watched a few of the workers as they wiped down and polished the railing. When they finished, they gathered their cleaning supplies and walked to the steps. Before the last worker stepped down, he stopped to glance over at Jack. He didn't say anything, but he had a certain look about him. A look of nervousness. As he climbed down the steps, Jack walked over to the rail and watched as the men joked with the worker about how he felt. Jack knew better, though. Everyone was on edge, but not everyone would admit to it.

The sun made its last appearance as it slowly sank into the ocean. Jack expected the moon to get a little brighter, but it didn't. Just when he closed his eyes to enjoy a nice breeze, Ben and Henry came walking up. "Hey, kid, there you are. Henry and I have been looking all over for you."

Shortly afterwards, Sam and Finnegan arrived. "Hey, is this a private party?"

Sam had an unopened bottle of wine, so he popped the cork. Finnegan held the glasses as Sam poured. As everyone raised their glasses, Ben made a toast. "Here's to not sleeping a damn wink tonight." Although everyone laughed, they knew Ben was right. Of all nights, nobody was going to tempt fate and sleep.

Finnegan took a moment to look out over the water. It was still calm. The stars were shining and the moon was dim. He could sense an eerie feeling in the air. When he noticed the talking had stopped, he turned to find everyone staring at him. "Well, gentlemen, seems that God has played his hand. The conditions are almost exactly like the night *Titanic* went down." Nobody said anything because the frightened looks on their faces said it all. Finnegan's words cut through their veins like a knife. Before anyone could respond, Finnegan gave them something else to ponder. "May the Lord keep you in his hand and never close His fist too tight." Finnegan took a deep breath and smiled. "That's an old Irish saying I heard when I was young." With a chill in the air, everyone had stopped drinking and the conversation grew stale.

With more curiosity than not, Jack tried to lighten the moment. "I've been wondering about something for some time now. Aren't we supposed to christen a ship for good luck before its launch?"

Of course, Finnegan had an answer for anything to do with ships, but it wasn't exactly what everyone thought he would say. "Well, Jack, my friend, we're not exactly launching *Titanic*. She's already in the water. Not everyone knows this, but *Titanic* never had a real christening. They raised her flag and shot off three rockets. Not really what you would call a traditional launching. Traditionally, christening was a way of appeasing whatever sea god or gods were being worshiped at the time. The Ancient Greeks had Poseidon and then his son Triton. The Romans had Neptune. It was their way of praying for the safe passage and protection of the seamen. As far as *Titanic* is concerned, I don't think it mattered either way. Our Almighty Lord did what he did, and tonight, whatever happens, he will have his way again. I'm not here to dispute Him."

With nighttime starting to settle in, there was a stiff chill in the air. Henry decided to retrieve another bottle, so Finnegan and Sam went with him. With a not-so-offensive smirk on his face, Jack turned to stare back out over the water. "Well, Ben, what'ya think is gonna happen when I walk into Kotter Industries and storm the boardroom?"

Ben walked over to the rail and looked over. "Well, I have no doubt you'll be a royal pain in Robert's ass." With a short pause, Ben could tell Kotter Industries wasn't really on Jack's mind. "So, kid, what else is bothering you?"

Jack thought about the question. "I gotta be honest, Ben. For the second time in my life, nothing is bothering me. I feel absolutely nothing. Just like the night I thought Lilith was going to punch my ticket. I just feel a certain peace. I'm actually looking forward to getting back to work. I think what Finnegan said must have struck something inside me."

Ben could see a peace within Jack. "Finnegan and his old Irish sayings. Which one are you talking about?"

Jack pondered the question momentarily. "Well, I guess whatever happens is going to happen regardless of what you, me or anyone else does at this point, so why worry about it?" Jack smiled because he knew Ben's nerves were on edge. "Don't worry, Ben. We have a modern communication system in place and there are two Coast Guard cutters off the coast of Nova Scotia."

Ben took Jack's words to heart in order to feel some kind of relief, but it wasn't working. "Alright, kid, whatever you say. What'ya say we go find the others so I can drink my worries away?"

Jack turned back around and stared out over the ocean. "You go ahead, Ben. I wanna enjoy the quiet for a while."

Over the next few hours, Ben and Henry drank and played poker while Sam and Finnegan did a stern to bow check of the ship. At 10:00 p.m., everyone went their own ways. Ben decided to stay near the wheelhouse, while Henry passed out with his bottle in the dining hall. Finnegan was busy double-checking the engines, while Sam checked and rechecked all the ship's instruments. Jack made his way to one of the first-class cabins, in particular, the cabin Mr. Thomas Andrews occupied during *Titanic*'s maiden voyage. As he lay in bed resting, it seemed his mind played some tricks. As the ship floated stationary, it constantly creaked and bellowed. At one point, Jack thought he heard footsteps and voices creating a commotion outside his cabin, but when he opened the door, there was nobody there. Every now and then, the temperature would rise and fall in the cabin, but he laughed it off as a possible malfunction in the system.

At 11:00 p.m., Jack made his way to the wheelhouse. Ben, Finnegan, and Sam were already there. Shortly afterwards, Henry came stumbling in. "You boys didn't think I would actually miss this historic occasion, did you?" Still with half a bottle in his hand, he passed it around for everyone to have.

As the time continued to count down, Finnegan spoke into the radio and had all pertinent personnel in place. Most of the workers who stayed behind lined the starboard side of the ship. The night became deafly silent and the only sound was the ticktock of the clock. There were no safeguards, no tugboats, and the only warning system was the single lookout up in the crow's nest, just like the night of the sinking.

With very little moonlight and only the ship's lights to keep the pitch black at bay, nothing much could be seen, but nevertheless, the crow's nest reported no activity. *Titanic*'s engines were started and the ocean started to churn. All eyes were on the clock as minutes ticked down to seconds.

Finally, with everyone's hearts pounding with every second going by, the clock struck 11:40 p.m. The exact time *Titanic* struck the iceberg. As Jack glanced over at Finnegan, a small alarm went off on his wristwatch. With the awful feeling of pending disaster still fresh in his mind, Jack barked out one simple order. "Let's get the hell out of here."

Suddenly, *Titanic* came alive and everyone cheered. Already pointing towards New York, she slowly started to move forward. It wasn't very long before *Titanic* was cruising at 21 knots per hour. The night air was crisp, but nobody cared. Even Ben walked out onto the deck in order to get the full affect.

Although one milestone was surpassed, most of the crew was still on edge. There was still the time when *Titanic* breathed her last breath as she sank beneath the waves, at 2:20 a.m. on the morning of April 15. Just a few hours away. Eventually, it became too cold to stay outside, so it wasn't long before everyone found themselves moving towards the lounge area. With watery eyes and yawns all around, some people fell asleep while others forced themselves to stay awake. As 2:20 a.m. came and went, the occupants of the lounge started to thin out. By 3:00 a.m., everyone was asleep in their cabins.

Later that morning, it was a dream come true. The sun was shining and breakfast was being served. *Titanic* was clear of Iceberg Alley, which put everyone in a better state of mind. After breakfast, Henry and Ben decided to take a trip down memory lane and utilize the now old-fashioned workout facility. With his work behind him, Sam was finally able to somewhat relax. Although he knew the ship backwards and forwards, he decided to take a tour and enjoy all that *Titanic* had to offer. With a photo crew on hand, Jack also toured the ship, taking as many pictures as possible. He even popped in on Ben and snapped a picture of him on the row machine. Jack quickly vacated the area when he realized Ben wasn't very happy about it. Finnegan was a different story. There was no relaxation for him. His time to relax was when *Titanic* was finally in port and docked. While New York prepared for the arrival of the iconic ship, the people aboard enjoyed nothing more than a lazy day.

On April 16, everyone was back to work. The crew constantly conducted maintenance checks as the workers polished and shined *Titanic*. Throughout the day, an occasional small plane would fly over, but nobody paid them any mind. By nightfall *Titanic* was only hours away from port. As Jack lay in his cabin, Ben came knocking. When he opened the door, Ben quickly walked in. "Listen, kid, I've been hearing a lot of weird sounds. I can't sleep while I'm on this tub."

Jack laughed as he poured a couple of stiff drinks. "Come on, Ben, it's just your mind playing tricks on you. I've never known you to be afraid of anything, let alone believe in ghosts."

Ben sat down and gulped down his drink. He then grabbed Jack's and also gulped it down. "Listen, kid, I'm not kidding. Let's speed up this floating barge so we can get the hell off this godforsaken thing."

Just then, Henry came knocking. Jack wasted no time in letting him in. "There you are, you old rust bucket. I knew I'd find you here."

Jack conveniently forgot to tell Ben and Henry about his experience just a few nights earlier, but had no problem with telling Henry about Ben's ramblings.

After a few laughs at Ben's expense, Henry let them in on a little secret. "I gotta tell you, Benjamin, my old eyes aren't getting any younger and I know I drank pretty heavy the other night, but I swear I saw some pretty young woman running around up on the poop deck after our little party. Ghosts or no ghosts, what'ya say we go have ourselves a little fun?"

Like a spring chicken, Ben was up out of his chair. "Woman?" Ben grabbed the bottle from the table and walked towards the door. "I've never been with a phantom woman before. Might be a little strange, but fun." Like a couple of kids, Ben and Henry walked out and scurried down the hallway.

After they left, there was another frantic knock at the door. Thinking Ben and Henry were scared and came back, Jack opened the door. He looked up and down the hall, but saw nothing. Unaffected by the incident, he slowly shut the door and went to sleep.

A few hours later, on April 17 at 4:00 a.m., Jack joined Ben and Henry on the bridge. Shortly afterwards, Sam and Finnegan came back from making their rounds. Pier 59 was the original destination of *Titanic* and it was still in use. Located off 11th Avenue on the west side of Manhattan, it was home to a 100,000-square-foot multimedia center and New York's only microbrewery, called the Chelsea Brewing Company. Dubbed the Chelsea Piers, they were still a formidable presence within the community.

Within the hour, New York was in sight. The dock manager had been contacted and everything was in place. Thousands of people lined 11th Avenue and the adjacent piers for the docking of the world's most famous ship. RMS *Titanic.*

The media had helicopters in the sky and cameras set up at every angle possible. New Yorkers and visitors from all over lined the shorelines and bridges just to be part of such a historical occasion. Exactly 100 years to the day, *Titanic* sailed into New York Harbor as though nothing had ever happened. When she entered the upper bay, she was met with a barrage of boats and small crafts. As she slowly moved towards her final destination, assigned tugboats followed behind. At 5:00 a.m., *Titanic* gave way to the tugs and she was guided into position for docking. For the icing on the cake, *Titanic* sounded her whistles as if to breathe her last sigh of relief. People cheered as though they were victorious in war. In a sense, they were. Against all odds and everyone's better judgment, Jack and his team raised glory up from the depths of hell and gave her back the dignity she'd lost so long ago.

Titanic stood high and proud as New Yorkers were awed by her presence. She was magnificent. When the docking bridge was extended, the workers and crew commenced their timely exit. Although extremely proud of their accomplishments, they were never so happy to be on dry land. Finnegan wasn't much on sentimental goodbyes, but he did thank Jack and Ben for allowing him to be part of something that brought pride back to his family. Wanting no recognition, he disembarked then disappeared into the crowd. By that time, the sun was up and shining bright. Henry's daughter was there waiting to take him back to Maine, but before he left, he promised

Ben he would come back for a visit during the summer as long as the trip involved women, cards, and booze. After an hour or so, the crowds started to disperse. It was a Tuesday, so people had to start their workdays. After all the hoopla was done, Sam was anxious to get back to California. His plane was leaving later that night, so he had a lot to do.

The official tours of the ship wouldn't start until the weekend, so most everyone was gone by 9:00 a.m. A few news crews hung around for pictures and interviews, but afterwards, it was just Ben and Jack. "Well, kid, congratulations on your success. Your father would have been so proud. I wish he was still here to see this."

Jack looked around then eyed the ship from stern to bow. "Yeah, I know what you mean." As he looked towards the bridge of the ship, he squinted his eyes as the sun beat down with a ferocious glare. As he tried to fight off the bright morning sun, he could see the outline of a well-dressed man staring back as to say "job well done."

"Hey, Ben, I thought everyone was off the ship."

When Ben turned around, there was nothing to see. Whatever Jack saw was gone. "Yeah, kid. Everyone is off. We did a sweep of the ship an hour ago. What's wrong?"

Jack paused as he continued to squint, but it was no good. "Nothing's wrong. I guess the sun makes your eyes see strange things."

Just then, Casey pulled up with the limo. When they climbed in, Ben could see Jack's mind was going in every direction. "So, kid, penny for your thoughts."

Jack smiled as he laid his head back to rest. "I remember reading a quote from Dr. Ballard. He said when he found the *Titanic,* it was a nice feeling to finally put those souls to rest, but I think that was a little premature. I think, now, any souls that were on that ship when it sank can rest in peace."

Ben smiled with pride. "I know I said your father would've been proud, but I'm also proud of you, kid. After all the arguing and bickering back and forth, you followed what you thought was the right thing to do. So, kid, what's next for Kotter Industries?"

Jack opened his eyes and picked his head up. "I don't know. We'll have to wait and see what the future brings. You don't happen to have any more old boxes from my dad laying around, do you?"

Ben shook his head and laughed. "No, kid. If I did, I probably wouldn't give them to you."

The following week, Jack had a small ceremony for Victor. Ben and a few friends were there, and of course, the media. There were no physical remains, but within the casket, Jack placed a picture of *Titanic* and an old piece of wood with a rusted bolt through the middle. The wood was a section of A Deck, which was the last place anyone had seen Victor alive. In his heart, Jack knew his dad could finally rest knowing Victor was at peace.

After a few brief passages read from the Bible, Jack shared his gratitude as everyone slowly left the cemetery. Afterwards, Jack stayed behind to visit at his father's grave. "Well, dad, I've done your bidding. I brought Pop home and hopefully placed his soul at rest. Just so you know, in the process of this massive blunder you left me, I lost the only woman I ever loved. My best friend Connie died, and I nearly lost Kotter Industries. Luckily, Ben has been such a great friend, because without him, I don't know where I would be right now. I hope you don't have any other surprises in store for me, because I have to tell you, Dad, I've had enough. I love you, but I'm here and you're not, so I'm going to run this company the way I feel it should be. Between you and Ben, with all the wisdom and knowledge over the years, I should be okay. Oh, yeah, one more thing. Thanks for trusting me with such a wonderful task."

In July, Jack was welcomed back at Kotter Industries with open arms. Robert wasn't happy, but nobody gave a damn. Given his new track record, Jack was overwhelmingly voted in as chairman of the board. At about the same time, a board of directors was also voted in for the *Titanic*. Of course, Jack was also the chairman there. First order of business, *Titanic* would spend a year in New York, open for tours daily, before embarking on a goodwill trip around the world.

With 2012 being an election year, it wasn't long before Kotter Industries was faced with new challenges. Once again, Jack was being pulled in various directions, but with his newly earned experience and Ben just a phone call away, he didn't mind.

Through it all, the one thing he missed the most was the Wiley Roadster and showing off *Fringe*. Shortly after working a long day, he decided to swing by and have some fun. Before he could drive onto the lot, a brand new Lamborghini Murciélago pulled up alongside him. When Jack glanced over, he saw Ben with a big smile on his face. "Hey, kid, long time no see. I gotta tell you, I'm loving life. Sleep all day and party all night. Can't beat it, and I'm betting that American muscle can't beat my Italian style."

Jack hit the gas and smiled. "One thing you taught me, Ben, don't bite off more than you can chew, and you're about to get a mouth full."

Just then, the Mopar brothers pulled up alongside Ben, one driving a new Challenger and the other a new Charger. Ben's smile quickly turned to a frown. "Well, well, look who it is. Tweedle Dee and Tweedle Dum. If I were you, boys, I'd take that junk to a scrapyard." Ben gracefully raised his hand and gave the brothers the one finger salute then turned back around to Jack. "Hey, kid, one final lesson to keep in mind. It's a long way to the top if you wanna rock and roll." There were a few more playful hits of the gas pedals, then all four cars blasted off.

A few minutes later, Ben found himself on the side of the road. His Italian dream machine let him down. After all the trash talk, he forgot to fill it up with gas. No worries, though. As he watched Jack and his pals race away, a convertible with two young women drove up. "You need a ride, old man?"

"Perfect timing." Ben pulled out his little bottle of all night sex pills and smiled. "First off, I'm not that old and second, hell yeah, I'd like to ride you all night."

Jack may have raced off into the sunset, but that wasn't the end. He went on to guide Kotter Industries through tough times and made sure the company stayed in stride with the top corporations of the world. Ben's world became simple. Eat, sleep, drink, women, then more women. Not necessarily in that order. As for *Titanic,* she completed her goodwill trip around the world and made it back to New York safely. There were no reports of ghosts or any strange happenings.

As for Bria, she grew tired of trying to avoid all the places where she and Jack had spent time together, so eventually, she put New York City in her rearview mirror. It wasn't a big loss for New York. Ethan wasn't too happy with Jack's triumphant return to Kotter Industries, so he sold his interests and tried being a stay at home husband. Bad idea. Ben was right all along, Bobby Jo became really tired really fast. After the divorce, Ethan lost everything. Jack briefly thought about trying to help, but then he recalled all the grief Ethan caused him. He'd finally realized Ethan was a false friend and it served him right for being such an asshole. Jack helped the Mopar brothers get in on the ground floor of Kotter Industries, and when a person says ground floor, that's exactly what it means. They worked the midnight shift cleaning offices from the top floor to the bottom. No doubt the Wiley Roadster women were glad those perverts finally had respectable jobs. And then there was Lilith. She was transferred to a new facility where she remained under close observation. When she wasn't being restrained with a straightjacket, she liked to draw pictures of Jack using nothing but a crayon and her memory. In the end, one would hope that crazy bitch doesn't wander off again. But living in such a dysfunctional world, one just never knows.

The end ... maybe.

CPSIA information can be obtained at www.ICGtesting.com
Printed in the USA
BVOW01s1744101113

335939BV00002B/59/P

9 781592 999835